MW01244071

The Ballad of Lacey Jay

A novel by

Larry & Barbara Payton

Bloomington, IN Milton Keynes, UK

 authorHOUSE®

AuthorHouse™
1663 Liberty Drive, Suite 200
Bloomington, IN 47403
www.authorhouse.com
Phone: 1-800-839-8640

AuthorHouse™ UK Ltd.
500 Avebury Boulevard
Central Milton Keynes, MK9 2BE
www.authorhouse.co.uk
Phone: 08001974150

First published by AuthorHouse 3/26/2007

ISBN: 978-1-4259-8009-2 (e)
ISBN: 978-1-4259-8007-8 (sc)
ISBN: 978-1-4259-8008-5 (hc)

Library of Congress Control Number: 2006910626

Printed in the United States of America
Bloomington, Indiana

This book is printed on acid-free paper.

Life is like a ball of yarn
Kitten plays with while you're gone.

Slaps it 'round the livelong day
Over'n under ev'ry whichway!

'Til it's gone and in its place
A spiderweb fills the space

A hundred knots bright red shade
with tangled loops that kitten made

I'll untie the snarls and knit a shawl
And wrap it warmly 'round you all.

Wrapped now in the wooly red,
I hug my babes then off to bed.

Written by Lacey Jay
Performed by Sunshine Autrey

1

Slowly, he climbed the fuzzy staircase from sleep to consciousness, memory of some innocuous dream already fading as his mind cast off its sleep shroud. Around him, the blue shadows of familiar furnishings in the windowless bedroom were more ominous than comforting. He was cold.

I must have left the window open.

Lucas Peterson shivered in the chill of the pre-dawn morning as he stumbled from the bedroom. He walked numbly out to the northern window in the kitchen/dining area at the rear of the shotgun apartment. With units on both sides of him, open windows was the only way to move any air through the old adobe fourplex.

Sure enough, the curtains billowed with the cool March morning breeze. It was another of those high-desert mornings when the temperature could easily vary 50 degrees from yesterday's highs — or from today's warmth, for that matter.

He pushed the aging casement down, then plodded back across the frigid linoleum and crawled in beside the beautiful blonde coed he'd met last night, and drew her towards him. She was cold, too.

"Damn, sweetheart, you're cold as ice, but we both know you're not frigid, right?" he said into her ear, letting his warm breath caress her coolness.

She didn't stir.

1

"Are you still asleep, darlin'?"

No answer.

Raising to one elbow with a sense of déjà vu, he looked into her eyes. The pale blue orbs stared back at him, open but unseeing. Panic gripped him by the throat. The alarm inside his head left a metallic taste in his mouth. A bit of vertigo accompanied shaky knees as he swung his feet off the bed to the floor. He felt the urge to vomit.

The lifeless form of Beth Miller lay motionless in the center of the bed, the sheet and blanket partially covering her nude body.

Not again, please Lord, not again!

Six months ago, someone had killed Evelyn Billings the first woman he'd ever loved. Her violent death had devastated the second-year student at New Mexico Western University. That she was found dead in her own bed that they had shared that evening, not only traumatized the sophomore, but made him a prime suspect. The coroner said the girl's hair had been pulled back and down so savagely her neck had snapped.

The emotional impact on Lucas wasn't diminished by being cleared as a suspect after a thorough interrogation and polygraph by Silver City police. They didn't have any other suspects and little to go on. Maybe it was someone out to frame him for her murder. Could it have been a former suitor, jealous now that he wasn't the one sleeping with the long-legged blonde beauty, who had done this?

No, some madman was turning his carefully cultivated world upside down. A person jealous over Lucas and Evelyn would not have known about Beth. That scenario was shattered now. He was only becoming aware of the stench of flesh just beginning to decompose, the same smell that had been present when he'd woke with Evelyn's body next to him in her bed last September.

Lucas feared he might never be able to get that odor out of his nose.

Somebody was out to get him. Who? Lucas didn't have a single enemy that he knew of. He was terrified. In a panic, he picked up the phone to call the police, but then placed the receiver back on the hook and reconsidered. Police would definitely attempt to pin this one on him. He knew they would revisit Evelyn's homicide to bolster their case in this second killing. He had lived in this sleepy little city most of his life and realized people around here would be deeply disturbed by such gruesome crimes.

Murder was as foreign a concept to Grant County as the Gila Rodeo would be to Tokyo. Police would be under a lot of public and official pressure to quickly identify a suspect and clear these cases. Lucas knew he would become the fall guy for both. And, if framing him was the killer's objective, the murders would cease with his arrest and assure his eventual conviction.

Lucas had to put his fear on the back burner and think this through. Hastily, but not carelessly, he devised a plan. It hinged on an assumption that no one knew he and Beth had spent the night together.

Beth was a sweet girl he had met last night at a drama club presentation of *"Strolling Thru the Woods"*, a parody of Hansel and Gretel. He had been attracted to the tall, leggy blonde cast as Gretel first by her laugh. That she resembled Evelyn was probably in the mix somehow, too, he figured.

He had approached her after the show and they had gone for a late coffee. Finding nothing open, he took her to his apartment and they had sipped coffee, then cognac, and laughed for hours. By the time they were ready for bed, Beth had decided she would like to spend the night.

Beth and Evelyn had been very different people despite their physical similarities. Beth was an intellectual and an artist, where Evelyn had been a bit of a tomboy. But both were adventurous free spirits in bed.

Lucas sat recalling Beth's surprising offer to stay the night. She had been so much more aggressive and sexually confident than Evelyn …

Stop thinking of her as a person, Lucas. Focus on the task at hand.

The thought was like being drenched in cold water. With it came clarity about his situation. He knew he needed to leave Silver City immediately, probably leave New Mexico altogether. Go to Texas, maybe further east.

But, first, there was the matter of the body.

There was no blood. By the way Beth's head lolled as he examined her naked corpse for any evidence that might tie him to it, he guessed that, like Evelyn, her neck had been snapped.

Lucas' mood wavered between grief and panic, but he realized he couldn't give in to either emotion. He had to get her out of his little apartment on First Street. Instead of trying to hide the body, Lucas decided to return Beth to her home, an inexpensive apartment not far from the campus.

Rigor mortis had come and gone, so he was able to fold the body at hips and knees. He stripped the bed and bundled the compacted body in the sheets, tying the corners to keep everything in place. Next, he emptied his wicker laundry hamper into the washer and stuffed the wrapped body into it. Then he remade his bed, just in case the police should visit the apartment. He cleaned up the remnants of their drinking and love-making, then walked through all the rooms, double-checking to be sure there was no indication he'd had company last night. He found make-up items she'd left out on the bathroom counter. This prompted him to locate her purse. He removed her earrings and dropped them in her handbag along with the cosmetics.

As he worked the hamper from the car outside the dead woman's apartment, he realized this would be the last time he would use this little five-door Toyota econobox he had shared with Evelyn. He didn't have a ride of his own; the car had belonged to her. When police cleared Lucas as a suspect in their daughter's death, Evelyn's parents had told Lucas that he could use the little Tercel as long as he was at the college.

He had attended Evelyn's funeral services with her family, who had been anxiously hoping the handsome boy on the verge of manhood would some-day be a member of their family. Lucas had the same hopes and dreams. He ached for the normalcy he observed all around him, but had never known. The dysfunction in his own family was such that he shared it with no one, not even Evelyn. His intention was that he would peel away the layers of secrecy about his childhood only for her, and only one at a time. In truth, he might never have found the "right time" for such revelation. The horrors of the things done to him and, in turn, by him, filled him with a self-loathing so intense he submerged it completely in smiling affability.

Lucas was extremely popular, and it wasn't just his handsome features and athletic body. He befriended the friendless on campus, the nerds, the poor, the disabled, all the unpopular and, in so doing, drew those a little closer to acceptance by others. If you were a friend of Lucas Peterson, you had to be pretty okay.

Lucas felt bad about using Evelyn's money for his getaway. The joint account held nearly $4,000, only a modest amount of which came from his labors. Most had come from Evelyn's parents to defray their daughter's college ex-penses for the coming semester. They had told the young man,who they had expected one day to be their son-in-law, to use the money for his own ex-penses. They had steadfastly believed in Lucas during the police investigation of Evelyn's murder, and felt vindicated when he was cleared.

He felt even worse about leaving Silver City, With its rich Wild-West history, its legacy of mining, ranching, and agriculture, and a terrific year-round climate. Like Evelyn, he had grown up bouncing between Silver City and Deming, just over an hour to the south. The city is nestled at the foothills leading into the Mogollon Mountains in Southwestern New Mexico, part of the wilderness comprising the Gila National Forest.

Lucas loved the wilderness, and spent nearly every weekend on its wild trails, backpacking and camping, or simply hiking. Evelyn had shared that love of the outdoors, often accompanying him up Highway 15 to his favorite trailheads. Sometimes Evelyn's parents came on the day trips with the young lovers.

The couple had talked of marriage, and he had planned to propose to her on one of their frequent day trips to the Gila Cliff Dwellings. The prehistoric architecture of the ruins of the homes cut into the mountainside are the most significant depiction of the life of people of the Mogollon culture who disappeared in the 14th Century. It was the couple's special place. They had even spent a night making love in the ruins unseen by the State Forest Rangers who regulate visits up the mountainside. Accomplished hikers and climbers, they had come in from the wilderness side, avoiding the man-made trail used by the tourists who flock to the Gila Wilderness — the nation's first designated wilderness area — every year.

Lucas felt the weight of the small velvet box in his pocket. Unknown to Evelyn, Lucas had been carrying around an engagement ring for the entire week before her murder. It had cost a month's income from fixing the eclectic array of junkers students drive around campus, everything from routine maintenance to complete engine overhauls. He could do it all. Even now, the ring was in his pocket. He knew he would have to pawn it somewhere — someplace where he wasn't known, someplace where whoever was doing these things to women he loved wouldn't be able to find him.

He hastily scribbled a note to Evelyn's family, dropped the car keys into the envelope, packed a duffel and his tools, drew all the money out of the joint account he had shared with Evelyn, and hit the road. Inside the duffel, along with clothes and toiletries, were the two sheets he had used to transport Beth's body to her apartment. He had reasoned that his semen or body hairs or other evidence on them would be too coincidental if they were ever found by the police.

The duffel and the mechanic's tool box would have been a daunting burden for a lesser man, but Lucas wasn't slowed as his long strides carried him through the hilly streets of his birth city to the southeastern edge where US Highway 180 became a real highway.

He stopped and looked back at the hodgepodge of buildings. Shacks and houses, fields and empty lots abutted each other in a community where city planning and zoning were still years from reality. Sadly he reflected how the town might change in the future and lose its personality. Someday, all those old adobe buildings dating from the 1800s would disappear, not all at once, of course but slowly — one by one. He said a silent prayer that he might live to return someday before that happened. Knowing that he would never live here with his sweetheart as he'd dreamed.

Lucas could not have predicted that it would be a quarter of a century before he returned to the place of his birth.

2

Hitching a ride out of Silver City is never difficult, even with a duffel and the heavy toolbox Lucas carried. Rides, although short hops from town to town, are easy enough. The crime plague and deadbolt locks of big cities hadn't yet become the curse of urban life for this high-desert oasis. The mechanic's tools told any passing motorist that this was just another workingman. Someone would stop.

Rev. William Benton spotted the young man alongside the divided highway. The hitchhiker was clean, well dressed for this rugged area in jeans, boots, and a leather jacket. Probably a mechanic looking for work. The minister was on his way out of town to visit a parishioner in Hurley, 15 miles away.

Reverend Benton let the aging Datsun coast to a stop on the broad shoulder of the highway and watched in the rearview mirror as the hitchhiker loped toward the car, carrying the toolbox as easily as an overnight bag, a duffel slung across his back.

"Thanks," Lucas said as he reached the car. He quickly opened the rear door and deposited the toolbox and duffel on the back seat. "Don't worry, I keep my toolbox clean. Won't hurt your seat." He opened the front door and folded his tall, muscular frame into the old sedan.

"Lucas," The hitchhiker said, extending a hand, grasped warmly by his benefactor. "How far you going?"

"Just to Hurley," the minister replied. "Call me Reverend Billy."

"Ah, a preacher."

"Yes sir, 26 years now. Going to visit a shut-in down here. She's too old to always make it to services anymore and sometimes can't find a ride even when she is feeling well. And where are you going?"

"Deming, to see my uncle. I work in his garage Saturdays. I'm taking engineering at WNMU."

Lucas didn't really intend to stop and see uncle Bo this trip; he planned to keep going, to get out of state. Beauregard "Bo " Duchamps was his father's younger brother and he really didn't want to see him or to answer questions about college or his mother, questions that Bo would be sure to ask. Lucas kept quiet and let his chauffeur do the talking. Reverend Billy talked enough for both of them.

"I can remember when it was New Mexico State Teachers College, before it got university status. I moved here in the 1950s," the preacher said. "I have a wonderful little church, Adobe Flats Church of Christ, charismatic, you know.

"Do you have a church home here?" he asked after getting no response.

"I sometimes make it to chapel at the college."

"Well, come see us sometime. If you're only in Deming on weekends, you might want to make our Wednesday night prayer services."

"I might do just that." Lucas didn't plan to return to Silver City. Two unsolved murders dictated it was time to move on.

"That was North Hurley back there. I'll drive on through Hurley proper so I can let you out on the highway, easier to get a ride," Reverend Billy said.

Years from now, the Rev. William Benton would see a story and photograph in a tabloid at the drugstore and remember the last words of his encounter with this handsome young man as they shook hands across the front seat: "Pray for me, Reverend Billy."

3

Lucas watched as the preacher made a U-turn and headed back toward Hurley. When the sound of the old Datsun's engine had been replaced with the forlorn silence of the southwestern New Mexico landscape, Lucas turned back south, his boots crunching on the graveled shoulder of the highway — the only sound.

In the distance, mountains appeared shrouded in lilac and lavender, a decidedly tender apparition of what the lone walker knew were the rugged mountains between himself and El Paso, the notorious Texas border town grown now to a prosperous city. Above him, the desert sky was clear and clean; over the mountains more than 100 miles away, tall cumulus clouds promised rain, a vow broken more often than kept in this part of the world.

Walking with his back to traffic along the highway, a two-lane ribbon paralleling railroad tracks stretching miles across the desert landscape, Lucas didn't bother to put out his thumb. Traffic is scarce in this lightly populated area. Only when he heard a car would he turn to face traffic, stretch out his arm, thumb pointing toward the clear sky.

It took nearly two hours and his purposeful stride has taken him nearly eight more miles, but the fourth car that passed him going south stopped with a squeal of brakes. The late-model pickup truck had probably been doing better than 80, pretty much the norm for this stretch of road, and had shot past him before deciding to stop. The driver put the truck in reverse and backed onto the shoulder and continued backing until about 40 feet from him

The thirty-something blonde behind the wheel of the late-model pick-up gave Lucas a dazzling smile as he walked up to the driver-side door. "Hop in, sweetie."

Lucas returned a smile as bright as the one received. He deposited the toolbox in the bed of the truck directly behind the driver's door. As he walked around the front of the truck, he made eye contact with the driver.

Beautiful, sexy, even if she's older'n me.

He opened the door and hauled his athletic frame into the cab of the truck. "You goin' as far as Interstate 10?"

The blonde appraised the well-built, tanned young man. "Honey, I can go a lot farther than that."

"Las Cruces, El Paso?" Lucas asked, hopefully.

"That's not what I was talking about, but sure, I can get you there." Her eyes flashed wolfishly. She licked her lips, winked, and put the truck in gear. The woman turned on the radio. An ill-tuned country station was playing a slow, romantic ballad.

Lucas talked about college life, about fixing cars. The miles began to roll by but the landscape didn't change. Sand, long stretches of barbed wire, prickly pear and yucca by the hundreds.

Lucas' hand brushed the woman's knee as he attempted to tune the radio, not quite on station; she smiled at him and pressed her leg against his hand lightly but noticeably.

A sexual encounter was the last thing on Lucas' mind, but he looked at her. She looked him straight in the eye, not a shred of coquettishness about that look.

Maybe we can relieve a little tension at that.

Lucas placed his palm on the inside of her knee and slowly slid it up the inside of her thigh. The blonde reacted with a quick intake of breath as he passed the hem of her short skirt.

They were approaching the City of Rocks, a natural rock formation almost always deserted. The man/boy in the seat beside her shuddered; she didn't notice. This is where he buried his mother's body many years ago, and the reason for the chill that made him shudder. It's also where she had buried his father's murdered corpse six years before that.

The blonde quickly turned the pick-up left at the entrance to the City of Rocks and drove up the dusty road to the first outcropping of large rocks. She pulled the truck out of sight behind the formation. By this time her passenger was massaging her through her panties. She slammed the car into park, killed the ignition, and turned toward him, pulling her right knee up onto the seat to give the probing hand better access.

"I don't even know your name!" But she didn't ask him to stop.

"Call me Luke." He slowly slid a finger inside the leg of the panties.

The blonde sighed. "Call me Mona."

Two fingers plunged into the moistness, hitting Mona like a jolt of electricity. Grasping both sides of the younger man's head, she kissed him fiercely, then she pushed him against the door, tearing at his belt and zipper until his quickly engorging erection was in her hand.

"I have a quilt and a blanket behind the seat," she said huskily.

"Great," Lucas moaned, reacting to her urgent pulling at his manhood.

Releasing her hold on him, and reluctantly removing his insinuated hand, she opened the door and jumped down from the pick-up. Lucas hastily readjusted his clothing and hopped out to walk around the truck.

Mona released the seatback latch and removed a folded, Burberry throw, basically, a lap blanket. Next she pulled out a thick, old and worn quilt. "Be a dear and spread this for us, then put my Burberry over it. It's really soft."

Lucas quickly unfolded the quilt and spread it on the driver side of the car, putting the smaller blanket on top of it. Mona hastily stepped out of her panties and tossed them through the open door of the truck. They came to rest on the edge of the driver seat, followed by her blouse and bra. She immediately sank to the blanket and rolled onto her back, the miniskirt bunched at her waist. "Oh, Hurry Luke, please."

Lucas stripped off his pants and shorts, kicking off his boots to get the legs of the jeans over his feet. They kissed fiercely, and, with no foreplay, he plunged his entire length into the willing woman as she arched her back to receive him.

For a 19-year-old, Lucas knew a lot about pleasing women; his mother had seen to that. He varied the tempo and the length of the stroke each time he felt Mona get into a rhythm. Each change was like starting fresh, and with each variation, she screamed in ecstasy. By varying the tempo, Lucas was also able to forestall his own climax.

The dry, cool desert air evaporated the sweat of the lovers as they twined together beneath the afternoon sun. After only a few minutes of Lucas' expert lovemaking, Mona's orgasms began. Over and over again, her body tensed, arched, and then relaxed. continued. When she relaxed, he would slow until her passion would again begin to ignite.

God, he can go all day; this guy's fuckin' superman!

Again she began to climax. This time, she quickly pulled away and grasped his member with both hands, enjoying the slippery coating of her own juices.

I want it in my mouth. I don't usually like the feel of it, but I want to taste him!

"No, don't do tha ..." Lucas groaned.

The blonde quickly brought her lips down around the burgeoning head of his cock. She died so suddenly she didn't feel the impact of the huge rock that crushed her skull.

4

Lucas awoke to find himself in the bed of the truck, dressed and alone, his head resting on his duffel. The sun was beginning to set.

The sun shouldn't be setting for a couple hours yet, and how'd I get into the truck? Where's Mona?

He looked over the edge of the truck bed and saw Mona, face-up and motionless on the quilt. Dazedly, he went to her. She was still naked except for the little skirt at her waist, She was dead, her face a mask of surprise — and blood.

How did this happen?

But now it was beginning to sink in. Lucas knew. Had it been he who murdered Beth? Evelyn? With revulsion he considered the possibility that he had been the person who had snapped Evelyn's sweet neck that night six months ago. Lucas had no memory of the deaths of the two Silver City women who had died in his presence, just as he had no recollection of what might have happened to this woman.

He inspected the body. A modest amount of blood had pooled under her head and nearly covered a rock the size of a grapefruit laying on the Burberry blanket beside her. He looked at his hands. The right hand was covered with dried blood and his left also had traces. He followed a blood trail back to the truck and saw bloody handprints; he must have climbed up into the bed before he blacked out.

13

Thinking quickly but with purpose, Lucas wrapped the body and the rock in the quilt and blanket and unceremoniously dumped it into the pick-up bed. He drove into the desert south and east of the rock formation. There, he stripped the body of all clothing and jewelry.

Teeth! They can identify her from dental records.

Lucas opened his toolbox, removed a pair of pliers, and commenced the grisly task of pulling all the teeth from the woman's skull.

He checked the body one more time, then buried it in a shallow grave about 60 feet up the foot of a mesa behind a small juniper. He knew that desert vultures and other carrion eaters would strip the flesh from bone, and that coyotes would carry any meaty bones to their lairs, effectively making the job of recovering all of the remains impossible, even if she were someday found.

He went through Mona's purse, removed out all identifying information and money. He scooped the bloody teeth from the desert sand into the purse, and then bundled it in her clothes. These he'd leave in a commercial dumpster in a municipal area later. He used her blouse and undergarments to clean up the truck bed as best he could. He would finish the job at the Deming Coin-Op Car Wash.

Lucas was surprised to find just over $1,300 in the dead woman's purse. His assets were growing. With the cash from the joint account he had shared with Evelyn, money wouldn't be a problem during his exodus. A library card from Las Vegas, Nevada, listed her as Mona Richter.

Maiden Name. Aha! I remember; she married old man Harper, who died and left her filthy rich.

Sure enough, her checkbook was in the name of Mona Harper. Now, he also had a truck, at least until the woman would be missed. That could take awhile. There was no ring on her finger, so maybe there was a chance no one was going to be looking for her for awhile, but he still needed to get out of New Mexico before she was missed.

First he had to do something about the truck.

As a mechanic in Deming, he was familiar with Mexican chop shops and had even done some engine rebuilding for some guys he figured were stealing and "remanufacturing" American vehicles to sell south of the border. He would find someone in El Paso or Juarez who would love to get their hands on this new truck, someone who would trade him a legal older vehicle, no questions asked.

Lucas didn't understand exactly what was going on, why women in his life were being killed, most likely by himself, but he was getting really experienced at disposing of bodies.

5

Lacey Jay hoped she could afford a new dress for the junior prom, it was such a special occasion. The all-state running back, the most popular guy in their school, had asked her to go with him.

Dude was the one bright star of their little school, which played six-man football. Although he'd never played the big game, colleges were already courting the rock-hard athlete — who wrestled steers and rode bulls in his spare time — with full athletic scholarship offers. His gentleness off the field, his affable smile and his refusal to limit his availability to any of the various high school cliques made him the most popular boy in town. His blue eyes and unruly black hair also made him the most sought-after escort on the dating scene.

I guess I should be thankful I can at least afford a dress from Goodwill, even if Miz Edie had to drive me to San Angelo to get it.

She had been doing chores for Eyidie Nwaigbo — Miz Edie — nearly every weekend since the first of the year. But the old black woman didn't need a lot of help, a couple hours each Saturday to vacuum and dust. It was easy work; the teenager's best friend and former babysitter kept her house nearly spotless on her own.

Lacey didn't know that the arrangement with her Nigerian neighbor was more one of charity than need. Eyidie knew the teenager's pride wouldn't let her take money if she just offered, and she knew her mother, Velma Jay, couldn't spare much, what with the chemotherapy and all. Widowed only three years ago when Kyle's liver finally surrendered to years of alcoholism, she was diagnosed with lung cancer just before last Thanksgiving. The couple could be the poster models for anti-alcohol and anti-tobacco campaigns. The old black woman figured that the alcohol just got to Kyle before the cigarettes could. Both were chain smokers in a time when filtered cigarettes were for the young, or as Kyle would say, "pussies and queers."

Eyidie understood, however, that there are pressures on a teenager to have enough financial freedom to go places and do things with her friends. She had asked Velma's permission to hire Lacey for her little chores.

Lacey dug through racks of dresses smelling of other women's cologne for one that would be pretty and would fit her. A couple of sundresses caught her eye and she headed for the dressing room.

The salesgirl — a pin on her chest said her name was Janine — opened the door and offered to assist.

"No, thank you, Ma'am, I just want to try these dresses on." Lacey felt strange being waited on. Usually, she was the one doing the fetching for her parents.

"Well, Sunshine, you just let me know if I can help," Janine said with a wink. "Got a date this weekend?"

Lacey felt herself blush. "Yes, Dude Autrey asked me to the junior prom. It's tonight, and after that, we're going to a party."

"The Dude?" she said, her eyes widening. Even in San Angelo, 80 miles north of Sonora, everybody knew of Dude Autrey, and loved him. And in Sonoma the dark-haired Adonis and sports hero was the closest many of them expected to ever get to a real celebrity.

"I know about those parties," the woman added. "My own was a blast. What I remember of it, I mean," she said with a laugh. "I'd smoke a little pot and drink a little beer. We were into free love and going with the flow back then."

"That can't have been too long ago," Lacey said. "You don't look that much older than me."

"Thanks, Hon, but I saw my teens a long time ago, and most of my twenties, for that matter. Sure hope you have as much fun as I did." She went back to the other side of the store to see if the two elderly women who had just walked in needed help.

Wow! He might expect me to go all the way, but I hardly know him.

Lacey figured that any other girl in school would probably be glad to give up her cherry to Dude Autrey. Tears began to leak from the corner of an eye. It wasn't that virginity was a particularly prized possession in this part of the world, but being a virgin made Lacey feel more like something special. Being special isn't the way most of the high-school kids thought of folks who lived in those trailers out by the rodeo grounds.

What am I going to do?!

Then she thought about Dude. He was so kind and easygoing. He could, of course, have any girl he wanted; he wouldn't need to force himself on anyone. Then it occurred to her, how would she fee if he *didn't* try to get into her pants. The thought made her laugh. She just might force herself on him.

A light tap on the door. "You okay, honey? I found a dress for your important night, a lot better'n those ol' sundresses you took in with you." Without waiting for an answer, she handed a hanger with a decidedly adult cocktail dress through the door, black satin with cutouts across the collarbones and the shoulder blades. "If you're gonna compete for attention from the likes of Super Jock, you'll need to bring your A-game to that party."

Lacey felt like Janine had read her mind; it made her blush. "I think tonight's gonna to be a real important time for me," she answered through the door." I surely hope this dress is cheap. I don't have much money."

"Just humor me. We'll worry about money later." The interaction between her and Janine sounded just like Lacey'd always wished she and her mama could talk.

Who am I kidding! Mama never shopped for anything but booze for her and Pops and bologna and Kool-Aid for us kids.

Janine was helping the two elegantly dressed elderly ladies check out at the register when she heard a very unladylike whistle from the dressing room. "It's so sexy," Lacey said. "I love it."

"Lemme see," Janine said. The two other customers looked at each other.

When the girl self-consciously opened the door and stood in a pool of her own discarded clothes in the tiny dressing room, Janine smiled appreciatively "You'll knock 'em dead."

"You really think it looks okay?" Lacey looked over her shoulder into the mirror at the back of the dress.

"I think you look like of of them fashion models! Come out here and walk for me." Janine instructed.

Lacey walked out in the sexy, clingy dress — and rubber flip-flops. To Lacey's dismay, Janine roared with laughter. To make matters worse, the other two women were hiding their own giggles.

"Get back in there until I get you some decent shoes. Size 6, I'd guess."

"Yes ma'am," the teenager said sheepishly.

Within minutes Janine had bagged the other customers' purchases and plucked a pair of shoes from a rack. She returned to the dressing room with a pair of strappy black stilettos in patent leather. "Honey these'll turn every head in the place, if you don't turn an ankle first."

Lacey retreated to the dressing room to slip on the nearly brand new shoes. This time when the walked out, Janine was the one to whistle.

"Walk for me."

Janine, knuckles under her chin, right elbow resting in her palm at her waist, watched the woman-child sashay across the aisle. Lacey had already developed a woman's hips, not the slender boyish butt of most of her classmates.

"Mmm, mmm,, mmm. It just needs a few accessories and you're good to go, girl."

"You're awfully generous with my money," Lacey said with a laugh. "Okay just for grins, but I'm sure I can't afford all this."

The two young women peered through the glass counter at the costume jewelry inside. "What about those little pearl studs with the matching necklace? That's all you'd need with that dress and those heels." Janine removed the pieces from the showcase and slipped the studs through Lacey's pierced lobes. "Now, don't you look cosmopolitan?"

Janine pinned Lacey's hair up high on her head, brushed her cheeks with blusher, and then fastened the pearls behind the teenager's slender, graceful neck.

Lacey Jay gazed at the stranger in the mirror on the dressing room door. "Is that really me?"

"Nobody else but!" Janine placed a hand on Lacey's shoulders. "I think your date will flip out."

"Look, I can pay you a little every week until this is all paid for, if you'll let me. My name is Lacey Jay and I work two days a week. I'll give you everything I make until we're square."

"I can cover you on that, pleased to meet you Lacey Jay." The saleswoman extended her hand. "I'm Janine Casagrande."

"What a wonderful name," the teenager said, taking the offered hand in a firm grip.

Neither the girl nor the woman knew that this scene would play out several times over the coming years. Janine's counsel on clothes and boys and life in general filled a void in the life of the young girl whose own mother wasn't equipped to the task of turning a girl into an adult. In the process, the age difference between the two melted and they became unlikely friends. Janine's importance was amplified when the cancer in her lungs claimed Velma during the summer. She and Eyidie Nwaigbo became steady counsel as Lacey Jay made the difficult transition from girl to woman, and they would all three remain closest of friends for the rest of their lives. No one would guess that the youngest life would end earliest.

6

Lacey had only been partially right. The Junior Prom was the beginning of their romance, and Dude had asked her to come to his graduation dance the following month. After the party, she and Dude had done some typical teenage making out, but Dude didn't press for more than Lacey offered. Nervously, she'd let him place a hand on her breast as they kissed, but Dude had read the stiffness of her body and slid his hand down to her waist. They saw each other at least once a day between the two dances, and Lacey knew she was in love with the small-town cowboy.

They'd spent nights together before, but had never gone "all the way", although they'd been together practically naked. If "All the way" was the home run, they'd rounded third base on more than one occasion. It wasn't that Lacey was unwilling, just a bit reluctant. That Dude respected her reluctance was one of the things she loved about him most; beneath that tough cowboy was a man who could be a gentleman.

Dude gave Lacey the big news the day of the graduation dance. A scout from Baylor University had tapped him for one of a handful of full-paid athletic scholarships the Baptist school could offer. He had hoped for it, but had already prepared himself for the likelihood that he wouldn't get a college education. The confirmation phone call had come last night and a letter of acceptance was on its way. The coach would be by in a few days to have him sign a letter of intent.

Now he was going to a big university. He knew Lacey would be a little disappointed in having their last summer together cut short; he would have to be in training camp in about three weeks. But he had a plan.

Dude was waiting when Lacey emerged from Eyidie's trailer after her regular Saturday cleaning. "Let's go to the Nook before it closes and get a soda."

"Can't I change out of these clothes first?" Lacey spread her hands to show the dowdy duster she had worn for the morning chores.

"Only if you can hurry; it's already 1 o'clock and the Nook locks up at 2."

"Three minutes, no more, I promise!" and Lacey tore across the yard and into the trailer she and Dude would someday inherit when her mother died — along with the payments.

As the teenagers sat in the booth at the coffee shop sipping sodas and sharing an order of fries, Dude not only gave Lacey the news, but told her his plan. "I suppose we'll have to get married so you can go with me," Dude said as he pulled her tight against him. "I can't think about football knowing you're here without me and I'm there without you."

But Lacey was elated and petrified at the same time. "It's me who should worry, Dude," Lacey said. "All those rich college girls for you to choose from — I'd lose you for sure."

"No way, Babe," Dude said while he nibbled her ear. "You and me are a set."

"Do you really mean that, Dude?" she asked. "I'm not especially pretty or anything."

"Don't you say that about my girl," he joked, now nuzzling her neck. "My girl's the prettiest, sexiest, and, mmmm, the tastiest in all of Texas. think I'll eat this ear … oh, wait. I got something."

From his hip pocket, Dude extracted a small box, slightly squashed on one corner where Dude's weight had sat on it. Lacey felt the heat rush to her face and all those other places Dude's attention had always awakened. He took a modest little diamond solitaire ring from the box.

"Lacey Jay," he asked solemnly, "will you share my hitching post for the rest of my life?"

Not the most romantic proposal a girl could hear.

24

Lacey didn't know whether to laugh at his corny proposal or to cry from the intense joy that made her heart feel like it was going to explode out of her chest.

"Yes, you crazy cowboy! Yes! Yes! Yes!"

Only Lacey's diary and her best friend, Janine, ever knew her thoughts the day that Dude proposed.

Does he truly love me or is it just the fear of going off to Baylor alone?

Lacey told herself it wouldn't matter in the long run.

I'll be Lacey Jay Autrey for the rest of my life, Dude's wife. If it ain't love now, it will be; I'll make him love me more'n he ever loved anyone.

Tonight, she decided, she would offer no resistance. She would allow her man to claim her. The teenager couldn't have foreseen the changes that would eventually come in life with her gentleman cowboy — the arguments, the drunken rages, the other women, the beatings — all that would come years later, after the children were born.

7

The first time Lacey left Dude was just before their wedding. The bachelor's party had included a group of buckle bunnies, one for each cowboy. Dude couldn't turn that down, now could he?

In retaliation, Lacey Jay headed for the only place she knew Dude wouldn't go — Janine's little farmhouse on the way out of town. Janine Casagrande, a remarkable free spirit of the '60s, took Lacey in and provided wise counsel regarding men in general and men like Dude in particular. She once had lived in a commune in California before heading back to Texas in the late '70s. Now her farm was almost a commune of its own.

The two women's friendship, which had blossomed from that meeting during Lacey's junior year of high school, now bridged the age difference with the trust and affection each held for the other. As for Lacey, she loved being with Janine because, unlike her parents and even her fiancé, Janine never made her feel childish.

"You'd a made a damn good Hippie, girl," she once told Lacey. "Too bad you were born too late."

Janine introduced Lacey to Brock Taylor, a gentle and caring man who soothed her injured ego and made her feel womanly again. What Dude took away from her with his philandering, Brock gave back to her. Their friendship began innocently enough with a few walks around the old farmhouse, which Janine had inherited and now used as a sanctuary for any lostlings she found, as long as they were willing to participate in the communal lifestyle she'd brought back with her from California.

For a few months, this included Brock and Lacey.

The middle-aged Hippie encouraged the two young people to nurture themselves, especially in love. "When a soul is as malnourished as yours, Lacey, take love where you find it. Brock is a decent man. You're not married to that arrogant bastard Dude, so why not spend time with Brock?"

Lacey felt uncomfortable with the sexual undertones of her friend's suggestion; she was — in Dude's vernacular — jailbait, still nearly a year shy of that number where she's supposed to be a woman. But she had to admit Brock Taylor was easy to be around, and Dude had ended her virginity the night of the dance.

Well, I ended it; it was my idea.

She and Dude had only had intercourse twice. He had been petrified of getting her pregnant, so he'd used a condom each time. Now here she was, isolated from the rest of the world most days and no one to know what goes on. And Brock looked so good, and she was so horny after her brief taste of the joys of sex.

Janine busied herself with her baking while Brock and Lacey spent time together. She sold her pottery, flowers, vegetables, and herbs along the roadside to make a little money on the side. She supplemented this with her part-time job at the Goodwill store. For her part, Lacey earned her keep in the garden. Brock's contribution was taking care of heavier chores around the little farm.

Between tending the vegetable garden in back of the house and the flower garden in front, Lacey spent the afternoons curled up in a corner bedroom with her guitar and her music, or in long, intimate conversations with Brock. It was an idyllic summer. Spending so much time together, Lacey and Brock became lovers as well as friends.

"You know I have a record, don't you Lacey?" Brock asked one day as they sat on the porch of the old house. "Otherwise I'd ask you to marry me."

Lacey laughed. "You think Dude Autrey's pure as the fallen snow? That man's been bailed out so many times, the bail bondsman has a rubber stamp with his name on it.

"Just so you ain't no convicted wife killer, there's nothing you could say that would change our relationship."

"Well, pot, marijuana, was my downfall back in college. Got caught with a couple joints in the ashtray of my car. Those days are behind me and I'll probably go back to school this fall."

Lacey moved closer and curled up against him. She looked into Brock's deep velvet brown eyes. "Why are you telling me this? I don't expect us to get married. I never said I wanted it. I only wanted this time to sort out what I do want. I'm still engaged to Dude and neither of us has asked to break it off."

"You haven't decided? I know you want to sing and to write music. You have a poet's soul and every one of your songs tells a story. You should continue with it, and I'm not sure that's possible with Dude Autrey."

She nodded. "I intend to continue to write and to sing. Just don't know if I can make much of a living at it."

"With the right help, you could. I don't know anyone in the business or I'd help. If it's meant to be, it'll happen. We both will know our way when we find it." He reached over and touched her face with his work-roughened hands. Tilting her face up to his, he drank deeply from her lips, tasting the sweetness of her. He leaned his body toward hers and pressed her down onto the cushioned swing seat. He ran his fingers through her unruly hair.

"I love you, Lacey Jay, but I don't think that's enough for us right now. I know we'll be friends if not lovers from now on."

She batted her eyelashes at him. "Is it because I'm so cute?"

"Cute isn't a word that fits you, Lacey Jay. No, you're definitely not cute.

"Cute is for puppies," he said. "You're one hell of a beautiful woman, a sensuous woman, a sexy woman but not at all cute," he said as he unbuttoned her blouse.

The summer love affair made Lacey feel grown up. But even as a teenager, she knew the relationship wouldn't last. Brock was her port in the stormy relationship she was still committed to with Dude. For his part, Brock, like Dude, had college plans. He would be gone once September rolled around, and she would probably be in Waco with Dude.

8

With summer winding down to an end, Brock put an end to the relationship with his decision to return to Sul Ross State University in Alpine.

This was fine with Lacey who had always intended to give Dude a second chance. Their wedding was scheduled for Labor Day. Dude would be finished with the early practice and have a long weekend before returning to Baylor. She looked forward to accompanying him to Waco.

The coach made Dude give up the rodeo, saying it was too dangerous and that a rodeo injury could affect the entire Baylor football program. What the coach really was saying is that everyone was expecting big things from the West Texas Flash, as the media had now christened him. Reluctantly, Dude gave up his favorite pastime.

Bidding Janine goodbye, Lacey headed back to Sonora. The farmhouse called Forlorn, Janine assured her, would always be there for her refuge from life's daily grind and woes, a promise fulfilled many times in years to come as Lacey and her daughters became frequent guests while Dude was away on the rodeo circuit.

She knew now that she would return to marry Dude. Over the years, she would come here for a few days from time to time when she and Dude were having troubles, and sometimes when they weren't. Dude's rodeo career kept him on the road, and the farm would become a favorite retreat for Lacey, and eventually, for her children as well.

31

But never would she cheat on her husband, Her time with Brock was a wonderful secret memory, not to be repeated.

She made sure that Dude would know where she was, though he seldom showed any interest in coming with her. Lacey suspected Dude's strict Baptist upbringing made him uncomfortable around a real, live hippie like Janine.

At the wedding, she wore a second-hand lace top and satin miniskirt in front of the JP as though she were wearing an elegant ball gown. Dude wore his Levis with a starched white shirt. He handed Lacey a bouquet he bought at the HEB store and removed his Stetson from his slicked-down hair. Lacey didn't even mind the bulge of the Skoal* can in his hip pocket. Beside him stood Carl Hansen, another rodeo cowboy and Dude's best bud. Lacey's matron of honor, not surprisingly, was Janine Casagrande.

The only sad moment came when the Justice of the Peace asked "Who giveth this woman."

Lacey had hoped her mother could hold off the slow progress of the lung cancer that had been slowly devouring her instead Eyidie gave away the bride.

"Baby," her mother said from the bed at the hospice, "I would love to be there for you and Dude, but I don't think I'll last the summer. Just one too many cigarettes, I guess.

"Just know on that day that I'm proud of you." Within a week, she was dead.

Lacey had promised her mother she wouldn't smoke and that she wouldn't let anyone smoke around her children. Dude's Skoal was a compromise, but she intended to nag him out of his nasty snuff-dipping habit.

Janine took wedding pictures with her Polaroid*. The snapshots would fade like the smile on Lacey's face in the next few years. But when her girls found them, they'd be able to make out features on their parents' faces that had a familial similarity to their own.

The couple rented a room in San Angelo for the weekend that come with free breakfast. Dude had stayed at the little motel once before, during a rodeo last summer. Lacey's summer fling at the Casagrande farm had shown Lacey what lovemaking could be, and she surprised her new husband with her expertise.

"Wow, put a ring on your finger and you become a hellcat in the bedroom!"

For the first time in his life, the young cowboy made love to a woman without the inconvenience of a condom; for the first time, Lacey knew what it felt like to have her husband climax deep inside her. They weren't worried about pregnancy; both were eager to start a family. Neither knew, yet, that Brock had already started the process.

But the morning sickness arrived less than a month later. Dude was out of town again at a fall rodeo in Mesquite, just outside Dallas. Lacey counted back.

Oh shit! I'm carrying Brock's baby

9

Lacey heard Dude whooping and hollering as he entered the small hospital in Sonora. She could swear the baby recognized his voice, too, she wriggled and twisted up her face in disgust at the noise.

Dude had been on the rodeo circuit ever since losing his scholarship and being kicked off the football team in Waco. Good Baptist boys, even football heroes who can cover 40 yards in 4.3 seconds, are expected to pass midterms. He lost the scholarship mostly for academic deficiencies. The tiny school in West Texas didn't really prepare its football star for the pressures of a major school like Baylor. He'd slid through high school as a jock and teachers were reluctant to give him poor grades. As a consequence, he really didn't learn. Dude wasn't stupid, but his native intelligence didn't make up for the reality that he'd never really learned how to study or to apply himself academically.

So Lacey's cowboy came home to be a cowboy once more. For Dude, it was a relief. He could now pursue his true passion, the rodeo. But that meant he was on the road a lot, leaving Lacey at home where she filled her time writing her little songs and picking out melodies for them on her old Fender guitar.

For his part, Dude was as successful on the rodeo circuit as he had been on the gridiron. He began to win with enough regularity that he could maintain the household without a second job. It took a lot of time away from the young couple, however.

The young wife found herself pregnant and alone — and scared. But she'd never tell Dude such a thing. It was the being alone most of the time that really got to her. But the loneliness and the blues brought out her best writing, and she went at it with a passion. It wasn't that all the songs were sad; some of her best work talked about babies and family. But others were the opposite, carrying themes of worry, jealousy, and emptiness.

Lacey knew all about the "buckle bunnies", teenage rodeo groupies who competed with each other to bed as many of the big name riders and ropers as they could. She didn't kid herself; Dude was a fun-loving, good-looking all-American boy. She knew he got plenty of offers. She could only pray he didn't take them; in reality, she prayed only that he didn't bring home a disease or send some teenie-bopper home with a baby.

Once again, Eyidie, who had cared for Lacey when she was a baby, was called in to help out as Lacey neared term. Lacey was grateful the old woman was with her at the hospital when the baby was born

As they were preparing to take the baby home, Dude came bursting into the room loaded with packages and smelling of leather, hay, and sweat, familiar odors to the wife of a cowboy. Lacey had grown to love the smells, mainly because it meant Dude was doing something he loved and not drinking as much. Rodeo had its upside.

He carried a miniature Stetson for the baby, a stuffed dog, and a fistful of flowers for Lacey.

"How is he?" he asked his wife before inquiring anything about her own health and welfare.

"He's a she," Lacey replied. "Our first child is a little girl." She pulled back the covers to reveal auburn fuzz and a pouty little set of lips above a cleft chin. "Isn't she adorable?"

"Sure, a girl's okay, I just counted on it being a boy. You know to pass the name along. Maybe even named after Willie Nelson, did I tell you he was the star attraction with the Mesquite rodeo this year?" he gushed the words out.

"We could still use his name, only shorten the Nelson to Nell, maybe," she said quietly, "If you're set on that for the baby's name. Willie Nell sounds cute."

"Okay," Dude was more than satisfied. "That works. After this, I get to name all the boys, though, and you can name the girls."

He dropped the packages on the chair by the bed.

"You want to hold her?" Lacey asked. "You'd have to wash your hands really good first."

He shook his head. "Nope, hand her to Miz Edie, First, I want to give my wife a proper hello kiss."

"Wash your hands anyway," Eyidie ordered the cowboy, twice her size.

He obeyed with only a nod.

As Dude scrubbed his hands, Eyidie walked over to take the child from Lacey. "I suppose they'll be riding home with you?" she asked Dude.

"Damn straight, they will," he replied. "Did you think you'd get to keep my beautiful girls all to yourself?" He lifted Lacey up and nuzzled her neck before a passionate kiss. "Dang, girl, I missed you."

"I missed you, too, Dude," she said, "when I wasn't puking my guts out or peeing ever 15 minutes. At those times, I called you every cuss word I knew and didn't miss you a bit."

"I thought pregnant women only had morning sickness." He said as he sat down on the bed with Lacey in his arms.

"Somebody shoulda told the baby that," she said with a soft laugh. "Our girl saw to it I didn't eat anything she didn't like."

"If she helped you keep your figure, that's alright with me."

When the nurse came into the room, Dude placed his wife gently in the wheelchair, then took off like a madman, racing the wheelchair down the hallways.

Eyidie watched the young couple as they raced to the doors. She looked down at the baby in her arms. "Your daddy isn't ever going to grow up, Willie Nell. Like as not you'll be more mature than him in no time." She clucked her tongue. The little girl looked up at her with eyes that saw things clearly.

If I didn't know better I could swear the baby understood ... more than that, she agrees with me.

37

Eyidie would always say that Willie Nell was born old.

She followed them outside but put the baby in the infant car seat behind her mother as instructed by the safety guide. The hospital even provided them for those who couldn't afford them. "Time was folks were allowed to tote their babies in their arms in the car," the old black woman complained to Lacey. "Now everybody's got to be buckled in. Can't see no reason for it, if folks drive safe, the baby's more secure if its mama is holding it."

Lacey didn't argue with her friend, although she'd seen the film of unrestrained children being ripped from their parents' arms and thrown from the car. She knew Eyidie, as opinionated as she was, would always honor a mother's decision. She had done so for generations of kids in Sonora.

The two-car caravan made its way to the trailer park. Dude parked on the rectangle of cement beside his door. The park had concrete slabs for each trailer and in front of the slab, a parking slab large enough even for Dude's Suburban. Yet, the road into the trailer park was unpaved. Eyidie parked in front of her own little place directly across the trailer park driveway.

Dude helped Lacey inside. Eyidie unbuckled the infant and wrapped her in the receiving blanket and carried her into her new home.

"Little girl this ain't like Heaven where you just left with its angels but your mama's as close to an angel as I've met on earth here. Since your daddy stopped drinking so much, it's a sight more peaceful, too. If he can just stick to it, you'll have a good enough life. Heaven help us all though if he begins swiggin' again."

As she got to the porch steps, she quit talking to the baby girl and slowly made her way to the nursery set up for Willie Nell.

With the WIC program and other helping agencies, Lacey had fixed up one room for her baby. The bed had a rail to keep her from falling out. She had made curtains in pink and white checks, always hoping she'd have a girl first. Two dozen diapers hung in a cute little thing made from scraps of fabric and a wire coat hanger. All in all, it was a darling space for such a little wisp of humanity. Eyidie found a rocker at a garage sale that was painted to match the pink and white. The brightly decorated nursery succeeded mostly in making the rest of the furnishings in the trailer look pathetic. Lacey didn't mind. Her baby would have a lovely place, that's all that mattered to her.

Dude noticed all the changes immediately. "Where'd you get the money?"

"I saved it from what you sent, Honey." Lacey beamed with pride. "Isn't it pretty?"

"Guess so. Kinda frilly for my taste."

Lacey laughed her trilling little laugh and said, "She is a girl, Daddy."

"Daddy!?! I'll show you who's a daddy and who's a husband."

"Dude, we can't yet. The doctor says six weeks."

"Six weeks. I can't last that long! Bet you want me too," he said with a seductive grin.

"I had a kinda rough time, Dude. Stitches and everything," she said softly.

"Hell, I've rode with a broken arm. You can love your man with a few stitches, can't you?"

"No, Dude, I can't. It's important that we follow the doctor's orders. I think it'll be sooner than six weeks but not right away."

"What do we do until then, play cards?" he said with a snarl.

A tear crept down her cheek.

"Oh, Baby Doll, I'm sorry. I'm just disappointed," he said. "You know I would never hurt you. I'm just horny as hell."

Lacey dried her eyes and smiled. "I can do something about that. Drop them jeans, cowboy."

10

God, I love this guy. If he doesn't propose soon, I will.

Billie Jean Bollinger stared at Luke's rock-hard body as he peeled off his clothes. It was always the first thing he did when he came in from a day at Darby's Car Care. He'd kiss her with a peck, careful not to get any of the grime from his clothes on her, walk into the large master bathroom of the apartment they had shared for nearly two years. Strip, shower, shave, brush his teeth, wrap a terry robe around himself, and return to give her a more appropriate kiss.

As often happens, today's kiss escalated to the bedroom.

Still locked in a passionate kiss, Luke palmed her buttocks. Billie Jean wrapped her legs around his waist as he supported her by his hands under her ass as if she weighed nothing. At bedside, Luke leaned and deposited his sweetheart on her back, still between her legs.

Anxiously, the willowy blonde opened Luke's terry robe and he shrugged it from his shoulders. Naked now, Luke set about the enjoyable task of removing Billie Jean's clothes, which consisted of nothing more than a T-shirt and shorts. He simply grasped the hem of the tee in both hands and, in a single motion, ripped it open to the knit collar. His strong hands made quick work of the tough band of cloth at her throat, then Luke peeled the ruined garment away from her perky breasts.

Billie Jean ran her fingers through his thick dark hair as he kissed and sucked her bright pink nipples, bringing moans and writhing gyrations from the woman Luke loved. He trailed kisses down her body as his hands unbuttoned and unzipped her denim cut-offs. He slowly slid them over her hips as his kissed the finely trimmed, kinky blonde pubic hair.

He paused long enough to bring her legs straight up and to slide the shorts over her feet. Luke tossed the shorts over his shoulder and buried his face in her crotch.

God, he loves me so well. Today, he'll get a real surprise.

They met more than two years ago when Luke had stopped by the convenience store where she worked to ask directions to a motel. They'd started talking, and he asked her to join him for dinner. After a slow meal with more conversation than eating, she had followed him to the cheap little motel and spent the night. The next day, Luke told her he had decided to stick around. A mechanic with his own tools, it hadn't been hard for Luke to find work. He told her it never was for a man who knew his way around an internal-combustion engine. Within three months, they had moved in together.

Billie Jean dreamed of the day she would become Mrs. Lucas Peterson. Her long-time dream of saying goodbye to the dusty little desert town of Fort Hancock, maybe to a big city, like Houston or Dallas, seemed much less important if she was with Luke. She could stay here with him, give him children and a home. Her dream of a college education, a career, all of that gave way to love.

Lucas, too, had never been happier. He was deeply in love with this plain-spoken, sexy, funny woman. His fear that something terrible might happen to her had finally passed; he no longer sat up at night when the nightmares of beautiful dead women haunted his sleep.

Maybe it's really all over? Maybe this time will be different.

11

It had been almost seven years since Luke had buried the remains of Mona Harper at The City of Rocks, the last two of those, the happiest of his life. Before he had met Billie Jean, he had dated a few girls, one in Van Horn and two in El Paso. There had been no repeat of the incidents that had driven him out of Silver City.

Although he had originally dismissed the college murders as being committed by someone else, he had no illusions that he wasn't responsible for Mona's death. Although he had no recollection of any of the three events, he had a nagging hunch that they could all be related to fellatio. As a consequence, he had totally avoided oral sex ever since he secreted the body of the poor woman who gave him a ride outside Hurley.

Luke decided to test the fates six months into the relationship with Billie Jean. He had to know that he wasn't going to black out, then wake up to see the corpse of his lover.

He drove to El Paso where he shopped for handcuffs, two pair at pawn shops in a rundown neighborhood. The first one didn't have a pair. The second shop had only one. He found the second pair at the third pawnbroker.

Lucas then joined the tourists to pay his 25 cents to walk over the bridge crossing the Rio Grande into Ciudad Juarez. The famed Mexican border town of the wild west had long ago grown to a major city of more than 1-2 million inhabitants and was the largest city in the Mexican state of Chihuahua. But was still a place with few rules, rampant poverty and a corrupt police force that can't be trusted. It's also a place where any human desire is available at a price, usually not a very steep price.

He knew that once a tourist steps off the main streets, he's in a third-world country. Within minutes, he was approached by a pretty Mexican girl, who offered to take him to her bed for $15. She was beautiful. Barely five-feet tall with a baby-smooth complexion, Luke guessed she weighed no more than 100 pounds. She couldn't have been any older than 14. He also knew that he could cut her price in half, but he was on a mission.

Luke followed the young woman along back streets to an old apartment building. She led him up rickety stairs to a tiny flat. Luke appraised the setting. It was a two-room flat consisting of a living area with a couch, table, and kitchenette. Through a doorway, separated by colorful hanging beads was a tiny bedroom, surprisingly well decorated, if a bit too frilly for his taste. This location would do. If something awful happened, he could probably disappear into the narrow winding streets and find his way back to the bridge.

He prayed that would not be necessary.

"You give me dinero first, yes?" The question interrupted his thoughts.

Luke took two bills from his wallet, a $5 and a $10, and handed them to the girl.

With a shrug, the girl's sundress dropped to the floor at her ankles. Beneath it, she wore nothing at all. "You like?"

Luke smiled woodenly. He was already feeling guilty for cheating on Billie Jean, but he had to know. "I like. And I would really, really like a blowjob."

The girl's face lit up. Oral sex was much safer for the prostitutes of Juarez; it also meant she didn't have to perform the complex post-coital ablutions to clean her body before she returned to the streets that provided her livelihood.

She walked over to him, a walnut-colored angel, and gently pushed him down onto the edge of the twin-size bed. Silently, she knelt on the floor before him, unfastened his belt and zipper, and expertly slipped his jeans and shorts down together, lifting his hips to push them down to puddle at his feet.

"Wait," Lucas said. His jeans and shorts at his feet, he waddled over to his jacket draped over the back of the tiny chair by the lamp and removed the handcuffs. "Cuff my arms to the bedstead," he ordered.

The girl, already well experienced in deviant sexual preferences, didn't think this measured up at all to the wierdness she'd seen before. She surprised him with her expertise in slapping the cuffs on each of his wrists, then she hooked the second cuff of each pair to the bedposts.

Luke struggled a couple times to test the security of the fetters before relaxing. "I'm ready," he told the young prostitute.

The girl straddled his calves and took him in her soft hands and gently stroked it until he began to stiffen, then slipped her mouth over the head. Quickly, Luke's cock was a steel rod. He moaned as she licked the length of his erection while her hand continued to slide up and down, Then she took him in her mouth again, her head angled to allow the entire length to slip down her throat as she repressed her gag reflex.

Expertly, she plied her trade until, uncharacteristically, he climaxed in just a couple minutes. The girl licked and sucked him dry — and survived the encounter.

"You got nice dick. You can stay and fuck me later?"

"No, sweetheart. You have already made me very, very happy."

She took the keys out of his jacket pocket and undid the cuffs at his wrists. While he was pulling up his jeans, she started to undo the cuffs at the head of the bed.

"Leave them," Lucas told, then he took a $20 out of his billfold and gave it to the girl as a tip. "Can I clean up now?"

"Si, in there." The girl pointed to a door off the bedroom that he would have thought to be a closet. The bathroom was small, but she had it sufficiently stocked with clean washcloths and towels. She followed him in and washed his cock and her face with warm soapy water.

Then, after he had again pulled his pants up and fastened them, she hugged him tightly, then kissed him lightly.

"Thank you, señor."

His guilt assuaged by the positive outcome of his sexual experiment, an elated Luke returned to the US side of the border, and drove quickly home to Fort Hancock and to his beloved Billie Jean.

12

Billie Jean had never known a lover so conscientious, so attuned to her needs. Luke was a gentle, attentive, and patient lover. He was also the only man who had never pressured her to perform fellatio on him. The truth was, Billie Jean never really enjoyed the sensation of having a man's cock in her mouth. But all her previous lovers had expected it and begged or pressured her for oral sex.

I think I'll enjoy giving him that pleasure for the first time. He deserves it.

Luke lifted her and slid her further up the bed so he could get on his knees above her. But Billie Jean put her hand to his chest to stop him.

"You lay down, sweetie. Let Little Billie drive."

She straddled him but didn't mount his manhood standing stiff against her belly. Instead, she leaned forward and began covering his muscular chest with kisses, biting softly at his nipples as he had done to her. She licked her way down to his navel and tickled his bellybutton with her tongue, and they both laughed.

Billie Jean's mouth traveled down to his wild pubic hair and was pleasantly surprised to see Luke getting impossibly harder. Her ministrations brought moans from her lover just before she took him in her mouth as deep as she could.

"Mommy, don't!" Luke suddenly screamed.

The black-out lasted six hours. It was dark when Luke awoke in the blackness of the unlighted apartment, he switched on the lamp beside him. It was after midnight. Other tenants in the complex had long since retired for the evening. The sight that greeted him would burn into his mind forever. His beautiful Billie Jean lay in a heap on the bed across from the recliner where he'd awakened. The unnatural angle of her head and neck, the open, sightless eyes painted a familiar picture. His intended bride had died, obviously at his own hand.

13

It had been years since the killings had stopped; years since he had awakened to find a lover lifeless before him. Luke was confused. He had thought oral sex had triggered the events, so he'd had his little tryst in Juarez. The woman/child whore had performed the fellatio expertly and he had experienced no blackout.

So, why did it happen this time?

It wasn't that Luke didn't like fellatio. It was the first sexual feeling he'd ever felt when he was even too young to get an erection, Dixie would take his little penis in her mouth.

The little boy, starved for affection in a household of fighting and arguing, loved the sudden attention. He was his mama's little man. She held him and caressed him, and kissed him and stroked him and fondled him, and touched him places he'd never been touched.

Luke had felt loved by his mother for the first time.

When she asked him to love her back, to suck her nipples like he did when he was a baby, he went at it with gusto. She asked that he touch her and probe in her secret place. It made her feel good and he felt good that she enjoyed their playing.

"Kiss me there. Lick me there. Nibble on that little nub," and she had placed his hand on her clitoris. It pleased her, so it pleased the boy.

He had loved the physical play with his mother when he was seven, before he had any sexual feelings and before he had learned the ugly truth about incest and child sex abuse.

As he aged and became able to do more than perform oral sex and manual clitoral manipulation on his mother, he learned all the ways to please a woman. Dixie's unquenchable sexual appetite encompassed a broad menu of sexual acts and perversions. But a child doesn't understand the difference between the two.

As his education in the real world outside the one in her dingy trailer increased, be became more and more aware that what she was doing was wrong. But he learned all the ways Dixie knew to please a woman.

He also learned to feel *shame*.

Dixie could arouse Luke even when he didn't want to be aroused. That increased his shame. She taught him about intercourse, adding the word "fuck" to his vocabulary. She showed him how to fuck her in the ass without hurting her. She taught him about sex toys and about bondage, and about spanking and other forms of sexual sadomasochism.

In his spare time, the boy tried to research perversion in the school library, where there was little data. Finally, he went to the public library and found a wealth of information. As he read about what was going on in his mother's bedroom, his shame gave way to anger.

Luke felt dirty. He could show no interest in the pretty girls his age at school; they would probably think he was weird. Instead, he channeled his energy into sports and athletics. At age 12, he was a formidable opponent for other boys in his weight class on the school boxing team. He lifted weights for hours, not only at school, but at home in his room. The downside to this pursuit was that Dixie found the 12-year-old's body already more man than boy, and all the more exciting.

Then there came that night when he was 13 that his anger changed. It became a fiery rage inside his belly. The instinctive love of a child for its mother became hatred.

Hatred-fueled, his rage exploded. He had taken a knife with him to his mother's bed — their bed — and when she had kissed down his belly to his groin, he screamed and plunged the 7-inch chef's knife into her back.

Dixie, in shock, bit down. Luke bellowed, now not only in rage but in searing pain. She opened her mouth to scream, but was dead before it escaped her lungs. The broad-bladed knife had slipped neatly between ribs to transect her heart.

Luke looked at his now flaccid cock. It was a bloody mess, but the tears in the flesh were superficial. He figured the purpling color of bruising would take some time to disappear. More importantly, he had to make her body disappear and do his best to clean up the mess.

First, he took a shower, getting rid of any trace of blood on his body. He tossed his shorts and bloody T-shirt onto the warm corpse, and then wrapped the body in the sheets, blankets, and mattress cover and pad. Luckily, because the heart stopped pumping blood almost instantly, most of the blood was contained. He had not withdrawn the knife, so there was no spatter. He set about cleaning up any trace of sexual activity, turned the mattress, and made up the bed with fresh linen while he concocted a story to cover the disappearance of Dixie Peterson.

He slept until the wee hours of the morning, then leaving the lights in the house off, made his way out to Dixie's four-wheel-drive pick-up, opened the rear of the camper topper and lined the bed with a tarp. He returned to the darkened trailer house, sitting on 10 acres of scrubby land a half mile off Hwy 180 and almost equidistant between Deming and The City of Rocks. Using a penlight, Luke verified that there were no leaks in the two large trash bags taped around the bundled body. Clicking off the flashlight, he carried the murdered woman to the truck.

It was a 30-minute drive to the City of Rocks. He had been here once before, six years ago, to help his mother bury the body of the man who had impregnated her with Luke — Bobby Duchamps. He would use her story, to a degree, to explain her absence.

Dixie had maintained that Bobby had deserted her and left her alone to raise the boy. Even the Duchamps family had bought the story. They knew that Bobby hadn't bothered to marry Dixie even when she announced her pregnancy. They suspected, with reason, that Dixie had hoped the paternity test would encourage Bobby to marry her.

It hadn't. They lived together, but Bobby, feeling trapped with a manipulative, alcoholic woman, sought romance elsewhere. The night of his disappearance, he had been discovered parked in a campsite with another woman. Dixie found them naked in the backseat of his Pontiac LeMans.

He'd been afraid to come home for three days, but when he finally showed up at the trailer Dixie owned, she'd been conciliatory and had even suggested they get young Luke and the three of them go to Deming to a drive-in movie.

They were on their way home from the drive-in when Dixie said she was getting sick. Bobby pulled the pick-up to the side of the road and helped her out onto the paved shoulder. With no warning, Dixie pulled her .32-cal revolver from her pocket and shot him once in middle of the forehead.

She wrapped Bobby's ruined head in a towel and had seven-year-old Luke help her put the body in the back of the truck. They then drove into the grounds of The City of Rocks and on a bright, moonlit night buried the body on the side of a mesa in the desert behind.

It was another moonlit night as Luke drove the truck far into the wilderness, unmindful of the body damage the boulders and trees inflicted on the truck's paint as he maneuvered further and further from any sign of civilization. He finally sent it over a cliff into a deep ravine, more than 20 miles off any roads.

Dixie's disappearance wasn't immediately noticed, so Luke told his Uncle Bo that he thought she'd abandoned him, too. With Dixie's drinking and partying history, folks figured she might have run off with some cowboy wandering through, when they thought of her at all.

The rodeo cowboy had taken the boy under his wing, seeing that he got to school, that there were groceries in Dixie's beat-up old trailer, and eventually brought the teenager into his auto-repair business, teaching him a trade, while putting away money to send him to college in Silver City.

Luke continued boxing and weight training. The hard physical work of the garage wore on Enrico Luna, the other mechanic that helped him and Uncle Beauregard, but for the teenager, it was exhilarating.

He loved Uncle Bo and accompanied the cowboy on the rodeo circuit at times when it didn't interfere with his school schedule. When they weren't in the garage or at a rodeo, the young man and the old man would haul a horse trailer up into the wilderness to ride the trails and camp out under stars. These would become the troubled boy's favorite memories.

When he went off to college, he came home on weekends to work in the garage. Bo didn't really need the help, but he knew the young man needed to feel he was contributing to his room and board, and giving something back for the tuition money that Bo had put up.

"Luke, don't worry about the money," his uncle had told him. "It's a joy to watch you making something of yourself. Dixie taking off with that cowboy was the best thing that ever happened to either of us."

And until he finally moved back to Silver City from Deming, he drove past the City of Rocks twice every weekend.

14

Luke was in shock. Across the bed was the love of his life, the woman who was to bear him children and grow old with him. She wasn't breathing. She would grow no older.

Lucas didn't kid himself; he knew he had killed Billie Jean. He knew the horrible livid bruises at her throat were made by his own hands. Three times before he had found himself in a situation with a dead woman right after making love to her. But that was years ago. He and Billie Jean had been lovers and sweethearts for more than two years.

Why now!?

The trip to Mexico had been his test. He had somehow suspected that the trigger was oral sex, because that was the last thing he remembered in each instance when waking up — sometimes as much as an hour afterward. When the beautiful little teenage girl had orally taken him to a complete orgasm, with no other sexual activities to cloud the issue, he knew that wasn't the trigger, but he was still at a loss as to what really caused the blackouts. He hadn't wanted any of these women dead. His college sweetheart had been the first, then there was Beth, a quickie hook-up after a play.

The police had questioned him, but he had somehow passed the polygraph, since he really didn't know exactly what had happened.

He knew it wasn't because the two lovers' intimacy was growing. In fact, he had planned to propose to her this weekend, and had picked out a ring to buy on Friday, payday.

There were no emotional ties between himself and woman who had picked him up as he hitchhiked, just as there was nothing with Beth.

I'm a monster! I … I can't ever allow myself to get really close to a woman again.

He knew he couldn't abstain from women. Lucas was good and life was worth living when he had a woman at his side; and he was at his best when he was in love. He understood that he should be careful — and that he would always need to have an exit strategy. Lucas swore off women and off sex, knowing it was a vow he would not, could not keep.

15

June, 1988

The sudden, powerful nausea swept over her and Lacey awoke in the early hours with an immediate need to vomit.

Miz Edie must be makin' coffee and bacon.... Hell, that hasn't bothered me since ... since ... I was pregnant with Willie Nell!

Her brain accepted the fact but her conscious self, the woman who wanted to get to Nashville and on the Grand Ol' Opry denied the possibility.

Wishful thinking: *It's only indigestion from that Mexican food last night.*

Reality: *You shouldn't have finished off Willie Nell's beans and flour tortillas.*

Wishful thinking: *But I didn't want them to go to waste and my daughter didn't want them.*

Reality: *Did you ever think about a doggie bag?*

The argument with herself was fruitless. She needed to find out if she had a bun in the oven before she accepted the signing gig out at the Rusty Spur, a cowboy bar that offered her a chance to sing every Saturday night.

All that smoke isn't good for an unborn baby.

And she knew that if she was pregnant again, she'd only be able to work a short while before she began to show. She also knew they'd then ask her to

8

make room for someone who better fit a pair of tight blue jeans. She began to giggle uncontrollably.

She finally accepted the inevitable.

Lacey Jay Autrey, you're gonna be a mama again.

Dude wandered into the bathroom just then to find her wiping tears from her eyes and laughing like a goofball. "Let me in on the joke," he said, encircling her waist with his hands, his semi-hard cock noticeable against her backside.

"I can't get over how tiny your waist is."

"Hold that thought, 'cuz it's gonna change soon enough. Enjoy it while you can, Studly Do-Me-Right." She turned around to face him. "Your cock wants to celebrate. Methinks he thinks he did it all by himself."

"I'm always hard when I wake up. It's a pee-hard. Don't go getting ahead of me."

He turned to the toilet but then her words began to penetrate his sleep-fogged brain.

"You... you're knocked up again?!" he said slowly as he caught up with the conversation. Adrenaline pumped him full of excitement and the cowboy turned back to his wife. And he peed on her foot as he grabbed both of her shoulders

"Well, I didn't get there by myself. And you don't have to pee all over me. Besides, I'm not 100 percent sure yet."

"Then let's get sure," Dude said excitedly. "I'll run to Wal-Mart and get one o' them pregnancy tests." He put his softening cock into his shorts and ran to dress. Pulling on last night's jeans and a fresh shirt, he sat and tugged on his boot loops. A string of profanity told Lacey he was having trouble.

A giggle from his wife made Dude look up to see Lacey at the bedroom door, laughing hysterically

"What's so damned funny?" he asked.

"Honey, if you put those on the right feet, they might fit better."

"I'm puttin' the left boot on the left foot," He said with bewilderment on his face.

"But that's not on my foot, cowboy, and it's my boot," she said.

"I figgered when we bought matching boots we might run into trouble. Then I told myself, he's a smart man; he knows he can't put a size 10 foot into a size 6 boot."

"Okay, make fun of me. But please don't make me look ignorant in front of our kids, cuz it looks like we're gonna have a passel of 'em runnin' around here."

"OK," she said sweetly. "I'll just let them find out for themselves."

As though on cue, Willie Nell straggled into the room, dragging her Pouty Peggy doll by the hair. "Why's everybody laughing?" she asked, rubbing sleepiness from her eyes.

"Daddy tried to put on Mommy's boots," her mother replied. "Isn't that silly?" She cautioned Dude with her eyes.

"Don't say anything yet or it'll be all over the park by sundown."

"Well, the boot story's already out, don'tcha figure?" But Dude had read and received her message clearly — *don't mention the baby to Willie Nell.* He nodded. "I'm going to run up to the store, be right back."

"I want to go with Daddy," she whined.

"Not this time, Little Lady," Dude said. "Daddy has some private business to take care of."

"My birthday's not for ages and Santa's already been, so why can't I go?" she tuned up to bawl.

"Because I need you to help me make pancakes," Lacey said. "But only big girls can cook, crybabies aren't allowed in my kitchen."

The child sniffled and took one dramatic, hitching breath, "Well, okay."

In a few minutes, she and Lacey had girded themselves in frilly aprons and were hard at work mixing up pancake batter.

16

Sunrise, that's a pretty name.

Willie Nell sat fidgeting on the plump sofa in the living room of Miz Edie's little trailer. She strained to hear the sound of the Suburban. Daddy was bringing Mama and the new baby home from the hospital.

The eight-year-old mildly resented that her baby sister had such a fine name while she was named for the son her Daddy had wanted. All the kids at school treated her like a tomboy. Daddy had already started referring to the baby as Sunny, which didn't bother Willie Nell at all.

Muddled thoughts clouded the little girl's mind. She couldn't decide if she was glad there was another child or if she was jealous. Her mature nature forced her to admit she was both.

She didn't really want to have to share what precious little time she got to spend with Daddy, nor to have Miz Edie's attentions diluted. She had no misgivings about her mother. Willie Nell and Lacey bonded so strongly the child already knew it was unshakable.

Sharing her room would be a mixed blessing; she knew she'd love a baby in the house, but she also knew it would mean awakening in the middle of the night to her little sister's cry.

"Now, remember what I told you," Mama had told her. "You're a big sister now. With that comes a lot of responsibility. You must help Sunrise. Show her that she's welcome, right now."

There it was. Her ear recognized the familiar sound of her daddy's old truck coming down the caliche toward the trailers. Willie Nell bounded out the door, completely missing the three steps up to the trailer door, and was in a dead run before her nanny could make it feebly down the first step.

Willie Nell was at the truck when it stopped She stood solemnly and held out her arms so Dude could hand her the infant.

"Let's wait until you're sitting down. I wouldn't want us to hurt this little bit of a thing." He laughed as he said it but the older daughter knew he might be afraid she would drop her.

"Daddy, I've been practicing with my doll and with the cat, so I know how to hold something special and wiggly."

Both parents smiled at the very determined girl. Over the summer, she seemed to have grown into an adult.

Lacey knew Dude wasn't about to let her carry anything, including the baby. She also knew Willie Nell was less likely to have a mishap with the infant than was her cowboy father.

"Hand the baby to Willie Nell. She might as well get used to handling her right now," she told her husband, who acquiesced and gently placed the warm, soft bundle in his daughter's outstretched arms.

With the new baby at home, Willie Nell's enthusiasm didn't wane. She loved being a big sister. One night after Sunshine and Mama got home, the baby began to fuss. Willie Nell had been told that her mother needed to rest so she tiptoed into the room where the infant lay in a bassinette and lifted her. Both girls went into the kitchen where Willie Nell proceeded to warm a bottle while she changed the baby's diaper. Just about the time she got the baby tucked into her lap and noisily sucking on the bottle, Daddy came in.

"Girl, what are you doing? You could have hurt that baby!" Usually her daddy didn't scream or get angry unless he was drinking but this time, she knew he meant it. He was stone cold sober.

"I've been doing it ever since she got home, Daddy. I'm real careful. Mama needs her rest. You told me so. I can help a lot."

He shook his head. "I think while I wasn't looking, you grew up on me, Willie Nell. You're a full grownup inside a little eight-year-old body!"

Willie Nell beamed in pure pleasure.

All too soon, school began. Even the new crayons and pencils and tablet failed to keep her attention. She watched the clock counting the hours until she could go home to be with the baby, like there wasn't ever going to be enough time. She didn't know that the time she would get to spend with her baby sister would be cut short soon enough.

17

Lacey got the kids down, then spent a couple more hours going over her scrapbooks, waiting for Dude. He should have been home hours ago; he'd missed supper and had disappointed Willie Nell, who was hoping he could help her with her school project, a diorama of a ranch scene. She finally put the scrapbook diaries away for the night, and crawled into bed alone just before midnight. Lacey hadn't yet fallen asleep when she heard the clatter outside; Dude Autrey was finally home, and he was drunk again. Dude's old Suburban hit the trashcan with more noise than damage and the motor sputtered to a stop. She heard him curse as he slammed the door on the battered truck disguised as a station wagon. He clomped up the steps to the trailer door and fumbled, trying to open it.

With a sigh, Lacey got out of bed and went to let him in.

She smelled Dude before he crawled into bed with her. The stench of alcohol and some overpowering flowery scent clung to him along with his sweat and that of another woman.

"Dude," she said, with a calm she didn't feel. "Don't come into my bed after being with someone else and expect me not to notice. I don't know how much longer I can put up with this."

"What makes you think you deserve any better? Any other woman would love to be in my bed, have my kids and live your life."

The retort did it. It hurt and it shattered the measured calm Lacey had attempted to maintain.."You bastard! You really think tonight's buckle bunny would like the beatings and black eyes that go along with living with you?"

65

she said in a hissing whisper. "Or doing without so you can drink yourself into oblivion?"

"You're not much of a wife. I've had better fucks on the road than what you dole out when you're in the mood, occasionally." He punctuated his scathing statement with a snort. "Some women know how to please a man."

"You don't wait until I'm ready for you and it hurts." She couldn't keep the whimper out of her voice." Maybe then I could enjoy sex, too."

"Enjoy it? Wives ain't supposed to enjoy it. Whores enjoy it."

Lacey bristled. "Whores get paid to enjoy it. That's their only talent, pretending to enjoy your inept fumbling and quick rides." She couldn't stop the pent-up feelings. They were a flashflood of venom.

He matched insult for bitter insult. "Talent? What makes you think you got any? That singing of yours? Hell, our old tomcat sounds better than you on any given day!"

When she replied, "I don't see no championship buckles or trophies with your name on them." Dude snarled and pulled his punch just before it connected with the side of her head.

Lacey gasped and pulled away.

"You're just like your mama. Exceptin' she could cook."

"If you ever got home when it was fresh cooked, to eat with us. at a respectable time like other families …"

"I'm not changing my life to be like some pussy-whooped wimp like you want for a husband. If that's what you think, you got another think a coming."

"I ain't asking for much, Dude. Just some consideration like you used to show me."

He began to snore and mutter in his sleep while she lay rolling his words around in her head. Lacy took a quilt and went into the room with her girls. Willie Nell wrapped her arms around her mother and Sunny's sweet breath warmed Lacey's heart.

I've got to get out of here before one of us kills the other.

Next morning she'd gotten the girls up and sent Willie Nell off to school before Dude woke up. The baby sat in her highchair awaiting the spoon Lacey held out. "Come on little darlin', eat it all gone."

The baby giggled and pounded on the metal tray.

Lacey began to sing,

You need to eat to grow my little brown eyed baby girl.

Your mama loves you more than anything else in this world…

About that time, Dude sashayed in, clapping and dragging his boots across the floor. "Now, ain't that right pretty? You two kids having fun?" He opened the refrigerator, pulled out a Budweiser longneck, and opened it with the magnetic church key he kept on the side of the old Amana.

"Fix me something to eat, Lacey girl. That baby can wait while you get your work done. Why ain't she feeding herself?"

"She's still too little, Dude," Lacey said, lifting the baby from the highchair onto her lap. "And you don't need to start drinking this early. Get yourself some toast and coffee while I finish with her and then …"

The backhand caught her on the ear and the impact sent her toppling from the chair. Lacey landed hard and the side her head hit the hard, linoleum floor as she rolled to keep from landing on the baby in her arms.

"Don't you fuckin' talk to me about my beers," he bellowed.

Lacey sat up on the cold linoleum, dazed, Dude snatched the overturned chair and, with both hands, smashed it down on her shoulders. The rickety chair splintered and Lacey lost consciousness and slumped onto her side, the infant rolling from her grasp.

Dude stomped out the door, across the wooden porch and down its steps to the Suburban and peeled out.

The screaming baby jarred Lacey back to consciousness. She blinked and staggered to her feet, her right shoulder and arm numb. She lifted the infant and labored her into the highchair with her left arm. The highchair was as wobbly as the chair Dude had cracked over her, but the tray would protect the baby while she assessed the damage her husband had inflicted. Lacey stumbled to the sink to splash cold water on her face. "I'll get you fed then we'll get the hell out of here," she said turning back toward Sunshine.

Lacey reached for the infant and a stab of pain seared across her shoulders and neck. The pain buckled her knees and made her gasp for air. Kneeling beside the highchair and looking up at her baby, she felt a wave of nausea.

I think that sonuvabitch really hurt me.

She rose gingerly, stumbled to the sink, and raised her left arm to lift the wall phone mounted above the cracking Formica countertop. Leaning against the cabinets for support, she dialed.

"Miz Edie, I'm hurt bad. Can you come help me?"

From the trailer across the road her friend said, "I'm comin' child. You just sit tight."

Her lifelong nanny/friend/confidante assisted her to the couch, then went into the bathroom and returned with bandages and Mercurochrome. "That man's already been drinking, there's a nearly empty pint of vodka sitting on the back of the commode."

"He certainly caught me by surprise. Dude isn't at all violent unless he's been drinking. Honest, he isn't."

"But he is one mean drunk when he's in his cups," Eyidie responded.

Carrying baby Sunny in one of her powerful arms, Eyidie supported Lacey at the waist as the two women hobbled to Lacey's car, looking for all the world like they were participants on of those three-legged races at the county fair. Once the baby was secured in the rear seat, Eyidie gently helped her injured friend into the passenger seat and buckled her in.

"Let me run in and get your keys and purse, sugar."

In less than a minute, Eyidie was back. She hauled her hefty frame behind the wheel, and headed to Lillian M. Hudspeth Memorial Hospital, the only major medical facility in Sutton County.

In the emergency room, Lacey learned she had suffered a hairline fracture of her left clavicle, and a bloody laceration low on the back of her scalp.

"You're lucky," the emergency room doctor told her. "An inch and a half lower and he could have broken your neck, probably killed you."

Even as she heard the diagnosis, Lacey knew she wouldn't sleep in that trailer again tonight, maybe never again.

18

During her recuperation at Eyidie 's where Lacey and the girls lived after leaving Dude, she found herself drifting back to a summer when Brock loved her and Dude left her alone. She knew the outcome of that romance was inevitable. Brock became the Rev. Brock Taylor and she became Mrs. Dude Autrey. She loved Dude, but knew down deep that happiness would be a rare commodity in this relationship. Love had nothing to do with. Her belief was that life just happened. A girl graduated high school and either went on to college (if she had parents with money) or beauty school if she needed a "career" she could afford. If all else failed, she waited tables, babysat, or married. Those were the viable options open to small-town West Texas girls in the '70s. As a child, Lacey had always thought her life would be like an old Doris Day and Rock Hudson movie. She'd raise the kids. He'd work then return to a home cooked meal. They'd ask how one another's day went and really listen to each other. Isn't that what married folks do?

Well, if that was true, I wouldn't be here in this sofa bed tonight.

She recalled when she had found herself with time on her hands while Dude was out breaking bones riding bulls, she took her old Fender and made up silly songs for the girls. Her first dream, a romantic life with Dude Autrey, was shattered. Now Lacey returned to a dream from her youth: Nashville. Everybody said her songs were cute. She carried a tune really well, even sang in the church choir for awhile even though Dude didn't like her leaving the girls with Eyidie too much.

69

"Miz Edie pokes her nose into our business too deep," he growled one night after about a dozen too many beers. "I don't need her thinking we don't love our kids enough to watch 'em ourselves", which meant (in Dude-speak): Lacey should stay home and take care of the kids.

Her mind went to a specific night in her house trailer when Dude was out on the rodeo circuit. Reverend Taylor had dropped by to see why he hadn't seen her at choir practice lately. By now, their relationship was totally transformed from their teenage romance. She even attended his church. The wisdom and care she had loved in him as a teenager was what she appreciated most now as an adult. He was her minister, and a true friend. He was, of course, married. His wife was the office administrator of the little Methodist church on the east side of town.

The preacher arrived, bearing pizza and colas. the girls were playing paper dolls cut from catalogs. She and Brock had talked about Dude's drinking and Brock had suggested she give her husband time to find sobriety. Dude had dabbled a few times in Alcoholics Anonymous, but had yet to make a real commitment to staying sober. Reverend Taylor felt the time would come; but Lacey wasn't so sure.

She had tried Al-Anon and found it helpful, but she didn't always make the meetings, using her children as a reason. "That's not the reason, that's the excuse," her Al-Anon sponsor had told her. Beverly Watson's husband now had seven years of sobriety in AA.

Easy for her to say. She's forgotten what it's like. Herman doesn't drink anymore.

Lacey knew she was rationalizing, but the truth was that she had yet to clear the hurdle of shame that confronted her when she talked openly in front of the other women about her husband's drinking and the way he treated her.

"Can we sing some songs, Mommy?" Willie Nell said, snapping Lacey out of her reminiscence.

"Yes Lacey," Reverend Taylor agreed. "You can't get out of this by saying you can't sing," he remarked with a twinkle in his eye. "I know better. I've heard you at church and choir practice. I'd love to hear one of your original songs."

"But they're for children, my children," she said softly.

"I'm just a big kid at heart."

He sat and held the youngest while Willie Nell hovered at his shoulder. Lacey finally agreed to sing them all a song at Willie Nell's urging.

At first she tentatively plucked at the strings and lowered her head until her hair made a curtain covering her so she couldn't see his response to her music. She sang of puppies who played with little girls, of angels who watched over them all and of course, of mommies who sang to little girls.

"Angels fly so close to me

"I know always safe I'll be ..."

Reverend Taylor clapped his hands and Baby Sunrise clapped with him. "Yaaay, Mommy."

"Bedtime, Ladies," Lacey announced about 8 o'clock. "Let's wash our faces and put on jammies. Then you can come out and thank Reverend Brock for your supper and say your goodnights."

She lifted the eight-month-old from his knee, brushing his thigh as she passed by.

Thank goodness for long hair covering my face. I know I'm probably forty shades of pink.

She blushed not so much from remembering their past, but from the subject she needed to discuss with him tonight.

After the girls were down for the evening, she walked to the front of the trailer where Reverend Taylor was sitting at the dinette. "Too late for a pot of coffee?"

"Well, that's one vice I haven't given up for my calling. And if you still make it as good as I remember, I'd be a fool to say no."

Lacey's mind whirled as she busied herself with the Mister Coffee. She had no idea how to approach this conversation. She had never been afraid of a man before — not even when Dude attacked her — but Reverend Taylor terrified her right now. She bit her lower lip, and turned to face him.

"I have something really important to tell you, not as Reverend Taylor, but simply as Brock, because it concerns you as much as me."

Reverend Taylor's attention perked up, but he held his tongue. His training told him not to press but to let Lacey feel her way through whatever was on her mind.

Lacey was shaking noticeably as she took down two coffee mugs and poured two cups of fresh, strong coffee. "You still take it black with one sugar?"

"Ten years later and you remember. I'm impressed."

"We need to talk about what happened back then," Lacey said, her voice barely a whisper.

I was really hoping she was past that teenage romance.

Reverend Taylor looked into the steaming cup. "I suggest we say a little prayer before starting this conversation."

Lacey nodded solemnly, and they joined hands as Reverend Taylor said a simple prayer for guidance in their exchange. The calm words and the focus on the spiritual aspect of what was to come calmed her somewhat.

"You know Dude and I were married only a month after our time at Janine's farm or commune or whatever you want to call it."

"I remember."

"I never told you, Brock, but I was pregnant when I married — with Willie Nell. She's your daughter, not Dude's." The words tumbled out of her mouth in one long breath.

Reverend Taylor's eyes widened. "You're sure. You and Dude didn't ... you know ... before the honeymoon?"

"Twice, but both times using condoms. And I was on the pill, which I gave up because I couldn't get refills out there in the country."

"I can believe it. So, what do you want me to do?"

Lacey had tears in her eyes, trying to spill down her cheeks. "Nothing, Brock. Neither Dude nor Willie Nell knows about you and I, and I want to keep it that way. I just thought it was only right that you should be aware."

"I'll have to pray for direction, Lacey. I've never kept secrets from Ruth, and I don't know if sparing her feelings justifies keeping a secret now."

"That's up to you. I would never ask you to mislead your wife. I'd hope that you two could keep it out of the community rumor mill, though, for my daughter's sake."

"That's a given, Lacey. This wouldn't be the first time I've been entrusted with a family secret, you know. I am a minister, remember?"

Lacey smiled slightly and rubbed at a tear. Then she gave a light chuckle. "This has been so big inside my head all these years, but we sit here and kinda shrug it off."

"I call that the 'magic magnifying mind'. Secrets do that, you know." Reverend Taylor said softly. "You know, Lacey, this is all part of God's plan. There are no accidental children."

Lacey felt 50 pounds lighter after she said goodnight to Reverend Taylor. She allowed herself to think back to those wonderful days at the commune, without the guilt and shame that had always accompanied those bittersweet memories. She knew that now they would always be precious, and would never again fuel regret. To wish it had never happened, she realized for the first time, would be to wish away Willie Nell, her bright, insightful, creative daughter and the joy of her life.

19

Lacey didn't know if she would ever live with Dude again. The reality of her situation weighed on her. Her two daughters might have to rely on her alone to provide for them. Eyidie had already said she'd help out, but Lacey knew the old woman wasn't much better off than she was.

I don't know how to do anything that can make me and my girls a living!

The thought devastated the young mother. If she divorced Dude, she knew he'd be responsible and offer up some child support. But he couldn't afford to maintain two households on just his rodeo winnings.

Lacey walked across the caliche' to Eyidie 's trailer and rapped on the door.

"Come on in, Lacey."

Holding the screen with one hand and opening the door with the other, Lacey chided her neighbor. "So, how'd you know it was me?"

"Who else? Just logic, dear. You're the only person besides them girls of your'n who ever pays old Eyidie any never-mind."

"Don't try to get me to pity you Eyidie Nwaigbo! You know more people and are beloved by more people than anyone else in the county. You raised half of us as kids, for that matter."

"And some of you turned out OK, I reckon. What's on your mind, Lacey?"

"I need your wise counsel, as usual. It's about money."

"Only a fool talks about something he doesn't know anything about. That's why men are always talking about women."

The quip broke Lacey up. She had needed a laugh, and Eyidie knew just how to bring her out of the doldrums.

"But two heads are better than one. You're probably worrying about paying the bills, right?"

"As right as rain in West Texas."

"You're probably going to whine about not having any work experience or skills, right"

"Uh-huh." Lacey had long ago become used to the canny black woman being able to read her thoughts.

Eyidie was standing in the center of the living room with her arms crossed across her sizable chest. "I figure a woman who can put food on the table for a husband and raise children has to have plenty of skills."

"But who's going to pay me for them?"

"Aw heck, girl. Waitressing ain't no different from what you do for your family every day. You're still just puttin' food on the table. And you also cook, you clean house, you shop, you care for children. But you're best at singing and song-writing.

"Tell you what. You go talk to Sarah at the Breakfast Nook. Tell her I sent you, and she'll probably find something there you can do."

Lacey remembered Sarah from her childhood. Eyidie had babysat Sarah Lockhart and her brother, Timmy, at the same time she had cared for her.

Why did I let go of those childhood relationships?

She was starting to get a little enthusiasm. "And right down the street is the Rusty Spur. Maybe they'd let me sing sometimes on weekends when they have bands in."

"Only if you got a band behind you, baby."

And just like that, Lacey deflated, the enthusiasm evaporating in the reality that waiting tables was her only choice.

"Of course, Timmy's got a little band now. He struggles some, but they play at the Spur on occasion."

"Miz Edie, is there anything goes on in this town you DON'T know?" The wheels were turning in Lacey's head. "And I'll ask Sarah for Timmy's number when I see her right after I leave here."

Eyidie poured two cups of tea and motioned Lacey to join her at the dinette. The two women drank in a truly comfortable silence, as only long-time friends can.

"Don't go to the Breakfast Nook too early," Eyidie said finally, refilling Lacey's teacup. "Let the lunch crowd finish up and get out so Sarah could spare you some time.

"You can take your lunch here with me. An old woman craves company, you know."

Lacey brightened at the prospect of enjoying Eyidie 's beans and cornbread, a staple in this little trailer ever since Lacey was a child.

"No red onion for me, though. I'm going job-hunting!"

20

Sarah Lockhart remembered their days together as little girls playing at Eyidie's, and offered Lacey work on the spot.

"I can only offer you two days a week right now as the relief girl, and the days will vary each week according to who's off. But when someone quits, or forces me to fire their butts, then you can work full time. Is that OK?"

"Fair enough. And thanks, Sarah." And just like that, Lacey joined that portion of the population she referred to as the "wage slaves".

"I got kids, too, gal," Sarah continued. "A boy and a girl, Denny's seven years old and Ariel's eight."

Sarah told Lacey that if she got in early, she could eat breakfast free. The coffee shop opened at 6 AM, but the cooks came at 5. "I'm usually having my French toast and coffee by 5:30; feel free to join me any day.

"We close at 2 and everybody's out of here by 3 o'clock, but the relief girl doesn't do clean up, so you'll be able to leave at 2. You can start tomorrow and work Friday as well."

"What's the pay?"

"Minimum wage plus tips. But as pretty as you are, you'll do well on tips. Just remember that the customer is always right."

"Hah! I'm married to a cowboy; I'm used to the customer always being right."

Lacey's joke brought a smile to Sarah's face. "You'll do all right, but you'd better get to bed early until you get used to this grind."

Lacey didn't bother telling her that getting up early is routine when you're cooking breakfast and packing a big lunch for a rodeo cowboy and getting a kid ready for the rural school bus, which came earlier than it did in town.

Lacey called Tim Lockhart from a pay phone outside the restrooms at the coffee shop. Yes, he remembered her. Yes, he had a band. No, they didn't have a singer. Yes, He'd be happy to listen to her.

After her first day at the Breakfast Nook, with nearly $25 in tips in her pocket, she drove to Tim's small frame house. He and two other musicians were setting up in the detached garage as she pulled in.

"Hey! You must be Lacey," the drummer said. "Boy, did you grow up nice."

The lead guitar player only whistled.

"You're Tim?" Lacey said, addressing the drummer, A slim, ruggedly handsome man with tattoos virtually covering both arms.

"And the Time Travelers," he replied. "Timmy and the Time Travelers, 'cuz we play the oldies, country oldies. How you like the sound of that?"

"Cool."

"That's Mac, our whistlin' guitar player; Jackie on the keyboard also plays a little bass," Tim said, introducing the band without bothering with last names.

"Lacey Jay Autrey." Lacey stuck out a hand in greeting, grasped by Tim. "Make that Lacey Jay. Autrey's in the dog house right now and I don't know that I'll ever let him out."

"Let's make some music, then," Tim said. "You know 'Your Cheatin' Heart', I'm sure."

"You bet."

Lacey wasn't ever nervous about singing, not even in front of complete strangers. It came to her as natural as breathing. The Hank Williams favorite had been recorded by dozens of artists, she preferred the Patsy Cline version, and did her best to imitate it.

"Wow!" Jackie, the keyboard player, silent until now, exclaimed.

"We may have to rename the band if she's our lead singer," Mac said, echoing Jackie's sentiment.

"You're good enough to get us out of this garage and in front of some audiences." Tim's statement made it unanimous.

"I like your sound," Lacey told the trio. "Are we all together?"

And just like that, Lacey had a band.

Lacey parked at the Breakfast Nook, not wanting to park in front of the bar blocks away. Elated by the prospect of being self-supporting for the first time in her 28 years, she was walking on air anyway.

The mid-afternoon sun didn't brighten the Rusty Spur with it's painted-over windows. A bartender disinterestedly wiped a glass while a single customer nursed a draft beer. She knew the bar all too well; she had dragged or carried Dude out of here often enough. She'd even accompanied him on occasion when they'd have a dance band. That was only on Friday and Saturday nights, but not every weekend.

"The boss around?" Lacey asked the man behind the bar. She knew Edna Stackhouse, the owner, who had inherited the bar when her father was stabbed by a drunk more than 20 years ago. Edna was a tough old bird, but Lacey knew she loved old-time country music.

"Edna's in the office, through that door," he said pointing toward the bathrooms. Down the hallway were doors marked "Cowboys", "Cowgirls", and "Private". She rapped on the latter door.

"It's not locked," said a raspy female voice by way of invitation.

Edna looked up from her bookkeeping, a cigarette dangling from her lips, a halo of smoke around her head. "Lacey fucking Autrey! I'll be damned. What you doing here girl; too early to be looking for Dude."

"Dude and me are separated, Edna. I got something else to talk to you about."

"Hey get in here and pull up a chair," the bar owner said.

After Lacey had moved a straight-back wooden chair close to the desk, Edna asked, "Are you OK?"

"I'm fine. I just started working down the street at the Nook. I'm not here looking for a job, well, not exactly."

"And what does that mean?"

"I want to sing here on weekends!" The words tumbled out of Lacey's mouth in a rush. Singing was easy. Asking for a chance came hard to the woman who had spent her life as a wife and mother.

"Can you sing? I know you got a pair of lungs on you; I've listened to you cussin' out that no-good cowboy of yours often enough."

"I can sing," Lacey replied. "And I'm good, honest. It may be the only thing I'm good at."

"Got a band?" Edna was a woman of few words.

"You know Timmy Lockhart?"

"… and the Time Travelers. Good musicians, but not a decent voice in the bunch. Yeah, I know 'em. You might be just what they need." The older woman looked at Lacey coolly. "And you're right pretty. That'd make my cowboys happy for sure.

"Tell you what, you and your boys can come over here Friday afternoon, say at 5 o'clock. You sing me a couple songs and if I like it, you can come back and try your act out on my crowd at 9:30. If they don't toss you out, you're good for $100 a person."

"Would that be regular-like?"

"Baby steps, little girl. Take baby steps," Edna cautioned. "I don't commit a bunch of bucks unless I know I'm gonna make a bunch of bucks. We can talk about a repeat performance Saturday morning."

Lacey's head was spinning. It was coming together.

Why didn't I do something like this years ago?

She knew the answer to the unasked question in her mind. She was a mother first.

21

It was already dark even after the switch to Daylight Saving Time. She figured it was probably after 9 o'clock. Lacey sat at the Formica table in the old house trailer, her daughter Sunrise on her lap. Wistfully, she browsed through a weathered notebook, one of four, which formed her diary.

She tried to picture herself as a young girl. The portrait in her mind caused a foul taste in her mouth. Memories of baking soda for toothpaste, watered down Kool Aid and bologna sandwiches twice a day sprang to mind. Standing in line with food stamps and having to put back items when her arithmetic failed her. The shame of wearing dirty clothes to school when Mama ran out of quarters for the Laundromat. Daddy hitting her mother if she asked for more money. His money was for "necessitaries", he'd say.

"Don't come whining to me because you spend every penny. You should be able to manage on what I give you!"

She flipped through pages covered with schoolgirl scribbles about how some-day she'd make it to the Nashville.

Well, Daddy, I'm on my way, no thanks to you, you sonuvabitch.

Lacey Jay had dreamed of being a Country-western singer her entire life. She had married the husband she'd always wanted, Rodeo Star Dude Autrey. Her lovely girls, Willie Nell and baby Sunny, were the joy of her life. Why not go for her ultimate dream?

After winning the talent portion of a beauty pageant to crown Miss Sonora, she goes on to win the contest outright, is spotted by a Nashville talent agent, and is asked to come to the music capital of the world to cut a record!

Her daydreams were all variations on that same theme.

Tucked into the small spiral notebook she'd used to capture the pain and indignities that defined her childhood, and which later provided inspiration for her songs, she located the letters — fan letter she'd written to her idols: Dolly Parton, Loretta Lynn, Tammy Wynette, and, of course, Willie Nelson.

Dolly Parton, was more like her in background if not bust size.

Loretta Lynn used the same grammar Lacey spoke — hillbilly-hick — as some called it.

Let them laugh, they'd be laughing out of the other side of their mouths someday.

Dolly and Loretta both made it despite their lack of schooling.

Then there was Willie Nelson for whom they named their first-born, now in school. The country star sent a letter but thought it had been a boy who bore his name. His letter said, "… I hope little Willie learns from his mistakes and gets a better start in life. Just tell him to have all the fun he can clean and sober."

Tammy Wynette had only sent a photograph with a signature, no letter. But hey, she was married to a drinker, too. Lacey knew how precious time was to the wife of a guy like that. Her own mama was married to a drunk and she had continued what Al-Anon called "the cycle".

Lacey kept the letters in spite of all the fun Dude made of them. He had ripped Tammy Wynette's picture. Yellowing Scotch tape held it together. So what if Tammy hadn't written a personal note. She'd encouraged Lacey to bear the turmoil of her life without abandoning her dream.

If it hadn't been for her dreams and Eyidie, Lacey's childhood would have been worse. Hand-me-downs from garage sales and thrift stores, and home haircuts didn't keep the little girl from dreaming of sequined denim, ostrich-quill boots and her own personal hairstyle, well, maybe Dolly's hairstyle.

"Woo-woo, things sure are changing for me and my kids! Dreams can come true."

She wrote in purple ink when she could, but the notebook was a riot of red and blue and black and green inks running up the margins in the notebook. Among the colors was occasional fading pencil script from when all the ball-points in the house were dry.

22

As Lacey adjusted the microphone and looked out over the audience, she said, "I read somewhere that Patsy hated these songs I plan to do tonight. Maybe hated is a strong word but she didn't want them to be all that was remembered about her. I call 'em hurtin' songs—WALKING AFTER MIDNIGHT, CRAZY and I FALL TO PIECES. They brought her fame all over the nation." Her last words were nearly lost to the applause they evoked.

When her listeners began to calm down, she continued, "Can you believe it was 50 years ago? My all time favorite is the one I usually close with SWEET DREAMS."

She strummed the strings of her guitar until it waned. "I prefer songs about the talk-back-to-men who don't treat me right—like my Dude. Y'all might remember him from one of those stools over there. But I kept on lovin' him hopin' he'd get it right if we kept at it."

She sang one of Patsy's hurting songs then continued her ruminations, "I like my acoustic guitar; it's real to my roots and I don't want to pull up my roots. I've been know to dust off a few songs like Willie Nelson does. That's why I didn't object when my husband wanted to name our firstborn after Willie. By the way, she's a G-I-R-L. I'm working on a song about that, too."

Two hours later, she did the bridge for SWEET DREAMS as the evening wound down. As the last chord from Lacey's guitar was still reverberating through the smoke-filled room she removed the strap from her neck, grabbed Mac's hand, and bowed with her lead guitar player. Lifting her head to stand tall after the applause stopped, she looked into the eyes of a man who looked out of place in the little cowboy bar. Slick was the word that sprang to mind.

She tried to ignore him but he'd have none of it. "Hold on, there, Lacey," he said reaching for her.

"I don't like to be grabbed, and if you don't want me to whack you over the head with a long-neck, you'll stand back."

Lacey wrested her arm from his grasp as Mac walked up behind her. "This guy bothering you, Lacey?"

"Nothing I haven't dealt with before, Mac."

"Whoa, missy. I think you're confusing me with one of your drunken cowboys that come in here," he said.

"I've heard that particular line about a hundred times, mister, so you'd better just leave."

"Just settle down and hear me out. Then if you want me to go, I will." He raised his palms in the air and took a step backward.

"Whatever you're selling or giving away, I don't need none."

"How do you know if you won't hear me out?"

"Shit, you're dressed like a pimp, so if it's a roll in the hay ..."

"Look, I really can help your career. While the prospect of a roll in the hay sounds appealing, I'd prefer your drummer, he's yummy. But I don't mix business with pleasure.

"Even more than the sound of your lovely voice, the sound of a cash register is what rings my bell."

Although still a bit steamed, Lacey made no effort to leave, so the stranger continued. "I'm Buck Milton, Big Buck, you know. I scout for a record label."

That got Lacey's attention as well as that of Mac and the rest of the band.

"I been hearing about you and your singing for days before I got here. You have quite a following for a little gal from Sonora, from El Paso to San Angelo, anyway."

"Let's say I believe you, what do you want from me?" Lacey knew what was coming but was afraid to admit it to herself.

"I want to make a tape to take back to Nashville with me, that's what. I'll secure a studio and we'll do a rough cut and see what the label owners say."

"So you want to be my Colonel Parker and make me the next Elvis, figuratively speaking?"

"I'd just like to be your agent. Colonel Parker robbed that Mississippi boy blind, you know," Big Buck replied, extending a hand.

Lacey took it. "Gotta include my band, too."

"Deal."

"You know there ain't no studio anywhere around here, don't you?" Tim told the would-be agent.

"Except in my motor home," Big Buck said with a wide grin that exposed two gold teeth.

Lacey and the Jayhawks, the quartet decided, would be the billing for the gigs at the Rusty Spur, but the recording would be under the name of The Jayhawks.

The band and the singer meshed well and Big Buck was effusive in his praise after the two-song demo tape was finished. "Let's paper this deal up. I'll need each of you to fill out one of these contracts."

He handed out the boilerplate forms to the band members, then he took Lacey aside.

"Listen, Lacey. You're the star of this outfit. They're signing as a group. I need you to sign as a solo artist. That way, if the band breaks up, I can still represent you by yourself."

"Does this mean I'm going to Nashville?" she asked breathlessly.

"It means I can get your name and your voice before people. That's what it means." Big Buck motioned the band to join him.

"I'm an agent. To put it in less than elegant terms, I'm a door-to-door salesman and you're my product. There's no promise today that I'll do anything but get this tape listened to. The rest is out of my hands until someone tells me they want to buy my product. When that happens, you'll hear from me."

Lacey and the Jayhawks nodded soberly.

23

November 1990

Bang!

It sounded like someone was shooting. Lacey sat bolt upright in the cramped little twin-size bed, trying to wake up.

Bang, bang, bang! Again.

Not gunfire. Someone's hammerin' at Miz Edie's door!

"Lacey Jay Autrey! Miz Edie! Lemme in. I gotta talk to Lacey. I need to see my girls."

It's Dude. Lacey carefully wriggled from beneath the sleeping forms of her two daughters, grabbed a robe, and walked through the trailer to the door.

"Shush up, Dude! you'll wake everybody up!" Lacey spoke through the door, uncomfortable with the idea of letting her so-called husband have another poke at her.

"Aw, babe," her cowboy drawled. "I wuz drunk. You know I'd never do nuthin' to hurt you. I love you. And I love those girls, too."

Lacey knew what Dude was saying was true.

"I been on the wagon ever since, and I swear I'll never touch another drop if you'll just come home."

She slid the chain off the "too late" lock, turned the deadbolt, and cracked the door.

Damn, that man looks good when he's sober and cleaned up.

Dude stood looking up at her, hat in hand, a pitiful expression on his face. The night wind whipped through his curly black mop of hair and he shivered beneath the denim jacket.

"I couldn't live without you, you know that Lacey Jay."

"Shit! Come on in, Dude," Lacey whispered. "I'll make us some coffee. Just keep it down."

Dude continued his litany of apologies and promises as Lacey busied herself with the coffee.

He's like a puppy, so cute and sweet.

The drinking had started in college, as it often does. Sure, he'd had some beers in high school, but she'd never known him to get wasted.

Dude was accepted at Baylor University on a football scholarship. Right away, he was struggling with the academic requirements, while making the starting team as a freshman. The presssure of athletics and study needed an outlet. Alcohol provided it.

In the end, he couldn't maintain academic eligibility and was in danger of being kicked off the team. The school put him into a tutoring program, but the attention required for him to do the work began to affect his performance on the field.

Dude's drinking increased. Both the tutoring and athletics suffered all the more. Lacey felt helpless during this period. She pleaded, she nagged, she cajoled, she threatened. The drinking didn't stop.

She knew her husband loved her with all his heart and soul. In high school, he had been so attentive she feared he might smother her in a marriage. Instead, he had provided her wings, encouraging her every endeavor whether exclaiming at a favorite recipe or clapping and cheering when she would sing one of her little songs.

Dude finally lost his football scholarship and with it any interest in pursuing a college education, and if she took him back, she'd most likely always be just the wife of a rodeo cowboy.

24

One night, after a couple of weeks of behaving well, Dude fell off the wagon one more time. Lacey knew when he didn't come directly home from San Angelo's Tom Green Rodeo. He'd won the bronc riding event and had called to tell her his news. An excited Willie Nell was eager; she had a surprise for him.

The sound of the telephone at two o'clock in the morning chilled her. She was awake, but had put the girls to bed at 10. Lacey was always jumpy when the phone rang. when she knew Dude was out drinking,

Good Lord, don't let anything bad happen to Dude.

She had repeated this same silent prayer more times than she could count. Once again her fear was washed away. Gene Durbin, owner of Concho Junction, a San Angelo honty-tonk was on the phone. "Lacey, sorry to wake you. I had to take Dude's car keys tonight; he just isn't in any shape to drive home; I'll let him sleep it off in the back room and send him your way when I open up for the lunch crowd tomorrow."

"I was awake, Gene. But thanks — for the call and for letting Dude stay over," Lacey answered. "At least now I will be able to get some sleep, too."

Lacey didn't know whether to feel disappointed or relieved. Willie Nell had baked her very first cake from scratch and was as nervous as a kitten to see if her daddy would like it.

"Daddy had to stay overnight in San Angelo, he should be home for lunch tomorrow, sweetheart." Lacey told one more lie for Dude. She knew this was what her Al-Anon sponsor called 'enabling' behavior, but she didn't have the courage tonight to break her little girl's heart one more time.

Durbin walked a sober Dude Autrey to the old Suburban. "You got a better woman than you deserve, asshole," he told his frequent customer. "If you come in here again, I'm gonna put you on a three-drink limit."

Dude started the truck, gave Durbin a two-finger salute to the brim of his cowboy hat, and drove off. As soon as he was out of sight of the bar, he reached under the seat for the pint of Jim Beam.

Hair of the dog, Dude, old pal.

It didn't take the whiskey very long on an empty stomach; Dude wasn't in much better shape when he arrived at the trailer than he'd been after four hours of partying last night at the Junction.

The Suburban lurched to a stop half-on, half-off the parking pad in front of his home, and he tumbled and stumbled out of the truck. Willie Nell ran arms out for him to lift her up as he always did when he returned from a rodeo.

The little girl's shriek of delight sent a knife through Dude's skull, which housed the King Kong of headaches, brought on by drinking away a hangover. When Willie Nell jumped up on him, he nearly fell, and shoved her away.

"Watch what the fuck you're doing," he slurred. Then he slapped her. Hard. The blow toppled the child to the gravel, bleeding from a busted lip.

Lacey had just made it to the door and witnessed the awful sight. She bounded down the steps to her stricken child.

Dude turned and, without a word, climbed back into the Suburban, started the engine, and left.

He felt as if he'd been doused with cold water and fed three pots of strong black coffee. In his rearview mirror, he could see Lacey's furious face. He drove straight to the VFW hall. Today, he wasn't going to get a drink, he needed to talk to his sponsor. Dude always wondered about his AA sponsor. Carl managed the VFW bar.

"Sounds like you may finally have reached bottom, cowboy. At least I hope so," Carl said as they both sipped the strong, black goo that passed for coffee at the VFW. They sat in one of the meeting rooms, not the bar.

"I can't drink ever again, Carl. I think I hurt my baby. If my wife doesn't sue for divorce, she's a fool."

"Asshole, she's a saint. And she's an Al-Anon. Comes by it honestly. Her daddy, was a friend and a drinking buddy of mine, died of alcoholism you know. Children of alcoholics usually either become drunks themselves, or go off an marry 'em. You're lucky you're not both drunks, or your kids wouldn't have a goddamn chance in hell."

"I know," Dude said miserably.

25

"I been goin' to AA meetings, Lacey Jay."

Dude's voice pulled Lacey back to the present. "How long?" Lacey kept her back to her husband seated at the dinette. It had been three months now and she hadn't forgotten what he had done to Willie Nell, who would have a small scar at the edge of her lower lip for the rest of her life. The two stitches to close up the cut were well done, but the scar would always be visible, particularly whenever her daughter tanned in the Texas sun.

"Got my 90-day chip tonight," he said with some pride.

Lacey spun to face the man she had married 10 years ago. She was livid. "I love you, you no 'count bastard, but if you ever lay a hand on me again, I won't be leaving you. I'll kill you. Do you understand me?! That goes double for the girls, you even look like you're going to lay a hand on one of them, I castrate you with a rusty razor blade!!"

"Does that mean you're takin' me back?"

"Tomorrow, and without the girls. They'll stay right with Miz Edie until you and I talk this whole thing out and until I feel comfortable we're all safe with you.

"Now you go back to the trailer and get some sleep," Lacey said firmly, then softer added, "I'll be knocking on your door in the morning, sweetie."

True to her word, Lacey walked across the graveled drive, under the carport and up to the trailer she and Dude had shared since he had started working the rodeo circuit. She rapped twice lightly and let herself in. Dude was at the stove.

"Biscuits in the oven, Sausage and eggs cookin'. Hope you're hungry."

"Got coffee?" Lacey sat at the dinette, positioned so she was facing the kitchen and her husband.

"Finished brewin' coupla minutes ago. Lemme get you a cup."

"I know my way around this kitchen, love. And you don't have to seduce me with breakfast. Here's a news flash: I'll be sleeping with you tonight."

Dude laid the turner on the counter beside the stove and stepped toward Lacey, wiping his hands on the ridiculous apron he'd donned to protect his new jeans and rodeo shirt.

As Lacey rose, Dude enveloped her in his sinewy arms and kissed her fervently. After the long kiss Lacey continued the embrace, laying her head on his shoulder.

"Dude, we can have it all if you can stay off the booze."

26

A frosty New Year's Eve, Lacey held the microphone above her head, the overhead kliegs bathing her face in a sweaty glare as she belted out the last words of Patsy Cline's "Sweet Dreams."

She felt lucky to get the gig at the Rusty Spur; it had helped with Christmas a lot to be able to sing on Friday and Saturday nights. Since New Year's Day was Monday, the club had let her come in Sunday night as well.

The Patsy Cline oldie was always her final encore song. This time, she included it in her regular playlist. There would be no encore tonight; she wanted to get home to her family.

"Sorry, I can't do encores tonight. I'm superstitious. Don't you know that the way you begin a new year is how you'll end it? I'm headin' home to kiss my babies and say howdy to a new year, even at two in the ayem."

The singer clicked the old corded microphone into its holder on the mike stand, turning a deaf ear to protests from the crowd. "I'm gonna have to get one of those new cordless mikes when I make the big time," she told herself.

Lacey didn't stop to remove her stage makeup or flashy outfit. Going home to Dude and her girls was the only thing on her mind. She stopped by the small dressing room — in reality, just a powder room next to the women's rest room — just long enough to grab her old shearling car coat. The little sequined denim jacket wasn't any protection on a night like this.

Texas winters don't bring a lot of snow particularly this far south, but sleet and ice are staples in January. In dismay, Lacey appraised the sheet of ice covering the parking lot as the wind tried its best to drive straight through her sheepskin-lined coat. It would be a nasty drive. Hopefully, there'd been enough tractor-trailer traffic to wear off some of the ice — New Year's eve, sleet, freezing rain, a mess.

The sound of the sirens in the distance weren't particularly disturbing to her as she exited the little bar into the cold night air. It was New Year's Eve; all the local cops, the EMTs, and the highway patrol would have their hands full tonight with the combination of weather- and alcohol-related carnage out on I-10. she knew the girls were at home or with Eyidie if Dude was out carousing.

On those rare occasions when Lacey sang, it was always too late to get the kids up by the time she got home. She and Dude had agreed with Eyidie that if no one could make it home by midnight, the kids slept over. The kids loved crashing on Eyidie 's overstuffed divan after an evening of being spoiled by homemade cookies, hot cocoa, and her bedtime stories.

God, I hope Dude got home in time to pick up the girls, It's New Year's, and I need to hold them.

Dude's new sobriety wasn't much comfort; he'd fallen off the wagon more than once in their 11-year marriage, and New Year's Eve was just the time for him to pull another drunk. Lacey was thankful she didn't drink anything stronger than ginger ale on nights she performed.

Driving carefully and attentively on the icy roads, she neared the little trailer park without incident, but dread began gnawing at her gut when she saw the police car as she pulled into the trailer park. It looked like they could be at her trailer.

Hard to tell from this distance. Lord, please make it not so.

The police cruiser, lights flashing on the bar across the roof, was parked on the cement pad where Dude normally parked the Suburban. His old truck was nowhere around.

The cops are at my house. Something's wrong. If that son-of-a-bitch has hurt my kids, I'll kill him.

Slamming the beat up old car into park, she bolted out and across the sleet-slick gravel to her trailer. A young highway patrolman inside met her at the door.

"What's happened?" she screamed, quickly becoming hysterical.. "Are my kids alright?!"

The young policeman gaped at the sequined cowgirl apparition accosting him. She shoved two hands at his chest forcing him to step back, "Are my kids OK? You tell me right now!" Lacey's eyes riveted those of the young cop angrily from beneath the gaily festooned Stetson atop her amber curls.

Eyidie walked into the trailer behind her and gently pulled the sobbing woman away from the dumbstruck officer. "It's Dude, Honey. He wrecked that old Suburban. He's dead."

"I want to see my girls. They're still with you aren't they?"

"No," The black woman and lifelong friend broke Lacey's heart. "Dude came by for the little ones about 11 or so. Said he wanted to begin the New Year with his girls, but ..."

Lacey interrupted. "Oh, no." She sank to the ground on her knees. "Did they ... I mean are they hurt too?"

"Willie Nell ran away when she saw that other woman with Dude; she's inside my trailer now, and crying. Dude took the baby though, buckled her in the backseat of that Suburban like you always told him to. That's what kept her from being killed, but she's bad hurt, sweetheart."

27

Lacey felt her world fall apart.

This is all a grotesque mistake. I'll walk inside and my girls will be fast asleep in their beds. I'll take off my makeup and my smoky clothes, and then fix me a cup of tea. Yes, that's what I'll do. I need a cup of tea.

"Miz Edie, you're gonna fix me a cup of tea while I take off my things. I smell like an ashtray," A hysterical Lacey reinvented her reality. "We won't wake the girls. It's too late. We'll tell them about their daddy in the morning."

"Child, Willie Nell knows, and Sunny was with Dude. Lord, I wish she wasn't, but God's truth, girl, she was." Eyidie put an arm around the shivering woman and led her toward her bedroom. "You just change and get that stuff off your face. You can go to the hospital to check on your baby. I'll see after Willie Nell. This policemen says he'll drive you."

"I'm here, Miz Edie, Mama," a small voice whispered from the door. It was Willie Nell. "Am I in trouble cuz I didn't go with Daddy? Maybe it wouldna happened if I hadn't run off; I didn't like that lady with him. He smelled like beer, too."

Lacey lost it. "He was taking my babies with him and his whore after drinking? And I was trying to support us the only way I know how!" She slammed her bedroom door and plopped across her bed. Eyidie opened the door and drew Lacey up into her arms.

"Dear Jesus, Miz Edie, how could I have been so blind? I had to have Dude, the hunk, the stud, the football hero. How dumb can one girl be?"

"If you hadn't been with Dude," Eyidie chastened, "these two wonderful children would never have been born. Now you go get yourself pulled together. Sunny needs her mother right now."

Woodenly, Lacey smeared cold cream on her face, wiped it off with tissues, and pulled her hair back. She quickly wriggled her way into a sweater and jeans, replaced the lacquered cowboy boots with an old pair of work boots, and snatched her shearling from the couch where she'd tossed it earlier. She paused on her way out just long enough to kiss her oldest daughter and thank Eyidie.

Lacey rode in silence as the police cruiser negotiated the icy streets to the hospital with lights flashing. The young trooper gave up after a couple failed attempts at conversation and focused on keeping the powerful car under control. Parking beneath the shelter at the emergency entrance, he helped her from the car and escorted her into the ER.

"I'll be back in an hour to take you home, Ms. Autrey," the young man said after he introduced her to the ER head nurse.

Emergency treatment had already stabilized the child's vital sights, but admission and the real treatment for her injured required Lacey's signature. Tears blurred the words, but Lacey wasn't reading anyway. She signed at the red X, and then sat. In silence, she waited as the hands on the sterile-looking wall clock crept slowly around.

"Mrs. Autrey, "the doctor's voice sounded like he was in a tunnel, "we did all we could for the baby, but ..." Dr. Daniel Houston's young face was drawn, tired, stubbled with yesterday's beard after several hours in the operating room.

"She's not dead!? Dear God tell me she's not dead!"

"No, but she'll be lucky to be able to walk again. The internal injuries, we were able to repair. But one of her legs was severely damaged, crushed by the weight of the vehicle. She'll require several surgeries just to save the limb. It's anybody's guess if it will ever be strong enough to support her weight."

28

As Lacey completed insurance paperwork and surgery authorizations in the early hours of the New Year, she spotted the same cop who had brought her to the hospital last night

Was that just an hour ago?

"I'm Lacey, and that's my baby Sunrise in the ER."

"Jimmy Wheat," the young man responded.

"How did it happen?"

"I'm sorry, Ms. Autrey, I wasn't the investigator. But Sheriff Cross is on his way here to speak with you."

As if on cue, Sheriff Alvin Cross' black and white cruiser passed under the ER entrance carport. The Sheriff parked in one of two spaces near the entrance reserved for police cars. He spotted Lacey as soon as he opened the door. Shaking the water and sleet from his insulated jacket, he strode across to her, hat in hand.

"I'm awful sorry, Lacey. Dude was a friend, even though he and I had a run-in or two, but only when he was drinkin'."

"Oh, Alvie ..." Lacey wrapped her arms around the rotund figure of the smallish sheriff and collapsed against him sobbing.

As the sobs lessened, she released her grip on Cross and stood up, taking a handkerchief that had materialized in his chubby hand.

"… *Sniff* … was he … was he, uh, drunk, Alvie?"

"All I can say right now is that the Suburban smelled of alcohol, and we found a fresh beer can in the floorboard," the sheriff reported in a monotone. "And Nancy Poteet was with him. Carl, down at the VFW says she was totally sloshed, been drinkin' all night.

"I sent one of my deputies to talk to Eyidie Nwaigbo. She said your oldest daughter refused to get into the Suburban cuz of the alcohol. Said she was 'fraid to ride with Dude."

Lacey's tears stopped abruptly as her anguish yielded to rage.

"That bastard was bragging about his sobriety just this morning!" Lacey balled her fists and hissed, "He'd better be glad he died in that wreck or I'da kil't him myself."

A passing nurse put a hand on her shoulder. "You want something? I could get Doc to prescribe something to calm you down."

"Fuck you! I should worry about not being calm? That's my baby in there and they don't even know if they can save her leg. My husband's dead. I should be calm???"

Lacey's hands shot to her cheeks. "Oh my God! Poor Billy. Does he know about Nancy, Alvie?"

"Yeah, but don't think about him," the sheriff said. "He could become your worst enemy in the coming days if tests show Dude was, in fact, drunk."

"That's a car insurance issue, Alvie. Billy and Nancy are friends. Anyway, they can't get any money from me; I ain't got any." Lacey thought, for the first time, about the future and her girls. "I ain't even got a job, no high school diploma, no skills.

"Aw, shit. Alvie, what am I gonna do?" Lacey's sobs began again.

Alvin extracted himself and nodded at the nurse. "Can doc give her a shot or something?"

"I bet he would. Let me go get him."

The nurse returned with Doctor Houston in tow. Doc had a full hypodermic in his hand.

"Here's something to make you feel better, Lacey Jay," he said as he pushed up a sleeve. Lacey didn't protest while Doc swabbed a spot with alcohol and deftly inserted the needle.

"Alvin," he asked the sheriff, "she'll be getting sleepy soon. Doesn't need to be driving with this stuff in her. Can you run her home now?"

"You bet." Sheriff Alvin Cross spotted Lacey's shearling jacket, wrapped it around her shoulders, and embraced her as he walked her to the police cruiser.

29

The shower in the bathroom was Lacey's place to cry. The world would never hear her sobbing nor see her tears.

In a small place like Sonora, off the main interstate highways, Lacey'd be lucky to get a big tipper much less a big-time agent to hear her. In order for her to begin to travel to larger towns and get better gigs, she had to find a place for Willie Nell. Lacey began to investigate the availability of places where a girl like Willie Nell could live and grow up to become something better than a saloon-singer and part-time waitress. So the search began.

Now she was facing the hardest decision she'd ever made in her life — whether to struggle on welfare and some minimum-wage job to raise her girls here in this ratty trailer, or to place them in the care of others while she tried to realize her dream of a singing career to make a new life for them all. So, only in private could she get the release she craved whenever she saw a little girl, especially one in leg braces or a wheelchair. "Sunny!" her mind screamed, but it never was her crippled daughter.

The little towheaded princesses in pretty dresses that she pictured in her dreams laughed and lived in a lovely place with other children for playmates. Food aplenty filled the table daily. They wanted for nothing.

Would they miss me? I hope so, but not so much they're unhappy and have to find a private place to cry.

109

Once she shut off the water in the shower bathing her face, Lacey vowed she would allow no more tears to stream down her cheeks, either. The vow only held until the next time she saw either a beautiful little girl with Willie Nell's somber expression or Sunny's little pixie face. The cycle would be repeated then. Lacey's agony would provide more fodder for new songs.

I wish for days of wet floors with tiny footprints

Left there while the children played

Now, the footprints are memories

If only love had stayed and no one strayed

The incomplete lyrics comforted Lacey while she labored over another song filled with the emotions crowding her heart. All of her songs, still hidden from the world, were full of her feelings. The process of setting them to words was comfortable, cathartic.

Lacey Jay's muse was heartache.

Sunny was at the hospital in Dallas, where she would spend much more time in the next few years than she would at home. She lived in a children's home between treatments except for those rare occasions Lacey could bring her to Sonora for a visit.

The hospital where Sunny would be treated was created by Scottish Rite of Freemasonry. Texas Scottish Rite Hospital for Children in Dallas is one of the nation's leading centers for the treatment of pediatric orthopedic conditions, as well as other conditions. Lacey was referred there immediately after Sunny's injury. All treatment would be free.

She could go to school and socialize in a safe environment where her injury wouldn't make her feel unaccepted. The literature promised that the program treated the "whole person" and not just the injury or disability. That comforted Lacey and softened the edges of the hard choice she was to later make.

The call to the state Child Protective Services was much harder ... to surrender her darling Willie Nell to the care of the state, to be adopted, or worse yet, to be passed up for adoption and spend her teenage years in an orphanage.

The reality of life fueled Lacey's determination. Dude's death left a few debts, but the trailer had been free and clear. She had to borrow against it to bury Dude. The insurance company wrote a check for the Suburban, which was totaled. But the total value of the old truck wouldn't replace it with anything newer than five years old, maybe newer if she went for a compact car.

Lacey felt as though a piece of her heart had been amputated. How she missed her kids! Every little girl's giggle or squeal felt like a thousand cactus needles in her flesh. As soon as she got the money gathered up, they'd be together. Sunny would have her leg fixed. They'd be a family again, almost. Instead of Dude being away at a rodeo, he was dead and gone. That couldn't be helped. What's done is done. There's no second take on life. No practice sessions warming up for the real thing—life just happens.

But the real problem was her lack of education or a marketable job skill. There was simply no way she could provide a decent life for her little girls. The Masons and the Baptists had more to offer, and she was grateful, if saddened by the reality.

Lacey got out her old guitar and began making the rounds of the local honky-tonks to try to sell the only skill she had, her music.

30

Willie Nell stood on the brink of her teens; her daddy was dead, her sister crippled, she was separated from her mother who was struggling just to take care of herself. It was time for her to grow up, she figured.

In her own mind it wasn't much of a stretch from age 10 to 13. Every day she'd look in her mirror expecting to see the beginnings of a woman's figure. She even asked Miz Edie about "the period" all the girls were talking about.

What a blessing, to have that feeling and know I'm a woman at last!

But it didn't come at age 10 or even at 11. Since her birthday fell just right, she was somewhat younger than some girls in her grade. To hear them tell it, a few months was a lifetime of difference.

Them and their training bras and tampons!

"It will happen soon enough," Miz Edie told her.

How can I not want to be all grown up?

She had decided that being a little girl was no fun. A her age, she stood half a head taller than boys in her class and her mother told her she was too old to play football or wrestle with the boys.

But I'm too young to go on dates!

It wasn't that she wanted to hang around with boys anyway. The Babtist-run children's home would be strict about that aspect of her social development; that much she'd already figured out.

She was beginning to yearn for the right to wear lipstick and high heels, to go dancing, to get a manicure like Mama, to do all those delicious things that grown ups do. Life will be so exciting. Mama told her not to rush things. Willie Nell knew her mother had rushed some of her decisions. She promised herself she wouldn't marry early like Mama did.

Even at her tender age, Willie Nell recognized that her mother's situation was terribly sad.

A widow before she's old.

It was true this pre-teenager had a certain wisdom not always found even in adults.

Willie Nell was, as Miz Edie had described her when she was just a baby, "an old soul." She wanted to go to college and become someone with a career, a writer, and live like people she saw on on TV. She understood that people didn't live like the characters on Dallas or Knots Landing. She had already observed the haves and the have-nots around her.

She understood that not all Texans have lots of money. She didn't expect to become rich, but she knew she could become productive and live a life of sufficency.

Mama wanted to be a big singing star and all she's got is local honky-tonks and the VFW club. If I were Mama, I'd go get on TV like Tanya Tucker or Crystal Gayle.

Her conversations with her mother began to sound just like the daydream conversations she held in her head. After awhile, Lacey began to think like Willie Nell. She, too, wanted a better life for herself and her girls. The baby was already being cared for at the Scottish Rite Hospital in Dallas, and an anonymous donor was paying for her stay at a nearby Baptist children's home so she'd be close to the medical care she would need most of her childhood.

Her life would improve. Doctors had told Lacey that Sunrise would be able to walk, possibly even run and jump and do everything. But before all of that, there would be multiple surgeries, each followed by painstaking physical rehabilitation.

Willie Nell decided she deserved the opportunity to better her own life.

One night on a visit to Sonora, the teen went to work with Lacey instead of spending the night with Miz Edie. By now, the girl was 12 and the "period" she had wished for had shown up for the first time two months ago. Tonight, she sat at the counter rather than at a table. That way, she didn't take up one of the available "tops" where some customer with spare change could leave Mama a tip. If Willie Nell took up a table, there would be one less "top" to generate business and Mama's chances for tips.

Nobody had to tell the young girl this reality; she figured it out on her own. just like she knew that if she sat with a group of other girls, no good-looking guy would come up and talk to her. Of course, if she sat by herself, she also ran the risk of being thought of as stuck-up.

Twirling fries in a pool of catsup, Willie Nell thought about articles she'd read in Seventeen, the magazine for teenage girls. She couldn't wait to try some of the fashion, decorating, and dating tips out when she got older. She didn't expect to find the love of her life in Sonora, the boys here either grew up to be cowboys or sheep shearers if they stayed. If their dreams included any sort of careers, they went to one of Texas' seven metropolitan areas to study something. Some, of course, would go to San Angelo, only 80 miles north, to work in a hospital or in a warehouse or factory.

But there was this one boy. He wrote for the newspaper. Ezra Hamilton was a smallish boy, four years older than her, but shorter and lighter. He said he was a "stringer" for the Devil's River News, Sonora's only paper, turning out a weekly column of news about high school activities and sports. Occasionally, he would get to broadcast a feature on KHOS, the local AM radio station. Willie Nell thought she might like to be a writer. But she didn't want to just sit at a typewriter all day like little Ezra. She already doubted if her energy level would allow her to sit all day like he had to do.

Maybe TV was the place for her. They didn't have one at the trailer park, but the café had a small one and her friend, Adele, had a set of her very own in her bedroom — An RCA color set! During a sleepover at Adele's last summer, Willie Nell had sat mesmerized in from of the 'boobtube' as Adele's father called it. The children's home had a large TV in the common area, but house-parents monitored when the kids could watch what shows. They considered News programming too intense for children and television was off from 4 o'clock until prime-time programming began at 7 pm, but not very many good series withstood their scrutiny.

As she glanced up from her french fries at the little black-and-white set in the diner, Willie Nell saw a local feature about local girls who were studying drama at the San Angelo University.

How cool is that!? Maybe I can go there and do that someday!

A plan began to form in the girl's head. Drama and communication would go hand in hand in the world of TV, she figured. And just like that, the pre-teen girl had decided her career path. She would major in communications and minor in drama. The only difference was that it would not be at San Angelo, but at age 12, she hadn't even dreamed of being able to attend a big-time school like Southern Methodist University.

Mama came back to the counter to get the coffee pot and refill cups in the room that were emptying. Her laugh floated back over to Willie Nell. The girl turned to look at her beautiful mother. Her slim body bore no evidence of being a mother of two, certainly no one would think this radiant woman with the rich, lustrous auburn hair could have a daughter approaching her teens.

How long has it been since I've heard Mama laugh?

Willie Nell had always loved to hear Mama sing. She's sang occasionally, not like before. And now her songs — once were full of fun and joy — are full of loneliness and sadness. This sudden awareness startled the girl.

Huh! I never realized that Mama wasn't happy either.

31

She would still be alive had she not changed her hair color. But the rowdy crowd of cowboys, both ranch and rodeo types, drinking and dancing a Saturday night away at the Rusty Spur seemed to appreciate the newly blonde look of Lacey Jay.

The Rusty Spur was a clone of hundreds of West Texas honky-tonks where a day's hard work can melt into a night of hard play, hard liquor, hard music, and soft women. However, Lacey was thankful for any gig in a joint close to home. In this small-town bar she'd always been a hometown favorite. Both the bar and her trailer court were on the outskirts of Sonora, a 90-minute drive south of San Angelo.

Lacey Jay Autrey had reverted to using her maiden name onstage after horny cowboys had found their way to the little house trailer on more than one occasion. Twice, Dude had been forced to protect his wife from the unwanted suitors, and sent one to the hospital with a broken nose. Lacey decided her two girls didn't need to witness those kind of events, so the name Autrey now appeared on nothing having to do with her professional life.

Dude's death hadn't changed that. To the outside world, she was Lacey Jay, but her bank accounts, her children's school and medical records, everything not connected to her career, all carried her name as Lacey Jay Autrey. More often than not, these days, she would forget to include the name of her late husband during introductions and simply met strangers exactly the same way she introduced herself to audiences: "Hi, I'm Lacey Jay"

117

Although a widow and available, Lacey seldom dated. But the loneliness was beginning to take a toll on her. She missed her children, she missed Dude, and she missed the feeling of being held and loved. So she changed her hair. Tonight, if she met someone interesting, she wouldn't close the door on seeing what might develop.

The songbird's beauty had mesmerized Lucas. And the cascade of blonde hair framing her face and tumbling down over her shoulders brought a familiar stirring to his loins. Yesterday, her auburn tresses, now transformed to dazzling honey gold and streaked with highlights, were just as striking but probably wouldn't have drawn his attention; he was an admitted sucker for blondes.

Lacey finished the first set of the night and abandoned the stage for a 10-minute break, heading toward the crowded bar.

The stranger intercepted her at the bar. "Let me buy you a drink."

Lacey seldom interacted with the guys who spend their time in the little bars and honky-tonks where she eked out a meager living singing old country standards. To her, these men were all clones of Dude Autrey, her late husband, who almost killed their daughter in the same crash that took his life.

But this guy's different; too clean cut and soft-spoken to be a barfly, and not really a cowboy. "Just a ginger ale, please. I have to get back to my guitar in another 10 minutes. Otherwise my pawnshop might repossess the damned thing."

"Ginger ale it is, then," Lucas said, a flashing smile bisecting his rugged, tanned face. "Just wanted to meet you. You're really good, you know. You should be in Nashville."

"That's my dream — and my intent." Lacey felt a flutter of excitement.

This guy's a hunk! And polite!

"I'm not much of a drinker, myself. But I like to show up when there's live music.

"Name's Lucas, Lucas Petersen. But please, call me Luke."

"Hi, I'm Lacey Jay. Pleased t'meet ya." Lacey sized up the handsome stranger, her eyes lingering an extra millisecond on his crotch.

Damn! Why do I do that?!

"I was born and raised right here in Sonora and I know I've never seen you before. Where are you from?"

"Just got here from New Mexico. I may stay a spell if I can find work."

Damn! I don't want this guy leaving town right away. Pickings for a widow with kids are slim enough.

"What do you do?"

"I work on cars. I'm not certified or nothin' but I been fixing 'em ever since I was a kid in New Mexico." He continued to look into Lacey's eyes.

"Then this is just the town for you. Most of these oilfield guys drive clunkers that spend as much time in the shop as on the road."

Whew! He's turning up the heat for me.

It had been a long time since Lacey had felt the stirrings that had her a bit flustered at the moment. She gulped her soda like a dying man in the desert.

"Can I buy you another ginger ale after the show?" He noted the empty glass with a chuckle.

"Honey, you can buy me a six-pack of Coors after I get off that stage." Lacey laughed. "I just don't like alcohol to deaden my throat when I'm singing."

"Then I'm nailed to this barstool for the night." Luke winked and Lacey again felt her face flush.

I might get nailed myself before the sun comes up.

She hadn't been with a man since the night Dude Autrey had picked up the baby, rolled the Suburban down the side of an arroyo, breaking his fool neck, killing a female companion, and crippling their infant daughter.

Damned drunk! What was that, four years ago?!

Still blushing, Lacey waved a coy fingertip goodbye and turned toward the makeshift stage where The Jaybirds, her accompaniment trio, were setting up to start the second of three sets they would perform tonight.

The crowd hooted louder with each new drink and each new rendition of the country classics the group performed.

Lacey ended the third set with one of her own songs, "A Ball of Yarn", making sure the recorder was on before beginning. The audience roared its approval as Lacey took her bows before leaving the stage and walking toward the stranger at the bar.

"How'd you like that last one, Mister Mechanic?" she beamed. "I wrote it myself."

"Wow! Let's make that two six-packs. That was as good as anything Hank Williams ever done."

"Let's take 'em back to my trailer, then," Lacey escalated the evening's potential.

32

It was 9 o'clock the next morning when Eyidie shuffled across the sparse, yellowed grass and dirt and huffed up the steps to the rickety landing. She knocked perfunctorily on the trailer door, and let herself in.

"I'm here, child and ol' Edie sure needs her caffeine fix today." The two women had shared this morning coffee ritual for years. "I got Willie Nell ready for church but the bus ain't made it by yet."

The sickly sweet smell of flesh beginning to decompose assaulted the old woman's nostrils and made her eyes water. "OH my God, No!" Eyidie rushed out the door and crossed to her own trailer. Willie Nell, visiting for the weekend from the children's home in San Angelo, gaped as the sitter bolted to the phone and dialed 9-1-1. Mindful of the presence of the pre-teenager, Eyidie made every effort to stay composed.

"Send an ambulance to Lacey Jay's trailer. I think she's hurt."

"Eyidie?" Sally, the sheriff's administrative aide is also the town's daytime 9-1-1 operator, exclaimed, surprised to hear from Eyidie Nwaigbo, a second-generation Nigerian a legend of wisdom and kindness in this small town.

"It's me, but send the ambulance to Lacey's place."

"Well, it's sure as shootin' not Dude actin' up this time. Not unless he's learned how to slap that woman around from beyond the veil!" the woman quipped mirthlessly, then asked, "Is Willie Nell alright?"

Everyone in town also knew Lacey's daughter spent as much time at home as possible, even though she lived in a church home 80 miles away. Much of that time she was with the old black woman whenever Lacey had a singing gig. "I kept her last night. She's in my trailer. Get someone out here fast."

Randy Gunn, a 22-year-old Sonora sheriff's deputy found the body of Lacey naked, face down in the back bedroom of the trailer. Justice of the Peace Hobson, who was also the de facto coroner for the small West Texas town, had seen a few deaths, but almost no murders. When he got the call from the deputy, he immediately called Doc Houston to the crime-scene to help him with the investigation. In this Texas county, nobody touches a thing until the head honcho, usually the JP, gets on scene. But Hobson knew he would want a licensed doctor this time.

Even in October, trailers get hot in West Texas, the close confines of the trailer, the heat, and the odor of decomp encouraged the two men to work quickly. "She's been strangled," the doctor said.

"The eyes show petechial hemorrhaging and there are bruises on both sides of her neck; the hyoid bone has been crushed. Man, this dude was strong!"

"I don't see any sign of a struggle, Doc."

"I don't think they were struggling at all. This woman appears to have had sexual intercourse, vaginal and anal, just before her death, and it doesn't look like it was forced — no tearing, no bruising. Wait. There's semen on her hand and on her face."

Sheriff Alvin Cross arrived as the two were finishing their preliminary work at the murder scene. He talked briefly with Eyidie before entering the trailer. Eyidie labored up the steps to her own trailer. She had calls to make, but the list — people who would really care that a woman named Lacey Jay Autrey had gone to her maker — was very small. She would have to call the children's home in Dallas where little Sunrise Autrey was fighting her own battles with multiple orthopedic surgeries. Lacey had no other family. Dude's family, would have to know, of course. She would notify Janine, then Sarah, then boys in the band, and finally the owner of The Rusty Spur and the VFW commander. She wouldn't worry about the funeral home. They wouldn't get the body until after the police investigation and autopsy, and then Reverend Taylor would take care of arrangements.

"Missus Nwaigbo says Lacey was singing at The Rusty Spur last night," he said as he ducked his head to enter the trailer. With his Stetson and western boots, the sheriff stood nearly seven feet tall.

With no fanfare, he began rummaging through kitchen cabinets and the spice rack. "Here's something." He called to the deputy, the JP, and the doctor. "These dopers haven't yet learned the first place we look for Mary Jane is in the spice rack, usually in an oregano tin."

The deputy emerged from the back bedroom. "You found weed?"

"Yeah, Randy. Hell, I didn't think Lacey'd touch this shit."

"Coulda been drug-related, sheriff."

"Damn! We ain't had a real murder in this town in years. Not since old man McGarritty shot that rancher who was boinking his wife back in ... when was that?"

"'66 wasn't it?" the deputy recalls. "Heck I was just a kid."

"You're not much more'n a kid even now," Sheriff Cross reminded himself.

The young deputy sniffed at the tin of marijuana. "Pretty stale. Been here a good while."

"Hell, it mighta been Dude's stash," the sheriff told his young deputy. "That was one hard-drinkin' bastard; I'd expect him to keep some weed around, too. She may not have even known it was there. But I'll let the coroner know we'll need a full toxicology report on Lacey's body."

"Who's Dude?"

"Aw, Randy. You ain't too young to remember the football hero turned rodeo cowboy, Dude Autrey. Killed hisself in a one-car wreck out on a farm road 8-10 years ago. He was Lacey's husband, a real hell-raiser.

"And I want you to go back there in that bedroom and see if you can find any evidence of recent drug activity. I'll check out here in the living area."

"Sheriff," the doctor interrupted, "I got enough to get a DNA sample from the semen this guy left behind. I'll get it to a lab in San Antonio today."

"Get me a tox screen, too, Doc."

123

"Randy, I want you to interview everybody who was at The Rusty Spur last night. I want to find that son-of-a-bitch who Lacey brought home with her. Hell. Get all our guys in on the interviews or it'll take us forever."

None of the men knew that the killer had already moved on and that this murder would sit in a cold-cases file for the next 14 years. The fingerprints in the trailer, the DNA, the descriptions from the interviews, none of the evidence would match any police database in the country.

33

Luke continued off and on to have encounters with women, not always with the same result. Yet, over the past 25 years he had left a trail of bodies across from New Mexico, across South Texas, in Louisiana and back across North-Central Texas as far as Dallas. More than 20 women had died at his hands, some of whom would never be found.

The mechanic could remember details of only one killing; it was the only one he had planned and carried out, the grisly murder of his mother. At age 13, after six years of constant sexual abuse, the child named Lucas had used one of Dixie Peterson's kitchen knives to kill her. Ironically, he had disposed of her body exactly as she had gotten rid of the corpse of her common-law husband, Bobby Duchamps.

As she buried the body of Luke's father in the desert beyond the City of Rocks, she had sworn her little boy to secrecy. Everybody believed her when she said Bobby had abandoned her and her illegitimate son.

Luke had kept in touch with Uncle Bo in Deming with an occasional phone call and cards, sometimes with a photo. But it had been years since he'd even contacted the one relative still living.

The young mechanic had tried to avoid women, but his occupation meant he would meet women in the natural course of working on their cars. His natural physical attraction would make a certain number of women approach him.

Like that woman in the pick-up truck in the New Mexico desert in 1981, many of the women he met were the aggressors. If Lucas didn't flirt or come on to them, they'd initiate things on their own. Many of the women success-

125

fully performed oral sex with him. Dozens of times, these encounters were enjoyable and didn't result in anything out of the ordinary.

"It's like Russian *roulette*," Lucas realized.

34

Nacogdoches, LA - April 1999

Sharon had stopped at the grocery for a few things on her way home and both arms were loaded down with brown paper bags as she made her way through the portal to the courtyard. She had been pleased when a downstairs apartment facing into the center of the complex had come open. She had spent the past two years upstairs facing the oil-stained, pot-holed parking lot and the noisy street beyond it. As she had anticipated, the apartment was quieter, cooler, and much more pleasant, just because of its location.

Nearing her door, book-ended by the two ornate planters she had bought within a week of moving, Sharon was pleasantly surprised to see Lucas, walking toward her, his muscular body and toothpaste-ad smile making her knees tremble just a little.

Lucas always sat at one of her tables at The Cotton Patch the past summer between school semesters. In only her second year at the Nacogdoches, Louisiana, elementary school, she supplemented her meager schoolteacher paycheck in the summer at the popular little diner.

"Luke! You're a welcome sight. Haven't laid eyes on you since school started. What are you doing here?"

"I just brought Miguel's car back, Miz Atlee," he said, continuing the conversation easily. "Patching that radiator just isn't going to get the job done; he needs t'spring for a new one."

"Well, Mickey's kinda tight-fisted," she replied "but with that houseful of kids and with Marie preggers again, he does have to watch his nickels and dimes."

Lucas only shrugged.

"So, how are you getting back to the shop? Mickey going to take you?" she asked.

"I'll hoof it. It's barely three miles; take me less than an hour."

"Let me put these groceries inside and I'll drive you."

"I couldn't put you out like that."

"No trouble. Give us a chance to get to know each other a little," she said, lowering her chin coyly.

Nothing was wrong with Miguel's car. In fact, Mickey didn't even know Lucas was anywhere around. That's how Lucas always planned these first encounters.

He took more than half of her load, held them as she unlocked the door, then followed her into the cool, clean, modest apartment.

"Just set them in the kitchen," she said. "I'm going to change first, if you don't mind."

"Go ahead, I'm in no hurry."

"No hot date tonight, Luke?" Sharon asked through the bedroom door that she left carefully ajar.

"I don't date much, really."

"What's wrong with the girls in this town?!" she giggled. "Be a dear, Luke. Come unzip me."

Sharon had unpinned her schoolteacher hairdo and a shock of blonde curls cascaded provocatively around her face and shoulders. As Lucas entered the bedroom, she turned her back to him, lifted her hair off her neck and leaned slightly back so her hips came into contact with the crotch of his jeans.

Lucas slowly slid the zipper down its length — ending several inches below the waist of her panties.

"While you're back there, could you undo my bra?" She heard his breathing quicken and deepen. It might be awhile before she would get him back to his garage, she thought.

Lucas fumbled with the hooks on the bra, and Sharon laughed softly.

"You haven't undressed many women lately, have you, Luke?" She turned toward him, staying very close, reached behind her back and deftly unhooked the bra. Shrugging her shoulders forward, she let the front of her dress and the bra straps fall down her arms, holding them in place with an arm below her breasts.

Lucas stared at the tops of her more-than-ample breasts, seeing pink semicircles of her aureoles peeking up at him. As she unbuttoned his work shirt, he clumsily helped her out of the rest of her garments — he always played it clumsy although he'd performed this ritual dozens of times, if not hundreds.

The muscular young woman pushed Lucas down onto the bed falling with him, her mouth on him in a passionate kiss. He returned the ardor, and his body began to respond. She abandoned the kiss, reared up beside his body, and placed both hands on his erection. "Luke, they shoulda named you 'Longneck.'" Mesmerized, she slid her hands along the shaft, up-down-up-down, and it continued to grow.

Moving her mouth down his body in a continuous barrage of licks and kisses, she reached his groin, taking the firm protrusion with the silken texture into her mouth.

35

Flashing lights slow traffic into the small town. An ambulance, fire truck, police cars — some marked, some not — sat at odd angles in the grass at the edge of the road. Up a slope about 30 yards, flashlights and floodlights danced and wove through a stand of trees. Lovers walking in the woods found the body two hours ago. The couple searched the carpet of fallen leaves for a suitable spot to spread a blanket to stargaze through the bare trees.

A naked foot, barely visible beneath a pile of leaves ended their plans for a romantic evening. Both were still at the station being detained for interrogation.

Instinctively, Atlee drew his service revolver, although there was no threat at the crime scene. The killer was long gone and the area crawled with patrolmen, detectives, and crime scene investigators.

He really wanted to shoot somebody. If it isn't the animal who snapped this girl's neck, then SOMEONE!

His rage surprised him, but knowing that fact doesn't ease it at all. The beautiful blonde woman was found naked beneath a pile of leaves at the edge of a stand of trees just off the highway between downtown Nacogdoches and the Interstate. Her body wasn't battered, bruised, or bloody. In his 35 years as a policeman, Atlee has seen the worst of what man can do to his fellow man. But for the leaves, she could be sleeping. Whoever placed her body here had some feeling for the victim. The eyes are closed, the broken neck not obvious — until patrolman Billy Turner tried to feel for a carotid pulse and her head fell over at an awkward, unnatural angle.

"We have fibers, Sarge!"

"Don't touch them, Turner," Atlee yelled. "Let the CSI boys recover them."

"Gotcha!"

Atlee noticed he was still holding his service revolver. With a sigh he holstered the weapon and secured it with the hammer guard.

"You need to go home, Atlee." It's Molly McKenzie, the lead CSI. She placed her hand on the meaty shoulder of the career policeman.

He turned toward her.

Sergeant Abraham Atlee was crying for his daughter.

36

"Your looks and your vocabulary don't go together. You sound like a long-shoreman in high heels!"

Claribel Simpson studied the young woman Joe Mosier had accompanied to the Assignments Desk. "You may fit right in at the cop shop, if they don't chew you up and spit you out."

Mosier, the Station Manager, had told Willie Nell that after 90 days as a probationer, or probie, a decision would be made about where she would spend her time as a news intern.

"Here at KTKO, we all cover a lot of territory, trade those stilettos for track shoes if you want to keep up with me," the City Editor told her.

Willie Nell gave out a loud laugh.

Mosier admonished her, "Claribel's not kidding. At an age when most writers are ready for retirement, she can still run circles around most of the young reporters. But I expect you to keep up with her. If you can hack it, she can teach you the ropes in half the time of anybody else in the organization."

"Not really," Claribel added. "I can help you learn to write it; but I can't make a reporter out of you. That's strictly a matter of your makeup. It takes a mix of guts, intuition, character, and a healthy dose of mule-headed skepticism. Those you have to bring to the party just to get in."

So began Willie Nell's training period at the all-news station.

So far, I've been told I need to talk like a lady around Claribel, but not to wear heels because she's always in fucking high gear. A lady in tennis shoes?

"Okay, spit it out. I hear those wheels turning in that freshly graduated 'I-know-everything' head of yours!" Joe said to Willie Nell.

She shook her head at the comment. "No, sir, I was just thinking how fucking little I do know about how a big station like this is run and how to fit in."

What an ass kisser you are, Willie Nell

"Ass kissing around here is done by Derek Prinz," Claribel said. "You need to learn some of his traits, particularly if you land in the cop shop. But we sure as hell don't need two of him around here," her new boss said.

Another fucking rule. Derek is the brown-noser, not my job.

"Joe, Mister Mosier," Willie Nell began.

"You had it right the first time. We're not all that formal around here with the misters and the misuses," Joe's smile gave her another sign of welcome to the group.

"So far, all I seem to have heard are the don'ts. What exactly am I to do?"

Joe waved a hand toward Claribel. "She'll let you in on the assignments. As City Editor, she does the assigning and training of the reporters and interns. Meet mother hen, mother advisor and mother confessor."

"Only in the very loosest of terms," Claribel said with a laugh. "I have no desire to listen to your romance or your credit problems. If it's about work, I'm all ears."

"You don't have to worry about that. I don't have much time for dating. I have a little sister to care for and a new career. That should occupy most of my day."

Ugh! I'm still brown-nosing. Cut the crap, Willie Nell.

"That's what I like to hear," Claribel said, "Although I don't believe a word of it. Sooner or later, some hunk comes along and you gals make up for lost time. But until then, I'll cram your head so full of the news biz that your dreams will be about headlines and deadlines."

"I'm ready, willing and eager to learn at your knee, Claribel." Willie Nell pledged. "And that's not ass-kissing, that's the fucking truth! … Oops, forgive my French."

"For the next few days it's the cop shop, then. Prinz seems to have a turnover of interns, and he's short-handed right now."

Claribel escorted the new reporter with her fresh degree from the University of Texas at Dallas to a grouping of four desks. "This is the cop shop, and this talented young man is Derek Prinz, the chief crime reporter for the station.

"Derek, this is Willie Nell, and she's all yours. Try not to chase her off."

"Are you all signed up with the W2's, I9's and all that other administrivia required by bureaucrats?" Prinz flashed a brilliant on-camera smile.

37

Willie Nell was dumbstruck; she barely nodded. She'd watched Derek Prinz on camera for most of her years at UT-Dallas. He was as familiar to the J-school students as the coach of the Dallas Cowboys.

"For the first two days, I want you to follow me around like a puppy. Your primary job will be to observe how I speak to people and to take names of people to whom you're introduced. These people will be your contacts at the police station and the Dallas County Courthouse. We'll also meet attorneys, emergency responders like EMTs and firemen, and folks in the morgue, the medical examiner's staff."

Willie Nell took notes.

"For God's sake, don't write down everything I say!" Prinz pulled a small, silver object from his shirt pocket. This is a digital recorder. I can start or stop it just by touching the front of my shirt unobtrusively. Beats taking notes most of the time. Spring for one from your first paycheck. For today, use mine."

Prinz tossed the tiny recorder to the reporter wannabe and spent a few minutes showing her how to operate it. "A charge is good for eight hours of recording. Don't try to save money buying less memory; that's pennywise and pound foolish," he advised.

The cop-shopper opened his desk and pulled out another recorder identical to the one he'd loaned Willie Nell. "I always keep a spare charging in my desk." He dropped the freshly charged recorder into his shirt pocket.

"Let's see what kind of stomach you've got. We're off to the ME's office — that's Medical Examiner. I'm anxious to find the cause of death of a vagrant found out behind the fairgrounds in South Dallas."

Willie Nell was impressed with Prinz' self-confident walk and carefully cultivated skill in talking to sources. At the ME's office, he didn't wrinkle his nose at the odors of chemicals with the undertone of putrefaction. Willie Nell, on the other hand, gasped at the sudden onslaught of her olfactory system.

Prinz dove right in, introducing Willie Nell to each of the office staff. Willie Nell repeated each name as she shook hands, a trick her mother had taught a little girl who was always entering poetry-reading contests at the library. "You gotta remember these folks who judge your recital; make 'em your friends, then just read to your friends," she'd preached. The little recorder also heard the names and titles and faithfully saved each one for posterity.

Prinz pushed through a double door that whooshed shut behind the two KTKO staffers. "An exhaust fan pulls air through the door so fewer germs and contaminants leak into the air outside," he explained.

After meeting the Chief Medical Examiner, Rose Billups, Willie Nell followed Prinz further into the bowels of the department where bodies on gurneys awaited technicians to tend them.

Prinz buttonholed a handsome woman with blonde hair and a slim but sexy body despite the white lab coat. "This is Anita Polanski, my favorite cop. She's a crime scene analyst and works closely with the ME's office." he said. Willie stuck out a hand.

"Sugar, you don't want to touch this glove with bare skin," the woman said with a wry smile. "Derek, get this girl some gloves, you dork!"

Prinz reached into a box of loose gloves and extracted four. He handed two to Willie Nell and pulled the other two over his own hands. "Sorry, Anita. I forgot."

"Forgetting in this place can get you dead, Derek ... you too, Willie Nell."

"So, what happened to my derelict at Fair Park?" he asked a forensics technician named Damon.

"Alcohol poisoning. No murder, nothing suspicious. Just another wino whose lifestyle killed him. Most of the folks here die from the same affliction."

"Alcohol poisoning!?" Willie Nell was incredulous.

Anita pulled the rookie reporter aside, "Most folks die from their lifestyle. The glutton dies from a heart attack, the doper from liver failure, the smoker from lung cancer. Their lifestyles were their afflictions and their cause of death."

"I get you. That's a good perspective; can I use it?"

"Sure, just not for attribution. I'm no philosopher." Anita laughed and Willie Nell found herself liking her instantly. The slender blonde possessed an earthiness that Willie Nell enjoyed. She didn't know that this hip and cool woman, 10 years her senior, would become her best friend in the near future.

The reporter would come to appreciate that when she wanted to let her hair down, her relationship with this scientist could fill that need. She became Willie Nell's sounding board, a woman she could trust to discuss things with — things AND feelings. She got the distinct impression the latter were not all that welcome in the newsroom.

38

Her mood was as gray as the threatening sky over Dallas this morning. It was the end of summer when autumn often announces its arrival in North Central Texas with thunder and lightning and cool, cool rain.

"Don't call me Sunrise!" The angry 16-year-old rails at the houseparent. "My name is Sunny Autrey!" Outside, a flash illuminated the gray clouds like an exclamation point.

The gray mood wasn't helped by the reality that tonight was her high school junior prom. All the kids but her would be dancing. She would wear an evening dress that would hide the ugly metal brace that allowed her to stand and to walk, somewhat awkwardly, without a cane or a walker. But she would be, as always, a wallflower. Boys had stopped asking her to be their date for the prom after she broke into tears when Jeffrey Bell had asked her and she'd turned him down.

Jennifer, working her way through a social work degree at the University of Texas as a caretaker for kids at the home for crippled children, rolled her eyes. She's read the case files and knows the mercurial teen before her had issues far beyond her disability — her murdered mother as well as her father, who died in the same car wreck that crippled her.

Sunny, a beautiful near-woman despite the lightweight metal brace on her left leg, watched the clouds piling one on top of another as they prepared for the pending light and sound show. Her lower leg and knee were crushed when the roof supports collapsed in the overturned Suburban. She would have died along with Dude Autrey, had her mother not always insisted on the child car seat.

After countless surgeries, the leg was well formed, all things considered. But the bones inside the lower leg weren't much more than stacks of rubble, ruins from that accident when she was less than a year old. The rebuilt knee was the most important accomplishment, allowing her to hobble along in her brace, but without a wheelchair or crutches. Although physical therapy had given her most of the musculature of leg, the bones still wouldn't support it. She knew that soon, when doctors were sure her growth was complete, they would surgically implant metal rods to do the job the bones cannot.

"I'm sorry, Sunny," Jennifer says. "It was just a slip."

"Sunrise was just a sudden inspiration in my mother's Hippie phase. I hate it."

"I know. You've told me often enough about your alcoholic dad and your honky-tonk mom."

"Can you believe she abandoned her children so she could be free to try to see if she couldn't visit every honky-tonk in Texas during one lifetime!" Sunny fumed.

"You've still got your sister, Willie Nell," said Jennifer, soothingly. "And you know she loves you very much."

"You're right of course; and I am grateful," the teen said, slowly calming. "But I feel like I'm going to be a burden on her when I'm booted out of here on my 18th birthday.

"And I know that's part of the reason Mama put me here. But why Willie Nell? She's not handicapped, and she was older and not all the trouble that a baby can be. . ."

"Stop that kind of talk right now!" Jennifer snapped.

"You're bright, creative, and sometimes even civil," Jennifer chided her ward. "Your sister will welcome you into her life."

"She can't afford to take care of me during those years of more surgery."

"Get off your pity pot! Lotsa good Masons are paying for the surgery; all she would need to do is feed you and keep a roof over your head. And the way you eat, girl! It'd cost more to feed a coupla goldfish."

Sunrise, Autrey was a direct opposite of her sister. Where Willie Nell was tall with chestnut hair, Sunny was a scant 5 feet tall with gorgeous brunette curls naturally framing her gamin face. Willie Nell was blessed with a large, sensuous mouth with full lips above a cleft chin. Sunny's bowtie mouth, though cute, didn't make for a sensuous appearance.

Both women were slender, but the teen's body was still a couple of years away from developing the womanly figure of her sister, if it ever would. Sometimes Sunny didn't understand how two sisters could be so different.

She was three when the two were split up. The crippled children's home took Sunny because they were better equipped to tend to her substantial rehabilitation needs than was the orphanage near the university.

Dallas was a good place to grow up. It drew more than its share of wealthy investors to keep businesses thriving and was the home headquarters of more than a dozen Fortune 500 companies. Its not-so-publicized technical industry was situated in a large area off Central Expressway known as "telecom corridor". Technically, the area was in Richardson and abutted Plano, one of the cities wealthier suburbs. Downtown Dallas boasts an arts district with a state-of-the-art symphonic hall, a fine arts museum, several galleries and ateliers, and the famed Nasher Sculpture Garden. These are served by the McKinney Avenue Transit Authority, a private non-profit corporation which restores and operates antique streetcars, some dating back to the 19th Century.

Nightlife and live music bookend the downtown district. The West End, a redeveloped warehouse district, offers nightclubs, fine dining, and an upscale mall built into one of the refurbished warehouses. At the east end is Deep Ellum, an edgier entertainment area with smoky jazz joints and eclectic clubs and eateries.

Educationally, the city boasts Southern Methodist University, Southwest Medical School, the University of Texas at Dallas, a seven-campus community college system, and many others.

Willie Nell had graduated from UTD with a degree in English and a minor in journalism. Sunny looked forward to attending UT's Arlington campus to "paper up" her already considerable computer skills.

Sunny always figured she and her sister got their brains from their mother because from what she heard about Dude, he had been a mental midget, even if he was a terror in the Baylor Bears backfield.

Her party-girl mother, Lacey Jay, had married herself a stud-muffin.

In fairness to the children's home, which was affiliated with a world-class crippled children's charity hospital, Sunny had a comfortable room in an attractive residence hall where she was free to pursue her interests as she pleased, as long as her grades were acceptable and she made all of her therapy sessions.

The teenager considered it the final irony in her life that her greatest talent and her greatest passion should be the same of her deceased mother for whom she held such fierce disdain.

The children's home was glad to make the piano in the sitting room available for their young prodigy. The counselors hoped that, through her music, Sunny would be able to express the anger bottled up within her. As they began to notice her ability to play, by ear, almost any tune she heard they approved piano instruction for Sunny Autrey. Abigail Ahrens, a retired high school music teacher, visited the home three times a week.

"Sunny," Abby told her early on in their relationship, "you play with a lot of emotion, and that's a good thing. But you will need to find music that is appropriate to the feelings you're experiencing. Writing and composing would probably be as rewarding to you as playing."

Now, eight years later, the music therapy had worked up to a point. Sunny's anger was still there, but the antisocial behavior and attitudes had long ago been scoured away. Abby was gratified to notice that fewer and fewer of Sunny's own lyrics and compositions were on themes of anger, self pity, and loss.

Sunny closed the door behind Jennifer and noticed the elevator had just stopped on her floor. It might be Willie Nell.

Studying herself in the mirror, Sunny appraised her appearance. The paint-stained cut-offs had to go. Even though her sister knew Sunny's passion for art and supported her efforts enthusiastically, she wouldn't' disrespect Willie Nell's visit by greeting her like a slob. As she ripped off her work clothes, the thought of her big sister quickly brightened Sunny's spirits.

The doorbell rang.

"I'm not dressed," she yelled over her shoulder as she streaked toward the bathroom. But the front door opened. She had given her sister a dorm-room key long ago.

"Like I haven't seen your bare butt before?" Willie Nell yelled after the sprinting naked form of her kid sister. She banged on the bathroom door just seconds after Willie Nell had slammed it.

"Can't a sister have a little privacy?"

"Can't a sister take a pee?" Willie Nell retorted. "You don't have any parts I don't have. Seriously, you can be such a prissy pants."

"Give me a minute and I'll be out." Sunny looked frantically for clothes, which were laying in the living room — at Willie Nell's feet.

"Any longer than a minute, you'll need a towel to mop up out here"

"Don't be such a baby! You can hold it a bit longer. I'm getting dressed."

"In what? I'm looking at a pile of what seems to be your clothes."

Sunny slowly opened the door and peered out at her sister. "I was gonna change, but you caught me in the middle."

Willie Nell unceremoniously dumped the armload of paint-stained clothes into Sunny's arms, walked to the toilet, pulled down her panties, and sat.

Sunny struggled to slip into her own underwear. "I don't know why I bother with panties. They're such a pain with this damn brace."

Pettily, Willie Nell chided her sister: "Crotchless panties would solve your problem. "Next you'll want to go braless, too. Of course you could pull it off; God knows you'll never be able to fill my cups."

"Most gals with big tits are dummies," Sunny parried the gibe. The sisters, as always, teased each other without mercy. "The bigger the boobs, the smaller the brain."

As she thought about it, Sunny added, "I must be a fuckin' genius."

"Watch your mouth, young lady!"

"You're the one with the foul-mouth rep; don't you lecture me." Sunny knew she had her sister's number now. Willie Nell's penchant for colorful language was legendary even though she tried mightily to overcome it. It had started with their parent's constant arguing, she had confided to her sister, who had been too young to possess more than a fuzzy idea of her life before the children's home.

145

"Besides bringing me a full bladder, what else have you got for me?"

From her purse, Willie Nell extracted a felt bag with a drawstring. Sunny recognized it. Her mother's pearls, bequeathed to Lacey Jay's then 10-year-old daughter, who had yet to wear them, were held in her outstretched hand.. "Just these."

"I know she left most of her jewelry to me since I'm the oldest, but tonight demands something special and these are definitely all of that," Willie Nell handed her sister the bag. "Her diamond and pearl studs are there, too."

Sunny smothered her big sister in a warm embrace. "You've always been the most generous person I've ever known." Tears were appearing at the edges of her eyes. "I'll get these back to you tomorrow."

"They're for you, sis. I'm not the little-black-dress-and-pearls type of girl. Keep 'em, with my love."

"There's something else," Willie Nell said, soberly. "Something important you need to know right now."

"Boy can you turn serious on a dime, Sis. What's the big hoo-hah?"

"It's about Dude — and the wreck."

"I told you never to mention that man's name to me! You know that." The younger girl bristled.

"Dude may not have been drunk that night, Sunny. I talked with Miz Edie, and she reminded me of a sobriety celebration we had just days before the accident. He'd been sober three months."

"Drunks fall off the wagon all the time!" Sunny wasn't going to give up a lifetime of hatred that easily.

Now woman and girl were at odds again, both near tears. It happened way too often. Willie Nell had to change to subject, or she'd lose it altogether. "And if that damned boyfriend of yours breaks the string on these pearls, I'll personally castrate him."

Sunny laughed just as a tear broke free to roll down her cheek. She wiped it with the back of her hand. Both sisters knew there wasn't a boyfriend and that Sunny would show up at the prom alone. "Then I better keep him outta your line of sight, just in case. He'll be here in less than an hour and I have lots to do to get presentable." They both also knew Jennifer, as usual, would drive Sunny to the dance.

"I can take a hint. Thanks for use of the potty … and I want all the juicy, nasty details about tonight when I pick you up tomorrow. We'll talk more about our mom and dad then. I need to, and I think you do, too.

"Right now, I got a staff meeting at the station."

"What?" Sunny said excitedly. "But you're not a senior reporter. You told me you're not allowed at staff meetings."

"That was then, this is now, squirt. Actually, I'm just supposed to sit in. Joe has some sort of idea for the cop-shop beat that apparently includes me. But my days at the real staff meetings will come in time." Willie Nell spun daintily, opened the door, and with a finger wave was gone, the door closing softly behind her. Willie Nell could not have foreseen that the coming meeting would end so disastrously, or that it would become the defining moment of her career.

39

Willie Nell's first real staff meeting began a little off-center to say the least. How could a newly promoted investigative reporter with a dynamic new TV news station in a major metro market like Dallas maintain poise and dignity with a black eye and taped ribs?

She was to sit in the cop-shop seat and do investigative reporting for KTKO, a new non-network 24-hour news station. Her debut was during sweeps. The black and swollen eye and scraped cheek were definitely drawbacks. Amid whispers and swift intakes of breath, she entered the conference room to be introduced to her associates as an equal member of the news staff after only a year as a junior reporter and a six-month stint as an intern. That in itself might be hard enough for them to swallow but her appearance would raise eyebrows, too.

Station manager/news director Joe Mosier took his seat at the head of the table; he motioned for Willie Nell to sit in the first chair on his right, a seat previously occupied by Prinz, who had been the lead reporter on the cop-shop beat, which consisted of a team of four writers. She looked around the room for another chair, or a maybe large hole to fall into. With no other option available, she sat in The Chair.

"'Morning folks, as you probably know, Derek is no longer with us. His actions resulted in his firing and Willie Nell's appearance. If anyone has a bone to pick now is the time. Before you speak, though keep in mind that this is a done deal. She's hired. He's fired. You're either part of the team with her at the helm or you're outta here. No discussions, no other suggestions."

The floor director, Eddie Sikes, tentatively raised a hand. "Comments allowed, Joe?"

"By all means," Joe chewed on his unlit cigar.

"I think we're going to have to be creative in shooting around her ...er ... flaw, physical flaws, I mean."

"If the big networks can shoot around pregnant stars, surely you can find a way to shoot Willie Nell without the viewers being offended."

"Actually," one of the others commented, "why bother? It might even give us an edge if we show what the SOB did to such a good-looking gal."

Willie Nell bristled a bit at the patently sexist remark, but quickly resumed her professional demeanor to remark, "I don't think we want the pity vote. Although it might garner us a few more viewers."

The promotions director spoke up. "I for one think we should start sweeps with the story about our former glamour guy going postal and assaulting his partner. The public has a right to know the story.

"If we don't tell our side of it, you can bet the other stations will."

Joe turned to Willie Nell. "He does thrive on adulation and popularity. It'd be just like him to use this as a story, the poor misunderstood reporter replaced by a female ..."

"You're still in the big chair and will take the heat, Sir but ..." Willie Nell rose, wincing as the cracked rib and dislocated shoulder protested the strain.

"This all happened four days ago. All the media ran with assorted versions of the story. I would prefer we ignore it altogether. The public knows about the assault and when they see me, they'll know the consequences. Leave it at that. . I'll tell my story to other media, if need be, but with dignity, not flash.

"I vote we take the high road, Joe."

Willie Nell's nervousness about acceptance by this room of experienced news pros evaporated in the warmth of the ovation that followed her statement. So ended her first staff meeting at KTKO. Time would tell if the station would ignore the story or feel forced to say something. She hoped to God there would be a breaking story of more importance by the evening crime news slot. She would soon wish she'd been more careful in what she hoped for. The real facts were not all that pleasant to recall.

40

It had happened two weeks ago, when Willie Nell had been an unofficial presence at another staff meeting. Not being senior staff, she normally would not have been asked to sit with the news station's war council.

Mosier had called the meeting to discuss a new format for the prime-time crime report. He wanted Derek to share camera time with his young reporter, Willie Nell, in a co-anchor format.

Prinz was unhappy. His knuckles whitened around the pencil in his right hand. He clenched and unclenched his jaw.

"Do you have a comment, Derek?" Mosier asked.

If the reporter was resolute in his situation, his face lied. "I suppose all that's to be said has been said," boss." The pencil succumbed with an audible snap. The rest of the news staff felt the tension in the room. The ancient mechanism in the large leather chair was the only sound as Joe shifted his weight.

"No, all I said was how would you like working on camera with Willie Nell?"

Prinz shrugged. Willie Nell sat dumbfounded.

"You both look good on camera. The two of you could create a dialogue on the dry stuff to make it more interesting.

"You've got a certain charisma, or whatever the hell the current word is, and Willie Nell, not to be non-PC, but you're a doll."

Willie Nell smiled with just a hint of reddening.

As the seething senior cop-shop reporter gathered up notes taken during the staff meeting, Willie Nell sat waiting for someone else to speak.

Taken aback at Prinz' attitude, Willie Nell mulled over the situation. Was he actually in fear of her taking over his job? Finally, she spoke, "I think I'd like to try, Joe. I believe that my rapport with the Police Chief and the forensics lab, I'd be an asset." She glanced over at her associate. He gave her no positive vibes. "While I realize I'm not a seasoned reporter like Derek, I can pull my own weight."

Prinz' usually sexy sneer only looked sinister to Willie Nell when he spoke, not at her but to the station manager. "I for one don't think she'll be able to pull it off but then ..." Raising his arms and shrugging, he sat back down for Joe to react. "I'll do whatever you decide, Joe."

"That's not good enough, Derek," Joe said, slowly. "If she's not ready to be on camera, then you didn't do your job. You were assigned to train her when she interned. Now, get outta here, both of you, and think about it. I want to see both of you first thing in the morning."

"I'm not taking anything away from you, Derek!" Willie Nell placated the obviously angry man. Nodding to her boss, she continued. "I'll let y'all talk it over. After all, Derek is the head of the crime news team." She gathered up her own belongings pushed back the wheeled leather chair and left the conference room.

Within seconds, Prinz was rushing after her down the long hall to the staff's exit.

"Don't you turn your back on me, you upstaging bitch!" I don't intend to share airtime with a rookie like you. You think your pretty face and sexy body allow you to climb over me?!"

Willie Nell froze in her steps. Prinz grabbed her shoulder and turned her around.

"I can't believe you really can believe that about me after ... after ..." Willie Nell was sputtering in shock at this surprise attack.

"There's damned little I can do about your cozying up to Joe, brown-nosing, fucking him for all I know, but I have seniority and I intend to see that you don't become grafted to my side."

Willie was dumbfounded.

"Who else have you been sleeping with? Eddie, maybe?"

"What's gotten into you?" She turned to leave the group of news offices once so sacred to her, now somehow an alien and treacherous wasteland with no familiarity.

"My contacts all dried up," he yelled after her "You stole them from me." He was ranting now and out of control.

"You're the reason you don't have any contacts now! You're vanity and ego take up a whole room by themselves." Willie Nell regretted the retort as soon as she said it. It would only fuel the argument. Better to beat a silent retreat. Willie Nell shook her head and turned to leave the irrational man.

"I didn't say we were through talking," Prinz shouted, suddenly aware of staff members staring at them. He lowered his voice, "I'll let you know when I'm done."

But Willie Nell was out of earshot by now and headed toward her Honda Pilot SUV.

His stride gobbled up the distance between them as they crossed the parking lot. She had no idea how close he was until she beeped opened her SUV and climbed inside.

Prinz grabbed her arm and yanked her out of the high seat of the Honda Pilot dislocating her shoulder. The surprised woman landed hard onto the blacktopped parking lot, abrading the side of her face.

"You— " Her words hung in the air, followed by a scream of pain. as Prinz kicked her in the ribs.

Willie Nell tried to sit up and the pain made her almost pass out.

Bastard busted some ribs.

The thought moved woodenly through her mind just before a huge fist landed on the already-scraped side of her face.

Willie Nell fought to remain conscious.

I can't see out of my left eye. Where are the security guards? Is he going to beat me to death?

A man hovered over, barely discernible through the damage and the tears.

"Please. Don't ... " she pleaded. He took her arm. Willie Nell screamed in pain.

Pete didn't know the shoulder was dislocated. He immediately released her right arm and put a hand behind her left shoulder. "Lie down, paramedics are on the way. And we don't know what kind of internal injuries you may have.

Willie Nell reacted to Pete's familiar smell of grease and motor oil by relaxing and letting him ease her down to the tarmac.

"Derek ..."

"Shhh, He's gone. I got him off you, and he ran away." Pete didn't tell her he'd busted Prinz' nose and knocked out at least one tooth.

She knew this gentle mechanic; he had recently been tuning up the "Elephant," the affectionate epithet for the news department's van.

Staring down at the blood in her gravel-scraped palm, she tried to take a deep breath. "Goddam that hurts! The bastard broke my ribs and I can't breathe—what if he punctured a lung?"

Pete handed Willie Nell her cell phone he'd recovered off the seat of her truck. "I called 911 for you, now lie still."

"I don't want publicity on this, Pete. It'll show up in reports and be on every news show and in every paper," she protested.

"Too late, they're on the way. Besides, you may have broken ribs; you can hardly breathe. I'm not about to risk to any more damage by picking you up," Pete had assumed control of the situation.

It felt good to Willie Nell for someone else to take charge so she could just lie back and wait. "You're right. But I hate to think of being in the news instead of writing or reading it." She sighed. "I thought Derek was a pro."

"Me, too." Pete brushed chestnut hair back from her face. "It's a shame."

Willie Nell glanced around, but couldn't find Prinz in the growing crowd of onlookers, many of whom were coworkers who had witnessed Prinz' assault.

Where did the cowardly S.O.B. go? I feel like I've gone three rounds with the Championship Bully of the Year.

The ambulance arrived at the same time as the security guard. Pete went into attack mode, "Security my ass! Where the hell have you been while this lady was being assaulted by the pretty boy reporter?"

"It's okay, Pete," Willie Nell said. "You were here. That's important to me."

As the paramedics prepared her for the trip to the hospital, Pete scoured the parking lot for her assailant. Not a sign of him. The muscular mechanic cracked his knuckles and clenched and unclenched his fists. *You better be hid good! If I find you, you'll wish you'd have crawled into a hole and pulled it in after you.*

Mosier came rushing outside, took one look at Willie Nell on the gurney, and turned on his heel towards his vehicle to follow the Mobile ICU to the hospital

Pete intercepted him. "Mr. Mosier, It was Derek Prinz who beat her up."

"I'd guessed that much, Pete, but thanks for helping Willie Nell. Don't know what could have happened if you hadn't."

"He's lucky." Pete rammed his fists into the pockets of his greasy jeans. "I heard the fracas and went to look, I yanked him away from her and punched him, and he took off. I didn't go after him 'cause Willie Nell needed my help more'n he need a beating."

"The police will find him, Pete. They have a soft spot for that young lady. I'd bet money Derek's in jail before the day's over. You can get back to work now. Everything's under control."

"D'ruther go with you. See she's okay, if you don't mind."

When the two men arrived at the hospital, Willie Nell was already in the ER. In addition to the shoulder and facial injuries, two ribs were cracked, what doctors called a green-limb-split. Before they got her sedated, the paramedics, nurses, and doctors learned a lot of new phrases to add to their profanity dictionary.

41

Much of the soreness had dissipated — unless Willie Nell tried to move — but the horror of the assault haunted her, awake or asleep. The nightmares made sleeping almost impossible. If not for the drugs Dr. Ecklund prescribed, she felt like she might never sleep again. It wasn't that Prinz would be the last person she'd expect to attack someone; she knew his ego, but to attack a woman and co-worker? Beneath that suave exterior a volcano of anger and inferiority lay well hidden, until that late afternoon in the parking lot.

"Got a good-looking guy coming to see you," Anita said. Her best friend, Anita Polanski, was a crime-scene analyst for the police department, and a forensics pathologist for the medical examiner. Her fashion-model good looks belied both her age and grim profession. Willie Nell had gotten to know the willowy blonde, logically enough, at a crime scene, after a uniformed cop had tried to bar the reporter entry to an apartment where a grisly murder had left the shotgunned bodies of four drug dealers.

"Let her in, you sexist dog. If she hasn't seen worse yet, she will, if she stays on the cop-shop desk very long." The two were immediately best buds.

Anita and Pete were her first visitors, both present when she woke up from the sedatives they gave her for the minor surgery that cleaned and repaired some deep gashes on one palm. Doctors were discussing getting a plastic surgeon for her face to keep the two wounds there from scarring.

"I don't mind the scars, but they can really cut short the life of an on-camera reporter," she'd told Anita.

Her friend really did not have to announce the cop who was waiting to see her. Willie Nell had seen him, and was glad that it was Patrolman Bobby Justin interviewing her. He was a good guy, the chief's nephew, and a guy capable of rising through the ranks without his uncle's help. She'd come to know and respect the young man through her job as a crime reporter. He and his uncle were people she treasured. Few reporters would dare claim friendship from the ranks of the police department, where newshounds were often persona non grata.

But Bobby was here to interview her, to interrogate her, basically. Her uneasiness at the process lessened the moment he stuck his blond crew-cut head in the door.

"Ready for the third-degree, Willie?" most cops omitted her middle name when addressing Willie Nell.

"Not sure I can do this, Bobby. I'm usually the person who asks the questions, not the one on the answering end."

Bobby laughed easily. "Only reason I wanted to be a cop was to have a license to interrogate all the beautiful young women."

The light banter was a common tool for both of them, used to keep a subject calm while easing into the interview.

"Okay if I ask you a personal question, Willie Nell?" Bobby cleared his throat before asking, "Were you and Derek close — personally?"

Without thinking, she shook her head, only to have it rebel in a spasm of pain that shot down her entire body. "No, we didn't even date. We worked together. I thought he respected me. I certainly had no reason to think that he'd ..." a near-sob caught in her throat.

The cop handed her a glass of water with a straw sticking out at an odd angle. "That's some shiner you got there, kiddo! And stitches. You'd take a great mug shot about now." Bobby's look was more tender than joking. He held the glass for her to take a few sips then placed it back on the table.

"I've got a shiner?!" Willie Nell giggled.

"What do you think of that? Why didn't someone tell me? I would have made myself presentable for you." In mock coquettishness, she hid her face behind bandaged hands.

"What happened to your hands?" Bobby asked. "Did he hurt them too?"

"Asphalt scrapes and such, I suppose. Stitches in my right palm, probably landed on a piece of glass or something," she said. "Now, what do I have to say to get that scumbag a little time in the Crossbars Inn?"

"He's in jail right now, Willie Nell," the young officer said. "But to keep him there, I have to know if you did anything to provoke the attack."

"Yeah, I got invited by Joe to share his spotlight," She answered bitterly, "I had turned from our brief verbal confrontation, walked to my car, and was putting the key in the ignition when he attacked me."

"That's the period I want to hear about. We have witnesses once the attack started, who have given me the blow-by-blow report." Bobby turned a little more serious.

"What about before? Was there already some bad blood between you? Professional jealousy? Anything?"

Willie Nell sighed. "Not that I was aware of. If he harbored ill will toward me, he hid it well."

Bobby looked at his notepad. "When he grabbed you, did you take a poke at him or say something?"

"I fucking wish I had!" anger flared in the undamaged eye. "But I was on the ground and had been punched or kicked several times before I even knew what was happening. All I could do was roll into a ball to try to protect myself."

"Willie, you know we almost consider you one of our own, and I can tell you I don't think our DA's going to take what he did lightly. That man's got a near pathological hatred of child abusers and woman beaters. Derek'll be doing good to see the light of day for a year if the DA gets his way."

As though reporting a story that happened to someone else, Willie Nell gave all the details she remembered to the patrolman.

Bobby laid his notebook aside. "I won't be writing this answer down, but just be up-front with me. Is it possible that Derek's motives could have been colored by the fact that you *didn't* have a relationship? In other words, could he have been angry because you turned him down?"

Willie Nell thought for a moment. "Bobby, I know when a guy's interested, even if he isn't hitting on me overtly. Derek never indicated anything but a professional interest.

"And, since you're not writing this down," she hinted, "I will admit there was a time I would have been interested. I was an intern taken under the wing of a big-city crime reporter. It made him seem sexy.

"But the more I was with him, the less I saw him as a crusader for the truth, and the more I saw him as an opportunist who didn't much care who he stepped on in his climb to the top; he wanted Joe Mosier's job, and Joe is nearing retirement age."

Bobby picked up the notebook, pocketed it without adding any further notes, and turned toward the door.

"Don't I need to press charges?" Willie Nell asked. "Or something?"

Bobby turned in the doorway. "You know better than that, after all that time you spent at the cop shop. The PD will file even if you don't. Lord knows enough people saw what happened that it'll be a slam dunk to get him indicted, with or without your statement."

"Guess we better be glad Pete showed up when he did.

"Bye, kiddo."

Later Willie Nell mulled over the facts she had shared with Andy. It didn't feel like it happened to her; she was disassociating.

It must have happened to someone else.

42

Today

A spic-and-span Pete strolled down the hallway of the Dallas Presbyterian hospital on his way to Willie Nell's room. The chattering and tittering of female voices tickled his imagination. He could picture the pretty young reporter lying in bed all bandaged up due to the sonuvabitch Prinz beating up on her. The other voice had to be her friend from the crime lab.

Anita! now, he could get a good look at that gal. She'd been the first one to show up as soon as Willie Nell was admitted and assigned a room. A tall, willowy blonde, maybe in her 30's, although you'd never know it to look at her. But her education and 10-year tenure with the police department made him do the math.

All sorts of quick snapshots of her rolled around in his head. Mostly, of how'd she'd look naked with him balanced on his palms as though he were doing push ups. But he'd be naked, too, and the exercises they'd be doing would be of a private nature.

I haven't been this excited over a woman in a while. She's got a great body and all that gorgeous hair. I want to grab myself wads of that blonde mane and just smell it.

Taking a deep breath, he entered the room after a perfunctory knock. "Is everybody decent?" he asked.

"Well, we got clothes on," Anita flipped back at him.

161

The two women began to giggle again.

"Want to let me in on the joke?" he asked.

"Girl-talk shit, that's all," Willie Nell said through her injured mouth. "I don't think you'd be interested in it."

Pete thrust forward a small bouquet of flowers that he'd picked up at the local grocery store, the green cellophane crinkling as he did so. At his side he held a bright red box of chocolates.

Willie Nell, didn't reach for them because of her bandaged hands. Instead, she nodded toward the rolling table that served as dinner tray, desk, and make-up stand. But he continued to hold them.

"Pete, you're spoiling the hell outta me. First you save, my life then you bring me flowers and these fuckin' chocolates I can't eat."

"Sorry about the candy, I plumb forgot about you having a hard time chewing 'em." Although he was talking to the injured woman, his eyes darted back and forth between her and her visitor.

"I'll enjoy them, though," Anita quipped. "Andy won't see these at all, Willie."

"Is Andy a special guy friend of yours?" he asked Anita.

"Not really, we work together — sort of," she said, stepping forward to relieve this shy, good looking guy of the flowers. "Why do you ask?"

"Well, I wouldn't like anyone messing around with my girl," he said.

"Your girl!?" Anita shot back, "I'm nobody's girl."

"That didn't come out right. What I meant was if you're HIS girl, I didn't want to make a pass or ask you out or anything." He purposely played the embarrassed suitor so he could better size up the woman.

There she goes again, staring at my crotch. Wonder if I should ask her now or wait?

While he was mulling over the situation, he found himself taking inventory of Anita's assets as she walked to the private toilet to get water and a vase for the flowers.

She's just my type even if she's a bit feisty. I may just ask her now.

162

Anita walked back out of the rest room with Pete's flowers now well arranged in a simple vase . "Pete," she said. "If you're not busy after our visit with Willie Nell, want to take me for a beer and a game of darts?"

The invitation caught the mechanic by surprise. "Does a bear sh ... uh, live in the woods?

"I mean, I couldn't think of a better idea."

Anita leaned down and gave Willie Nell a gentle kiss and a private wink. Pete, candy still in hand, looked around for somewhere to set it down.

"I think Anita has designs on those chocolates already," Willie Nell said with a laugh. "You two have fun."

Pete let Anita walk ahead of him out the door, mainly to check out the action of her hips. She moved like liquid sex to the elevator.

She's gotta be great in bed; she's just oozing sensuality.

He turned to her when the elevator doors closed. She kissed him just before the door opened, tongue teasingly playing with his own.

Grabbing his hand just as though nothing had happened, they walked to her car, a shiny dark blue '63 Corvette. She tossed him the keys. "Drive for me."

"Why'd you do that?" he asked.

"Don't you like to be the driver when you're with a lady? I thought you'd love driving this great old 'Vette."

"I do, I would, I mean," Pete stammered. "I don't mean that. I mean why'd you just kiss me in the elevator?" He stood there looking down at the woman while the sunset played in her long blonde locks, turning them first reddish then pink then gold. She opened her own door and slid inside.

She shrugged sending the waves of hair into motion. "I wanted to get it out of the way so I wouldn't be thinking about it all evening long."

She strapped herself into the seat belt. "That wastes a lot of time."

He got into the drivers' seat.

"Right." Pete walked around the car and slid in behind the wheel, and started the engine.

"Buckle up, please," Anita ordered.

This chick is a major turn on. Hope the lovemaking's as good as the kissing. He closed the door and started the engine.

Pete did as he was told. "Bitchin' car! Your ex-husband's or your daddy's?"

Anita bristled and Pete could feel the sparks of energy between them. "Did I say something wrong?"

"Wow, excuse me," Pete said, contritely.

"Not likely. I think you can get out of my car now."

The ice doesn't melt quickly with this one.

Pete extracted himself from the low-slung roadster and again apologized.

"Anita, there's no excuse for my statement, except that my mind was far ahead of where we are right now."

"Yeah, about six inches ahead of your zipper, you mean." With that, Anita slipped behind the wheel.

Whew, fiery. I like that, but I'll have to watch my P's and Q's with this one.

"Can I at least call you sometime?"

"Sure. I'll get over your insensitive chauvinistic jerkiness — someday." Then the irate blonde drove off leaving two long streaks of black rubber in the parking lot.

43

After her discharge four days later, Pete drove Willie Nell home. Tenderly, he helped her from the pick-up. She walked slowly up to her apartment door and with shaking hands tried to insert a key into the lock. At her second attempt, Pete took the key ring from her and opened the door.

He stood just inside the door near her small table containing her phone and a message board.

"I'll come back later and drive you to the station. I got to get the Elephant ready for when you get back to work."

"That's not necessary, you know. The station can send a driver. Joe already offered."

"I didn't suggest it, Willie Nell. I said I was gonna do it. Now, call when you're ready." He scrawled his number on her message board.

"Pete, I don't know how to thank you for all you've done. The flowers, the visits, and now the driving me back and forth." She looked at the man who had gone from just Pete the mechanic to a good friend in a matter of hours.

"Okay," she decided. "Let a girl get presentable then I'll call so you can transport me again." She tiptoed to give him a quick peck on the cheek.

Driving back to his apartment, Pete decided to wash up a bit better than usual, and not for Willie Nell, although she definitely was a class act despite her "colorful" language.

Pete had been attracted to Anita, who spent a lot of time with Willie Nell at the hospital. Anita also seemed attracted to him, despite their fireworks this afternoon. He'd call and apologize, try to get things back on track. The kiss in the elevator had been full of passion and promise, even thought he'd stuck his foot in his mouth later on.

Pete answered on the first ring. "I guess you're ready now?" he said to Willie Nell.

"My offer still stands, Pete. I can call the station and have them send someone."

"And do me out of the honor of escorting the heroine back into her arena? Not on a bet. I'll be buzzing your door in what … 15 minutes. Is that OK?"

"And I'll be escorted by the hunkiest guy in Dallas. Just get those gorgeous pecs and abs and glutes over here young man."

"Older'n you by a long shot, but I'm on my way."

Pete had been right about the heroine's return. Joe, alerted by Pete, had the whole office turned out on the front steps of the station to greet a red-faced Willie Nell. Inside, there were chips and dips, cookies, and other finger food along with an assortment of cold drinks, coffee and iced tea.

Her computer terminal screen was invisible — covered by cards and letters of well wishers taped to it in layers until the well-wishes were simply taped on top of more cards and letters.

"The public considers you a star, young lady," Mosier said, walking up behind her and putting a hand on each shoulder. At his touch, the tears that had threatened when she saw her work station, escaped and rolled down her cheeks.

"Your bottom drawer is full of more letters, mostly unopened. I had to stop; got a newsroom to run, you know."

Willie Nell turned and put her arms around her boss. "And it's time I started pulling my weight. I'm ready for my marching orders, boss."

"You know those cases you had requested from cops all around the state? A bunch of 'em have come in; I have them in my office," Mosier told her. "I guess you can start there. The police still haven't done anything with those three local women who were killed, but two of your cases from outside are close enough to consider them as part of the general Dallas-Fort Worth Metroplex. There was one in Wylie and another in Rowlett."

"Right in our backyard! We gotta nail him before he moves on."

44

"Damn, Willie Nell! I can walk into a ring of armed cops at a bloody crime scene without so much as a tingle. Why am I so nervous about tonight?" Anita, a 10-year veteran City of Dallas Crime Scene Analyst, fidgeted with the upscale lingerie she'd just taken out of the Victoria's Secret box.

"Hell, I'm not even sure how this stuff goes on."

Laughing, her best friend snatched the crimson panties from her, taking the two stringy edges and pulling them across her abdomen. "The lace is on both sides of the crotch so it opens for his ... whatever."

Anita felt herself redden at the thought of the crotchless panties. And the bra was just as revealing, with cutouts in front so her nipples would be exposed.

"Try them on," Willie Nell prompted. "And watch your language. You hang around cops too much."

"And reporters." Anita swiftly stripped naked in the middle of her living room. "Here goes nothin', then," she said, recovering the size 5 panties from her friend and tossing them back into the box. Scooping up the pink, black, and white box, she scampered to the bathroom, black ribbon still taped to the bottom of the box trailing behind, along with Willie Nell.

Anita critically studied her nude reflection in the large mirror behind the sink. Would Pete like it? She was slim. Too slim? The rosy tips her smallish breasts — Too small? — pointed up perkily. The tuft at the juncture of her thighs confirmed her natural hair color.

"How old do you think Pete is, Willie?" Anita asked, slipping into the cop-shop argot of leaving out Willie Nell's middle name. She stepped gingerly into the flimsy panties, working them up long legs and over flaring hips, pulling the thong tight between her ass cheeks.

"I'd figure he's 40-ish, maybe older. That hard body of his makes it hard to really guess.

"That man's gonna go crazeeeeeeeee," Willie Nell said with a mock wolf-whistle as Anita pirouetted in front of her. She folded back the tissue paper and extracted the royal blue bra, which matched the panties, as well as Anita's eyes. "Pinch your nipples girl so they'll pop outta these holes."

Blushing, Anita took the push-up bra and shrugged into it. "Do me up, would you Willie Nell?"

Her friend fastened the single clasp behind Anita's back.

The image in the mirror shook Anita to the core. She had expected to look a little trampy, like some street prostitute or a vision out of a teenage boy's fantasy. What she saw was an incredibly beautiful woman — fashion-model beautiful in her mid-30s. The sheen contrasted to her creamy skin, and the color made her blue eyes seem a deeper blue and larger somehow. The scanty panties made her legs look impossible long and shapely.

"So, what seductive plans do you have tonight for the lucky Mister Pete?" Willie Nell interjected, breaking Anita's reverie.

"Whatever he wants."

"That hunk? Sweetie, he'll want it all!"

"I hope he doesn't want me to do oral sex on him! Ughhhhhh!"

"You don't like taking a man in your mouth?" Willie Nell arched an eyebrow.

"It sounds so gross, sucking a penis."

"Honey, little boys have penises. Men have cocks. And I, for one, love it. It's one of only two times in the event I feel really in control."

"The other time is ...?"

"His climax, of course. Right at that moment, he's totally out of control, trying to hold back and not able to stop the inevitable." Willie Nell said, smirking. "But let's get back to the ol' blow-job issue."

"Now whose language needs to be cleaned up!?"

"Every man loves the thought of a woman sucking his cock," Willie Nell continued, ignoring her friend's jab. "It's a power thing. One fellow might think of it as putting him on a pedestal; another might think that it abases the female and exalts the male, but damn few would turn a good BJ down, especially if she were to let him cum in her mouth."

"I don't think I can let him put his penis … um … cock in my mouth and suck on it, let alone let him cum. What if I gag?"

"This is the first time; don't feel you have to let him shoot his wad down your throat. And you don't have to swallow it. If it happens, just let it flow down your chin. Guys like that.

"Another thing, you don't have to take it in your mouth right off. Work up to it. Lick the tip. Lightly. Then run your tongue up the shaft. Lick the head some more and jerk him with your hand while you're doing it. He won't complain."

"I … I've never … "

Willie Nell cut Anita off in mid-stammer. "It's a rush to feel a man go from soft to rock-hard in your mouth, Dearie."

"I'm not saying I'll do it, Willie Nell, but you make me think I oughta consider it. Try new things, y'know."

"You just think a little later. Right now, we gotta get you out of this rig before you start thinkin' too hard and ooze all over it."

So saying, Willie Nell expertly popped open the bra clasp she'd just hooked, bringing a laugh from Anita. "let's hang these over the shower rod a couple hours to air. And you might spray them with some of your perfume. Guys like that."

Anita peeled the panties down her body and tossed them to her friend. When Willie Nell had lovingly smoothed out each wrinkle as she draped them over the rod, Anita misted each with her White Diamonds cologne. Then she wrapped herself in her silk bathrobe and walked Willie Nell back to the living room.

"I better go now, dear. I'm expecting Sunny to come by my place shortly. And you gotta start getting ready for your big night. But think over what I told you. Believe me, I know all about men and what they like," Willie Nell said, embracing Anita sisterly.

Anita opened held the door for her friend. As Willie Nell ambled down the three steps to the sidewalk, she said under her breath, "I most certainly will think about it — a lot."

She plopped on the sofa, the silk robe falling open from the waist down. Anita was alone for the rest of the afternoon. She began planning the seduction of her boyfriend. Although they had flirted with that invisible line, they still weren't yet actually lovers. They had fooled around, a lot of heavy petting and fondling; she had once massaged him through his jeans until he ejaculated, making such a mess of the front of his Levis that their night out consisted of drive-thru rather than their favorite Italian restaurant, Bertones.

She had never been the aggressor, the initiator. Tonight that would change, she promised herself. Just thinking about it was exciting her. Anita traced the open robe from the belt down her abdomen, around her bellybutton, through the soft kinky pubic hair to her pantyless womanhood.

"How the Hell am I supposed to wait three more hours as horny as I am tonight?" she said out loud to the empty room.

45

The one-column header over the short cop-shop story, clipped years ago from her tiny hometown paper, paralyzed Willie Nell Autrey as she sat in a corner at Starbucks with her first cup of the morning.

SONORA, TX — The nude body of promising local singer Lacey Jay was discovered Sunday morning by a deputy sheriff responding to a 9-1-1 call.

Police reports indicate the woman's neck was broken, but the official cause of death is pending a complete autopsy. The body was unclothed, but officials say there were no signs of sexual assault.

Homicide investigators were investigating the Rusty Spur nightclub where Ms. Jay last performed. There have been a number of recent drug-related arrests in the area and police suspect the murder may be tied to local drug traffic.

A small quantity of marijuana was reportedly found inside the mur-

dered woman's mobile home at
Happy Trails, a trailer park just outside of Sonora on State Loop 467.

The clipping was one of several scraps of information in the large manila envelope; there were playbills from bars and clubs where Willie Nell's mother had been singing the last few months of her life; a pawn ticket for some cheap jewelry and her prized 35 mm Nikon; a worn business card from an auto-parts chain store; and files on Lacey Jay's many domestic disputes with the late Dude Autrey, the only person in the world that Willie Nell knew who would be capable of murdering her mother. The fact that Dude was already three years dead when Mama was killed kinda let him off the hook, Willie Nell figured.

The envelope was one of eight Texas police cold cases collected to see if they could be connected to suspicious deaths in the Dallas area. Inclusion of her mother's case momentarily unsettled the young crime reporter. Her mother's death, following the tragic loss of her father, had orphaned her and Sunny. Worse, yet, it had estranged the sisters, sending each to a different children's home.

It had been the frustration with police efforts to find her mother's killer that had eventually caused Willie Nell to gravitate toward the cop-shop beat at the television station where she started as an intern. She would deny such a simplistic cause for her choices because she wasn't really aware of the influence her mother's death had on her entire way of life.

As much as Sunny disdained their mother, Willie Nell loved and missed her. Looking at photos in the envelope of Lacey performing, on stage, the young woman was transported to a dreamland where an angel in purple sequins sang with a voice like melted butter and honey on a biscuit. Mama's music had touched her heart in ways no one else had since.

True, at the age of 10, Mama had placed her in the children's home. As an adult, Willie Nell understood the pain such a sacrifice must have been for the young, widowed mother with no way to feed, clothe, and keep a roof over her family's head. It had been a hard life even when Dude Autrey was alive. When he was killed and her baby sister horribly injured in the wreck, the load on Lacey grew exponentially. Dude's estate consisted of nothing so much as over-limit credit cards, a barely serviceable Chevy Suburban rigged to haul his horse trailer, and a good roping pony. Truck and trailer were already a decade past their prime and now the truck was totaled. At least the trailers were paid for, both the one for horse and the one for the family. Selling the horse and trailer barely raised enough to get Dude into the ground. After the funeral, Lacey was truly on her own.

Where Sunny saw her mother as a bar-hopping party girl who dumped her kids because they slowed her down, Willie Nell understood that waiting tables, bartending, and a few singing gigs were about all Mama had going for her after Dude's untimely death.

Her old anger at the Sonora police department returned. The local Sheriff pretty much shrugged off the murder as being of the "doper–offs–doper–and–who–cares" variety. Interview transcripts indicated her mother had left the bar where she sang that night with a good-looking man, but he was never interviewed. "Probably left town," a paper quoted the sheriff.

In other words, who gives a flying fuck. You assholes probably couldn't find your cock without instructions.

Dragging out a laminated map of the state, Willie Nell located each of the murder locations with sticky tabs. Starting with the three most recent, all in Dallas County, she worked backward by date. It was the similarity and peculiarity of these three murders that prompted her to consider there may have been others by the same perpetrator, a serial killer. The chief also included two more cases from outside the county but still within the Dallas-Fort Worth Metroplex. One was in Rowlett, which occurred in February of last year, and a second in Wylie, a body found the past summer that likely had been killed last October. Both suburbs were just east of Dallas.

Willie Nell looked up to see Joe Mosier walk in. He didn't see her and walked straight to the counter and ordered a Grande quad Americano. Willie Nell was standing at his elbow when he turned around.

"I need another set of eyes to look at this, Joe. I'm at a loss."

"Hey, you mind if I get my heart jump-started first," referring to his daily four shots of espresso with hot water. "Meet me back at the office, we'll talk."

Willie Nell was waiting by the station manager's locked office when he returned with his travel mug of caffeine. Mosier slipped his keycard into a slot and unlocked his office. "I have a busy day ahead, but come on in. I can give you five minutes."

In addition to a large, well-used, and weathered oak desk backed by a wall of bookshelves, and facing an equally worn leather sofa, the editor's office has the ubiquitous "interview" table with four chairs.

Willie Nell rolled out the map on the round table. On it, colored round tabs with dates mark the sites of each of the cold case murders and the three fresh ones in Dallas. "These red dots were supposed to give me a trail of murders, if these were all committed by the same person." Willie Nell's agitation was palpable. With an erasable felt-tip, she connected the trail according to the dates of each, laying out a route of terror spanning nearly two decades.

"See? Instead of a trail, I have two lateral lines crossing the fuc ... frigging state. The southernmost starts just east of El Paso and runs through small towns and cities to just East of Houston. Then, two years later, the second line starts in North Central Texas at Marshall and makes almost a straight line to Dallas."

Willie Nell drew in a deep breath and exhaled slowly. "Joe I really do believe we have a bad-ass serial killer and that he continued east into Louisiana and maybe further before the bastard started back our way."

"That's quite a leap for a rookie reporter," the editor said, rubbing his chin, already showing gray stubble by early afternoon. "But I suspect you could be right. We'll need to get some help to expand our probe into Louisiana, though. You know that as soon as the police see your work, they'll call in the Feds, don't you?"

"I just hope the sunovabitch didn't start on the other side of the Rio Grande."

Mosier straightened up. With both hands to his back, he arched. "Let me get the legal department to clear the way for us to get some cooperation with Louisiana and New Mexico cops. Do you have any friends at the FBI offices over in the Earl Cabell Federal Building?

Willie Nell quickly furled the map into a tube again. She turned toward her boss, "I really need to take this map to Chief Justin. He needs to know that these local murders are almost certainly connected and that he's looking for a very dangerous guy."

Mosier acceded to his reporter with a nod, showing none of the trepidation he felt for the inexperienced woman diving into a story most likely way over her head. When he heard the elevator ding in the hallway, he knew she was out of earshot, and he reached for the phone.

Police Chief Andrew Justin glanced at his caller ID before answering the phone. "This is Andy, how's tricks in the sound-byte world, Joe."

"I need a favor, Andy." Quickly, Mosier explained that an inexperienced, but sharp young reporter was heading his way with information about a serial murderer.

"I need you to assign someone to keep an eye on her, keep her out of harm's way. And I'd like to be kept in the loop on every step of the investigation, if the Feds will let you, because this will bring them in."

Justin and Mosier's relationship spanned 30 years from the days the chief was walking a beat in the mean streets of South Dallas and Mosier was the back-up guy for the cop-shop beat writer.

Mosier had stumped for promoting Captain Justin to chief of police when the Dallas City Council had wanted to spend $400,000 to form a search committee after the city manager had fired the former chief. The editor of a metropolitan daily newspaper sits at a pretty powerful bully pulpit. The council couldn't take the public pressure the paper exerted, so it accepted the Mayor's nomination of Captain Justin for the post.

Mosier was, of course, repaying his friend for the night Justin stopped a bullet saving the young reporter's life. But more than that, Mosier knew that Justin would be the best man for the job of cleaning up a corrupt police bureaucracy. No outsider could bring the knowledge of the intricacies of the Dallas department that Andy Justin brought to the job. The decision to back his friend gave Mosier a front-row ticket to the arrests of police administrators and other public officials as the new chief cleaned out his new fiefdom. The scoops resulted in a Pulitzer for the reporter and an upward spiral of success that put him in this big office.

Each owed the other favors that could never be repaid, and neither was reluctant to ask or grant favors when needed. Each knew neither would never do anything that would reflect poorly on the other.

"Get me Grady," the police chief told his administrative assistant. Grady Elliott was the best homicide detective he had, and a decent profiler. If Joe was right about this being a serial killer, Elliott was the right man for the job.

Willie Nell entered the elevator and pressed the button for the top floor where the administrative offices were located. Just as the door was closing, an ominous figure squeezed through. The man had to be as close to 7 feet tall as he was to 6. Willie Nell guessed his weight at the far side of 250. He looked directly at her and their eyes met. His hard, steely; hers like a doe caught in the headlights. Raised in a violent, alcoholic household, Willie Nell didn't intimidate easily, but she felt a shiver.

This is what a killer looks like.

She was relieved when the elevator door opened. She quickly scooted out of the car and turned toward the chief's office. She entered the outer office, "I'm Willie Nell Autrey from station KTKO. I really need to see Chief Justin."

"Go on in, sweetie, he's expecting you."

46

Pleasantly surprised, Willie Nell reached for the knob when a large hand extended in front of her and opened the door. "After you," the giant from the elevator said.

What's this mountainous asshole doing here?

"Grady, good to see you," the chief beamed, rising from his desk. "And you must be Miss Autrey. I've heard a lot of good things about you from the troops.

"This is our profiler, Grady Elliott. Grady, meet Willie Nell Autrey. She has something to show us."

Elliott's hulking figure was still intimidating, but Willie Nell sat beside him at the round table in the interrogation room, which the chief wisely chose for the meeting since it provided the most soundproof location of any room in the building.

At first, Willie Nell thought Elliott was overweight, maybe even obese. But when he slipped off the heavy trench coat, she was surprised at how muscular the dour detective was.

She didn't know that Elliott was a first-round draft choice of the old Houston Oilers as an all-American tight end out of Penn State. Elliott had blown out a knee in training camp, so he used his criminal justice degree to launch a career in law enforcement. Since joining the police force, he had continued his education, gaining a Masters Degree in abnormal psychology. He also had completed the coursework for a PhD in forensic psychology and was nearly done with his dissertation, an accomplishment he didn't want in his personnel folder. Elliott enjoyed his work but didn't want to carry the title "doctor" in the squad room. He also understood that he would have to fight off being fast-tracked through the ranks and out of the investigative sections into management.

The big man maintained his physique for a logical reason: his size and strength often took the will to resist arrest right out of a suspect. Although he could easily mop up the floor with most of the bad guys he encountered, his intimidating appearance kept him from having to get physical very often. She also didn't know that Elliott's prime directive from the chief was not only to solve this case but to protect the young reporter if the investigation ever got close to the serial killer.

Elliott listened intently as she carefully laid out the route and the links among the 10 cold cases and the three recent ones in Dallas. "Hell!" the giant cop exploded. "If these are all related, this guy could be criss-crossing the country."

"We better plan on taking our probe west, too, Grady, maybe even south into Mexico," the chief said.

Elliott took the marker from Willie Nell's hand and drew a thick line arrow across southwestern New Mexico from El Paso and another south from the border city into Mexico. "The guy probably didn't start in Texas."

Willie Nell was relieved and surprised that the profiler had grasped the significance of the map so quickly. "You need to study the case files to see if you can find a pattern. I was only able to find one. All the victims are about the same age, blonde, and were not sexually assaulted or mutilated."

"All blondes might rule out Mexico. What about the timeline?"

"It seems to be all over the place. Some murders are years apart, others only months. I thought of how a psychopathic pattern sometimes compresses, the longer it goes, but that doesn't really fit, either."

"Unless we don't have all the events accounted for," Elliott noted.

The thought that there may be several more murders not yet accounted for sent a shiver down Willie Nell's spine.

"We need to track down missing-person cases along this route within the timeframe our perpetrator was active in each area.

"Next, we have to see if we have cases that aren't perfect matches that may have been ruled accidental or death by natural causes. And there may be bodies yet to be found, we need to check for missing persons with similarities to the known victims. West Texas has plenty of desert land where a body could be hidden with no fear of it ever being found. The woods in East Texas and the wetlands near the Gulf provide the same kind of opportunity for a killer to dispose of a body."

The picture the profiler was painting forced the young reporter to consider whether she might just be in over her head. Willie Nell seldom backed down from a challenge, but she would sure welcome someone with Prinz' expertise right about now.

"You're a profiler," she said to Elliott. "Do you have any ideas about the person who did this ... uh, these?"

"The problem is that some of these are probably somehow connected. But the only common denominator we have so far is that they were all slim and blonde. But what we don't have may be as important as the similarities."

"What do you mean?"

"Well, Willie, what a cop expects to see isn't here. There's no sexual abuse, no apparent torture, and no mutilation. In fact, these crimes look like impulse murders; that doesn't fit with most serial killers, who usually plan their crimes so cleverly.

"Whoever did these murders, if they are in fact related, loses impulse control at some point, and commits these killings from out of the blue. That behavior isn't even in the books about psychopaths and sociopaths."

47

December 31, 1990

It had been a good day for Dude Autrey. He was sober, his family life was beginning to get back on keel. He was making progress in Alcoholics Anonymous, even sponsoring a 19-year-old kid.

It was New Year's Eve and he was going to get his girls and go out for a bite of dinner before Lacey got home from her gig.

A gallon of Blue Bell Rocky Road ice cream, that's the way to celebrate a New Year sober for the first time since I was 14.

The citizen's band radio set slung under the dashboard crackled to life.

"This is Warbird, Hey Rodeo Dude, you got yer ears on?"

Dude keyed his microphone. "The Dude is in the house."

"What's yer 20, Rodeo Dude. You in town or on the road? Over." The VFW post commander was better than Dude at remembering CB protocol, but only sometimes.

"On my way to run some errands around town, Carl. What's up?" (Dude often ignored radio etiquette of protecting identities, using CBers given names instead of their handles on the air).

"Hey good buddy, I'm down the VFW hall. Nancy Poteet is here, stewed to the gills. I called Billy, but his car's in the crapper. Wonderin' if you could take his wife home?"

"Sure, Carl. I got nothin' but time 'til Lacey gets home." Dude turned off Cornell Street and headed out Bond Road. When Carl Hansen told him to do something, Dude had learned to do it without asking questions. Carl was Dude's AA sponsor and had been responsible for finally getting Dude to seek help for his alcohol addiction. Dude figured he could pick Nancy up, then get the girls, drop the woman at Billy's apartment, get some Happy Meals at Mickey D's, and then stop by the HEB for the ice cream.

Ice cream's always the last, don't want it to melt before you get it home to the fridge.

Nancy was a mess, but Dude hadn't been sober long enough that he couldn't remember his own drinking days. He helped her out of the VFW and unceremoniously boosted her up into the passenger seat of the Suburban.

She'd be really attractive if she wasn't always soaked in whiskey and beer. Mebbe I can get one of the women in our club to do a Twelfth Step with her.

Dude figured that Anne Cook, now 20 years sober in AA would be a good one to ask, He recalled her saying that she'd never refused an opportunity to do a Twelfth Step — the Alcoholics Anonymous program's final suggestion that, to maintain their sobriety, recovered alcoholics should reach out to other drunks to help them get and stay sober.

But not today. Take it one day at a time Old Dude. Y'cain't peddle AA to a tosspot still in his cups. Go get your girls, spend a nice evening with your family, and be thankful that, but for the Grace of God, that would be you passed out over there in the passenger seat.

Willie Nell was excited to see her dad drive up in the Suburban — essentially an oversized station wagon on a pick-up truck frame — and barreled out the door and down the steps, the door banging loudly against the metal side of the old trailer. She slowed to a walk when she saw the redhead in the passenger seat, then she smelled the Suburban; it was like a brewery in there.

The 10-year-old choked back a sob and turned to run, just as Dude was climbing down from the driver seat. "Let me go get her, Dude, the baby's all ready for you," Eyidie, who had followed the girl out of the trailer, hollered from its stoop.

Dude had replaced his resentment for Miz Edie with gratitude. He realized she had spent more time as babysitter with his children than he had as their father.

That's changing right now, he promised himself as the gathered up Sunrise and her baby things. While he was buckling the baby into its car seat in the back seat of the Suburban, Nancy started making unpleasant noises.

"Oh Lord, Nancy, don't you go 'n' puke in my Chevy now!"

Dude ran around to the side of the Suburban and rolled down the window in case his passenger got sick, and then he trotted after the old black sitter. "Miz Edie, I'm gonna get Nancy home before she gets sick, if I can. Then I'll be back for Willie Nell, if you can calm her down."

"She probably thought you'd started drinkin' again, Dude. That woman there smells like a Saturday night honky-tonk. But you just run on along; I can deal with Miss Willie Nell."

Dude jumped in the Suburban and headed for Billy's apartment a couple miles further out of town. He figured he could still manage getting her into the apartment, plop her on the sofa, drive back to Eyidie's and pick up his oldest daughter, and then run the rest of the errands before Lacey Jay got home.

Damn, this woman stinks of beer. Just hope she doesn't upchuck before I get her home.

As he turned out of the trailer park, he felt something roll against his foot. Glancing down, he saw the open beer can sloshing all over the floorboard.

No wonder it smells like the Coors plant in here. Oh well, I spilt many a beer in this old heap myself. I'll hose it out in the morning.

Anxious to get Nancy home so he could get on with his evening, Dude nevertheless kept his speed 10 miles per hour under the 65-speed limit, as the weather and the fact that he had his baby on board dictated.

48

New Years Eve, 1990

Dexter Worley was in a bigger hurry. He had finally landed a date with Daisy
Hollister, who preferred to be called Holly rather than her given name. The
new Corvette with the T-tops hadn't hurt. She loved hot cars, and his was
the hottest around.

The country road glowed like glass under the New Year's Eve moonlight.
Dex goosed the accelerator and threw the low-slung roadster brutally from
one curve into the next. Speedometer and tachometer needles danced crazily
and tires screamed protests against the laws of inertia and centrifugal force
as they battled for friction.

Dex was running late, so he pushed the sleek red roaster closer to the limits
of its heritage, willing the machine to live up the reputation of its racing-bred
family.

It felt good. An ex-fighter pilot and a top-division amateur formula race driver,
he knew what he was doing. With reflexes honed at the stick of a Mach 2 jet
fighter maneuvering against ground-to-air missiles over Vietnam, Dex rode
the razor's edge along the isolated West Texas highway.

The junior Dexter Worley didn't see much difference in the split-second reactions required in the cockpit and those needed at the wheel of the formal
Vees he'd driven since he was 14. His mechanic father, Dex Senior, had been
his crew chief, mechanic, crew, and pep squad as Dex blistered the formula
racing circuit. He returned to his hobby after his military tour, investing in a

used race car that he and his dad quickly restored to its competitive best. They had begun to win regularly enough that he invested in a better machine and now made so much money racing that it nearly equaled his take-home from the small garage where he worked with Worley the elder.

Now there was going to be Daisy in his life. OK, Holly. His thoughts focused on the pretty, freckled librarian, the car a mere extension of himself.

My God, I'm getting an erection!

That realization was immediately followed by icy-cold reality, which snapped him to attention. He was entering a curve! Too fast!

The pavement of the shallow hill fell away as the road broke sharply to the left. Dex was in trouble. Years of flying the faster planes in the sky left Dex with lightning-fast reactions and his years on the racing circuit gave him an uncanny feel for the road. Now, everything that was to happen in the next two and one-half seconds would be only a matter of instinct.

Dex feathered the brake, then downshifted and increased pressure on the throttle; he could feel the wide tires fighting for more traction as his brain registered and computed the angle and back of the curve. His fingers pulled ever so slightly on the wheel to take an inside track through the apex of the curve. Although the maneuver would put him momentarily in the oncoming traffic lane, there was no other way to ride out the curve at this speed.

"Accelerate hard exiting the curve, now," he muttered this thought aloud, remembering the phrase as it had been drilled into him time and again. He would exit the curve into the correct lane without flying through the guard-rail.

Dex saw the glow of headlights from behind the rise a heartbeat before cresting the curve. He was at full throttle when the other vehicle emerged from the black night.

He backed off the throttle only a little, knowing the action would cause the sports car to drift back to the outside of the curve — if he could only keep it off the guardrail.

It was working! The reduced traction caused the Corvette to slip slightly to the right as Dex steered into the controlled skid, downshifted again, and slammed the accelerator to the floor. Angrily, the engine roared its outrage at the rough treatment. But true to its nature, the sports car obeyed the skilled hand at the wheel, gained traction, and straightened at the end of the apex.

It's working — rather, it should have worked; it would have worked, except for that fucking Suburban!

Dex didn't have time to consider the possible actions of the other driver. Like twin suns, headlights filled his windshield!

The other driver was seeking escape in the outside lane, expecting it to be unoccupied. The two cars were again in the same lane on a collision course.

Dude Autrey had only two choices: have a head-on collision at high speed, which would kill everybody in both vehicles, or crash through the guardrail and try to keep the Suburban upright as it plunged down the slope.

Like Dex, Dude had cat-quick reflexes. But he didn't share the other driver's skill and experience. The big forerunner of the modern SUV crashed into the guardrail just as the red Corvette screamed past the left side of the Suburban. Its off-road suspension was too high for the guardrail to engage the body and the Suburban reared up on it like a stallion in a rodeo, and flipped over it, rolling several times before coming to rest at the bottom of the grade.

Dexter managed to bring the Corvette to a stop, slammed the transmission into reverse, and in moments was at the mangled guardrail where the Suburban had gone over. Grabbing his flashlight he went hurtling down the embankment, half running, half tumbling down the icy, wet slope. in the darkness. The stab of light from the flashlight was little help.

Shining it into the upside-down truck, he could see the driver and passenger weren't moving. Climbing halfway in, he checked for life signs. He could detect no carotid pulse at Dude's throat. Turning his attention to the woman, he could tell she was dead without any examination. Her skull was crushed. Her face obliterated.

Sorry gal, even you buckle bunnies chasin' after Dude deserve better'n this.

Dex shone his flashlight into the backseat and saw a gory, mangled leg protruding from the inverted child seat. No chance the child had survived.

He thought quickly. No one witnessed the accident, and there were no survivors. No one had to know he was involved. A fatal accident would make it difficult to get sponsors on the Vee-car circuit; even worse, he could be sued for wrongful death, maybe even arrested for reckless driving. But would the investigation prove his role? After all, the Suburban crashed after crossing his lane.

"I was taking this curve and this truck, this Suburban, that drunk Dude Autrey came barreling around from the opposite direction, but wide. I think he tried to pass me on the shoulder 'cuz he would roll it if he tried to cut back on the curve." He practiced his story on the slow climb back up to the roadway.

49

Dex reached the Corvette and called the police on his car phone hard-wired into the console, the first one sold in Sutton County. He sat in the car and replayed his role in the accident until the police and ambulance arrived. Dexter Worley thought he would probably carry this secret to his grave.

The fire truck beat both the ambulance and the police to the scene and fire department emergency medical techs scurried down the slope to the wrecked Suburban.

The EMTs verified what Dex knew: both the driver and the woman were dead. But the baby was alive — Seriously injured, probably permanently crippled — but she would live.

The announcement about the baby sent a pang of guilt through the pilot/race-car driver.

This little girl now has no father, and she'll be a cripple the rest of her life. It's all my fault.

At the accident scene, investigators were wrapping up their paperwork. The friction of braking had melted the sleety slush to leave a clear imprint of the Suburban. Dude had been in the wrong lane already when he braked. But Dex was in the same lane and his braking skid marks crossed those of the ill-fated truck. They had cleared up the questions about the second set of Corvette tracks when Dex explained that he backed up to the spot where the Suburban went over the rail, and had gone down the slope to see if he could do anything for the victims.

The smell, the beer can, and reports that the woman was seen drinking heavily at the VFW were already in the report. The sheriff and investigators expected a routine autopsy to show that Dude was also drunk.

There was no rush since no other car was involved in the accident. Although it would give Billy Poteet the proof he needed if he wanted to bring a wrongful death suit against Dude's estate, they also knew that the attorney would cost more than the cowboy's meager belongings were worth. The basic auto insurance settlement would be more than that beat-up old trailer or the almost as dilapidated horse of his.

"There's never an upside to something like this," the sheriff told his investigator. "I was with Dude's wife, widow, at the hospital. There won't be enough money to pay for all the medical help that baby will need, let alone enough see this family through."

"Yeah," investigator Paul Purifoy replied. "And Billy's life has always been wrapped up in Nancy, despite her heavy drinking. Whether Dude carried 10 or 20 on his policy, there won't be much left after burying her. Not that Billy would care. You know he'll give her as fancy a send-off as anybody in this town ever had."

Sheriff Cross tossed his tape and flashlight into the trunk of his cruiser. "Miracle about the baby, really. That child safety seat saved her life for sure. Banged up like it had gone a couple cycles in a clothes dryer, though."

The investigator decided to confide in his boss. "Sheriff, I'm kinda shocked. I'm a recovering alcoholic, been sober 12 years now. I was at the meeting last week when Dude picked up his chip for 90 days sobriety. I never thought he'd go out this way, not after he came to AA. I've always been reluctant to tell you about my drinking, but my sponsor has been telling me for the past two years to tell you."

Cross chuckled. "Why shit, Paul. That's been the worst kept secret in the department. We figgered that out when you started showing up for work on time and stopped writing those reports that no one could make sense of."

"Really?" Purifoy gaped. "Why didn't anyone say anything."

"When someone makes that dramatic a change, you don't want to do anything to hex it."

Purifoy then did the other thing he'd always wanted to do to his old friend. He walked across the frozen roadway and gave the sheriff a hug.

50

"Not guilty, your honor," Derek Prinz muttered. The ex-reporter for KTKO's Texas News Time, looked glumly down at his manacled hands. Dressed in the ubiquitous orange jumpsuit of the Lew Sterrett Justice Center, Prinz was unshaven and his thick salt-and-pepper hair was uncombed. His red nose poked from between two puffed and blacked eyes, which matched the lip puffed grotesquely on the left side where Pete's fist had neatly extracted a tooth.

Prinz was extremely familiar with the Dallas County jail. For 12 years he had walked these halls with cops, attorneys, and felons and their family members. Last night was the first time he had fully understood the impact of the walls and the iron bars on those incarcerated.

During the first hour, he had mostly inspected the small room (out of deference to his profession, friends in the sheriff's department had arranged a private cell). By the end of the second hour, the boredom had set in. Prinz tried to relax on the bunk, but the cot wasn't particularly comfortable, and he was too agitated to lie still for very long anyway.

As the hours crept by, he relived the day's events.

That little cunt really fucked me over. First, she infiltrates my police contacts, then she cozens her way into Joe's good graces to begin pushing me off the air. Then she shows up at a staff meeting for senior staff, for God's sake!

Prinz' emotional state is slowly making the irrational emotional leap from anger and indignation to rage, from sanity to insanity. This has happened before and, for the most part, it had proved an asset to his education and career. In college, he was able to channel his rage on the football field to become an all-state linebacker. In his career, he had been able to harness its energy to push past other reporters to move into position for a promotion to assignments editor, a post he had coveted for the last five year. Then Willie Nell came along.

And so did that damned mechanic! I'll kill that fucker!

The courtroom was packed with a variety of orange jumpsuits, each with attending legal representation. In the gallery behind this group, all seats were uncustomarily full and there were writers standing at the back wall. The attack on one of their own had the press out in full force for the routine arraignment.

Prinz' lawyer presented a total contrast to his disheveled client. Dressed in a pale Blue Armani three-piece with thin, widely spaced navy stripes, Teddy "Tex" Reed was the epitome of courtroom chic. His dark hair, expertly manicured and styled, was set off by pale blue eyes (more than once they had been characterized as "the eyes of a gunfighter") and rugged countenance.

Indeed Prinz' counselor was a legend in Texas courtrooms. He first created a splash in headlines when he successfully defended the Highland Park mother charged with killing her husband's mistress by running over her repeatedly with her Escalade SUV. By carefully selecting jurors, he twice obtained mistrials by getting hung juries. Charges were eventually dropped and he pocketed the first of his now common six-digit fees.

"Your honor, this entire affair is a ghastly mistake. All of Miss Autrey's injuries occurred when she fell out of that large, very high-seated SUV of hers. Admittedly, my client exacerbated the incident when he reached to catch her, but only caught her arm."

"Yeah, right!" Joe Bark, the attending assistant district attorney stood. "And I guess you didn't kick her, you just kinda stubbed your toe on her rib cage — about five times, according to eyewitnesses." The young, smallish ADA's voice was strident, his anger over the case evident.

"Boys!" Municipal Judge Tabitha Guillemot's authoritative voice chastened, "save it for the courtroom or take it out on the playground. In my courtroom I will have decorum at all times. Is that clear?"

Mumbled "yes ma'ams" came from both tables.

When she was sure opposing counsels were going to remain calm, Judge Guillemot proceeded. "Does the district attorney's office have any bail recommendations?"

"Your honor," Bark bristled, "the defendant attacked and savagely beat and kicked a co-worker, and hospitalized her with serious injuries. We consider him a continuing threat to the woman's wellbeing as well as a flight risk. We are opposed to anything less than a cash bond of $100,000," the prosecutor said firmly.

"One-hundred-thousand dollars in cash? Ludicrous." The defense counsel rose. "Which is it counselor; is my client going to run away or is he going to stay and beat up this woman when she gets out of the hospital?

"Derek Prinz has been an asset to our community; he's hardly a criminal; he's a force in Dallas' fight against crime. As a professional police and crime reporter, he has kept the public informed and alerted to danger, and has helped bring dozens of real criminals to justice. To lock him up on a charge for which he will be proven innocent, is a grave injustice."

"Objection!"

"Sustained. Mr. Reed, we don't need your summation just now. Please be seated.

The judge banged her gavel. "Seventy-five-thousand cash or bond. Next case."

Reed turned to Prinz. "Relax. I have a bail bondsman already drawing up the papers; you'll be on the street in an hour. You'd better get yourself cleaned up for the photographers. I brought you some upscale clothes. A clean, well-dressed and relaxed person always looks innocent; keep that in mind."

Accurate on both counts, Tex Reed led his client down the steps of the courthouse 45 minutes after the arraignment. Dozens of reporters and photographers clamored for a statement, a photo, something for Page One.

Prinz emerged into the sunlight cleaned, shaven, and groomed. Clad in gray gabardine slacks, a Jhane Barnes polo shirt, and polished loafers, he would have been a picture of leisure elegance, except for the broken nose and busted lip. As instructed by Reed, he smiled and nodded, acknowledged individual reporters with whom he'd enjoyed a good rapport — and kept his mouth shut.

"You're going to continue to deny you beat Willie Nell Autrey?" asked one reporter, who had been in the parking lot during the attack. A barrage of camera flashes competed with the bright North Texas sunshine, partially blinding Prinz.

"Mr. Prinz has given me a statement and will say nothing more on the subject until the trial." Reed produced a stack of 150 sheets and began distributing them to the clutching hands of the news crowd, then jostled through the crowd to his waiting limo with Prinz firmly in tow.

Once the car was in motion, the lawyer turned to Prinz. "We can get the felony assault charge reduced to a Class A misdemeanor; that'll keep you from having a criminal record. And I'll make every effort to get you probation. If that doesn't work, we can go for a deferred adjudication. That way after probation — if you're a good boy — the whole record is expunged."

"So what? My reputation is ruined," Prinz said bitterly. "I'll end up writing for tabloids or radio."

"Not with deferred adjudication. Once you're off probation, relocate to another city and, when they do a background check on you, you're a virgin all over again. Just keep your nose clean between now and then."

Prinz should have heeded his attorney's advice.

51

The limo dropped Prinz at the high-rise in Dallas' Arts District in what locals referred to as "Uptown". Restored turn-of-the-century electric streetcars clattered along the street in front of the building, which housed his tony loft, which he had fortuitously purchased before the prices skyrocketed.

The TNT reporter — *if I still have a job* — didn't bother going up to his loft but headed straight for the parking garage, hoping Tex Reed had made good on his promise to send someone to the TV station to recover Prinz' car. Prinz loved the 20-year-old Porsche 911, and had painstakingly restored it over the years to better than new, using original parts most of the time, but often opting for new technology, which actually improved on the classic.

Using his keycard, Prinz let himself into the gated garage and rode the elevator to the third parking level. In his assigned parking space sat the silver Porsche. Prinz unlocked the car with the electronic fob and sat behind the wheel. He had to reposition his seat; whoever Tex sent to deliver it was shorter than Prinz' 6-1 frame. From the never-used ashtray he extracted the key he had given to his attorney, placed it in the ignition, and started the car.

OK, Silver Bullet, let's go hunting.

The silver Porsche stopped at the curb in front of a seedy bar on Industrial Boulevard, its mildew-blackened bricks and cracked sidewalks a stark contrast from the breath-taking view it commanded of the ultramodern Dallas skyline to the east out the dirty front window. Its proximity to the county lockup assured Elbert Dewhurst, the owner, of a steady clientele of lowlifes, cops, reporters, and attorneys. "Hell, they're all lowlifes, and the crooks are the best of the bunch," he was fond of saying to anyone sitting at the peeling Formica bar.

Prinz slipped quietly into the bar, impossibly dark, considering the sunshine outside. He waited until his eyes adjusted to the murk, and then carefully looked around. He didn't want any other reporters seeing him meeting with Little Mo. At the bar, Morgan Little sipped a good scotch. Elbert's bar had a surprisingly upscale list of spirits, considering the place was, quite frankly, a dump. His clientele— a steady stream of lawyers, crime figures, and police — demanded it.

Certain no one who would recognize him was sitting somewhere in the gloom, Prinz approached Morgan, a street-savvy career cop who would never rise above his current rank of sergeant. Little Mo, a few discreet people knew, supplemented his income as an enforcer and collector for some of his contacts. For his services, he received payment in cash and, as a bonus, in information that helped him hang onto his job despite a well-known drinking problem.

"Got a minute, Mo?"

The uniformed cop turned, the old stool squeaking in protest beneath his bulky frame. "Yo Derek, you look like you got beat with the ugly-stick."

"Yeah," Prinz shrugged and gave his crony a crooked smile. "Asshole hit me when I wasn't looking. Broke my nose and knocked out a tooth."

"I heard. But weren't you whaling on that Autrey chick at the time?"

Prinz decided to stick to his lawyer's line. "Damn, No! I was trying to catch her as she fell out of that honking big SUV of hers. Grabbed her arm, probably responsible for that injury, though.

"Next thing I know, this mechanic guy grabs me, spins me around and does a one-two on me."

"Mmmm-hmmm. So what do you want from me?" But Little already knew that he was going to be involved in some payback. Twenty-two years on the street gave him a nose for when people were looking to make trouble, and Derek flat reeked of trouble.

"I want the two of us to teach the young man some manners, that's all. A couple hundred for your back-up. I'll do the dirty work."

Little knew better. He'd been here before. The translation of Prinz' offer he figured was that Little'd hold the victim in his meaty arms so Derek could tune him up without the guy being able to resist in any way.

Derek's an ass, but money's money. And if I'm there, I might actually be doing the guy a favor. This fucker might decide to kill Luke if there wasn't a cop present.

"When do we do the deed, my friend?"

"How about I pick you up right after shift change? That'll give me a chance to locate him." Prinz pulled two crisp 100-dollar bills from his wallet. He knew Little always takes the money up-front, so he had driven through an ATM on the way to the bar.

"You know I can't let you kill him, Derek. But I'll back your play so you can be sure he'll not mess with you ever again."

"That's all I ask."

Business completed, Prinz nodded to Elbert, "Gimme a Shiner, and no wise-ass remarks about my eyes."

"Comin' up, Mr. D," the bartender, owner, waiter, cook, and janitor said, and drew a glass of Shiner Bock from the tap into an iced schooner.

"And you didn't hear a thing, right?" Prinz said as he stuffed a $20 into Dewhurst's tip jar.

Dewhurst placed the frosty dark beer before his long-time customer. "Hell, Derek, you know I'm deaf."

Little and Prinz sat silently until the cop finished his drink. "I'll see you about 4:30, then," he said, rising to leave. "I'll meet you beneath that old bridge down in the bottoms."

Prinz gave an affirmative grunt, waited a minute, then drained his beer, and left.

52

The Trinity River often jokingly referred to as the "Trinity Trickle", separates West Dallas from downtown. It rises in three principal branches: the East Fork, the Elm Fork, and the West Fork and flows to the coast, making it the longest river having its entire course in Texas. The East Fork rises in central Grayson County and flows southeast to a confluence with the West Fork, forming the Trinity River proper a mile west of downtown Dallas and flowing 423 miles to drain into Trinity Bay just west of Anahuac near Galveston. Its flood plain in Dallas is more than a mile across in places, and has been a notorious dumping ground for murder victims since the 1940s.

Prinz drove to the TV station and walked into the administrative offices a floor beneath the newsroom. He hoped news of his dismissal hadn't made it to all the clerical staff; he needed some information from accounting.

Not pausing at the reception desk, Prinz strode back to Ed Smiley's desk. "Hey, Grins, I need some help."

Smiley was anything but his namesake. Prinz always thought the accounting clerk looked like a Basset Hound. "What can I do for you? Just don't ask me for more mileage on your expense report."

"No, I just need the address of the guy who worked on our van. The Silver Bullet's acting up and I thought I'd see if he could work on a Porsche."

"Just a sec, let me look it up." Smiley turned his back on Prinz, and clicked a few icons on his IBM Workstation.

"Got it." He jotted the address and phone number on a sticky note and handed to the man he still thought of as the lead cop-shop reporter for the station.

"Thanks, I owe you one."

"Nah, now get out of here, I got work to do," Smiley replied and turned back to his computer.

Prinz left the building without incident, started the Porsche, and drove back to his apartment. He had some planning to do in the two and one-half hours before he picked up Little. He knew the garage where Pete worked, but Pete would know something was up if the man he helped send to jail approached him.

Little will have to handle that part.

He dialed the dispatcher and asked to be put through to Sgt. Morgan Little.

"Little," the voice crackled through Prinz' phone moments later.

"Mo, call me on a secure line. It's important." Prinz hung up before Little could reply. Minutes later, his home phone rang.

"Okay, I'm at a phone booth. What's up?"

"Can you take a cruiser this evening?" Prinz asked.

"Sure, I take one home often. There's a program that encourages cops to take patrol cars home and park them prominently, if they live in high-crime areas, and it so happens my sorry dump qualifies."

"Then we need to pick this Pete guy up in your car. You'll need to get him and bring him to me."

"Makes sense. But we need to meet between his job and the station. He won't be the least bit suspicious until he sees you."

"How about under the Woodall Rodgers Freeway at Continental? There's a makeshift parking area right there," Prinz offered.

"But if I come as a cop, he'll be able to identify me and the car."

"Then we'll have to kill him."

"You know better than that. And I already told you I can't be involved in something like that, you bastard."

"Relax, relax. I'll think of something. Wait! Do we have anything on him? Something criminal that could be used against him?"

"Sorry, Derek, he's clean as a whistle. The suits ran him after your altercation. Not so much as a parking ticket."

"Shit!"

"What about this? I pick him, then have to drop him to answer an 'officer needs help' radio call!"

"How will you fake that?"

"I'm dating the dispatcher," Little said. "By the way, you got a piece?'

"You mean a gun?"

"I don't mean a gumdrop, idiot. How else are you going to get him into the car with you?"

"Yeah, I sometimes carry a .380 Beretta. Where do I bring him?"

"How about along the north side of Bachman Lake. I'll be in civvies. I'll also wear a toboggan cap that unfolds into a ski mask. He won't be able to ID me, but he'll know you."

Icily, Prinz hissed into the receiver, "I want him to know it's me." Then he hung up.

53

Daylight Saving Time had arrived a week earlier and the autumn sun was already almost gone, the end of another day for most employees of the little garage. Hidalgo's Car Repair sat at the end of a strip shopping center in West Dallas, its fading name above the bay doors facing the busy divided street. In an open bay, a lone mechanic had just wrestled a tire onto the rim of a city utility truck. Pete would close up the shop when he finished with this truck; the water department supervisor would pick it up first thing in the morning.

He leaned the long truck-tire wrench against a stack of old tires and wiped his brow, unmindful of the police black and white parked out near the street. After a long pull from the lukewarm bottle of Ozarka spring water, Pete located the battered hubcap and banged it into place over the lugnuts. He was finished. He stretched, wiped his hands, and went to the employee bathroom to clean up. Reynaldo, the chief mechanic was leaving as he walked in.

"You lockin' up tonight, Pete?"

"Yup, in another five or ten minutes."

"Then I'm outta here, goodnight."

"'Night, Ray."

Little watched Reynaldo walk to his Honda Odyssey and drive away. As soon as the van was out of the parking lot, he started the cruiser. While Pete was cleansing his hands and fingernails with alternating administrations of Lava soap and Goop™, Little pulled the squad car closer to the garage and got out.

He was leaning against the open-bay doorframe when Pete returned from the restroom.

"You Pete?" Sergeant Little asked the young man.

"Yes sir, what can I do for you?"

"I was sent by the detectives to fetch you. They got a few more questions."

"I'm here by myself; can you wait for me to close up?"

"Sure, son. No hurry."

While Pete straightened up and balanced out the register, Little called the dispatcher on his cell phone, not wanting the call to show up in the radio log. "Sandy, it's Mo. I need that radio call 15 minutes from when I hang up. I'll stay on the line until my suspect comes out, then I'll hang up."

"I'll time it to a tee, sweetie. Don't you worry about that."

In less than five minutes, Pete had closed and secured both service bays, turned on the alarm system, and was locking the front door. Little severed the cell-phone connection.

"Should I follow you in my truck?"

"No. you'll need to ride with me."

Pete reached for a rear door. "No, sit up here. You're not under arrest or anything."

Little drove from West Dallas on Singleton Boulevard, a direct line to downtown where Pete assumed they were heading. When Singleton crosses the Trinity River, its name changes to Continental Avenue, which enters the downtown area from the west at the northernmost end of the high-end clubs and shops that make up the West End, a well-known party venue for the well-heeled young Dallas professional set.

Parking is at a premium in the West End, a one-time warehousing district where little land was left for the kind of parking retail requires. For that reason, some of the land beneath the overpasses at Woodall Rodgers Freeway — a short, busy connector between Interstate Highways 35E and 45 — is used for parking, dark, and manned by attendants only during prime time, which is the cocktail hours for the bars in the West End.

Little timed his trip expertly. While on the half-mile span across the river, the radio crackled alive. "All cars in the vicinity of the Crescent Hotel, officer down, shots fired."

Little keyed his microphone. "Unit 23 responding,"

He turned to Pete. "I gotta drop you somewhere right now! That parking area under Woodall Rodgers — we go right by there."

The policeman toggled the lights and sirens and then slammed the accelerator to the floor. The big Ford Crown Victoria's rear squatted slightly before it shot forward with a roar, Little weaving through other traffic scurrying out of the way.

"I'll let you off at that parking lot up there and either I'll pick you up within half an hour, or I'll call the detectives to come get you."

Taken aback by the sudden developments, Pete can only manage a "whatever you say, officer," as he cinched his seatbelt tighter.

The Crown Vic plowed to a halt beside a shabby, unattended parking attendant's shack. Pete was barely out of the police cruiser when it took off, with squealing tires and a hail of gravel, toward the hotel a few blocks on the other side of the freeway.

Pete spotted a couple small folding chairs, apparently intended for customers to sit while waiting for their cars, and took a seat.

What the hell can these detectives want with me?

"Why, looky here." Prinz emerged from behind one of the concrete supports for the 10-lane freeway over their heads. "Never know what kinda vermin you might find under these old highway stanchions." Cat-quick, Pete rose and turned toward the smaller, wiry reporter in a single motion.

"I wouldn't if I were you." Prinz leveled the black Beretta automatic. "You and I have some unfinished business, my friend." Derek put the gun into the pocket of his light windbreaker, continuing to point it at Pete.

"You know my car, don't you — that silver Porsche over there?" Prinz motions to the car with a nod. "And for a treat, you get to drive."

Prinz escorted Pete to the sportscar, unlocked the doors with the remote, and ordered Pete to get behind the wheel. He then walked around the front of the car, keeping the gun inside his pocket pointed at Pete through the windshield. Prinz handed Pete the keys only after he had buckled his seatbelt, and removed the gun from his pocket. "Start the engine and get up onto I-35 North," he ordered.

Pete was thinking fast and frantically. Slowly, he relaxed. Prinz hadn't caught the transition, but his quarry now was icy calm.

Derek intends to take me out somewhere and kill me.

He reasoned that his captor would drive to somewhere remote, a location where a body might never be found.

That's what I would do in his place.

It suited Pete just fine. Prinz' little plot had a fatal flaw; he had turned control of the car over to the victim, which meant the gun was useless as long as the car was moving.

Pete controlled the Porsche like he'd driven it all his life. He darted out of the parking lot onto Continental, under the railroad bridge just before the entry ramp, and barely slowed to make the sharp right onto the ramp. By the time he entered the moving traffic, the little car was purring along at 80 miles per hour.

"Slow down, you asshole," Derek said threateningly, jamming the muzzle of the automatic into Pete's ribs. "Don't do anything to make us conspicuous."

What are going to do, shoot me and send your precious Porsche out of control at 80-plus?

The ex-reporter ordered his captive to stay left at a split to follow Airport Freeway heading west out of town, entering the suburb of Irving. "Cross the bridge and exit onto Grauwyler," he ordered.

Pete now knew where they were going. The Trinity Bottoms where police often find bodies left by street gangs and organized crime. He also knew about the levee. That's where he'd have to make his play.

Prinz directed Pete to make the U-turn and then to swing onto the dirt road that ran to the flood-control levee, which ran on both sides of the river bottoms. While turning onto dirt road atop the levee, Pete surreptitiously thumbed open his seatbelt, but didn't let the tensioner draw it away where Prinz would notice. Then he downshifted and stomped the accelerator. This time, Pete ignored Prinz' commands to slow down. Twisting the wheel to the right, Pete let the front of the car tilt down the slope before whipping it to the left and leaping out onto the rutted roadbed, landing in a roll. The sandy soil and grass between the ruts cushioned the impact and he rose, unhurt to watch the driverless car tilt, then roll. It gained momentum as it went, crashing through small trees, underbrush and exposed shale, rolling completely to the bottom to crash top-first into a tree.

Peering down at the car, Pete saw no movement. He turned to walk back toward the highway, but changed his mind. Prinz might be hurt bad; he couldn't leave him like that.

Pete scrambled down the grassy levee to the demolished Porsche. Looking in through the windshield frame, he could see Prinz, in obvious pain, struggling to release himself from the seatbelt.

"Toss the gun out, and I'll help you." Prinz didn't hesitate, the gun landed ungainly at Pete's feet.

"I'm hurt bad. I can't feel my legs at all."

Pete climbed halfway in through the windshield; Prinz' door was against the ground. He released the catch on the seatbelt. and Prinz screamed as his body fell the extra three inches to rest against the door. "I think my back's broken. Oh God! What am I going to do?"

"Tell you what I'm gong to do," Pete replied. "I'm going to get rid of this gun and go get some help. I don't dare move you, and you shouldn't try, either."

"Why should I trust you, you bastard?"

"What else can you do, fool?

Pete scrabbled back to the top of the levee and sprinted back toward the highway, remembering a strip center where they exited at Grauwyler Road.

Prinz was barely conscious when the firemen and EMTs reached the crash site. Gingerly, the rescuers managed to get his battered body onto a back board and strapped down.

At the emergency room, Prinz' self diagnosis proved prophetic. He had suffered a fracture of two vertebrae and a severed spine, as well as a ruptured spleen, broken collarbone, and a concussion. All but the spinal injury could be repaired with time. But Prinz would never walk again.

54

The next morning, Sergeant Morgan Little had a visitor at the station house.

"Where can we talk?" Pete asked the dumbfounded police officer.

"Uh ... follow me," Sergeant Little led his visitor to an interrogation room, checked the observation room and audio controls, then motioned for Pete to sit.

"I'll stand."

"Look, it wasn't my idea. Me and Derek were just supposed to rough you up a little."

"The Trinity Bottoms isn't a place you take someone to beat 'em up; that's where you hide the body afterward," Pete said angrily.

"But ... but we were ... um ... at Bachman Lake, not in the bottoms. When Derek didn't show, I went home. I figured the little chickenshit had wimped out."

"Well, Derek's in the hospital and his Porsche is totaled, I have his Beretta, and you're about to put in your retirement papers. Do you understand me?" Pete had lied to Little; the Beretta was already at the bottom of White Rock lake.

"Wait a fuckin' minute, bub!" Little made took a half-hearted stab at playing the tough guy, but it wasn't going to work. He was as white as a sheet and his face was sweating. "I just picked you up, then I got that call and dropped you off. I didn't have anything to do wi- ..."

"Save it!" Pete cut him off. "I saw you shut down the recorders for this room, but I have my little digital recorder right here." Pete tapped his shirt pocket. "You just said you and Derek were going to ... what was it? Rough me up a little?"

Little sat. "Derek won't talk, so what else ya got," he said with false bravado.

Pete noticed that the man's pallor now was accompanied by a tremor. "Now why would you think Derek won't testify against you?" Pete smiled wryly at the cop. "He's got an aggravated kidnapping charge while out on bail for assault. You know the weasel would roll over to save his own hide and the DA would cut him a sweet deal in a heartbeat to get a dirty cop."

"You think?" Slowly, the truth of his situation dawned on the old, overweight cop.

"Aw fuck!"

"You quit. It all goes away. Otherwise, I press charges. Your call."

"I quit, I lose my retirement, most of it, anyways, and I got 18 years on the force," the police sergeant moaned.

"How much you get if you're convicted of a felony, fatso?"

"Ah, hell." Little's shoulders sagged, then he shrugged resignedly. "Tell you what," he said slyly. "if you can keep both me and him out of it, you got a deal. Derek'll probably get a wrist slap on that assault charge, first offense, y'know. Just as well. The little shit couldn't hack hard time anyway."

Pete didn't care what happened to either of the men. Little would never know that he had walked to his desk with nothing more than a bluff. He had no intention of ever letting the issue go into the legal system. It would have been his word against the two of them and Prinz might even make a case for Pete causing his injuries. With the gun at the bottom of the in-town lake, there was no evidence of self-defense.

"I expect you to be a civilian at the end of the month, then. Don't make me come back again."

"I won't. I won't. I promise," Little liked the prospect of keeping his ass out of jail; he wouldn't double-cross the man who had the recording and the gun. He was getting off lighter than Prinz at any rate.

Neither man knew that Prinz would never see the inside of a jail cell again. Judge Joe Bark would allow the crippled man to plead to a Class 1 misdemeanor and request deferred adjudication with 10 years of probation. If Prinz toed the line, the charges would disappear totally at the end of his sentence. If he got into further trouble, he could be ordered incarcerated for the entire term.

55

After more than three decades in law enforcement, Atlee still liked the big Fords, even since his retirement six years ago. He pressed the pedal down on his civilian Crown Victoria and the massive car accelerated to 79 miles per hour. Another tick on the speedometer and he'd be 10 miles over the limit and draw the attention of any radar patrolmen on the Interstate.

Although cops routinely deny it, professional courtesy would probably get him no more than a warning, if that. But the stop would take up more time than he'd save if he drove any faster. He'd already spent six years on this case and had only recently begun picking up a trail. He couldn't afford any delays right now as he crossed the Louisiana state line and entered Texas on I-20.

It had been six years since Atlee buried his only child in the well maintained old cemetery in Nacogdoches. The only two women he ever loved lie there, his daughter, Sharon, and her mother, Celeste, who died in childbirth.

The years of retirement had done nothing to soften the policeman's physique. Nearing 65, he was in excellent health and doing the kind of work for which he was trained. He was investigating the murder of his daughter. He had found a remarkably similar case in Baton Rouge, which occurred four years earlier than the murder of Sharon, in 1995. A third case turned up in Liberty County near Cypress Lakes, Texas, a cold case dating from 1992.

Atlee was anxious to get to Marshall, less than 100 miles from the border. Arnold Boyette, an old friend of his, had called last night and said he was getting ready to relegate a four-year-old case in Marshall to the cold-case vault.

Boyette, a fifty-something patrol captain now, was also on the four-man panel which decided when a case was too cold to actively pursue. He had been surprised when he'd read the case file at the meeting last week. A young, blonde waitress murdered in her home. The unusual aspect was the evidence of sexual activity, but not of sexual assault or mutilation. He'd only heard of one similar case — the slaying of his friend's only daughter. Boyette knew that Atlee was looking for similar cases and, although there are regulations against sharing closed cases without clearance, he made the call.

Boyette was waiting at a diner just off the Interstate when he spotted Atlee's big Crown Vic. He sounded the horn although his was the only black and white parked at the restaurant.

Atlee parked beside the police car, locked the Ford, and climbed into the front seat beside his friend. "Thanks for the heads-up, Arnie."

"Don't thank me yet. I don't have the case file." Boyette said. "Since you and I last talked, we got a request from Dallas for anything fitting a profile of a killer that's been active there very recently.

"The profile fits our case, so we had to ship it off. I'm sorry. But that profile also fits the details of Sharon's murder, Abe."

Atlee, far from disappointed, was elated at the news. "Don't apologize. This is great news!" Atlee felt the trail getting warmer. "The cocksucker's been in Dallas, maybe within the past few months!"

"I brought some notes and clippings of the newspaper coverage." Boyette handed a large brown envelope to his old friend, which Atlee opened eagerly.

The woman had a resemblance to his daughter: slim, blonde, and attractive. Reports said there were no signs of forced entry and no evidence of sexual assault, although she had been involved in sexual activity not more than two hours before her death — possibly at the instant of her death from a crushed skull. She had been clubbed with a pottery vase that had been on the bookcase-type headboard.

"That's another thing about these cases," Atlee said aloud while reading. "The cause of death varies in each case. It's like a crime of opportunity.

"In some cases, he disposes of the body; in others, they lay where they were killed."

"So. What now?" Boyette asked.

"I'm heading for Dallas. Can you get the particulars on exactly who it was requested the information, then call them? Tell them I have information about some other cases that could involve the same perp."

Boyette nodded. "Not a problem. If you have a cell phone, I can even try to get you an appointment, then call you to confirm it. How's that?"

"Spectacular, old buddy." Atlee scrawled his cell phone number on his notepad, tore it off, and handed it to Boyette. "The food here worth eating? I'm starved."

"Let me buy you lunch, then. Call it Texas hospitality."

In less than an hour, Atlee again had the cruise control of the big Ford at 79. He'd be in Dallas in a little over two hours. As the car gobbled up miles, he added the new information to his mental database. The killer had made a U-turn. From Cypress Lakes, located near Houston in southeast Texas, he'd crossed into Louisiana and surfaced with a murder in Baton Rouge in southern Louisiana. A few years later, he strikes again more than 100 miles north in Nacogdoches. Now he's turned east back into northeast Texas. leaving a victim in Marshall, and possibly in Dallas and, if so, very recently.

Near Terrell, 60 miles east of Dallas, the cell phone rang.

"Speak to me, Arnie."

"I spoke directly with Dallas Police Chief Andrew Justin. He patched me through to this profiler, a detective Elliott, Grady Elliott, I think. He's heading up a Task Force and — get this — there's a reporter sitting in on this thing!"

"A reporter?"

"Yeah. Seems like she tied all these murders together. Her mother was a similar victim out in Texas, and there have been three victims in the Dallas area." Boyette took a deep breath. "The chief says the woman has promised to sit on the story until there's an arrest."

"Bullshit!" Atlee exploded. "I know those media hounds. As soon as they have a name, they'll run the story and our guy'll jackrabbit.

"Look, Arnie. I got one more favor. Call Chief Justin and ask him to keep any information I have other than your case to himself. I'd like to hold my cards long enough to meet with this Task Force, and especially with this reporter dame."

"No sweat. I didn't tell him what you know because I don't know it myself. You churned outta here so quick we didn't get to talk much. Besides, you had your mouth full of chicken fried steak most of the time."

"And he still set me up an interview with this Elliott guy? Now that's a co-operative attitude. For the record, old buddy, that was the best eatin' I've had in a blue moon. I'm signing off for now, traffic's getting heavy as I get closer to the city."

"Bye, Abe. Good hunting." Boyette clicked the disconnect button on his cell and sighed.

I'd hate to be in that guy's shoes when Abe finds him.

56

Elliott wasn't expecting a lot from his interview with the retired Louisiana cop. But the chief said do it, so he'd keep an open mind. He was surprised when the man called him direct and asked if he'd invite the reporter to their meeting.

A cop who really wants to talk to a reporter? What's that about?

Willie Nell answered on the second ring, just long enough for her caller ID to display Elliott's name and number.

"Hi, Grady. What's up?"

"If you're available, I got a Louisiana cop who wants to talk to the Task Force and he specifically requested you be present. Can you be here in … say, two hours?"

"With all my fuckin' bells on." She penciled the appointment onto her desk pad. "We need all the information we can get."

Elliott cleared his throat. "While I have you on the line, Willie, I want to thank you for the job you've done of keeping any information about our killer off the air. You know I wasn't gung-ho about having you this close to the investigation."

"I knew none of you would be, and that I'd have to overcome a lot of skepticism. But this bastard killed my mother and left my sister and me orphaned. I absolutely will never do anything that could jeopardize getting him put away."

Willie Nell knew she didn't have to do any research on this Louisiana cop before the meeting. Elliott and the Task Force would already be on it. With time to kill and unable to concentrate on any of the other pieces she wanted to write today, she dug out her files to refresh her memory about as many details as possible.

If this retired cop has cases from Louisiana and maybe from other states, this will all fall into the FBI's lap pretty soon. Might be about time to give my Fed friend a heads-up.

Willie Nell dialed the number of Special Agent Johnson. He answered on the third ring.

"Federal Bureau of Investigation, Special Agent Johnson."

"Don't be so formal, Marty. You're such a fuckin' stuffed shirt sometimes. Probably happened when you passed 50. "

"Willie! How's my favorite talking head?"

"Rushed, old man. So just listen, would you? Remember that case where I theorized a serial killer had crossed into or out of Texas at the Louisiana border?"

"Uh-huh. But you didn't have enough to really launch an FBI investigation, as I recall."

"Well, expect a call from Grady Elliott later today if my hunch plays out. I think the Task Force is about to be handed some corroborating evidence. But what I'm hoping is that this local Task Force and the Task Force you will undoubtedly muster can work together — at least until or unless we learn the killer has left the state."

"Willie, you're a riot. You're not even a cop and you're wanting the entire metropolitan police force and the FBI to put their investigations under the control of a mere slip of a girl." The FBI agent was laughing into the phone.

"Mere slip, my ass. And you gotta admit I'm easier to deal with than fighting all the turf wars that go along with trying to maintain cooperation between local cops and the Feds."

"That's true enough. Tell you what: get me an invite to sit on the Task Force, maybe bring some of my folks on board, and we might be able to use the Dallas bunch as the core to a larger operation. Bounce that idea off Chief Justin and Detective Elliott and get back to me."

"You got it sweetie. Can I bear your children? Or would Susan get upset at the suggestion?"

"She'd tell me that if it would get my snoring out of her bed, go for it."

"Deal's off. No snorers allowed past my front door. Thanks for the offer. . . and I mean about the Task Force. Buh-bye for now, handsome."

Willie Nell clicked the disconnect and hit the speed-dial number for Chief Justin.

"Justin."

"Andy, it's me."

"Willie! Won't I be seeing you shortly anyway? Not that I don't enjoy our chats."

"Got a suggestion, Andy. This serial killer thing is going to go interstate at today's meeting, and that will mean FBI involvement. Rather than losing control, why not suggest to Grady that he invite Johnson to sit in today's meeting as a consultant to your Task Force?"

"Not bad thinking, little lady."

Willie Nell rolled her eyes at the chauvinistic remark, glad the chief couldn't see her. "Thank you, Andrew."

Chief Justin got the message. Willie only called him Andrew when she was upset with him.

I'll see you in ... what? Forty-five minutes, then."

Without waiting for a reply, Willie Nell severed the connection and walked to Joe Mosier's office.

She rapped lightly on the polished oak door and peeked in. "Got a sec, Joe?"

"Sure, Willie Nell. Come on in."

Willie Nell briefed her boss about the Louisiana cop asking to visit the Task Force and about the implications that it would take the investigation across state lines, bringing the FBI into the picture.

"But I can't run anything, right? So why do you bother telling me anything in the first place?" Joe smirked. "I swear, I think you run this station more'n I do, young lady."

"I just want to be sure that when this story finally breaks, we're going to be the firstest with the mostest on the airways, boss," she said sweetly.

"I will have the story already written with blank spaces for currently unknown data. You just need to know it could break in days. But it might still be months away."

"I appreciate your efforts and the way you've been able to stay on top the other cop stuff while you're working with the Task Force."

"Don't embarrass me, Joe. You know my staff writers are carrying the load for me. I can't thank you enough for letting me go after a story with so much personal meaning for me."

"If it were my mother, I'd probably attempt to do what you're doing. But I doubt I'd be as good at it as you. Derek was a fool. He could have kept the status quo and you'd have ended up making him look good. He wanted my job and he could have ridden your coattails right into this chair."

"Well, don't look at me. I don't want it."

I wonder if I really mean that. Was Derek right? Am I maintaining a high profile just to build my rep?

Willie Nell knew she didn't have any hidden agenda, just an abiding determination to seek out the man who killed her mother. This little self check — evaluating any underlying motives for her actions — was something Lacey had passed down to her daughters. Willie Nell valued this technique which had helped her maintain her integrity in journalism, a field where integrity means everything, and in an environment, television, where it often means little. Prinz had been a case in point; to allow his shallow indictment to deter her would be a discredit to her mother's legacy.

"Joe, you know I'm a grunt; just send me to the front lines. And that's where I'm heading right now. Bye."

57

Chief Justin allowed Elliott to commandeer the executive conference room as headquarters for the new Task Force. He understood that the trickle-down effect of this decision would put the executives in his personal conference room and that he would have to scrounge around for a place for him and his assistant chiefs to hold their own staff meetings. Most likely, these would now take place in the employee break room. The troops would squawk, of course, but they'd really raise hell if he tried to use the ready room for his meetings.

Two sheets of typing paper taped together defaced the regal double French doors to the executive conference room. The makeshift sign, written in blue Magic Marker*, indicated this was home to:

Headquarters

Task Force LJ

A detective had thought of the name to honor Willie's mother. The title also was innocuous enough that not too many questions would be asked.

The chief poked his head into the room.

Elliott looked up from a computer terminal. "Hi, chief. We're getting the geek squad to install all the hardware and explain it to the luddites in the crowd. Also, I'd like you to sign off on allowing us to work with the FBI. Otherwise, they'll take over the investigation altogether and we'll be out of the loop. I've talked to Johnson and he's willing if you are."

"Go for it, Elliott. But I wonder why Johnson wants to hook up?"

"Three reasons: First, we already have an investigation in progress; second, we can get the technical resources in place faster, and, probably the most important reason of all, Willie recommended it."

The police chief laughed out loud. "Elliott, if that gal ever leaves the TV station, you and I will have to watch out for our jobs."

"She's got a cop's eye for detail, that's for sure," Elliott replied.

The chief nodded. "She's also having a Louisiana cop sit in on our meeting, did you know that?"

"She ran it by me first. Guy's not a cop anymore. He retired after his daughter was murdered to do his own investigation. There's a chance it's related to our task-force cases."

"OK Grady, just be careful that the guy doesn't wind up having his own agenda. We can't have a vigilante on the Task Force."

"Don't worry. I checked this guy out. He's an A-Number-One career cop who's always followed the book."

"But personal feelings about a case can be dangerous."

"Warning taken and noted. I'll ride a close herd on Mr. Atlee."

"Thanks, Grady. I won't keep you from your work. The meeting's in another half an hour.

As if on cue, the elevator doors opened to discharge a single rider, Willie Nell. Chief Justin was closing the doors to the conference room when he saw her step out of the car into the lushly carpeted and paneled hall.

"Willie!"

Her houndstooth slacks and bright blue sweater followed her svelte curves and drew men's attention. That she didn't seem to know how lovely she was added to her beauty. Although a petite woman, she had that carriage that exuded confidence, inborn and not effected at all.

Willie Nell turned and, recognizing the chief, gave him a dazzling smile. "Hey there, boss man. You sitting in on our little tea party, too?"

"Don't think it's a good idea, Willie. Too much brass in these kinda meetings tends to stifle creativity. I'll be in the loop for all the Task Force reports anyway. Grady knows I have his back if he needs me; I'll leave it in his hands."

"Is he in there?" Willie Nell gestured to the massive doors with the task-force sign.

"Yep. Up to his elbows in co-ax and power strips at the moment. But the techs are really doing the work. Go on in," the chief said with a wave as he turned toward his own office.

The young reporter poked her head inside just as the chief had done moments before.

"Don't just stand there. Come and help. You're the one who put all this in motion, you damn well better be willing to do some of the labor." Elliott smiled broadly to indicate he was just having some fun with her. "Actually, the techs say they're only about 10 minutes away from having everything online, so I guess you're off the hook."

Without waiting for a response, Elliott sobered. "Anything new?"

"My boss has agreed to keep task-force news a low profile. But you know the public will want something on the local cases."

"We can give 'em that. We just don't want to announce that we are investigating it as a serial case, at least not at this point."

"Damn, Grady, you're a lot more reasonable and sane than the Chief led me to believe you would be. He warned me that you're impossible for anyone to get along with."

"Did he now? And did he tell you that I eat fresh young reporters for breakfast? Two, over easy, to start each day."

He's flirting with me! Willie Nell angered, then quickly mellowed. He is kinda interesting, kinda like an intellectual grizzly bear.

Willie Nell huffed and turned her nose into the air. "The only way I'd be at your breakfast table is if you'd taken me to an obscenely expensive restaurant the night before. Face it, sweetheart, you couldn't afford a high-class dame like me."

Willie Nell hoped she was sending the right mixture of come-on and go-away messages to keep his interest. Just like she knew that now wasn't the time or place.

"I've gone to lunch with reporters and seen how you eat. They wouldn't let you in the places I take my dates."

Yes! He's interested. And he can certainly take it as well as dish it out.

Time to change the subject, Willie Nell decided. "Who'll lead the meeting, you or Agent Johnson?"

"Why I thought it was obvious, Willie. You're going to chair the organizational meeting of the Task Force, then we'll just take it from there."

Willie Nell sank into the nearest chair in shock, slipping off her 'kitten-heeled' pumps.

"Before you say no, listen to me." Elliott pulled up a chair facing her. "You're the one who brought us the information that tied this stuff together; and you're a neutral party, so neither Dallas PD nor the FBI can be accused of stacking the deck to claim any turf.

"Most of all, you have the trust of just about everyone who'll be involved."

"Who's going to be on your side of the table, then, Grady?"

"There'll be four of us, three besides myself, and you know them all. I'm probably the one you know least. Remember Jimmy Cates in Vice? He's the one who came up with the idea of naming the Task Force for your mother."

"Wow! I like Jimmy but I never knew he cared so much for me."

"And there's Helen Summers from Narcotics and Ed Soames from Ongoing Investigations, what you might call 'Cold Case Files'. How's that sound?"

"Wonderful — except, why Narcotics?"

"Helen's got a 15-year record in Homicide before going over to the narcs, and we don't know but what we're looking for someone who goes off on these women under the influence of some substance."

Willie Nell could see that Elliott had given everything a lot of thought. She also knew that, chairing the organizational meeting, she'd try to see that he was named chairman of the Task Force if at all possible. A gentle tap on the door interrupted the conversation. Then a tanned, lined face appeared between the double doors. "You must be Ms. Autrey. I'm Abraham Atlee."

Recovering quickly from Elliott's suggestion that she chair the preliminary meeting — which was more like acting as emcee until they could decide on a chairman — Willie Nell slipped her shoes back on and stood and walked toward the door as Atlee let it close behind him. "Welcome, Abraham. Come in and get comfortable. The others should be arriving soon."

"Thanks, and just call me Abe."

Elliott extended a hand. "Grady Elliott, I'm a detective lieutenant and a criminal profiler. I hear you have some information for us."

"And I hear you have some information for me."

Willie Nell put a hand on Grady's arm. "Let's not talk shop boys, not until everybody's here. That's how information falls between the cracks."

Grady knew the reporter was right, and nodded. He stood and escorted Atlee to the coffee buffet and each of the men drew steaming cups in porcelain mugs — No paper cups for the executive conference room. While the two men exchanged pleasantries, Willie Nell opened her leather portfolio to a blank legal pad. She began outlining the meeting agenda. She would have each person stand, introduce himself, and give a brief bio. Then she would pass out copies of the cold cases. She would brief the group on the travel route or routes and the timeline, then ask Atlee to add his cases to her presentation.

She fully expected that Agent Johnson would want to explain the FBI's position on Federal jurisdictional requirements and limitations.

She would end with Elliott, who, she hoped would have been able to draw some kind of preliminary profile of the serial killer and maybe get a handle on when and where he might strike next.

While she was busy planning the meeting, Johnson arrived with two other agents in tow. Elliott, knowing Willie Nell was rushed at the moment, intercepted the trio and steered them toward the coffee. As he was introducing himself, the three Dallas detectives filed into the room, nodded toward Willie Nell, and approached Elliott.

"Nice digs, Elliott," Soames observed. "Who'd you have to kill to get us a setup like this?"

"Thank the chief, Ed. He had to give up his own conference room to the suits in order to get us this place."

A sound drew everyone's attention and they all turned toward the head of the large conference table where Willie Nell had placed her pinkies in her mouth and emitted a loud and shrill — and definitely unladylike — whistle.

"Sorry guys, no one thought of a gavel, and we need to get this party started."

58

Willie Nell sat at the head of the table with Elliott to her immediate right and Atlee on her left. Special Agent Johnson was positioned beside Elliott with Helen Summers to his right. A young FBI agent, Jeremy Merriweather, a computer expert, had the last seat on the right. Across the table, the third FBI representative, a middle-aged black woman named Naomi James sat between Jimmy Cates and Ed Soames.

"We really have a mixed bag here," she started. "And that's a good thing, since I'm the unlikeliest person in the room. But each of you brings something special to the group, and this case will probably use every single skill represented by each of you.

"In front of each of you is a computer terminal linked to NCIC, certain FBI links, and local and state police databases. Beside each terminal is a thick folder. Please do not open these until instructed to do so. Some FBI links are password protected, for obvious reasons, and access to those will be controlled and monitored by Special Agent Johnson. Martin, raise your hand if you would."

Johnson lifted his pen from his notepad and raised his right hand. "Don't be bashful about asking for information and access, people. We're a team."

Willie Nell stood up. "Let me introduce a guest for today, then we'll each introduce ourselves, even though most of us have met. At my left is Abraham Atlee, who recently retired from the Nacogdoches, Louisiana police department to pursue this case full time, for personal reasons. His information is the reason for this joint Task Force.

"Abe, now's the time to tell us what you know."

Willie sat and the gray-haired man with the sun-darkened skin stood, ramrod straight and steely eyed. "Gentlemen, and you ladies, too, If we're after the same guy — and I'm convinced we are — I have a burning interest in finding him. One of his victims was my only child, my daughter Sharon.

"When it was apparent the case would be relegated to the cold-case files, I resigned to pursue the investigation on my own. I have since found information that indicates the route of this killer moved from Texas into Louisiana, killing a victim in Baton Rouge Parish, before coming through Nacogdoches. From there, he next seems to have turned back through Texas, committing another murder in Marshall.

"Detective Elliott has since showed me files that indicate he also was in Hughes Springs, Rowlett, and Wylie. Dallas police think he may be responsible for multiple homicides here. I've been on this guy for six years, but your information convinces me that a single investigator could never work all this information on his own. I'm not on your Task Force and I have no law-enforcement credentials, but I'd like to make myself available for whatever legwork you might need help with.

"Thanks for hearing me out." Atlee sat down and all eyes turned toward Willie Nell.

"I don't have any credentials either, Abe. And after this meeting I'll just be an observer and willing gofer for this group. But I would like to ask Detective Elliott and Agent Johnson if they have any objections to asking you to serve on the Task Force."

"I have no objections, Willie," the senior FBI agent said.

"Nor I," Elliott added. "It might be good to have some eyes out there in the field that aren't constrained by the rules that go with a badge."

"Are you game, Abe?" Willie Nell asked.

"Count me in, and thanks for including me. I promise not to do anything to make you regret this decision."

Willie Nell knew she needed to keep the meeting moving. "Jimmy, you're next. What I want each of you to do is to give the group your name, your position, and a quick bio, going around the table clockwise."

Elliott finished up the task-force introductions. "Your turn, Willie."

Willie Nell blushed slightly. "Most of you know me as the potty-mouthed police reporter from KTKO-TV. I was interested in finding out how often crimes like these happen, and asked for and received some old case files, almost all of them cold cases. I was shocked to find that one victim was my mother, who was killed in West Texas 14 years ago. I also noted there seemed to be a route and timeline indicating many of these could be related."

"She turned her information over to Chief Justin and me, and we decided to put together a Task Force," Elliott interjected. "But it began to look like he might have entered Texas from the west and exited into Louisiana. When Mr. Atlee confirmed these suspicions, we knew the FBI would also have to be involved.

"I'm grateful to Special Agent Johnson for agreeing to a joint Task Force with local and Federal representation."

"Naomi, do you have something on your mind?" Willie Nell asked, noting the cross-armed, crossed-legged posture the agent had assumed.

"Doesn't anybody besides me have trouble with a reporter (she said the words with venom dripping from her voice) sitting in on our meetings?" Naomi looked around the table at the others.

"I assume you have reason to mistrust other reporters but let me assure you I have given my word to Marty and to Grady that I will sit on this story until we get the perp. I worked in the cop shop for my internship. The force to a man trusts me." She told the woman.

"Honey, I know the men trust you but I don't trust your skinny white ass as far as I could fling Grady — which isn't far."

Willie Nell clenched and unclenched her fists. "Naomi, when you know me better, you'll trust my skinny white ass as much as you trust your own. If time comes when you don't, you have my permission to kick my skinny white ass up between my shoulder blades."

"Permission!" Naomi sputtered. "You—" She scanned the smiling faces around the table and erupted into infectious laughter. "I will happily place my sensible size 9 uniform brogans in the seat of your designer trousers and willingly oblige."

"Naomi, I hate to correct you just when it's obvious that we're becoming bosomy buds, but I never pay retail. These are knockoffs."

Willie Nell was glad to see that interest in information exchange was picking up in the group; a good time to review copies of the cold cases and brief the group on the travel route or routes and the timeline. "Please open the folders beside your terminals. These are copies of the case files we have so far identified as possibly being victims of our serial killer. You will be free to study these at your leisure. Become as familiar with them as you can.

"Now, we need to move on to another important piece of business. You need to select a Task Force commander from among your ranks. And, as those of you who know me would suspect, I have a recommendation."

The rustle of paper gave way to murmurs. "Although Agent Johnson is the ranking law enforcement official in the room, I think you, Grady, are best suited for the following reasons:

"One, you're more familiar with the Dallas crime scene, and that's where this guy seems to be right now.

"Two, you're a trained profiler and we really need to get inside this guy's head in a hurry.

"Finally, the local population will be more comfortable with local rather than Federal leadership of the group."

Special Agent Johnson stood, buttoning his suit coat as he rose. Willie Nell felt a rush of panic.

Uh-oh. I think I overstepped my bounds, here!

"I agree with Willie. And I must say you have a good head for organization. But within the FBI, I will have to be the intermediary. The agency won't take direction from a local cop. That said, I'd rather someone else have to sit at the head of the table anyway. Take up the gavel, Grady and just give us our marching orders."

Willie Nell pushed her chair back. "Sit here, Grady. We'll change seats."

59

Elliott moved to the head of the table but didn't sit. "Willie, my first official act as commander will be to draft you onto the Task Force. Marty's right about your organizational skills, not to mention your analytical mindset. You will be an asset in this investigation and we would welcome your input.

"Does anyone else on the Task Force object?"

Agent James raised a hand. "But she's a reporter. We can't go broadcasting Task Force activities on the evening news."

"We covered that earlier Ms. James," Elliott replied. "Willie and her station manager have agreed to sit on the story until we have an arrest. In return, they get the exclusive. Considering the work she did to get us to this point, I feel it's the least we could do."

"Well, I for one have never had much luck trusting the media, but you're the boss." The FBI agent took her seat, staring at Willie Nell.

Elliott ignored the interplay between the two women and continued the meeting. "Let me also add that this Task Force is likely to grow as we find activity in more jurisdictions. The state police may want to put somebody on board, of course, and you can count on Louisiana wanting to send someone. If it turns out that he's been active in other states, we'll probably see some more requests for participation. And those who don't necessarily want to join the Task Force will damn sure want to be kept in the loop with up-to-date reports.

"I will set up a schedule of interviews so I can meet each member one-on-one. Marty, I'd like to start with you, if you have the time after this meeting."

"I'll make the time."

"Good. And I'll make a schedule over lunch and post it on the door. I want to get this out of the way as quickly as possible. This meeting is adjourned, but I want everybody to check the schedule. I'll have it up by 1 o'clock."

Elliott was interested in interviewing the senior FBI man first to get additional insight into the other two agents. Since he already knew the three Dallas Police representatives, he'd save them for last.

From Johnson, Elliott learned that Naomi James was a transfer from Washington DC, and had been responsible for tracking down two serial killers during her career. He also learned that she was a Yale graduate and a member of Mensa, a social organization of people with exceptionally high IQs. He wasn't surprised to learn the woman had been burned by the media on her last case, which resulted in her transfer, a de facto demotion.

Agent Merriweather was the local FBI office's top geek, a computer genius with a graduate degree in electrical engineering and computer science.

Johnson was punctual, as Elliott expected. During the interview, the FBI discussed the limitations of cooperation between the Feds and the police department. Elliott was relieved to know the restrictions would have little effect on the group's effort, and would only get sticky if more jurisdictions became involved and were unwilling to work within the framework of the Task Force.

Only the interview with Naomi provided any surprises. Elliott was amazed at her depth of knowledge about serial killers and with her past successes, wondering privately how such a sharp agent could reap the wrath of the Washington office.

He didn't have to bring up the subject. "I have some doubts about this Willie Autrey woman. I had a case blown out of the water by a reporter who broke confidence on a case that resulted in a mistrial and the release of a very dangerous individual."

"How did that come about?"

"The district attorney filed a formal complaint that I gave privileged information to the journalist, who put it into print in a way that was prejudicial to the case."

"And they decided to run you out of town?" Elliott tried to challenge the agent's ego.

"No. It was my idea. I knew my mistake would hold me back in the Washington office, so I requested the transfer. I figured I might as well go where it's warmer if I had to move anyway."

Elliott liked the matter-of-fact tone with which Naomi spoke of her transgression. He figured Willie's people skills would eventually win some level of trust from the older agent. So far, every law enforcement person who met Willie Nell Autrey had came to like and trust her. And Naomi's experience was simply too valuable to veto her as a member of the Task Force.

Following the interviews, the profiler had a good handle on the make-up of his team and had built a reference file of his talent base and he liked what he had to work with. The FBI had three members on the Task force, Johnson, a skilled agent, and leader, and two of his people, Naomi James and Jeremy Merriweather. He knew Merriweather; almost anyone in law enforcement in North Central Texas was aware of the skilled computer hacker, database expert and electronics surveillance genius. He taught Computer Science courses at the University of Texas at Dallas campus. In addition to his exceptional skills, he knew Jeremy to be a hard worker and a team player.

James was a different story, arriving in Dallas after some kind of dust-up in DC. But Marty assured him she was an incredible intellect and analyst. Her aggressiveness and ambition could be channeled, the FBI station chief told the Task Force commander.

Elliott's own team from DPD consisted of Jimmy Cates, Helen Summers, and Ed Soames.

Cates, he knew, was an outstanding investigator, instinctive, case hardened, and physically tough. Elliott had worked with him on more than one occasion and knew Cates was a good undercover guy as well as a top-notch detective.

Helen Summers was a rock. She had logged 15 years in homicide, and wasn't the least bit squeamish for a female (what a chauvinistic attitude, he chided himself). Helen was a good detective who knew the narcotics environment, and was an adamant feminist. She was also one of the best marksmen in the department, and had been a sniper with the SWAT team for awhile, a skill she'd picked up in the Marine Corps.

Ed Soames would be particularly valuable, he figured. The older cop was a cold-case expert with good instincts. With some classes, he could be a profiler himself. He was another guy that Elliott had worked with before.

The two question marks were Willie Nell and Abraham Atlee. He figured that Atlee's cop background couldn't hurt, and he was motivated. His daughter's death drove the man. But Elliott had to be sure that Atlee didn't develop tunnel vision. His daughter was only one of God knew how many women their quarry might have killed.

Finally, there was Willie Nell. A damned civilian whose chutzpah had landed her right in the middle of everything. But he liked her courage and focus. She was also a born leader, surprising, he thought, considering her age. He had to remind himself that the fact her matter-of-fact sensuality didn't really need be be a consideration.

60

Grady Elliott had the floor at the second meeting two days later. The detective had developed a preliminary personality profile of the Task Force's target.

"It is obvious that our killer's attacks were not premeditated. He did not bring a weapon to the scene but used whatever was there. If there was nothing, he used his bare hands, strangling two, snapping one woman's neck, and pummeling another to death with his fists.

"The unsub — Willie, that's detective-speak for unknown subject — does not dislike women. It appears that he actually was in the act or had just finished making love to each victim at the time of the attack. He is nomadic by nature, but may not have always been so. He is uncomfortable away from home, thus his turnaround to head back west. We may find that he originated in a desert environment such as New Mexico, Arizona, California, or even West Texas.

"He is attractive, perhaps handsome, and has no trouble starting relationships. So consider him well spoken, probably educated beyond the high-school level. Expect him to be gregarious and make new friends easily."

Elliott flipped the cover sheet on the whiteboard standing on an easel beside him. On it appeared a simplified map of Texas and western Louisiana with the approximate route of the killer, each victim location represented by a large red circle with the year written inside it. "Since he's been at this maybe 20 years or longer, he's in perhaps his late 30s to mid 40s. He could be older; we don't know when he started. Our earliest case in Texas appears to be in 1987. He's probably muscular and may work in a trade rather than a profession, despite his education. He will not appear dangerous or belligerent.

"Since all the victims are of a single appearance type, we know he targets slim, attractive blondes, exclusively. This could be a clue to his pathology. Most likely, he is acting out a scene with a significant person in his past in each relationship, perhaps his mother, or an early sweetheart. He probably also killed that person. She was a blonde, like all of his known victims."

Elliott paused. "Any observations, rebuttal, or additional information?"

Willie Nell's hand shot up.

"That doesn't play, Grady, my mother had long, luscious auburn hair."

"Not according to the case file. The report indicates Lacey Jay Autrey's hair was blonde at the time of her death, but that it was a coloring job."

"Son of a fucking bitch! How'd I miss that?"

"Probably because you saw what you expected to see. It's normal, Willie," Elliott said, trying to mollify her.

"If I'm going to make my living as a Goddam reporter, I sure as fuck better start paying more attention to my source information."

"Take it easy on yourself, or you won't be good to any of us on the Task Force. Anybody else have anything?" Elliott moved on, leaving the reporter to stew in her own recriminations.

Naomi raised a hand. "Expect him to take money, debit cards, maybe a vehicle from a victim. If he has limited means, he will need money to affect a getaway. Except for the Dallas killings, he's always moved on, or so it appears."

Johnson raised a hand and Elliott nodded to him. "Do not assume we have found all of his victims. As the murder in Nacogdoches shows, he is willing to transport a body to another location where it might not be found for some time."

"What if he just ... stops?" Ed Soames chimed in without raising a hand. "There have been periods of nearly five years between some attacks."

"Unless there are undiscovered bodies out there, heaven forbid," Helen responded.

"He won't stop," Elliott declared. "This pathology is too engrained. It's part of who he is."

"Can I add something?" Willie Nell asked.

A chorus of raucous boos and a resounding group "NO!" filled the room. The reporter was crestfallen, until everybody laughed.

"We've been waiting to ambush you, Willie," Jimmy Cates said, between chuckles.

"Have your say now that we've had a good laugh at your expense," Elliott told her. "We all figured you'd been too quiet, so we cooked this up."

Regaining her composure, Willie Nell stood. "I think he's a Lothario. I believe he loves these women until something happens that causes him to kill them."

"If that's the case," Atlee observed, "we need to find victim X, the first one, which means we need to be backtracking from that killing out there near El Paso." He looked at the map.

"I need to go to Fort Hancock and snoop around."

61

Grady Elliott paced around his two-bedroom condo like a caged animal. Restless. Angry.

He couldn't have told anyone what was wrong with him. At a subconscious level, he knew that there was little more to do but what he and the Task Force were doing to find this killer. That they had 15 cases to go on didn't help a lot. The evidence indicated he usually moved on after a murder. But there was a possibility that he had slain three different women here in Dallas, and a couple more in eastern suburbs.

He might have moved on, or he might have decided he liked the big city. Either way, there was little to do or learn until he struck again. That's where Elliott's anger was rooted. He felt helpless to protect the next victim. Somewhere in Dallas, or maybe west of here, a woman was going to be killed and there wasn't anything anyone could do about it.

"Like hell there's not!"

Elliott exploded out loud, rousing the sleeping German shepherd at his feet.

"Sorry, Sadie."

He reached down and scratched behind the retired drug dog's ears, eliciting a contented whine from his only roommate.

Elliott became a widower four years ago when breast cancer claimed the love of his life. Amy had been his childhood sweetheart and there had never been another woman before their three-year marriage, nor since. They had been childless, by choice, waiting for Elliott to get his gold shield as a detective, and the accompanying pay raise before starting a family.

The pretty, warm condominium had been their first home and it still whispered to him in her tender voice. The furniture, decorations, drapes, dishes, everything — they had picked them out carefully, together. Sometimes Elliott would fantasize seeing her coming out of their bedroom and up the hall to join him on the big sofa. He knew he was still grieving, and that work was his refuge. Right now, Elliott needed refuge.

He dialed FBI Special Agent Johnson at home.

"Johnson residence, this is Mandy," a tiny voice answered.

"Hi, Mandy, is your daddy home?'

Johnson was on the phone in seconds. He had already noted the caller ID. "What's going on, Grady?"

"I'd like to talk to you about assignments for the Task Force. Maybe the Starbucks on Beltline Road at Marsh Lane in an hour?"

"Should I round up my guys?"

"Don't think that's necessary just yet. Anyway, I'd like us to agree on a strategy first, then your team can get its marching orders from you rather than a local."

"Not bad psychology, Grady. I might try to recruit you for the bureau."

"Hah! Not on a bet. See you in an hour."

"Wait. I just had a thought. Let me see if Willie can come. She's pretty intuitive and I think her input might be helpful. I'll call her."

"Not bad psychology, Marty. A third party can help us with any differences of opinion and keep either of our teams from launching turf arguments," the Dallas Police profiler said, before hanging up.

And she's damn nice to look at, too.

Willie Nell was sitting and sipping a mocha latte when the two lawmen walked into the smallish coffee shop. "Hell, guys, I didn't even have a fuckin' siren and I beat you by 10 minutes."

"Nice to see you, too, smart-ass," Johnson retorted.

"Don't mind the suit, Willie," Elliott said. "Feds ain't got no couth when talking to a lady. We'll just let the Federal oaf-fishul buy."

"Unlike locals, us pros make enough money, I'd be happy to treat everybody. What can I order you, Grady?"

"Just a drip, thanks."

The FBI agent smiled at the young oriental girl behind the counter; she knew the agent, and smiled back. Johnson ordered the medium coffee for Elliott and a tall cappuccino for himself, the profiler joined the pretty young reporter. "What did Marty tell you we would be discussing?"

"Task Force assignments. Is that right?"

"Yeah. We need to get everybody working, and we have a lot of ground to cover with few folks."

Johnson sat down. "I asked her to bring them to the table and she said she would."

"I had a few thoughts on the way over here." Elliott began. "We know your computer guy, Merriweather, will be staying at headquarters, so let's get some communication equipment installed so all our people in the field will have a centralized comm center and can stay in touch with each other. He can run a comm center, can't he?"

"Yes, and we'll certainly need one. But why not run it through the police communications center?"

"We can't afford to wait for our dispatchers, 9-1-1 operators, and switchboard folks to triage our calls, or to misroute them. And the Peter Principle says that's probably exactly what would happen if we made it possible."

"You're right," The FBI agent conceded. "Then I think I should send Naomi to talk to police departments in southern New Mexico, and maybe even to Arizona. Her Washington connections might get some folks to share information who aren't used to working with Federal investigations."

The coffee arrived. "Need a refill, sweetie?" the oriental girl asked Willie Nell.

"Decaf non-fat mocha latte," she answered.

"And put hers on my card," Elliott said, handing the prepaid Starbucks card to the barista.

Grady found himself staring at the intriguing young woman. Worse yet, she had caught him staring at her at least once. He'd just smiled like a proud father, not fooling himself but hopefully fooling her.

Willie Nell stretched, riveting Elliott's attention to her lovely neck. He had to fight to keep his libido in check. When she'd toss her hair during the conversation, he would anticipate running his fingers through its silky strands.

His guardian angel perched on one shoulder cautioned: Watch out old man, you've just been celibate too damned long. Lust is a dangerous thing at your age.

The horny devil digging into the other shoulder teased: She's flirtin' with you. What's a little tumble with a sweet thing like her gonna hurt?

Angel: *She'd get a glimpse of me naked and have a laughing fit.*

Devil: *Make sure she's hot-to-trot and it won't make any difference how your body looks. Hers either for that matter, but truth is she's damned hot. No pun intended.*

While he was having this conversation with himself, he'd evidently missed part of the real discussion with his table mates at Starbucks.

"Sorry, guess my mind was wandering," he'd admitted, not about to say just where it went during its digression. "This case is taking a lot of my head-space, crowding out a lot of stuff like manners."

"What about Louisiana?" Willie Nell asked again. The girl had retreated to fetch her drink.

Elliott addressed the question. "I think Atlee brought us most all the information we're likely to need from there. I'll get Chief Justin to call and schmooze with the top cops in the two parishes involved to be sure our investigation doesn't ruffle any feathers."

Johnson was nodding in agreement. "I take it your guys are going to work within the state, then. That leaves us needing one thing we don't have: undercover investigators to backtrack this bastard and see where he came from."

"Why not Abe?" Willie chimed in. "He has no police authority, but no constraints, either. He did a good job in Louisiana and even in Southeast Texas, digging up the cases that have given us a route and a timeline for the rest of these murders."

"True," Elliott said. "He can talk to people who might not be willing to open up if a badge was shoved in their faces."

"And I can do some snooping, too, you know," Willie Nell added.

"Willie, I think you're going to have your hands full keeping the press at bay for awhile."

"Fuck you, Grady." Her pretty blue eyes suddenly turned icy. "I'm going to be involved in this Task Force, so you might as well get used to it. I'll start in West Texas where my mother was killed. I'm local; people will talk to me."

"She's got a point, Grady," Johnson said softly. Willie's outburst had turned all eyes in the coffee shop toward the small corner table where they sat.

"Okay then," Elliott conceded, "But I'm sending Ed Soames with you. He's an expert on cold cases. You'll probably cross paths with Abe. Keep your investigative imperatives separate, but share information freely."

"I can do that," Willie Nell said.

"I'll hold Jimmy back for now in case we have any new cases come in that he can bulldog for us. I expect the next incident to be in Tarrant County, probably Fort Worth. Jimmy can work with their locals on any fresh case."

"Who's that leave, then?" the FBI agent asked.

"Helen. I'm going to have her go over the Dallas cases again. She's a great investigator and knows how to take care of herself if she runs into a dicey situation."

"That just leaves you and me with nothing to do," Johnson laughed.

Elliott winked, "I think I need to take you under my wing and make a profiler out of you. Seriously, you and I need to pick the brains of some psychiatrists and psychologists to find out what makes this guy tick."

"Gotcha. And we can have Jeremy Merriweather do some Internet research along the same lines," Johnson agreed.

Elliott stood, a signal the meeting was over. "Now we can round up the troops and get 'em on the road." He walked through the door with Johnson, unaware of the pair of pretty eyes following him.

Willie Nell thought she'd seen him scoping her out. She admitted to herself that she'd thought about seeing if he was as muscular as he looked, too.

When things aren't quite so heavy, maybe I'll find out. I know he's interested. I can read it in his eyes when they look into mine.

62

Willie Nell and Ed Soames were wrong. Atlee wouldn't be covering the same murders they were investigating. When Elliott had rounded up Task Force LJ, Abraham Atlee had ideas of his own.

"I think I should start with the Fort Hancock case, then I want to go over to New Mexico and see if they have any similar cases prior to 1987."

"But the FBI's going to be looking into that," Willie Nell had responded.

Atlee wasn't asking for approval; he was simply informing the Task Force of his intentions. "I think they'll be taking a top-down approach, starting with the administrative brass. It could take months to work down to the street cop level. Since I'm no longer a law-enforcement official, I don't have to worry about the chain of command. If there's something there, I'll have it before these guys get done exchanging letters of authorization, emails, and phone calls.

"I suspect this guy started in New Mexico or Arizona."

Elliott stood with his arms crossed at the head of the Table. "Just for the sake of argument, why not from Mexico?"

"He's Anglo, to begin with," Atlee explained. "Not all the women he's killed would date a Mexican. My daughter, for one, was a bit of a snob as well as a closet bigot."

Willie Nell could see that it pained the retired police officer to speak so bluntly about his murdered child.

"She was also attracted to very athletic men, so I think we're looking for a guy who works out, or works in a trade that keeps him in good shape."

"Hey Abe," Elliott interjected. "You're after my job. That's a fair piece of profiling you just performed. And I, for one think you're right. But remember, this guy's been at this for something like two decades, so he's not a kid anymore. Let's figure from late thirties to fiftyish, at the top end."

"I'd consider the low end first," Atlee added. "Forty-something. My daughter was 24 when she was killed in '99. That was six years ago. I figure he was no more than 10 years older than her, that would make him ... say 34, or 40-something today. If he's a physical-fitness freak, he might pass for five years younger, or even more."

"Let's add that to our profile. Also, I think our guy may not be a psychopath or sociopath."

Elliott's last statement brought a murmur from the gathering.

"Let's say he goes into a rage or a fugue state during the course of love-making. What could cause something like that?"

"Drugs!" Helen Summers offered.

"Bipolar disorder!" Naomi James surmised.

"PTSD!" Atlee shot up from his chair. "Post-traumatic stress disorder! That's it!

"I saw a lot of that after Vietnam. My best friend suffered blackouts and flashbacks for years after coming home. And some of the guys in my platoon even had problems while we were still in-country.

"My lieutenant went ape-shit one night and started blasting away with his Colt Commander at snipers in the trees on the base, when nothing ... nobody... was there. I hear he killed himself shortly after he got home."

"I think Atlee's right, Grady," Johnson agreed. "We usually think of PTSD as only a wartime occurrence, but I've seen it in officers and in crime victims. Let's say some kind of trauma happened in this guy's life, and he flashes back to it, like a Vietnam veteran who still sees pajama-clad Viet-Cong on the streets.

"He may not even be aware he's doing it, at least at the time of the event. Or, perhaps, he's killing someone else."

"Damn!" Agent Johnson exploded. "You're saying he could have been interviewed in the initial investigations and was so forthright he wasn't suspected?"

"Worse." The profiler looked from Willie Nell to the local head of the FBI, then down at his hands. "He could have been dismissed after a polygraph exam because the truth to him is that he doesn't know a thing about the killings."

63

Perhaps because he was the same age Dude would have been, Willie Nell was drawn to Atlee and they become fast friends; or it could have been that she reminded the retired policeman of his own slain daughter; or maybe it was that they each had lost an important person in their lives at the hands of the killer both were determined to track down.

At any rate, Atlee and Willie Nell were, by now, in constant contact. When it wasn't at Starbucks, it was an email or a phone call to compare notes —or just to check in with each other.

"I look everywhere in Sharon's belongings for clues," he told her over pre-dawn lattes. "I hate to admit it, but I didn't know Sharon as well as I thought I did. As I went through her belongings, I found private things — not just woman things, but embarrassing things; a porno CD, marijuana paraphernalia, even sex toys … but I guess most single women these days have those. Some things I've learned I'm glad to know, but others, well let's just say I'd rather not even think about."

The effect of this simple revelation on Willie Nell was galvanizing.

Do I really want to know all about my mother's life after Dude's death? Or any of her private secrets for that matter?

She slapped herself on the forehead lightly.

That's not what woke me in the middle of the night! Abe went through Sharon's belongings…

"There wasn't a fly on your forehead, girl. So what's up? You just thought of something."

Willie Nell voiced her thoughts to Atlee. "Where did all my mother's things go that were in the trailer? Does Miz Edie know? Sheriff Alvie? I have to find them. She always carried a pasteboard hatbox with her. Carried her Stetson in it, but what else?"

The old cop sat silently, letting his surrogate daughter muse.

"Could a copy of her audition tape or any clues be in it? Her costumes? I want them even though no clues or stuff of any importance might be with them. But who knows?"

And there were those wonderful scrapbooks — her diary!

"So," Atlee said, "check first with this person, then the sheriff, even the trailer park manager. Somebody has to know. After all, as next of kin, that stuff belongs to you, and your sister.

"But not much can be done at 6 in the morning. so it'll have to wait till the rest of the world's awake."

Atlee sipped his quickly cooling latte, wishing he had ordered his usual Café Americano, a real eye opener consisting of three or four shots of espresso with a roughly equal amount of hot water.

"Damn it Abe, this fucking insomnia's gonna make an old lady outta me if I don't watch it. Too much coffee late in the day, then up before dawn for more caffeine."

"Too much worrying about the rest of us on the Task Force, Mother Hen."

Willie Nell was grateful that Atlee was smiling as he chided her.

"You're heading out from here, right?" Willie Nell needed to change the subject. If she thought much more about her mother and all the things she had that were still not accounted for, she'd burst into tears right here in public.

"I'll take the old toll road to Fort Worth, then I-20 out west to pick up I-10 on into El Paso. I figure I'll pull in around tomorrow night.... getting too old to drive straight through."

"I have a Thermos in my SUV; why don't you let me fill it with some good ol' Starbug's breakfast blend as a going-away present?"

Atlee started to protest, then realized it would be a slap in the face of this dear girl who wanted to do something for him. He acquiesced.

Willie Nell excused herself and hurried out to her personal gas hog. She returned with the large stainless-steel-lined insulated bottle, the Thermos manufacturer's top of the line. Beaming, she walked straight to the counter. "Give this a good, hot rinse and fill it for me please. Breakfast Blend."

After paying, she returned to Atlee at the little table. "Don't forget to pick up some fixin's before you go," she reminded him.

"I just use artificial sweetener, and I keep some in my ashtray since I'm a nonsmoker. And you're playing Mother Hen again."

Willie Nell laughed brightly. "Oh, I'm gonna miss you, Abie Baby."

Minutes later, she saw her Thermos on the drink counter, and rose to retrieve it.

"I'll get it, relax. You have the stopper in your hand, though." Atlee took the stopper and retrieved the coffee, added three packets of sweetener, and then sealed the bottle.

Willie Nell followed him outside to his big Ford. "Gimme a hug, you lug. You better drive like a fuckin' little old lady. If anything happens to you, I'd …" her voice trailed off.

Atlee saw the tears trying to spill and pulled her close to him. "You're special to me, too, Willie Nell. And if that big galoot Grady gives you a hard time, you tell him he'll have me to answer to."

"Grady's great," she sniffled, wiping an eye, but smiling.

"Well, I think he's kinda sweet on you, you know."

You're kidding!"

"God's truth. Probably afraid he's too old for you, though."

"Fuck. Abe, I like my guys to have a few miles on 'em," she laughed. "They got better stories to tell; and us writers are suckers for a guy with a good yarn."

"Maybe I'll return with a tale or two myself," he said as he strapped himself into the Crown Victoria. "Hope so, anyway. Hate for this to be a wasted trip."

Atlee closed the door, backed out of the parking space, and negotiated his way out of the parking lot that was quickly becoming congested with the "on-my-way-to-work" Starbucks crowd.

Hell, if Abe's starting his investigation, I guess I'd better get my skinny butt back to Sonora.

64

Willie Nell flipped open her cell phone to alert Eyidie that she was on her way back home. "I'm coming with some more questions. You think a wayward gal could crash on your couch tonight? I remember many a night spent there while Mama was working and Dude was out doing Lord-knows-what!"

"Well, you're a mite longer in the leg now, Sweetpea, but I reckon I could find a quilt or two for a pallet."

Both of them laughed. Of course, Eyidie wouldn't allow a guest to camp out in the living room, even though the couch made out into a sleeper sofa. She still kept the room where Sunny and Willie Nell slept as children as a guest room.

"It could stretch into several days, Miz Edie. I'm revisiting Mama's murder as part of a Dallas police Task Force. There's a real probability that whoever murdered her also killed several other women over all these years."

The old black woman gasped. "Goodness, baby, how'd you get wrapped up in such a thing?"

"I'm a journalist, Nana, remember?" Willie Nell was the only child who ever referred to Eyidie Nwaigbo in such a manner. It began when the old woman was babysitting her as a six-year-old and reading Peter Pan to her.

"I need to find the rest of Mama's belongings. There could be clues among them. Do you know where her stuff wound up?

"I recall a hatbox she kept with what she called her 'singing duds'."

"Well, we had to put 'em someplace safe and I didn't have room nor the heart to hang onto them."

"You didn't get rid of them?" Willie Nell was aghast.

"No, no, no child! I wouldn't do that. As survivors, you and your sister own them now. Reverend Taylor, Brock, told me to put everything in one of those storage warehouses you rent by the month. He's been paying that $50 rental every month since."

"Do you have a key, or do I need to call Uncle Brock … Reverend Taylor?" To Willie Nell, Reverend Taylor Taylor was a dear friend and counselor, a substitute for her absentee father who wasn't really ever there for her. Even before his death, the combination of his rodeoing and his drinking kept Dude estranged from his daughter. Despite the close confines of the little trailer, she remembered feeling like they were strangers as they'd pass in the narrow hall. This was her legacy from Dude after years of broken promises, the fear each night that he'd come home roaring drunk, the fear of the unknown that children of alcoholics know all too well. Underneath all that was the dread that one night he wouldn't come home at all, that the police would bring the news of the alcohol-induced wreck.

Willie Nell shuddered at the memories, glad she was on the cell phone and that Miz Edie couldn't see it. It had happened pretty much like that, like she had always feared it would, at least from the time she began to understand what her daddy was like when he drank.

"We were talking about Reverend Brock, baby girl, and you went all quiet. Don't you pay for these calls by the minute?"

Her old nana and dear friend's voice yanked Willie Nell from thoughts about that awful night. "I was thinking about Uncle Brock," she lied. She had gone to his church until she left Sonora, and he often drove the 80 miles to San Angelo to pick her up at the children's home to bring her to church some Sundays. She'd loved that. It meant she'd also get to visit half the day with her mama. Even now she still had trouble thinking of him as "reverend", and he preferred Uncle Brock, anyway.

"No, I told the preacher I didn't want the key. Figured if he was paying for it, he could be trusted." Eyidie explained. "I'll call him right now. He can bring me the key or go with us, whatever you want."

"No, I want to do this myself. It will be nice to see him again, but I probably need to handle it alone. If there's evidence there, I need to preserve the chain of possession, and I wouldn't be allowed to tell folks about it except members of the Task Force." Willie Nell closed the phone to break the connection, and continued her drive through the Texas Hill Country, her mind bouncing from memory to memory. Pictures of Mama as Lions' Club Queen. Even though it was January, she remembered, her mother was dressed in a spaghetti-strap evening gown, bare shouldered and without a wrap of any kind as she waved from a blue convertible.

Where is that picture now?

She recalled another picture, a clipping from the newspaper. It was Dude riding in the Sutton County Outlaw Days Rodeo. How Willie Nell had bawled, thinking her daddy had been an outlaw, until Eyidie explained that the cowboys weren't outlaws, and that was just a name for the rodeo.

What thoughts run through a child's mind when they're little.

"If that was sponsored by the Professional Rodeo Cowboys Association (PRCA), did that mean Dude was a pro?" she asked herself.

Of course he was a pro. He made the payments for the trailer and bought groceries with what prize money he'd bring home — after celebrating, of course, at one local honky-tonk or another.

Noting with dismay that all the cafes and truck stops featured the usual fried everything or else a greasy Tex-Mex menu, Willie Nell opted to continue driving up the caliche road to the trailer park and Eyidie.

Nana's always got something. I can just taste her red beans and cornbread with honey. Mmmmm.

Angora goats nibbled at the stubble of grass alongside the dirt road to the trailer park. Big dogs still ran up and barked at her car. Not many vehicles passed by on the hard-packed caliche road with its gravel.

A doe and her fawn lay in a shallow culvert a little further into the fields between the park and the highway. Willie Nell slowed down, trying not to spook them. She feared they might leap into her path. Hitting them wouldn't do much good to the SUV she drove or to the animals. She shuddered at the thought.

Not a lot had changed since she last was here. The pansies in the flower beds, the hanging begonia pot, and the rickety old rocker on the deck of the trailer. Eyidie's place. Couldn't be anyone else's.

She didn't honk; just parked and walked up to the three steps leading to the doorway.

Eyidie opened the door and her arms to the girl as she reached the top step. "You look tired. Get on in here."

"Tired, yep. And hungry!"

Willie Nell's memories of pinto beans and cornbread were accurate, they were as good as she recalled. Finishing a second wedge of buttered cornbread drizzled with honey, she leaned back in satisfaction. "That was good eatin', Miz Edie."

"Thanks, not fancy but it fills in the hollow spots," Eyidie 's usual reply.

"You said Reverend Taylor had Mama's things? How did that come about?"

"Well, the manager said he could store them for about $50 more a month than I could afford."

"How much did the trailer park manager ask?"

"Fifty a month," she replied with a grin. "You know with my income and my outgo about the same, there just wasn't any money for me to take on the responsibility. So, Brock said he'd be glad to see after them until you or your sister asked for them."

"I didn't even think about anyone having to store her things!"

"Child, you were 10 years old. How could you think about stuff like that? I know you had some real grown-up ways about you, but girl, you were still wet behind the ears. Reverend Taylor and me took on the task of settling Lacey's affairs. Him more than me, actually. It was like I lost my own child when your sweet mother was kilt."

Eyidie reached out and covered Willie Nell's soft, white hand with a callused, mahogany one. "I only kept one little picture, just like the one you got of her and Dude's wedding, the lovesick girl with flowers in her hair and the goofy grinning guy with the Stetson."

"I wondered if you might have any thoughts about who …" the young woman's voice broke, "… could have done such a thing to her?"

"I've racked this old head of mine and come up empty every time. Unless some drunken cowboy followed her home from the Rusty Spur, like I told the police …" She shrugged. "Don't have no new ideas on it."

65

The next morning, Willie Nell called Reverend Taylor at the church. He invited her to come by and pick up the key.

Reverend Taylor was standing in front of the church when she drove up. He handed her the key through the driver's window, and offered to go along. "A lot of those boxes are pretty good size. I also might need to move some of Lacey's furniture. Your furniture now," he corrected himself.

Willie Nell really wanted to talk to her old friend. He'd always been good at helping her focus. She had parlayed those skills to excel in college, and honed them to apply in her career. "Thanks for the offer."

"Let me tell my people I'm going." Reverend Taylor turned and walked toward the church door.

Willie Nell quickly jumped down out of the SUV and trotted after him. "I'd kinda like to see the old church."

"Come on, then." Reverend Taylor stopped at the coat racks just inside the door and pulled a weathered old Resistol˚ from a peg.

"That's the same hat you've always had, isn't it? I remember you in it when Sunny was born and you baptized her. Nearly 15 years ago?"

"I'm afraid it looks its age, too," the preacher smiled at the reporter and continued to his office.

He didn't sit down at the desk, but pressed the intercom button on the phone. "I'm going out for a bit with Willie Nell Autrey, Pauline. See if you can hold the fort down."

The elderly woman who worked only part-time for the modest church, blushed. "This fort could run on its own, you know that, Reverend Taylor."

Turning to Willie Nell, he winked. "I think you're entirely too modest, Pauline. Between you and my wife, you leave me little work but to meet with the flock and come up with the occasional topic for a sermon."

"Don't sin, tithe generously, treasure your family, and help the needy. Those are your four topics every month, year after year," the smallish woman chided, sticking her head out of the office door. "What time should I tell folks you'll be back?"

"Don't count on me being back today. I'll call you again when I get a better idea of what's what out at the Lacey Jay warehouse."

Willie Nell walked over to the woman in the doorway, extended her hand, and said. "I'm Willie Nell Autrey. Happy to see you again, Pauline."

A secretary often has more information than the boss — always stay on their good side.

"I remember you children. How's your dear little sister? Such a tragedy."

"We're fine. I'm trying to get a handle on exactly what happened to my mom."

"I won't keep you two, then." Pauline said, quickly returning to her own desk.

Willie Nell and Reverend Taylor got into his vehicle, a larger SUV with plenty of room for whatever she might need to haul out of storage.

Storage! I probably owe a fortune for storing this stuff all these years.

"Reverend Taylor?" she began. "... Brock ..."

"Brock's just fine. Used to be Uncle Brock when you were little but that was before ..." his voice trailed off.

"Yeah, a long time ago, before Mama died. I know."

"You were going to ask me something Willie Nell. Is it about your mother?"

"I just wanted to know to whom and how much I owe for the storage unit. I feel strange knowing someone was paying my debt all these years."

"I did that, and you don't owe me. You kid's couldn't pay it, and your mother was very dear to me, a special friend."

Reverend Taylor's face grew thoughtful, and he kept his eyes looking straight ahead. "I really want to talk to you about her soon, but not right now."

They drove to the mini-warehouse complex and the preacher was headed to the card-secured gate when Willie Nell shouted, "Stop! Stop this truck. I want to go to the manager's office before I forget." The big Hummer SUV had barely stopped when Willie Nell jumped down. "I'll just be a second. Wait here," she said over her shoulder, walking briskly through the glass door to the warehouse rental office.

An old man wearing clean but ill-fitting jeans and a too-large white shirt was behind the counter. Above a breast pocket, a plastic tag proclaimed "Manager".

"I'm Willie Nell Autrey and I want to change the responsibility of paying the storage on Lacey Autrey's ... well, my stuff. Bill me, not Reverend Taylor."

If he was surprised, the old man didn't show it; the manager merely nodded, asked for her Social Security number, and hit a few strokes on the computer with palsied fingers. "Where shall I mail the bills?" he asked.

She gave him the TV station's address in Dallas and began filling out the single sheet he handed her.

"Do you have the preacher's keycard, or will you be needing a second one?"

"I will have his," she said. "But I probably should have two more, one for my sister and another for Miz Edie."

"You'll have to put both names on that there form you're workin' on."

Willie Nell entered the two names, signed the form, and handed it back to the old man, who handed her back two shiny new plastic cards saying, "Your code is your warehouse number plus the last four digits of your Social Security number."

"You're off the hook," she announced climbing back into the Hummer. "I'll pay for the storage from now on."

263

"You didn't have to do that,' Reverend Taylor said softly.

"Yes, I did. I make more money than any Texas preacher, and you've done more than enough for this family over the years."

Reverend Taylor used his keycard, drove through the electric gate, and handed the card to Willie Nell. "Guess you'll want this and my key then."

As soon as he parked, Willie Nell jumped out of the car. "I think I can handle things from here out, Brock."

"I think I'll hang around anyway. You might change your mind. It's not a long walk back to your car at the church but if you need brawn, I have it."

Willie Nell took the offered card and key to a warehouse unit the size of a two-car garage; the door slid up into the ceiling like a garage door. She tugged at the corrugated steel door, trying to raise it, to no avail even with a generous amount of swearing.

As Willie Nell tugged, Reverend Taylor said softly, "Looks like it's been awhile since that one has been opened. Let me try." Reverend Taylor stepped around Willie Nell, grasped the handle, and heaved. The door slid up on rollers with a long, loud squeal of metal against metal.

She made no comment as he preceded her into the dark room. The preacher reached up and pulled a cord to turn on a single overhead bulb. When she began to scour the room with her gaze, he asked what she was looking for.

"Mama had this hatbox. She always carried it with her. It holds … held her purple Stetson and Lord knows what other shit. Sorry, I need to clean up my language around you, I suppose."

"I don't have virgin ears, Willie Nell. And I think that hatbox would be over on top of that chiffonier holding her costumes. Since I never opened it, neither the Lord nor I could tell you what's inside the hatbox." He grinned at her.

"Just put it in the Hummer. We have a lot of stuff to go through here."

"What are you hoping to find?"

"I haven't got a clue." Willie Nell suddenly laughed. "And that's the problem; we're looking for clues to turn over to the Lacey Jay Task Force investigating Mama's murder, along with about a gazillion others, all apparently by the same creep.

"Kinda eerie laughing about it, huh?"

Reverend Taylor smiled. "Laughter's often no more than a way to relieve tension."

"They teach you that in preacher school?"

"Some things are learned without you realizing it. For instance, you have a lot of anger and you cover it with profanity. Is that your way of avoiding closeness?"

"No psycho–babble, please. I just want an extra pair of eyes to help me look for anything relevant to their lives which might give us a clue to who may have been responsible for Mama's death. I'm not in the mood or the market for a shrink, thank you very much."

Reverend Taylor decided to wait before approaching any other topics, at least for now, including the biggie.

He found a box with Lacey's block letters declaring its contents to be keepsakes. "Here's one box you'd want to go through for sure." He hauled it out to the Hummer.

"Keepsakes, that covers a lot of territory," Willie Nell said. "I wonder what deep dark secrets I'll find inside?"

Reverend Taylor thought that was a perfect lead-in for what he planned to tell her.

66

They rode in silence back to the church, ostensibly to retrieve Willie Nell's vehicle, but Reverend Taylor asked her to come inside for a moment as soon as he parked the SUV. "I have something I'd like to share with you."

"If it's about Mama, okay," she said tentatively.

He nodded and led the way to the chapel. He sat on the front pew and the girl sat beside him.

Reverend Taylor sat very still and said a silent prayer:

Lord, help me tell her without her losing more respect for her mother. I want to make her understand that we were both very young and quite different people back then.

Reverend Taylor cleared his throat. "Another reason I'm glad you contacted me, Willie Nell is to tell you that Dude wasn't your father."

"What?" Willie Nell sat stunned by the blunt pronouncement from the preacher who had instructed her in her faith all the years she was growing up.

"That's a damned lie," she finally choked out in fury. "My mother loved that miserable drunk and took him back more times than Carter has little liver pills. I do not believe she would ever be unfaithful to him."

"No, darling girl. She was pregnant with you before they married. I didn't even know it until much later."

"What difference does it make when you found out? I still don't believe it." She folded her arms and caught her lower lip between her teeth. "Wait a damned minute. You trying to say you're my ... that you and mom... "

Reverend Taylor nodded. "You're my daughter, Willie Nell."

The fury Willie Nell felt was replaced by nausea and dizziness. This apparition was calmly destroying all of her cherished memories of her long-dead parents.

"It doesn't matter what you may think of me," Reverend Taylor said, breaking the silence. "Just know that your mother made her choice and that it was Dude she loved and married. She and I remained friends, but only friends."

"Yeah, right," Willie Nell's anger was back, but now it was brittle. "Sunny had our folks figured out better than I ever thought," she said, disdain in her wavering voice, "I was the one who was misguided. My mother was a fucking round-heeled party girl after all! She really did just dump us kids so she could live the honky-tonk life." Tears flowed unimpeded down her ashen face.

"I will not have you speak that way about your mother." Reverend Taylor's voice was stern. "She only told me about you after she decided to place you in the children's home. She had no choice. I was the one who suggested the Scottish Rite hospital for Sunny since it would be capable of bearing the expenses for Sunny's many surgeries."

"Well, Daddy," she said, her words dripping with sarcasm, "what does wifey-poo think about all this?"

He could feel her eyes boring into the side of his head, but he couldn't face her anger.

Staring straight ahead, the preacher replied, "My wife accepts the facts and would like to form a relationship with my daughter and her sister at a time you are both ready to do so. In fact, she's the one who told me to tell you. She's right; you two need a family. I'm here whenever you're ready to have me in your life."

"That'll be when Lucifer needs ice skates!" Willie Nell huffed. "Listen, Preacher Man, I'm not going to just automatically fling myself into your arms and say, oh Daddy we should go tell Sunny the good news," she said in a sing-song voice dripping with sarcasm.

"That's not what I expect at all. I want us to get to know each other and hopefully…"

Willie Nell slapped him with a resounding crack. "I am so damned fucking mad at you for keeping this secret from me. Why the Hell didn't you come to me when Mama died?"

He hung his head. "Go ahead and vent, I'm handy and strong enough to bear it."

"Handy my ass, Brock Taylor you're responsible for me having to bear all this alone. My sister's crippled—I was left without even the comfort of Sunny with me. I repeat—why didn't you tell me?"

"I was in my new pastorate. I didn't want to upset your life anymore than it had already been. I could use a million excuses. Truth be told, I was scared."

"Scared to tell your own daughter that she was yours?" She scoffed.

"No, scared I'd lose my wife and my congregation and that you'd hate me and your mother as much as you hated Dude for his drinking."

"So what's different now? Did you hear from the Most High? Did you get some sort of message from God that now was the time I could take the shattering of my life once again?"

Her words stung Reverend Taylor more than the slap had.

"My wife changed my mind. She wanted to know why we didn't know my daughter, our daughter existed, and why wasn't she allowed to get to know her? A girl needs a mother, even one with no experience. She and I want to learn to be a part of your life and Sunny's if that's possible." Tears escaped the corners of his eyes. "Do you think you could give us a chance, Willie?"

"I'll have to think on that. Right now, I'm on the trail of my mother's killer. My mind's full of crap right now and I'm not thinking as clearly as I could be. We'll take this topic up later." She paused and clutched the letters she'd found in her mother's hatbox.

"I wish Mama could be here to help me explain to Sunny all that's become apparent to me. For instance I know Dude wasn't drinking. The coroner's report says that as plain as your fuckin' nose on your face." She turned to Reverend Taylor, "Sorry, Pop. I have a lifetime of ingrained profanity to overcome. I know all you had to overcome is a fling with my mother. Resulting in — ta-da — me!"

"You couldn't be more wrong. I loved your mother but discovered I loved the Lord more and she decided she loved Dude more. We've always been close. When she told me about your being my daughter—I was overwhelmed but glad to acknowledge you."

"Better late than never, I suppose but hey, we're both too old for adoption. Back to my original topic of discussion. Me and Sunny and our … the people we thought were both parents to us." Willie Nell blinked as though an unpleasant thought occurred to her. "If I decide I need you to help me bring her through this with as little additional damage to her fragile psyche as possible, think we could pull that off?"

"I don't know, Honey, but I'm willing to do whatever we can to help your sister. How do you want to handle this?"

"Hey, you're the fucking professional with all the initials after your name. I'm just a reporter with a crazy mixed up kid sister who's saddled with a handicap. We'll just have to rely on each other's savvy in their own little niche. Besides, like I said, I've got a killer to find."

How can I not forgive him? It looks like he's turned his life around better than the man I always thought of as my daddy did.

Or did he? People say Dude was on the wagon and the wreck wasn't his fault. Guess they both made their own kind of restitution. For all I know, mama was as good a person as I always thought. Even good people make mistakes!

"When did you plan on telling me? What if I hadn't come back right now?"

"I hadn't made that decision. I figure the Lord would make it happen in His own time," Reverend Taylor said quietly. "And He has."

"You hypocrite! All this talk about forgiveness and taking responsibility. You pious son of a bitch, you've had ample time to be a father to me." Willie Nell's anger didn't abate as she paused to take a breath. "But, who was there when it counted? Not you. It was Dude, as disreputable as he was, he was there for us. He did what he could and so did Mama. Miz Edie was our surrogate grandma. We were a family."

Reverend Taylor sat solemnly and looked at this daughter he never bothered to know on an intimate level and winced inwardly at her words.

Willie Nell let the tears flow, not bothering to wipe them. "If you could be classified as anything, it's basically a sperm donor. Had you truly wanted to be a real father, you would have stepped up and claimed me. Why do you think Lacey told you? If it had been simply to unburden herself, she could have done that during one of your counseling sessions. She told you because she needed help with us. That was the time you should have …" A sob broke her composure and she wept heavily and loudly as she burst from the chapel.

Driving back to Eyidie's may not have been the smartest thing Willie Nell had done. She couldn't stop the tears, and they were blurring her vision.

Then her cell phone rang.

I'll be damned if I talk to that son of a bitch!

She yanked the little phone out of her purse and was relieved that the number calling was Ed Soames.

67

Brock drove home in silence, stunned by Willie Nell's outburst. Arriving at the comfortable brick home supplied by the church, he parked and steeled himself to discuss the exchange he'd had with Willie Nell with Ruth

"I've lost my daughter," Reverend Taylor wailed miserably between the fingers cupping his face as he sat on the edge of the sofa.

"That's not true, Brock. You abandoned your daughter, then rode in like a knight on a white horse to rescue her when she no longer needed you," his wife said, icily.

At that moment, the preacher realized that not only had he lost Willie Nell, he had forfeited the respect of the woman he loved. He also now feared his marriage might not survive his neglect of his now grown love-child.

"Ruth …"

His wife turned toward him, hands on hips.

"Can we … survive … this?" he asked, now fearing for his marriage.

"You self-absorbed, selfish, lazy bastard!" Ruth exploded. "That's the wrong question altogether. You should be worrying about whether Willie Nell and her little sister can survive the bombshell you laid on them just to assuage your guilt.

"As for us, of course we'll go on.

"Honey, I knew you weren't the bravest of the brave or the strongest of the strong when I met you. But I knew you were a good man."

Reverend Taylor was stunned for the second time this day, and by another woman. His sweet little choir-girl Ruth, who had meekly followed his lead through 20 years of marriage, was baring her feelings about him, too. And it wasn't pleasant.

"You went to seminary because you saw it as an easy life. You're a decent preacher, but you never had the fire in your belly like my daddy did," Ruth continued in a softer voice.

"But I loved you, so I overlooked your faults. Today was the first time I ever knew you to do something to hurt someone else, so I suspect the secret you carried all these years just got too heavy.

"Do I wish you were stronger? Yes, at least strong enough that you don't have to break the hearts of young women who have no parents. But would I leave you over it? Of course not.

"I love you, Brock. You're the only man outside my daddy I've ever loved, and you know it."

The preacher listened to the ugliness his wife was speaking and knew it was all true. Reverend Taylor found that he could take money from one parishioner to help another and be the hero of the story every time. He knew that he was accepted by the community as a good man without having to do anything more daring than preach to his congregation and listen to their problems.

A sliver of resolve ran through him. "What can I do to fix this?"

"My darling husband, I don't think there's anything you could say right now, but maybe I can pour a little oil on these troubled waters myself. Just give me directions to where Willie Nell is staying."

68

"This is Willie Nell."

"How's it going?" Ed Soames asked. "What can I do you for?"

"I have some things of my parents that I need fresh eyes to look at. You got time for coffee?" she asked.

"Can I take a rain check? Besides, you sound tuckered out. Let's get together later this evening. If I don't get some food and some rest, I wouldn't be able to solve a knock-knock joke!"

What she should be concentrating on was the serial killer, but Willie Nell thirsted for information about Dude's life and death. "I'd like you to talk to Dexter Worley about my dad's car wreck. His name was on the report as having called it in. See if he has anything more to add than what's written on the report."

Soames agreed. "If I can find out anything, I'll be sure to fill you in. So far, I don't have any leads on our cold case here in Sonora. Sorry."

"I didn't think it'd be easy. Too many years have passed. My own memories are askew, things I thought I knew proved wrong. Might be the same with everyone who knows something but just have filled in some blanks with impressions and gossip—not with facts. Later."

She flipped the phone shut.

Who would believe that my first major story would be about my own mother's murder?

Willie Nell headed back to Eyidie 's. The impact of her task weighed heavily on her mind, and her heart.

69

Willie Nell tapped her horn when she pulled up to Eyidie 's place. Within a few seconds, the deep chocolate face peered out the screen door, then unlocked it to let her young friend inside.

"What you got there, girl? I recognize the hat box as Lacey's. What's in the other box?" She closed the door behind them.

"I found these two when Brock and I went into the storage room. Since the mystery seems to revolve around what happened to both of them in death, I aim to find out as much as I can about them."

"Your folks weren't all that complicated, Willie Nell."

With a scoff, Willie Nell answered, "How little you know! Dude's not my father. I only found that out today. Or did you know?" She set probing eyes on her old nanny. Putting the boxes on the counter which served as breakfast bar, prep-station, and catch-all, she placed her hands on her hips in a gesture the elderly woman had often seen.

"Don't you go accusing me, girl. If I had known, and I didn't, it weren't my place to tell any of her secrets. How, if you want to say, did you find out?"

"He told me himself. He's known since before my mama died. Did you know he's been bearing lots of the expenses of mine and Sunny's?"

"You sure are full of questions. Mind if I brew us some tea and let's sit and talk in more friendly tones?" Without waiting for an answer, she turned to the cupboard and took out her teabags and began to draw water into a kettle. "Get the honey out of the fridge and see if there's any lemon in there."

Used to obeying Eyidie's directions, Willie Nell did as she was told. "Let's assume you didn't know any of this. Why didn't he tell me before this?"

"Depends on who he is, I suspect."

"Oh, sorry, it's the Right Reverend Brock Taylor, of all people. Now, ain't that a kick in the head!?"

With a heavy sigh, the old woman turned with a nod. "I can see that happening. She needed so much love. Never had much as a child. Her father, your granddaddy had an imbibing habit, too. Lacey spent most of her time trying to please him, then ups and marries somebody just like him. I will say this for your daddy, err Dude—he straightened himself out. Now, Lacey's daddy drank himself into the ground."

"That's no excuse, Miz Edie, for an illegitimate baby—" she choked on the words.

"Now, listen here, Missy, there's no such thing as an illegitimate baby. The parents did the deed not the child. Besides, if I can count and I pride myself that I can, you came along just after nine months. Maybe Lacey was wrong—though you do have the mark of your father on your chin."

"I wondered if anyone else thought about my having a cleft in my chin and Sunny didn't. I often questioned in my mind why we didn't look anything alike. She's so delicate and petite. I'm short but rather lusty like Lacey. It kind of makes sense now looking back. Reverend Taylor was so kind to us, taking care of the family when Dude was gone."

"That's just his way, Honey. He did that long before if as you say he didn't know in the beginning. With his calling, he always took care of everybody. Why he even tried to care for me—like I needed it!" she said with a huff.

The whistle of the teakettle drew her attention back to the business of preparing tea. She poured two cups over teabags. The women dipped and dipped again to get the color just to their liking. Then, Willie Nell stirred honey into hers and both squeezed some lemon into the brew.

"This is so much better than whiskey. Why couldn't Dude or Granddaddy get hooked on tea?!" Willie asked solemnly.

"You going to open those boxes and see what's inside?" Eyidie asked, stirring her cup with a clinking sound as the spoon struck the side.

"I'm scared. I want to know what's in here," Willie Nell's hands trembled as she spoke, "but then what if I find out more secrets than I can stand."

"You want me to do the honors?" her old nanny asked.

"No, as much as I'd like to forget I ever found these things, I need to know," she spoke as she continued to untie it, "especially since it might help find her killer."

The young woman untied the hatbox, removed the lid, and laid it aside. Reaching into the box, she withdrew a stack of letters tied with a ribbon, more of the spiral books like the others and an old cassette tape. "Do you have a cassette player?" she asked Eyidie .

"Round here somewhere. I'll look. You open up some of the books or letters. No sense in both us digging around here."

Willie Nell opened one of the books and began to read. Bits and pieces of familiar songs were scrawled there, along with notes about her and her baby sister when Lacey sang to them.

"My grown up little Willie Nell listens so hard to the words, it's like she wants to brand them on her brain," Lacey wrote.

"Sunny claps her little hands and tries to sing along. If one of the girls becomes musical, it'll be her. She loves music. Even tried to pick a guitar string but it cut her soft little fingers and she cried. When I get money enough, she ought to have a piano."

Willie Nell wiped at tears threatening to pour over her cheeks.

"Sunny, how could you think she didn't love us? One thing's for damn sure. I need to let you read this page if I have to hogtie you."

Eyidie came into the room just then and handed Willie Nell some mail addressed to Lacey. "I found these while I was searching for the tape player."

"One's from Nashville and it's not opened!" the girl exclaimed.

"I wouldn't open anyone's mail but my own. The postman left it here and I just plumb forgot about it."

"Don't you know what this means?" Willie asked.

"Not a clue," the black woman said. She wore a quizzical look on her face.

"She probably sent one of her tapes to Nashville. This must be an answer."

They inserted the tape and Lacey's contralto voice came across the years to her daughter:

> *Life is like a ball of yarn*
> *Kitten plays with while you're gone.*
>
> *Slaps it 'round the livelong day*
> *Over'n under ev'ry whichway!*
>
> *'Til it's gone and in its place*
> *A spiderweb fills the space*
>
> *A hundred knots bright red shade*
> *with tangled loops that kitten made*
>
> *I'll untie the snarls and knit a shawl*
> *And wrap it warmly 'round you all.*
>
> *Wrapped now in the wooly red,*
> *I hug my babes and off to bed.*

Both women now had tears in their eyes. Eyidie walked over and took the younger woman in an embrace and hugged her tightly. "How she loved you girls."

"I know, now, Sunny has to see it, too. I think I should just gather up all this stuff and take it back to Dallas.

"I'm supposed to be part of a task force looking into all this information about the victims. That helps create a profile of the killer and perhaps we can see what the common denominator is! So far, all I'm sure of is the women are about the same age, beautiful and blonde—he has sex with them but it doesn't seem to be rape. Either he drugs them or they're willing."

70

"You think you need to leave now?" Eyidie asked. "You just got here. Let's go through these things together, then you go back. Don't want no surprises among strangers, do you?"

"Not all of them are strangers, Miz Edie, but you're right about one thing. If I have a melt-down, I'd rather it was with you."

The old black woman hugged the girl close. "Now, let's see if I can shed any light on whatever's in those boxes."

As the two women sat down to dig through the boxes, a knock sounded on the door. A well-dressed, though rather ordinary woman stood at the door which Eydie opened.

Eyidie introduced the two women. "Willie Nell, this is Mrs. Taylor, the reverend's wife."

"Pleased to meet you," Willie Nell said perfunctorily and extended her hand.

"I'm not at all sure how I feel about it," Mrs. Taylor replied.

"Really? Your husband thought we'd get along quite well, even thought we should become family of a sort."

"That was before you were so rude to my husband and before you made yourself judge and jury over your parents."

Willie Nell squirmed a little under her scrutiny. "I don't know if this is something I should be discussing with you. It's between your husband and me."

"As his wife, Brock and I are a unit in big decisions. What concerns him, concerns me. I don't know how you could be so callous to him. When he found out from Lacey that you were more than likely his child, he wanted to be involved in your life. He rushed to the hasty conclusion that he'd lose all if he confessed to me."

Willie Nell nodded. "That's what he told me."

"I tried to convince him that if God could forgive him, so could I. After all, it was before we met and we – well, I'm unable to have children. You could have had such a different life."

"Ain't it the truth? I don't see what all this has to do with the cost of tea in China."

"Lord sakes," Eyidie remarked, "speaking of tea, I forgot to offer any to Mrs. Taylor."

"That would be lovely, thank you. Edie."

As she busied herself in the kitchen alcove, Willie Nell continued to browse through the items in front of her. "I admit I feel rather awkward, Mrs. Taylor."

The woman on the couch looked down at the young woman sitting cross-legged on the floor with books and letters scattered around her. "Funny, but I feel very comfortable. We should have met years ago. My husband was hesitant to intrude in the life you'd made for yourself. When he was in DFW airport one time, he came home telling me about seeing you on TV. He was so proud. I told him then, he should contact you but he kept making excuses."

"Mrs. Taylor, did you know Lacey, my mother?"

"She sang in our choir for a little while. My husband counseled her regarding her husband's abuse, or so I assumed. When she came to see him, she bore signs of bruising on her face although she tried to cover it with make-up. He'd never divulge anything a person told him in confidence. That's not his way."

"Mrs. Taylor ..." Willie Nell began.

"Do you think you could manage to call me Ruth?" She asked with a smile. "You call him Brock and me Mrs. Taylor; one might think I was his mother."

"Not a chance!" Eyidie said, popping her head back in the door. "You're much too young to be his mother. Here's your tea. I put a dollop of honey and a squirt of lemon in it. That's how me and Willie Nell take it."

"Sounds grand." She took a sip. "… and it is."

Willie Nell decided to start going through into Dude's things, rather than her mother's, since Ruth Taylor had joined tea party. If there was anything in Lacey's things about Brock …

I don't want to go there just yet. Not in the presence of his wife, of all people.

The hatbox contained little things she had yet to look over. Willien Nell dumped the box onto the floor in front of her. A resounding clunk drew everybody's attention to one item: a large belt buckle with a bull rider image on the front.

Willie Nell turned it over to read the inscription on the back:

Champion Bull Rider

Smoky the Bear Stampede and Rodeo

Capitan, New Mexico

"My dad, uh … Dude never set foot in New Mexico," Willie Nell told the other two women. "I went with him to a lot of the rodeos and I followed his circuit religiously and he sure as shit never won a buckle in New Mexico."

"Wonder whose it is?" Eyidie asked of no one in particular. "If somebody else found it, they most likely thought it was his and just chunked it in his box."

"That's mighty fucking interesting!" She flipped on her phone and dialed Soames' number.

71

"You got a phone call, says it's important, Ed somebody."

I just got off the phone with Soames; why would he be calling again so soon?

Willie Nell fought her way to consciousness, the dream of her mother singing to her already a will-o-the wisp and slipping away.

Good Lord! I don't even remember going to bed.

She took her cell from Eyidie.

"Hullo," she said, groggily.

"Up and at 'em! I got news." Soames said cheerily. "Let me buy you breakfast and I'll tell you all about it."

"Only if it comes with coffee in half-gallon mugs. Pick me up in 30 minutes. Gotta get my innards to working first."

She hung up and looked up. Eyidie was holding out a steaming mug. "Some things never change, Sweetpea. You and your mama weren't neither one any good in the mornings until that first cup of coffee."

Soames was on time and Willie Nell was still trying to dry her hair. "Fuck it! It can dry itself." Grabbing her purse and cell phone, she pecked Eyidie on the cheek on her way out.

At the Breakfast Nook, the detective and the reporter placed their orders for spinach and mushroom omelets, with bacon on the side and coffee.

"Okay, what's the big news, Eddie?" Willie Nell knew Ed didn't like to be called Eddie, but she had vowed that as long as he called her Willie instead of Willie Nell, he could live with it.

"The accident that killed Dude was Dexter Worley's fault!" Soames was beaming.

"But the tire tracks, the police report...."

"Misinterpreted."

The breakfast orders arrived and the two Task Force partners busied themselves for a few minutes doctoring the fresh, hot coffee and buttering the home-made biscuits.

After testing his coffee mixture and finding it to his satisfaction, Soames continued his report, explaining that Dexter, who inherited a wealthy car dealership, had nearly lost everything to drugs and alcohol after the wreck.

"He was just waiting to purge himself. When I said Dude's daughters wanted to know more about what happened to their daddy, well, he just lost it."

Soames explained about the lane-changing tire tracks and how Dexter made up the story that became the official report. Ed told Willie Nell that not only had Dude not been speeding, he'd not had anything to drink, according to the coroner report.

She could only nod. Willie Nell was surprised by her lack of surprise. She had already forgiven Dude for the accident after she learned he wasn't drunk. Soames was just giving her details, eroded by 14 years of their hard edge. But she knew someone else whose edge was still plenty sharp. Sunny.

"Wait, there's more," Soames continued. "I learned that The VFW commander at the time, Carl Hansen, was your father's AA sponsor, and the person who put that woman into Dude's Suburban that day. I talked to him. He verified that Dude was only doing a favor, taking a drunk home.

"He told me that you're the reason Dude sobered up and stayed sober for months before the accident."

Now Willie Nell was surprised, not only at Soames' revelation, but at the icy stab of pain that seemed to pierce her heart. With a gasp, she broke into tears, then sobs.

Soames reached across the table and placed a hand on her shoulder. "Willie, do you remember a time, shortly before his death, when Dude was in a drunken rage and slapped you when you tried to defend your mother?"

Tears had wrecked Willie Nell's mascara and she could only nod as she blew her nose into the paper napkin that was in her lap.

"I remember. If all this is true, it was the last time I ever saw him drunk," she managed between sobs.

"According to Hansen," Soames continued, "it was the last time he ever took a drink. He drove straight to the VFW and told his AA sponsor about the episode, and recommitted himself to Alcoholics Anonymous, making 90 meetings in the next 90 days."

She blew her nose and, still snuffling, replied, "I remember the night he got that chip for three months' sobriety. I was just a kid, kinda wondering what all the fuss was about for getting to walk up and get a blue plastic poker chip in front of a roomful of drunks."

Willie Nell remained silent during the rest of the meal and Soames let her have her time to deal with her feelings and memories. After the waitress had cleared the table, refilled their coffees, and left the check, she took a deep breath and finally spoke.

"Well, I found something, too," she told her partner. Willie Nell took the rodeo buckle from her purse. "This was with my mom's stuff. It's a pro rodeo championship belt for bull riding."

"Dude was a rodeo cowboy. Isn't it his?"

"That's what I thought, but it's from New Mexico. Dude never rodeo'd out of state. Out-of-state entry fees were too high."

"Then you're thinking it could have belonged to the man who killed her?"

"Why not?"

"Then you gotta fax a copy of it, front and back, to Grady."

72

Atlee had only been in Fort Hancock two days when he got the call from Elliott asking him to cross over to New Mexico to continue the investigation in Deming. It had been a relatively futile 48 hours; both of the victim's parents had died since the killing. A sister said that her mother had died of heartbreak. So far, he had only interviewed the sister and an aged aunt, whose failing memory did nothing but frustrate the ex-cop's investigation. In those two interviews, he had now spoken to just about the only people who seemed to have anything of relevance to the 1987 cold-case murder of Billie Jean Bollinger.

Marge, the sister, remembered that Billie Jean had a boyfriend, but neither she nor the aunt remembered his name after all this time. Marge recalled that police had cleared the boy after he voluntarily took and passed a polygraph test. The young man had left town shortly afterward, but that was no surprise. Fort Hancock wasn't the kind of town where young people wanted to live out their lives. Kids graduated from high school, went off to college, and seldom returned.

"Willie found something Abe, and I'd like you to follow it up, if you don't mind a side trip to New Mexico."

Atlee was enjoying the rugged desert and mountain landscape and the rich tableau of which blended Mexican and American Indian cultures with modern US technology. He had rented a hotel room in El Paso, only 50 miles west of Fort Hancock, with much better accommodations. As a bonus, he was near the Bridge of the Americas, one of four international bridges that cross the Rio Grande to Ciudad Juarez. But Elliott's call meant his sightseeing and shopping in Mexico would have to be shelved.

The Louisianan decided to keep the hotel room; Deming sits only 100 miles west of El Paso on I-10, a 90-minute drive. The hotel turned out to be nicely situated between the two areas where he would be investigating.

Elliott told Atlee about the belt buckle. Merriweather had learned that a cowboy named Beauregard Duchamps had won it for bull-riding in something called the Smoky the Bear Stampede and Rodeo Held in Capitan, New Mexico, during the summer of 1974. The Dallas Police computer expert had used the Internet to track Duchamps to Deming.

Atlee took down the address. "I'll pay him a little visit tomorrow."

"Be careful, Abe. We're looking for a really dangerous guy."

"I carry my Glock 27 in 40 caliber. That should discourage anyone who wants to tangle with me."

"What about a permit?"

"Got a Texas concealed-carry permit. Texas has reciprocal agreements with New Mexico and Louisiana to honor each other's permits. I really wouldn't need one in Louisiana, being a retired cop."

"Well, I'd like you to report in twice a day, morning and evening, until you get back to Dallas, if you don't mind."

"Will do. If you don't hear from me by 10 morning and night, call my cell immediately."

Atlee had another concern. "Do you know if Willie Nell carries a weapon?"

"The boys in homicide made her get one right off the bat. Said if she was gonna hang around with them, she'd better be able to protect herself, because they couldn't guarantee her safety in every situation."

"She's supposed to be a crack shot, growing up out there in West Texas."

"Glad to hear it. Hope she never has to fire her weapon other than on the range." Atlee knew all too well that possessing a handgun was no guarantee of security. His daughter had a permit, advanced firearm training, and three pistols. Yet, she had still been a murder victim. At least everyone on the Task Force knew what they were up against; his daughter never had a suspicion.

Atlee expected to do one more go-around with some of the Fort Hancock witnesses if he could connect the 30-year-old belt buckle to the victim there.

The retired cop awoke early, eagerly anticipating his trip to New Mexico. After his shower, he shaved meticulously; a holdover from 35 years in uniform — closer to 40 counting his four years as a Marine, which included two tours in Vietnam. At 65, he was still fit and a force to be reckoned with should the need arise.

Nacogdoches was a small, sleepy town with a college and several Old South homes, which had been converted to bed & breakfast inns for tourists who loved to while away a lazy day in the arts and craft shops along First Street on the banks of Cane River Lake. Serious crime was an anomaly in this little town; that's why Atlee had moved his daughter from New Orleans where he'd been a decorated cop for more than a decade.

He'd taken a bullet in the chest answering a silent alarm at a convenience store; it had nearly killed him, but his return fire had taken out the robber. After three months in the hospital, Atlee decided that his daughter shouldn't lose both parents. He resigned to join the force in Nacogdoches. It had cost him in rank; he would have probably been a captain by now in the Big Easy, but he never regretted the decision — until that night when Sharon's body was found under a pile of leaves.

Atlee sighed at the memory. He combed his close-cropped salt-and-pepper hair and brushed his teeth before putting on the starched khaki slacks and polo shirt. The Glock went inside his waistband at the small of his back, beneath the untucked shirt. A tan herringbone sport jacket with leather elbow patches and leather-covered buttons completed the ensemble. Now he was ready for breakfast.

At the hotel coffee shop, Atlee ordered oatmeal, orange juice, and coffee, and then handed the waitress — Rhonda, according to her nametag — the borrowed Thermos™. "Might as well fill this, too."

After bringing his food, Rhonda went back to the counter to fill the Thermos™. Sitting it in front of him with the check, she asked, "You staying here at the hotel?"

"For awhile. But today, I have to go to Deming. You familiar with the town?"

"Why sure, sugar. My parents moved there when they retired."

"I'm going to see someone and I wonder if you can direct me to this address" Atlee showed the girl the address in his notepad.

"That's on the north side." Rhonda told him. "Take a right on Highway 180. Berkley will be a little street on your right as you head out of town. If you get to the 26 cutoff, you've gone too far.

"Visiting relatives?"

"Just going to do some hunting," Atlee said cryptically, leaving the check and picking up the Thermos™. He tossed a $10 bill on the table, nearly twice the tab, and walked out.

"You forgot your change," Rhonda yelled after him, but Atlee just waved back over his shoulder, walked to the Crown Vic, got in, and drove away.

Rhonda smiled and waved at the departing white Ford.

Bet he's a cop or something; good looking. Too bad he's not 20 years younger.

He didn't look at Rhonda. He couldn't; she looked too much like his daughter. A lot of young women these days had that effect on him. Being tall, slim, and blonde was the American girl's ideal. Even Willie Nell resembled Sharon. But they were developing a relationship that he was beginning to really treasure. He knew she had no parents living, and he was beginning to feel that protective, fatherly concern for her. He knew it was a form of familial love. And Atlee really needed love in his life right now.

73

The flat, open terrain encouraged a heavy foot on the Crown Vic's accelerator, and Atlee was exiting on US Highway 180 North only 75 minutes after pulling out of the hotel lot in El Paso.

Rhonda's directions were accurate and within minutes of leaving the interstate he arrived up in front of a small frame house, well maintained, with a pick-up and horse trailer beside it.

Must be the place.

As he pulled into the rutted, graveled driveway, a man appeared on the stoop. He stood, arms folded, leaning against the porch post. Fiftyish, Atlee figured.

But still very much the cowboy.

Atlee ambled toward the porch, taking his time, sizing up the man who had emerged from the house. Jeans, a plaid shirt, and a weather-beaten Stetson. Boots were in about the same shape.

"Abe Atlee," he said sticking out his hand. "You must be Beauregard Duchamps."

The cowboy smiled broadly and clasped Atlee's hand with a firm grip. "Call me Bo. What can I do for you?"

"I'd like to chat with you a spell. Sure hope you have a good memory. I'm investigating things that go back maybe 30 years or so."

"Nice morning. Can we talk out here? I got iced tea in the ice-box."

Atlee sat on the stoop. "Sounds good, except for the tea. I've been mainlining coffee ever since I got up this morning."

"Well, I'm gonna have a glass; let me drag out a chair and you can sit in that glider hanging over there." Bo nodded toward a swing at the edge of porch.

Atlee rose from the stoop and stretched. His host disappeared inside the house. When Bo was out of sight, he transferred the Glock to the front of his trousers, sat on the swing, and arranged his coat to cover the weapon.

If this is the killer, I gotta be ready for anything.

Bo reappeared in only two or three minutes, opening the screen door with his butt, both hands full — a folding chair in one, a tall glass of iced tea in the other. He didn't react to the sigh as Atlee relaxed just a little.

Bo expertly opened the chair with a flick of the wrist, turned it, and straddled it to sit facing his guest. "Well, I'm an old rodeo cowboy, and I've been kicked in the head a coupla times over the years; let's see how good what's left of my memory can do you."

Atlee didn't want to mention the crimes at this point, so he started with the buckle. "I have an email photo of a buckle that once belonged to you. You won it at the Smoky the Bear Stampede and Rodeo back in '74, for bull-riding, I think."

"You think right. That was my last time with the bulls. I decided bulldoggin' and bronc-riding were safer.

"And wouldn't you know a damn calf kicked my shin and shattered my leg a few years back and I had to retire from the pro rodeo circuit."

"So, what do you do nowadays?" Atlee wanted to get to know this guy before he revealed too much information.

"I got a little garage in town. I keep mosta these cowboys' pick-up trucks on the road. Got me a good horse and still do a little barrel racing for fun."

Suddenly, Bo sat erect as a memory crossed his mind. "Y'know, I just remembered something about that buckle. I gave that to my brother's boy, Lucas. He really liked it, and I got more buckles than I do belts anyways."

"Your nephew, then. He or your brother here in town?"

"Nah. Sad story. Luke's Dad, my brother Bobby, left 'em when the boy was maybe 6 or 7. Dixie went to drinking and I guess honky-tonking around. I could tell the boy was really sad most of the time. Then his mother just up and abandons him, too. Disappears. I take him in … That was maybe a year or so after I'd given him this buckle in your picture."

"Mr. Duchamps, I mean, Bo, would you know where I could find Lucas?"

A pained expression flitted across the old cowboy's face. "I've kinda lost track of him since he went away to college. Oh, he calls me once in awhile, but I miss that kid.

"We had our troubles when he came here, but we got along OK after a spell. I could never get him to open up about his parents, though. I think he'da been a lot better off if he'd just talked all that shit out of his system."

Atlee desperately wanted to keep Bo talking about his nephew. "When did he go off to college?"

"Probably '78 or '79, I think. It was … yes … 1978. He was accepted at Western New Mexico University in Silver City. Wanted to be a social worker or counselor or something like that. Didn't really need to. He was a darn good mechanic of his own; guess he learned that from me. Took his tools with him to college; figgered he could pay his expenses mechanicin' up there."

"How far away is Silver City?"

"Maybe 60 miles straight up 180."

"So he came home often?"

"Nah. Had him a girlfriend. And he fixed cars on weekends. Didn't see much of him to begin with, and then it fell off to nothing. Called me once to tell me he'd dropped out. Haven't seen him since. Just very rare phone calls."

"Did he say why he'd left college?"

"His girlfriend. He said she was murdered and he couldn't stand being around their friends and the school. Said he could make a good enough living as a mechanic and that he didn't need a degree for that."

Atlee felt the pain and tension in the uncle talking about his missing nephew.

"Does anyone else in the family hear from him?"

"Ain't nobody else. A rodeo cowboy's got no time for a family, so I'm growing old alone now. And the only relative me or Lucas have is his mom, my sister-in-law, who's gone off God knows where." There was an edge of bitterness now, in Bo's speech as he tore open the wounds of loneliness.

74

A person might think Silver City, situated in Southwestern New Mexico, is at or close to sea level. Strangers are often shocked to hear its altitude, nearly 1000 feet higher than Colorado's 'Mile-High City', Denver. At 6200 feet, Silver City, the seat of Grant County, sits at the southern edge of the Mogollon Wilderness in the Gila National Forest. Some call the area the "high desert", which runs from El Paso across the southwestern edge of the state, including Deming and Lordsburg.

The Mogollon Keystone Forest, which stretches northwest from the Rio Grande Valley in southeastern New Mexico to Flagstaff Arizona, is known for its high-elevation spruce fir, Ponderosa pine, and Piñon juniper forests. Altitudes in the wilderness often approach 10,000 feet and in some places, exceed it.

Deming makes one think he's on the desert floor, but the small city sits more than 4300 feet above sea level. The 60-mile drive to Silver City seems flat, and the big Ford sedan gobbled the miles quickly. Atlee wasn't even aware that he was in a steady climb all the way, reaching 6200 feet by the time he arrived in Silver City. Parking in a head-in spot on North Hudson street, two blocks from the police station, the retired policeman was winded after the short walk. It was Atlee's first lesson about high altitude and thin air. In this part of the country, even a little exertion can sap a man's stamina, unless he's accustomed to it.

The name badge above the shirt pocket of the cop at the desk identified him as Sergeant Polk. He smiled at the visitor's red face. "Not from around here, are you?"

Atlee laughed with a bit of a wheeze. "How'd y'know? ... Never mind, if I can feel it, you can see it.

"My name's Abe Atlee. I'm a retired cop from Louisiana looking into the murder of my daughter, and related cases. I need cold-case files on murders of females back in the mid-'70s."

"If you're really a cop, you know I can't show you those." The smile disappeared from the local cop's face.

"Look, Sergeant Polk, I'm on a Task Force formed up in Dallas to chase down a string of killings across three states. I can have Dallas Police fax you confirmation, if you need it."

"I'm no hard-ass Mister Atlee, but if you can give me a name and phone number, I can check it right now; If Dallas PD vouches you, you can look at that old stuff. We're sure not doing anything with it."

"Fair enough." Atlee gave Polk Elliott's name and number.

The sergeant disappeared behind a partition to the administrative section of the building. Atlee took a seat in a well worn straight-back armed chair and waits.

"Chief wants to talk to you," Polk said, sticking his head from behind the partition. Atlee stood and followed the officer to a metal door with an opaque glass stenciled with the name of Chief Hector Velasquez. The sergeant rapped once.

"Come."

"Hec, this is Sergeant Atlee."

"Thanks Larry, go back to the front, someone might steal that old chair out there."

To Atlee, the chief said, "Have a seat sergeant."

"Thanks, but I haven't been Sergeant Atlee for six years now." Atlee sat down in a wooden chair across the desk from the nattily uniformed Hispanic cop.

"I'm kinda glad you're here," he began. "Silver City's not the sort of place where we see murders of this sort. We really weren't able to do much with the cases, I'm sorry to say. If you and your Task Force can develop some new leads, you're welcome to everything we have."

"Did you talk to Grady Elliott?"

"Yes sir, I did." The younger officer was falling into a respectful form of address to the 65-year-old man before him."

"Feel free to just call me Abe; may I call you Hector?"

"How 'bout Hec? Otherwise, no one here'll know who you're talking about."

A young Hispanic woman rapped at the door, then opened it. "Here are those closed-case files you asked for, Hec."

"Thanks Maria. Just hand them to Abe here."

Atlee took the proffered folders, noticing they were woefully thin.

"I was still a niño when these two women were killed, but I've been over the files several times," Hec said.

"No suspects?"

"None. And what always puzzled me is that they look like sex crimes, but there are no signs of struggle, no mutilation, no sexual assault — nothing that would indicate these women were anything but willing participants in recent sexual activity during or shortly before their deaths."

A chill ran down Atlee's spine. He'd seen this kind of report before.

"Was there a boyfriend?"

"Evelyn Billings had been seeing a couple of guys off and on. The other one, Beth Miller, wasn't seeing anyone that we know of, which doesn't mean much around here. The college kids and the townies keep their distance. If she was sleeping with another student, we might not ever know about it."

"I have reason to believe one of these women was seeing a kid named Lucas Duchamps."

"Never heard the name. The first one had a steady boyfriend and our department polygraphed him back then, but he passed with flying colors, from what I hear,"

"Maybe the Duchamps kid was seeing the Miller girl, then. His uncle said his girlfriend was murdered.

"The kid who was seeing the Billings girl has disappeared, that's for sure. Calls his uncle in Deming from time to time, that's about it," the chief said.

"But we have a piece of evidence that might tie Duchamps to another murder, one in Fort Hancock. That's in Texas."

Hec's face portrayed earnestness. "I know where it is. Just a wide spot in the road — sorta like Silver City was when I was a kid."

"Now that I have a name, I think I'm going back to Fort Hancock to continue my investigation. Can I get copies of these files?"

Chief Velasquez pushed the intercom button on his phone. "Maria, can you make Ex-roxes of those filed for the sergeant here?"

Within seconds Maria's smiling face was at the door. "Let me have them, sir," she said to Atlee.

"Only one request, Abe. Keep me in the loop on this investigation. We had a woman go missing back in those days. Neither her truck nor a body was ever found. Her name is Mona Harper, a young widow whose 70-year-old rancher husband, Roy Harper, left the Las Vegas showgirl Mona Richter very well-heeled."

"What about your own investigation?"

"I can get you that file, too. But keep it quiet; it's not officially a police matter, since no formal missing person report was filed. She was supposedly on her way to some beach resort in Mexico for a month of frolic in the sun.

"She could just as easily have decided Silver City's not much fun for a young widow with lots of money."

Driving back to El Paso with the file copies, Atlee played the two conversations over in his head. Lucas' mother "disappeared" as did a woman from Silver City. He now had turned up as many as four more cases for the Task Force.

And, I have a name!

As soon as that thought flashed through his head, Atlee knew he had to return to Fort Hancock.

75

Atlee drove back to his hotel in El Paso and, from there, made a conference call through the Task Force Comm Center.

"Who you want in on it, Abe?" Merriweather asked.

"Grady, Marty Johnson … oh, yeah, Willie Nell. Especially Willie Nell."

"Give me a few minutes to get everyone to a phone or radio, and I'll call you back."

Atlee laid out a change of clothes and took a quick shower. He was still wrapped in a terrycloth towel and hand-drying his close-cropped hair when Merriweather's call came.

"Atlee."

"You're on, Abe," Merriweather reported.

"Abe, Grady here. Hear you found something."

"Yeah, boss-man, a name."

"Wow. Not too shabby for a fuckin' has been."

"Willie! Who else could have that mouth. I love you, too. Better to be a has-been than a wannabe."

"Cool it, you two," The FBI agent interjected, "Let's have the name."

"Lucas Duchamps. He goes mostly by Luke."

"Do you have two sources for collaboration?" Willie Nell asked.

"The uncle gave that belt you found to his nephew, Luke, who disappeared in the mid '70s from the campus of WNMU in Silver City, and … here's the kicker: right after two coed murders."

Elliott whistled in appreciation. "Can I echo Willie's WOW?"

"There's more. A Silver City woman and her pick-up truck disappeared about the same time this Luke withdrew from college and hit the road. No body, folks thought at first she'd taken off with her late hubby's gazillions and moved to Mexico."

"So she could be a third victim," Elliott surmised. "I don't believe in coincidences."

"She could be a fourth," Atlee continued. "The boy's mother also disappeared, and the boy went to live with his only relative, his father's brother, at age 13. That brother is Bo, rather, Beauregard Duchamps, who put me on the trail to Silver City."

"Now what are you going to do, Abe? Head back to Big D?"

"No, Grady, I'm going back to Fort Hancock. I got damn little from the only two relatives of the murder victim there, but I didn't have a chance to check in with the local constabulary and see if there's a case file around somewhere."

"I have the cold case files, remember," Willie Nell said.

"Are they with you there in Sonora?"

"Yep, I X-roxed everyone a set for that first meeting, remember?"

"Yeah, but this one's pretty skimpy," Atlee noted.

"Then try the State Police substation closest to Fort Hancock. What are you looking for?"

"I'd like to know if Luke was the girl's boyfriend and if he was every questioned, maybe even photographed."

This got Johnson's attention. "The uncle didn't have photos?"

"Only kid pictures' not a lot of help since he's possibly in his 40s or 50s by now."

"Call him. Have him send the latest to the Task Force. Our FBI crime lab has a cool program that can predict how a face will change as it ages."

"You got it, Fed-man."

"Why don't I join you in Fort Hancock? Ed Soames can follow up the leads here in Sonora," Willie Nell suggested. "It's a straight shot across Interstate 10."

"I'd enjoy a second pair of eyes and ears on this case, that's for sure."

"Be there at noon tomorrow. Is there a fast-food joint or something there where we can meet?"

"You two figure out how you're going to hook up, I need to get everybody involved in this thing, so I'm off the air," Elliott said.

"Me too, Grady," Johnson said. "Want me to get my troops to the Command Center if they're in town?"

"Sounds good. Meet you there. I'll be with you in 15 minutes, Jeremy."

"Ten-four, Detective Grady."

76

Fort Hancock isn't much more than a wide spot along Interstate 10. Atlee parked the big, white Ford Crown Victoria just off the service road where it would be visible from the town's only off ramp. He leaned against the front fender, drinking from his ever-present insulated Starbucks mug, glad he'd stopped in El Paso. A burg like this wouldn't support such an upscale coffeehouse.

The Louisianan spotted Willie Nell's SUV exiting the Interstate 15 minutes ahead of their noon schedule. She parked alongside Atlee's car and opened her window. "Good morning, old man."

"Morning, Miss Tag-along."

"I brought the belt. Thought it might spur Mister Duchamps' memory."

"Good idea. Why don't you lock up that gas hog of yours and ride in a real car?"

"Just so you're not planning to conveniently run out of gas on some fuckin' back road and put a move on me, you old lech."

"I couldn't kiss you unless I'd washed that mouth of yours out with lye soap."

Willie Nell pecked the 65-year-old man's cheek. She had a lot of respect for this driven man, and a bond born out of the quest each had for finding out what happened to their loved ones. As they walked around the car to the passenger's door, she put an arm around his waist and leaned her head against his shoulder.

"Promise me you won't disappear as soon as this thing's over, Abe."

Atlee stopped walking and turned to face her.

She's so much like Sharon. I'd like to think my daughter would have turned out something like Willie Nell.

"Sweetheart, I'll be as hard to get rid of as a bad cold. As far as I'm concerned, you and I are family."

Willie Nell had tears in her eyes fighting to spill down her cheeks. "You know, you and I need to sit down and talk. I'd like to hear about your daughter, and I'd like to tell you about my mother. I think it would make my mother seem a little bit alive by having someone else who knows about her life, her dreams, and her music.

"But I'm still learning about her; that's why I wanted to go to Sonora."

The ex-cop took the young woman into his arms, and her tears lost their grip, carrying much of her make-up down her face.

"I'm not saying I'll stay in Dallas. I'm most comfortable in Cajun country. But I promise we won't ever lose touch with one another."

"Fuck, Abe," The reporter said, wiping at her face and accomplishing little other than smearing the make-up even more. "I'm not rooted in the cement in Dallas, either. I want to be a writer someday. Maybe a mystery writer. I'm learning the cop side of the things as KTKO's senior crime reporter. I'll probably want to travel, keep my perspective growing."

Atlee pulled a clean handkerchief from his hip pocket. "You need this, sweetie, otherwise folks are gonna think you're a raccoon."

Willie Nell laughed and leaned over to peer at her face in the side mirror of the Crown Vic. "I'm a wreck!" she laughed. Atlee opened the door for her to get in, and she immediately lowered the visor and began repairs to her face in the lighted vanity mirror.

"Get my briefcase, please Abe. It's in the floorboard on the passenger side; the door's not locked."

Atlee brought the briefcase and put it on the backseat of the Ford. Willie Nell pushed the remote lock button on her key chain and the Pilot's doors locked with a single beep of the horn.

"Deming, El Paso, or Silver City?" Willie Nell asked as Atlee floored the Crown Vic to merge into 80-mile-per-hour traffic on Interstate 10.

"None of the above, my dear. We're gonna visit the DPS substation and see if we can't get some more information on the case here."

"Well sir," the trooper at the desk, Jose Cruz, told Atlee, "those records are never kept at a substation. They're handled by our investigation division and by now, a 20-year-old case would be molding away in some basement or warehouse in Dallas ."

"I understand that officer Cruz; I just wondered if there might be someone still around who remembers the case." Atlee showed his police association retiree ID card.

"The investigator was Ben Himmelmann. He retired, of course, but still lives in El Paso. And he drops by almost every morning to have coffee with the boys during morning shift change."

Willie Nell brightened. "What time does he get here?"

"Sixish, almost every morning except Sunday."

"Thank you Officer Cruz," Atlee said, "Hasta mañana."

While they were strapping into their seatbelts in Atlee's car, Willie Nell chided him. "Hasta fuckin' mañana? Now I've seen it all, a Mexican-talkin' Cajun redneck."

"So what do we do today?"

"Deming, I suppose. How 'bout some lunch first? We can find something decent in El Paso. If you're a fan of Tex-Mex, it doesn't get any Texier or Mexier than right here."

Atlee had eaten at the little café once before, and knew it was clean, reasonably priced, and served homemade tamales that made him forget all about Cajun meat pies. At his suggestion, she ordered a tamale plate and iced tea. Atlee, deciding to be adventurous, asked for the chicken enchiladas mole. Neither was disappointed.

"Do you think Duchamps will be evasive, try to protect his nephew?" Lifting the cloth napkin from her lap, she wiped her mouth. Then hoisted the teaglass, drained it, and held it up to signal a needed refill. A busboy hastily rushed to fill it.

Atlee thought about it. "I really don't think so. He's a straight shooter, from what I can tell. If he suspects Lucas could be implicated in such vile crimes, I think he'd be forthcoming.

"What you young people don't understand is just how long 30 years is. How far back do you remember? Twenty years ago, you were only 4 or 5. What can you remember from then?"

"OK, Yoda, I get your point. Maybe the buckle will help him remember something. At least we can pick up the picture instead of having him mail it."

"If he hasn't already done so. Thanks for reminding me." Atlee opened his cell phone and punched in Duchamps home number.

The retired rodeo cowboy answered on the second ring. "Howdy, this is Bo, can I help you?"

"Abe Atlee again. Got a friend with me and she has a few questions. Can we drive on over now; we're in El Paso? We can pick up those photos, if you haven't sent it off."

"I only grabbed a few and they got as far as an envelope but it didn't make it to the PO yet. And I'll look around, I know I got some more. this time I'll have coffee, not tea. So, come on."

The two friends finished their lunch in the relative silence that some folks call small talk — where there's easy conversation, but nothing gets said, and then they hit the road for New Mexico.

When Atlee drove into the driveway, Bo was in the same posture as before, crossed arms, crossed feet, leaning against the same post.

"Whooeeeeeee, Abe!" he said, admiring Willie Nell as she exited the car. "You didn't tell me I'd be entertaining such a fetching filly. Shoot, I mighta even combed my hair and polished my boots."

"Don't you go giving a girl signals if you're not in the market, cowboy," Willie Nell said with a wink.

"This is Willie Nell Autrey, a Dallas reporter and a trusted friend. We can say anything in front of her without it coming back to bite us in the backside."

"I always trust a pretty lady; it's them old Cajuns a fella's gotta watch out for."

A jovial tone set for the interview, Atlee got right to the point. He opened Willie Nell's briefcase and removed the buckle and handed it to the retired rodeo cowboy.

"I thought… well, Willie Nell thought … that if you saw the real thing, it might spur your memory about your nephew around that time."

"The memories it brings back are kinda bittersweet. Back before my injury. I really enjoyed rodeo life. But I did just remember something. When I handed this to Luke, I told him not to let his mother see it. Dixie was always on my ass about giving stuff away. Well, Luke said something kinda strange."

"What was that?" Willie prompted.

"He said something like, 'She can't see anything from where she's at'.

"I thought at the time he meant because she had left. But as I think about it, I'm not so sure anymore."

Atlee cleared his throat and stood, motioning for Bo to sit on the porch swing. "I have to tell you something heavy, Bo. I … we believe Luke is implicated in a string of murders across three states, and his mother may have been his first victim."

Bo sat silently. After a few moments, he removed his Stetson and ran his hand through his hair. He stood.

"From our previous conversation, and that statement I told you about, I'm inclined to believe you. I love that boy; he's family. But wrong is wrong. What can I do to help?"

"Well, I'd like to see as many pictures as you can find," Willie Nell said. "I'll scan them at the TV station and mail them all back to you that same day."

Bo nodded, not speaking, and disappeared through the screen door as he'd done on Atlee's first visit. He returned with a serving tray holding a coffee pot, two cups, cream, and sugar. Setting the tray on a rattan ottoman near the swing, he said, "You might as well relax and have some coffee; I could be awhile. I'll go through every old photo album in the house."

77

Willie Nell had just poured herself and Atlee a second cup when Bo emerged from the house with a sheaf of photographs of differing sizes, dates, and formats.

"I found 12 that include recognizable views of Luke," he announced as he let the screen door slam behind him.

Atlee pored over them carefully, handing each one to Willie Nell as he finished with it. "I need you to do one thing for us, Bo," he said, not looking up. "Write Luke's approximate age at the time on each of these, would you?"

Turning to Willie Nell, he continued, "I think there's enough here for the FBI to have something to work with."

In no profession, perhaps, is time more critical than in journalism. That training spurred an idea from the young reporter. "Do you have a computer with Internet connection and a scanner, by any chance?" Willie Nell asked Bo.

"Actually, yes. I even have a cable modem."

"A 21st Century cowboy! My kinda guy. Is it OK if we scan these here and E-mail them directly to Marty? That way, the Feds can get started right away instead of waiting for us to get back to Dallas."

Bo nodded agreeably.

"Good idea, because we still have to talk to that retired DPS investigator, Himmelmann," Atlee agreed.

Still thinking about time constraints, Willie Nell suggested they call Him-melmann from Deming. "We may be able to get everything we need on the phone," she reasoned.

Atlee pulled out his cell phone and punched in a number. Covering the mouthpiece, the told Willie Nell, "I'll set it up through the Comm Center so they can monitor and record the conversation."

After explaining what he wanted, he told Merriweather to give them an hour, then put the call through. "I did that just in case we hit on something else while scanning these pictures," he explained.

All three went into the house and Bo directed them to a state-of-the art computer system with a Hewlett-Packard all-in-one scanner/printer/copier/fax machine. The computer was fast, and the Internet connection was always on. There would be no upload or download problems, so the two investigators set about the task of rendering the pile of photographs into electronic documents.

Willie Nell pulled a 512 MB flash drive out of her purse and plugged it into a USB slot on the front of the computer. "Save everything to this drive. Sorry, Bo, but we can't let you keep these photos. For the time being, they are evidence."

"She's right," Atlee added. "Even though I promised we'd get these back to you, it won't be until the investigation is over."

With the scanner set to its highest resolution, it recorded each photograph in detail, much larger than the 19-inch flat-panel monitor could display at once.

The young woman and older man carefully looked at each image.

Atlee thought about cropping each one to show only Lucas, but Willie Nell thought otherwise. "The settings and locations of these photographs give them context that we may want to revisit later in the investigation."

"You're a sharp cookie, Miss Autrey. Let's compromise. I'll keep the full shot and copy a second one for cropping. I'll give them filenames that will keep them together: 'View 1' and 'View 1 crop', for instance."

"I like it Abe. Do it!"

A confused Bo interjected a question: "Just which one of you is in charge of this thing, anyhow?"

Both Atlee and Willie Nell broke out in laughter.

"Grady is," Willie Nell said as soon as she was able to control herself.

"Yup, we're just a coupla working stiffs who seem to fit together well," Atlee confirmed.

"Clear as mud, you guys. But you sure do seem to end up on the same page a lot," Bo observed.

Willie Nell was changing the photos on the scanner while Atlee arranged the finished scans into files. "Here's something." She held up a picture of a college-age Lucas, shaggy-haired, bearded, and cuddling with a pretty young blonde coed.

"That was his girlfriend," Bo volunteered. "He sent it with a birthday card his first semester at WMSU."

Willie Nell turned the picture over and what she saw made her blood run cold.

In a neat handwriting, the chief read:

Evelyn and Luke, October 1980.

"Abe! Look at this!" Willie Nell pushed the picture under her partner's nose. "Wasn't one of those two Silver City murders named Evelyn?"

"Yes, but we already knew one of them was his girlfriend, what's new about this? I thought it was the other girl, for some reason."

"LOOK at the girl! Abe, she's the spitting image of my mother, and of all those other women in the cold-case files, including your daughter."

Atlee sat up with a start. "My God, you're right! Girl, this is as close to a confirmation as we might ever get."

"Don't write off Himmelmann. He may have even more." Willie Nell took the photograph out of Atlee's shaking hand and put it back on the scanner. "We need to get this done before our teleconference with that state cop."

313

Atlee returned to his tasks on the computer. "You know that the FBI photo techs can also render a likeness without all that facial hair."

"I'd be really interested in that. Abe, there's something familiar about his eyes." Willie Nell looked closer at the shot of Lucas with his coed girlfriend. "He's either been in one of my news stories, or in something I edited at the station, I think."

In 40 minutes they had scanned all 12 photographs, and Atlee had cropped nine of them to show facial detail.

"Twenty minutes to spare," Willie Nell beamed.

Atlee looked at the on-screen time displayed in the lower left corner. "I don't think we should do the phone interview."

"What! Why?" Willie Nell was shocked.

"We need to see him at the substation tomorrow morning, just like we planned. He needs to see these photographs. Let me call Jeremy and call off the teleconference. But he can make sure Himmelmann gets his regular coffee at the station house tomorrow."

78

Atlee and Willie Nell were already in the break room enjoying coffee and the donuts they had brought as payback for the cooperation of the state troopers assigned to the tiny substation.

Himmelmann showed up in his aging Volvo station wagon at 6 o'clock on the dot, having already been briefed by both Merriweather and detective Elliott.

Right off the bat, during the preliminary exchanges before the interview, Atlee decided the man's small, portly appearance worked in his favor. He had a highly analytical intellect, and his non-threatening appearance probably gave suspects a false sense of being in control. Himmelmann retired as a senior investigator in the Texas Department of Public Safety's Criminal Law Enforcement section. A quick computer check performed by Merriweather had shown that the DPS detective closed more cases than most of his peers in the department.

But Benjamin Franklin Himmelmann considered his investigation of the Billie Jean Bollinger slaying a personal failure. The Fort Hancock murder happened 18 years ago and had been the oldest of the case files Willie Nell had rounded up before Atlee's digging had unearthed the New Mexico killings, which occurred five years earlier.

For the second time, Willie Nell found herself fetching coffee for her senior partner as he interviewed the other retired cop. It surprised her that Atlee never asked; she just did it as a courtesy for the considerations he showed her.

Careful girl, you'll lose your standing in the damned Feminist Journalistic Society.

Himmelmann was looking over Bo's pictures, his mouth agape. "I interviewed this guy! I think he was the boyfriend. We even sent him to El Paso for a polygraph. But he passed completely, so we dropped him as a suspect."

"Grady told us that could happen, Mister Himmelmann," Willie Nell said, placing a cup of fresh coffee before him.

"Please call me Ben, Willie Nell," he said. "But how does a young kid like this know how to beat the lie detector?"

"He doesn't," Atlee took the question. "According to our profiler, our killer may commit the crimes in something like a black-out, and not have any recollection of actually killing these women. Under that scenario, if he says he didn't do it, in his own mind he's telling the truth."

"Good grief! No wonder I wasn't getting anywhere on this case."

"But you're the guy who's finally given us concrete confirmation that this Lucas Duchamps is our guy, so you're really responsible for us being able to go forward."

"Abe, how many people has this guy killed?"

"We have 15 that we can tie him to, two more that are probable, another that's a possible. And those numbers don't include any women he may have killed who are only listed as missing."

Willie Nell stood over the table looking directly into Himmelmann's eyes. "For your information, so you'll know where we're coming from, my mother and Abe's daughter are among his likely victims. Mama was murdered 14 years ago in Sonora; Abe's daughter was killed in Nacogdoches, Louisiana just six years ago. And right now, we have three unsolved recent killings in Dallas."

"Forensic evidence reveals that each victim had engaged in sexual activity either during or shortly before the murder," Atlee added. "None of his victims suffered physical or sexual assault, and there was no sexual mutilation either ante-mortem or post-mortem, nor signs of break-in at their residences."

Himmelmann jumped on the conversation thread. "So the women knew the assailant and had willingly opened their doors to him. That fits with Billie

Jean and the girlfriend photograph. They all liked him and trusted him. That also means he is probably handsome, maybe a gym rat, and very charming."

The chubby little detective lowered his eyes and sighed, then spoke to Atlee. "I can help. I'll also check and see if he has a Texas driver license."

"How do you think Elliott's going to react now that we've shown a picture of this guy to another retired cop who's not even a part of the Task Force?" Atlee asked Willie Nell.

"Oh, he'll have a cow."

All three investigators laughed loudly. Two puzzled troopers could only stare over the tops of their coffee cups and donuts, unaware that what they were seeing was a very effective crime-fighting team.

79

Himmelmann was a retired cop, but he still worked as a consultant to DPS on a part-time basis, so continued to carry a badge and a gun. He also supplemented his income as a public speaker, and maintained most of the contacts he'd amassed during his long career.

The Dallas investigator was as good as his word. A call to the Department of Public Safety started a flood of information streaming to the Task Force.

The trio had moved their conversation from the little police substation to a back booth in a short-order joint where they were eating a late breakfast. They had been on the phones for the past three hours. A setback in the investigation turned out to be lack of a current photograph of the suspect, which Himmelmann had expected to get from a Texas driver license. The team had also hoped to be able to follow a chain of addresses if Lucas had kept his license information up to date. Either he was driving without a license, or he was licensed in a state other than Texas, they assumed.

"New Mexico! Of course!" Atlee blurted. "Let me call Hec in Silver City."

"Heck? Who in the hell names a kid Heck?" Himmelmann asked earnestly.

Atlee and Willie Nell laughed loudly. "Chief Hector Velasquez of the Silver City police department," Atlee finally choked out between a fit of giggles, unseemly for the big, rugged ex-cop.

"You did say the Task Force was reimbursing me for my cell phone minutes and roaming charges, didn't you, Willie?" Atlee said as he punched in the direct number Hec had given him.

"Afraid not, old man." Willie Nell yanked her friends chain. "The Task Force has no funding. The Dallas cops will get expenses reimbursed by the city; The FBI covers Marty and his agents; the TV station takes care of me; and Himmelmann's a State employee, so he files an expense report each month.

"But you? You're a free agent, accent on FREE."

Atlee muttered under his breath, then said, "Hec! Abe here. Remember me? Good."

"I need a favor. Can you check with some of the state guys and see if Lucas Duchamps has a current New Mexico license?

"Great," he said, after a pause.

"I'll need a copy, preferably an enlargement of his current DL photo. Can you fax that to the Task Force number?"

Again, there was a pause as Atlee listened to the other end of the conversation which his two companions couldn't hear. "That's just great (pause). We're here in El Paso. Just left the Fort Hancock DPS substation (pause). You will? Great (pause). What time? (pause). I really owe you one, pal (pause). Yeah, you to. Thanks. Goodbye."

Himmelmann and Willie Nell stared expectantly as Atlee pushed the "End" button and closed the clamshell cellular phone.

"So?" Willie Nell asked excitedly. "What was all the rest of that?"

"He's going to send a copy for us by one of his men. It'll be at the substation by early evening."

"If it's the same guy I interviewed, we'll have narrowed this whole investigation to a single suspect," Himmelmann pointed out.

"And the manhunt begins," Willie Nell added.

The three returned to Atlee's hotel room and spent the hours going over the Duchamps photos.

"None of these were taken indoors," Willie Nell observed. "Except for the campus shots, they all seem to be in the desert or the mountains."

"The wilderness. This guy's a nature lover." Atlee extracted a shot showing Lucas at age 14 peering over a broad vista from a scenic overlook, one foot up on the railing beside a marker describing the scene and the local history of the location.

"This is up in the Mogollon Wilderness north of Silver City. See the inscription on the marker? It's a good bet a lot of these other pictures were taken in that area, too."

While they waited for a call from the troopers at the substation, Himmelmann ordered sandwiches and drinks for everyone. "That should pay for a minute or two of those roaming charges, Abe."

"Funny, really funny," The Louisianan grumbled.

The sandwiches arrived at the same time as the phone call from the substation. Willie Nell beat the men to the phone.

"A New Mexico State Trooper just dropped off a package for you and Abe," Trooper Cruz said.

"I'm on my way right now."

She turned to her partners. "You boys finish your dinner and I'll fetch the picture. We might have an interesting evening when I get back." Willie Nell had no idea of how prophetic her statement would become.

80

"Hello, beautiful," Cruz said, a white smile creasing his tanned Latino face as Willie Nell walked through the glass door of the substation.

"Bet you say that to every woman who comes into the station, Jose," she said, smiling back. "Whatcha got for me?"

"S'posed to be for Ben and it requires his signature." The trooper said. "but if you'll print his name on this form, then sign your own, I'll take it."

"I appreciate your consideration, Jose. We really are in a hurry to get a handle on this case. This guy has been leaving bodies across three state for more than 20 years, and he's still at it."

Trooper Cruz handed the manila envelope to the reporter. "Where are you a detective?"

Willie Nell gave the handsome young trooper a finger wave as she paused at the door.

"I'm not. I'm a reporter." She let the door close and walked straight to her Honda Pilot. Leaving the young state trooper slack-jawed. Although she was eager to open the envelope, she recalled Cruz' statement that it was really for Himmelmann.

Better let him do the honors.

Willie Nell let herself in with the keycard Atlee had given her. The two ex-cops were relaxed and enjoying beers as they chatted about the case, as well as others they had worked over their careers.

She nodded at the two men, placed her purse on one of the beds, and handed the still-sealed envelope to Himmelmann.

The retired investigator emptied the contents onto the coffee table: a photocopy of a page from an old NMWU yearbook, and a smaller envelope with a handwritten note taped to it.

"Abe,

"I don't know what you can make of this. There is not, nor has there ever been a New Mexico operator's license issued to a Lucas or Luke Duchamps.

"However, I checked up at the college on the guy we polygraphed and found his photo in the yearbook. His name is Lucas Peterson. I found an old license for him with an address in Lordsburg, and an address change for Silver City around the time of the murders. Here's a copy of the license and a 5 by 7 print of his yearbook photograph.

"Please keep me in the loop. If this is your guy, he's probably our guy too and good for two or three old cases here. But you'll still have to explain the polygraph results somehow.

"Sincerely,

The signature was simply, "Hec".

"Himmelmann, can you get another Texas search done under the name of Lucas Peterson?"

"I'm on it Abe," the retired Texas investigator said, already punching numbers into his cell phone.

"That's Lucas Duchamps!" Willie Nell said in disbelief. "I want to talk to Bo about this."

Atlee's face was a stormy countenance. "Yeah, me too."

"I said it first, I get to do it, "Willie Nell said in a mock little girl playground voice. "Give me his number."

"This is Bo, I'm out riding and roping or doing something else, just not here. Leave a message and I'll get back to you."

"Fuck, shit, piss, damn, motherfuckin' whore!"

324

"I think Willie Nell just got an answering machine," Atlee observed.

"Wow, what's she like when something really goes wrong?" Himmelmann said, his eyes wide.

"You don't even want to know."

"Well, partner, I guess Bo can probably guess you're not happy he's not home."

"Oh, shit. Did that go onto his tape? It did, didn't it."

"Uh-huh. Maybe you should use the mute button when you're gonna throw a tantrum."

"Eat shit and die, Abraham Atlee," a still disgruntled Willie Nell replied to the taunt.

Himmelmann interrupted the battle of words to announce, "I'm having a friend at DMV do a live check for Lucas Peterson to see if he has a registered vehicle, another is checking for a driver license. I could have some kind of confirmation in a matter of minutes."

"Ah, back to work Willie Nell, play time's over," Atlee continued to needle the young reporter.

"What are you thinking about now, girl? It's like you just left the room."

"It's too fucking corny to even talk about."

"I could use a good laugh about now, or at least a chuckle. Come on, give."

"I was thinking about a song Mama used to sing to us. Hadn't thought about it in years. We had this kitten that liked to get into Miz Edie's knitting basket. Miz Edie and I had spent hours, or so it seemed to me, getting this ball of yarn ready for her knitting that night. One day, Kitty took that yarn and batted and chased it and ran it all through the house. She pulled the yarn under, over and through every opening she could and when she couldn't, she'd tie it into knots and tangles trying. What a beautiful tanglement it was!"

Abe grinned. "What made you think of that?"

"Oh, I found some of Mama's things in storage and was digging through them before we got back onto the killer's track. You know. That song was in with a bunch of music and other songs we found. She wrote lyrics and music, Abe. I never even knew." Suddenly Willie Nell was weeping.

The retired DPS investigator didn't notice the interchange between the other two people in the hotel suite. He'd just received important news. Into his cell phone, Himmelmann said excitedly, "a truck? A pick-up. Registered in Richardson (pause).Yes, I know where that is; it's a Dallas suburb. And what about the driver license (pause)? Email me the picture. My old email address is still good. I can access it from here (pause). Yes, I'm still retired and still in El Paso. But doing a little sleuthing around for some of the working stiffs. Earl, you're a pal. I owe you one. Oh, send me a list of all the addresses where that license has been reissued (pause). No, that should about do it. I'll call you if I think of anything else."

"They found it!?" Atlee asked.

"Yep. Now I have to find a secure computer, maybe at the substation."

"Boys," Willie Nell interjected, "Did you ever know a reporter to travel without her laptop? Mine's in my trunk."

"The hotel has a DSL line over here behind the desk," Atlee said.

Willie Nell fetched the rolling computer case from the SUV, removed her Sony Vaio portable, plugged it in, and then turned to Himmelmann. "You drive Ben, it's your email."

The three anxious investigators were disappointed when Himmelmann's email file showed more than 40 messages, but none from the DPS Dallas investigative unit.

"Give it time, folks," Atlee said. "I need a Starbucks break anyway. Anybody want anything?"

"Nonfat mocha latte for me," Willie Nell sang out.

"I remember!"

"Maybe an Americano for me, then, since you're going," Himmelmann said.

"Be right back." Atlee left Willie Nell with Himmelmann.

"So, how does a reporter wrangle her way onto an official police task force, anyway?" he asked.

"I think they appreciated that I found links to tie some of these together. But I also suspect Chief Justin figured he could put me on the task force, swear me to secrecy, and not have me in his hair day in and day out with questions about the investigation."

"Andy Justin?" Himmelmann asked.

"Yeah, know him?"

"Yes ma'am. A real cops' cop. Headed my section until he got a detective gig in Dallas. Gosh, that was nearly 30 years ago. That he likes and trusts you is good enough for me. He was the best at sizing people up."

Willie Nell blushed, then the two sat and talked about Andy Justin, the life of policemen, and the interaction among agencies and departments.

"The public has the wrong slant on that issue," Himmelmann said. "Except for the Feds, most cops are more than happy to help out sister departments. It's at the government level that all the turf wars arise. We wouldn't have all these marvelous criminal databases for DNA, fingerprints, weapons, ballistics, and such if we weren't sharing."

"Well put, Ben. I've had nothing but cooperation from Andy all the way down to the cop on the street. They're really my favorite people."

"Who's your favorite people?" Atlee said from the doorway. He was holding a molded carrier with three cups and a bag with cinnamon twists sticking out of the top.

"She's a police groupie, Abe," Himmelmann said with a laugh.

"I suspected as much. That email come yet?"

"Oops. We got to talking and I forgot all about it. Let me check."

"And let me play waitress, since you're always having me get you coffee, you chauvinistic pig," Willie Nell said, taking the drinks and pastries from him. Atlee started to protest her statement, thought better of it, and relinquished his burden silently.

"It's here. They sent a J-Peg file of his driver license photo and it was current three years ago."

Willie Nell left the drinks on a nightstand and rushed to look over his shoulder. She gasped audibly.

The reporter took a step backward and sat on the bed, her hands over her face.

"Willie Nell! What's wrong?" Abe said, rushing to her side. "Are you OK?"

"I ... I, uh I know him, Abe. I know who this is. He's a friend."

Atlee looked over his shoulder at Himmelmann. "Can you get her some water? She might faint."

"Got it." Himmelmann quickly disappeared into the restroom, emerging with a plastic glass of water.

81

Himmelmann had pulled the drapes while Atlee lifted Willie Nell's legs onto the bed and put a pillow under her head. Taking the ubiquitous plastic hotel cup from the retired Texas investigator, Atlee cradled Willie Nell's head and tilted a little bit of water to her lips.

"Guys, I'm no goddam little old lady. I'm OK," she said, but continued to lie on her back looking at the ceiling.

"And you better fucking believe I'm the one who's gonna be calling that ass-hole cowboy who wasted so much of our time."

"Who is this guy and why did his photo floor you?" Atlee asked, concerned for the partner he had come to look upon as a daughter.

"His name is Pete something or the other. He saved me from a former reporter who attacked and beat me pretty badly. He dates my best friend. He was one of my first visitors in the hospital. Atlee, he even brought me flowers," she said, choking on a sob.

"He's as sweet as one of you fucking testosterone oozing Neanderthals ever get."

"Except that he kills people. Specifically, he kills women," Atlee pointed out the obvious.

"Let's call that damned Deming cowboy!"

"After dinner, perhaps," Atlee said. "Right now, I'm in charge and I'm telling you that you're going to rest."

After a surprisingly good room-service meal of Reuben sandwiches with potato soup, an eager Willie Nell took the land-line telephone Atlee was offering.

"You're a professional interviewer, Willie," he said. "I have no problem with you handling this part of the investigation."

"I'll put him on speakerphone when he answers, just the same."

"I got a better idea. Let's put it through the Comm Center and get that profiler of yours to listen in, too," Atlee suggested.

"Great fuckin' idea, partner," Willie Nell beamed, and dialed Merriweather's Comm Center line.

"Jeremy here."

"Hey, kiddo, is Grady around?"

"He's in his office, let me ring him."

"Not so fast." Willie Nell slowed the FBI geek down. "Before you do, let me tell you what I need."

Once she'd told Merriweather that she needed a conference call to Deming with Elliott participating, she hung up and waited for the return call. It took less than two minutes.

"Howdy, this is Bo, can I help you?"

"This is Willie Nell. Do you remember me?"

"Not likely to ever forget, sweetheart. Cute as a newborn calf."

"Right now, I'm an angry old heifer, cowboy."

"Uh-oh! What'd I do?"

"You let us waste several days looking for a Lucas Duchamps when he doesn't exist, that's what," the reporter growled, but her anger was already beginning to fade as she realized that this even-tempered old rodeo cowboy just wasn't a really deep thinker. She pushed the speakerphone button. "Abe and another investigator are with me; they'll want to listen in. And is it alright if I record it?"

"Fine by me. I suppose I need to tell you all about my brother and his illegitimate son."

Himmelmann and Atlee dragged chairs over to the bedside to listen to Beauregard Duchamps' interrogation. Willie Nell laid her tiny digital recorder beside the speakerphone.

"Back in high school, my brother fell for a cheerleader name of Dixie Peterson. They dated off and on for years, off mostly for the first 10 years or so. Dixie loved the honky-tonks, you see. And Billy — well, he was a teetotaler, so he couldn't share that part of Dixie's life."

"Did Dixie care for him?" Willie Nell asked.

"In her own way. Or, if she didn't care that much, she definitely needed him."

"How so?"

"I hate to speak ill of anyone, but Dixie's a roaring drunk. But Bobby, he just loved her so much he put up with her going out on him, coming home drunk, you name it."

"But then he went and got her pregnant."

"That woulda been Lucas?" Atlee asked.

"Yep. But Bobby wasn't sure the boy was his, so he made her let him get paternity tests. Luke was Bobby's boy alright, and that pretty much tied them together for the next few years."

Sardonically, Duchamps chronicled the fights and drunken rages that characterized the Dixie/Bobby relationship.

"He woulda left a long time earlier but for that boy. He loved his son. I was still surprised though when he up and took off."

"So, he abandoned them?" Willie Nell asked for clarification.

"Yeah. He couldna taken the boy, since they weren't married. Dixie didn't even put Bobby's name on the birth certificate; that's why he's a Peterson rather'n a Duchamps.

"Then Dixie starts coming around me for help. She didn't have any money really, just the tips she got running the breakfast shift at a truck stop on I-10. And she drank up mosta that."

The old cowboy's aged voice cracked as he painfully recounted his efforts to see that his nephew's needs were met. He started a college fund for the child without telling Dixie. He also taught the boy auto mechanics, working with him every day when Dixie was at the restaurant.

"He became a helluva good wrench-bender, I tell you," Duchamps said proudly.

"Do you know if Dixie mistreated or abused the boy after Bobby left?" Elliott asked.

"Well, she had a temper. I know she could beat the stuffing outta poor Bobby. But I never saw bruises or scratches on Luke when he was around, other'n those he'd get banging hands against an engine block in the garage.

"But he did change after his daddy left. He got quieter, more self-conscious.

"Shoot, he was the best-looking boy in high school, but he almost never dated. He seemed really, really shy."

Elliott began to suspect something. It made sense, but he didn't want to confront Duchamps with it right now. He might need him to testify, so he wouldn't take the risk of making him a hostile witness.

"OK, you guys," Elliott told his Task Force investigators, "Let this man get back to his life. You have what you need. You know the name and you know what to do with it."

82

Morgan Little couldn't believe what he was hearing from his contact in the Department of Motor Vehicles. He had dated Donna Ruiz a few times and the chubby young woman had been taken with the tough cop. Recognizing the woman's value as a source of information, Mo called her often and saw her enough to keep her feeling there might be a future for them together. She loved him and he led her to believe her feelings were reciprocated.

Little loved nobody. Donna fulfilled his need for sexual release a few times a month. In return, she cleaned his apartment every Sunday and provided him a window into confidential information in state computers. He had not told her of his resignation and didn't plan to do so. She was still valuable to him as an unlicensed private investigator for some unsavory individuals who paid well for a man with good connections within the law enforcement community.

"That gringo you had me check up on, Mister Mo, some other people are checking on him. There's some kind of task force here that asked for his picture and all his old addresses."

"Old addresses, not just the current one?" Little knew this was unusual. It also meant they were tracing Pete's past movements.

So good ol' Pete's been up to no good, and that's good news.

"Listen, sweetheart," he ordered the DMV data clerk, "See if you can find out what cases he might be connected to. I'll see if any of my old buddies can find out anything about a task force in the department.

"Thanks for the heads-up, darlin', and let me know if you learn anything else about this guy."

Little removed his shoulder holster and installed the trigger lock on his Colt .357 magnum revolver. Placing the pistol back in the holster, he locked the rig in his gun safe, removed the fake badge from his wallet, and drove into the city.

"How the hell are we supposed to conduct business in this room with all these people around?" Capt. Alvin Jackson complained.

"It's that damned task force," Asst. Chief Mickey Bundy pointed out. As chief of the Traffic Division, he had called his captains and lieutenants together to discuss allegations of sexual harassment against officers by women who had been stopped for traffic violations. "They're working with the Feds and some fuckin' reporter on a tri-state murder spree of some sort."

"Well, how can we discuss complaints against individual officers and keep their names confidential?"

"Look, we can clear the room when we get to the point in our meeting that we're naming names," the captain explained. "But there's no reason not to let these guys take their breaks just because we need a couple of tables."

Little, with his back to the conversation as he nursed his lukewarm coffee, smiled inwardly.

So they're looking at Pete as the doer! Bet Derek'd pay good money for this information.

Following his conversation with Donna, Little had decided today might be a good day to hang around the headquarters building downtown and see what scuttlebutt he could pick up. He would never have thought he could get this kind of an edge on the man who had blackmailed him into resigning, the guy who had put Derek Prinz in a wheelchair for life.

He knew that Prinz was working as a stringer for a couple tabloids, and had seen his byline a few times on the lurid covers of the tabs displayed at the grocery checkout.

"Maybe the chief would let us use his conference room when we're talking about something a little touchy," Jackson suggested.

"Worth a shot. Anytime the bigwigs aren't gonna be using it, he should make it available to the troops," Assistant Chief Bundy agreed. "I'll take it up with him after we finish. Maybe we can do the confidential part of our meeting there tomorrow."

"Yeah, the break room's not suitable for this kinda shit" Jackson continued. "Always a few of the guys around, and cops have big ears."

83

"You fucking slut! I know you've been shacking up with the county commissioner, and if you don't give me the lowdown on someone else, it's your story that appears on this week's cover, and your husband can see it on newsstands and in all the drug stores and 7-11's in town! Is that what you want?" Prinz was still browbeating his source for his main story this week when he saw the flag for an E-mail message from Morgan Little pop up on his computer screen.

The crippled ex-TV reporter now made his living writing for the nearly half-dozen tabloid papers and magazines in the area, using the telephone and the Internet as his primary sources of information. He knew the commissioner's mistress had inside information on County Judge Elmo Abramowicz and he also knew that she would soon break and spill her guts. By now, she was crying. He hung up on the woman.

Prinz' name gave instant credibility to anything he wrote. The public still remembered him from his time before the television cameras. That he had been arrested, fired, and disgraced was information the public had never received, thanks to a generous plea bargain that required he not appear on local television news shows and that he make generous restitution to Willie Nell and the station's insurance carrier for her treatment.

In Texas, the County Commissioner's court is headed by the County Judge. Although the story was small potatoes, anything about a county judge would guarantee him good placement, maybe even a cover. And that's what decided the worth of a story in the tabloid journalism. That Abramowicz had pulled strings to get police to reduce charges against his teenage daughter, who'd reportedly been rounded up in a drug raid, didn't rank alongside the unsolved murders he had been investigating with that bitch Willie Nell Autrey, but he could picture the headline:

Judge Uses Clout
to Save Junkie Daughter

Dallas, TX — County Judge Elmo Abramowicz again has abused his office, coercing Dallas police officers to soft-peddle charges against his teenage daughter rounded up in a major drug raid.

The judge reportedly threatened a narcotics detective if possible drug-dealing charges against his underage daughter didn't go away.

Melanie Abramowicz, 14, was released without bail only 30 minutes after her arrest, the People's Voice learned today.

The judge's daughter was arrested for drug possession, that much was true. The raid was only an unannounced locker inspection at her high school, however. An aging marijuana cigarette in a baggie was the only find, one of dozens in the school. The allegations of traffing and the rest the details in the story were fictions from Prinz' imagination. A retraction in a week or two would appear on a back page somewhere.

Derek opened Mo Little's email message.

Brother D,

What would you pay to be able to get back at Peterson? I mean get back real good.

Mlittle

Prinz pressed 3 on his phone to autodial Little.

"This is Mo."

"It's Derek. Whatcha got?

"Let's talk money first, man."

"OK, how much?"

"You tell me," Little said, cryptically. "Let's just say we can get him put in jail for a long, long time. But I want a clear 20 thou for the story."

Prinz whistled appreciatively. "I can't pay that kind of money, and you know it."

"But the tabs can. Take it to them. Tell 'em it blows the whistle on a serial killer who's the target of a three-state manhunt."

"Oh shit! Peterson?"

"None other. Just call your richest rag and tell the fuckers to get the money together — cash. Don't want the cops tracking this to find the leak, OK?"

"Damn! Mo, this story'll scoop that little cunt who took my job. She'll shit when she sees my byline on it."

"So you get two revenges for one price; is that 20-K starting to look like a bargain? Should I raise the price for my information?"

"Should I make you dead and write a story about another cop who ate his gun? Not much money in those; happens all the time," Prinz warned.

The journalist's head was spinning. He had wanted to kill the bastard. Now he could send him to prison for life, or to death row. That was even better. "Let's do it. Call me tonight and I'll give you a timeline for payment."

Prinz hung up and called the "People's Voice" syndicated headquarters in New York. Twenty-First Century Publishing printed 15 tabloids, 12 of them with multiple runs for different markets. Altogether, they appeared in more than 120 different metropolitan areas.

Prinz was already planning the best use of the information and how to get the tabs bidding against one another for the exclusive, when, four hours later, a woman knocked on the door to his condo. When Prinz opened the door, she simply handed him a canvas bag, nodded, and left. He rolled the motorized wheelchair to the window and watched while she got into a little BMW 325 and drove away. Only then did he open the bag.

It was all there. Five bundles of C-notes, 100 bills to the bundle. Fifty-thousand dollars! He would clear $30,000 after paying off Little. If Mo's story didn't check out, he'd call a special number and the woman would return for the bag. If all the money was there, she'd disappear. If it wasn't, the man on the phone said the company would see to it Prinz disappeared.

What Little neglected to tell the defrocked crime reporter was that he had also placed an anonymous call to Pete's home and left a cryptic message that he would be making the cover of all the tabloids in a couple of days.

The money's good, but this asshole doesn't deserve to enjoy his revenge too much.

84

The voice on the phone was venomous. "You deny, Chief Justin, that your Task Force L J is seeking a serial killer, and that they have narrowed that search to a single suspect, a man from New Mexico named Lucas Peterson, and known around Dallas as Pete Peterson?" The haranguing tone of the New York editor of the "People's Voice" left no doubt that Andy had only two choices: confirm the facts or refuse to confirm or deny them. Either way, the story would appear on the newsstands, and that would alert Pete and send him to cover.

Andy had liked the easygoing man who had intervened when Derek Prinz had attacked Willie Nell Autrey. They'd met at the hospital; Andy recalled that Pete had even brought flowers. At first, the city's top cop figured the man had designs on the young reporter — until he saw how he looked at Anita. The police chief sighed. His profiler, Grady Elliott, had warned investigators time and again that serial killers were, so often, very likable, personable people. In many cases, they held down responsible jobs, were active in church and community, and had no police record.

If they looked like the rank and file of the thugs and hoodlums his officers dragged in for violent crimes, it would be easier. First of all, victims wouldn't have lowered their guard to let people like that get close to them. The photo of Pete on the front pages of tomorrow's tabloids wouldn't be a mug shot, rather it would be a picture from his college yearbook of a handsome, clean-cut kid. A kid who may have left a trail of more than 20 bodies behind him since that picture was snapped.

Justin's first call after talking to the New York journalist was to Elliott, "Round up your guys and circle the wagons, Grady, the guano is about to fly."

As Justin detailed the call he'd just received from New York, Elliott wasn't as disturbed as the chief expected. "We've been lucky, Boss. As much as we've learned so far flying beneath the radar like this without the press catching on. I'm surprised we got this far."

"Only one question, Grady: can we get to Pete before this gets out?" Justin asked.

"No. Someone tipped him off. He disappeared a couple days ago. I sent Jimmy Cates and a couple of uniforms to his apartment. He wasn't there, so they went to that garage where he works. They haven't seen him and he didn't call in.

"He's skipped, chief."

"Fuck! Or, as Willie might say, fuck, fuck, fuck, fuck, fuck!"

"Kinda grows on you, doesn't she, chief? Me too."

85

Anita was used to being single and comfortable spending time in her North Dallas apartment, tastefully furnished despite the eclectic mixture of artwork on the walls. There wasn't anything on TV that interested her, so the forensics specialist poured herself a glass of inexpensive, but exceptional Beaujoulais Villages, settled into her worn but comfortable recliner, and started reading the new murder mystery, featuring a female medical examiner, of course. It was a comfortable routine; she often lost track of time in the pages of a good novel. Tonight, the exciting book kept her turning pages until way past midnight when the hours and a second glass of wine took their toll.

She was barely asleep when she heard the banging on the door. Wrapping a thick terrycloth robe around her, she retrieved her Smith & Wesson .38 Special from her nightstand and slipped it into her pocket.

In this town, only a fool answers a knock on the door at two o'clock in the morning without a weapon.

"Who is it?" she said through the door, not loudly.

Shouldn't wake the neighbors. Miz Abernathy would talk about it for a month.

"It's me, Pete."

Anita turned the thumb lock and rolled back the deadbolt, unlatched the burglar chain that she always fastened even though she knew they were useless. Then she opened the door.

Pete was agitated and fidgety. "Anita, I need to know — do you like me?"

The surprised woman smiled and shook her head from side to side. Realizing what she'd done she blurted, "I don't mean 'no' I don't like you, I mean 'no' I can't believe you're here in the middle of the night asking me such a thing."

She barely gave it another second's thought before she added, "Get your butt in here or Miz Abernathy will be telling everybody we were doing the big nasty on the front stoop!"

Pete stepped inside the apartment, and Anita locked the door behind him. He closed the distance between them in a step and took her in his arms and kissed her fervently. Anita melted into the embrace and returned his passion as Pete's hands moved inside her robe.

"I really like you, girl, and I want you."

"Me too," she said breathlessly.

"I want you to come with me, right now."

"Impetuous, are we?" Anita smiled at her soon-to-be lover. "The bedroom's this way," she said, taking him by the hand.

"No, I mean, let's go away for awhile. Right now!"

"And just where would we be going at this time of day?"

"New Mexico."

"Say what!?"

"I have to leave town for awhile. I'd like you to come with me. Can you call in tomorrow and get a couple weeks off?"

"Probably, but …"

"Toss some stuff in a suitcase and let's get on the road, then."

For some reason that Anita would never be able to explain to anybody, she complied. Unselfconsciously, she shed the robe and her pajamas. Naked before Pete, she dug in her lingerie drawer for a pair of sensible cotton panties and a sports bra and wordlessly put them on. As she pulled a pair of blue jeans out of another drawer, Pete turned her toward him, and kissed her again, hands cupping her well shaped butt. She could feel his erection against her abdomen, but pushed him away with a smile. "We'll have our time. Now, what's the weather gonna be like?"

"Nice, cool, but cold at night. Pack a light jacket and some warm socks. Oh, yeah. Something you can walk in the mountains in — boots or sturdy athletic shoes."

"I guess you don't mean cowboy boots. I'll have to get some on the way. My pink tennies are purely for the gym, not for mucking around on trails."

"And there won't always be trails where we're heading, so that's a really good idea, young lady."

A light sweater topped the jeans and sandals to complete Anita's traveling ensemble. Next, she began throwing things into a rolling suitcase as Pete ticked off items she might need. She checked her purse to be sure her wallet and badge were there, then retrieved the pistol from the robe in the floor and placed it with the badge. She retrieved a box of ammunition from the nightstand and tossed it into the open suitcase.

"Wow. You were expecting the boogeyman, were you?" Pete said appreciatively.

"Now I know you won't be flirting up the waitresses at the truck stops, Mister Pete,' she responded in kind.

Within 20 minutes, her suitcase joined Pete's own baggage in the back of the pickup and they headed toward the Interstate.

Between Dallas and Fort Worth, Pete exited I-30 at a convenience store that also had gas pumps. "Can you get us some snacks and drinks while I top up the tank?" He tossed her a Styrofoam cooler. "Better get a bag of ice, too."

As she quickly amassed a cache of chips, cookies, nuts, and canned sodas, Anita began to think about what she was doing.

Pete noticed the thoughtful look on her face as she placed the cooler and two plastic bags between the seats in the cab.

"What's wrong?"

"Pete, I like you — a lot … and I love what you did for Willie Nell. But are we ready for this? I mean … I hardly know you."

Pete's handsome face broke into a dazzling smile. "I hear marriage is a great way to get acquainted."

86

"Hello, Brat," Willie Nell said as her sister answered the phone.

"Back at ya," Sunny replied. "How's Brenda Starr, girl reporter, doing? Found out anything new?"

If you only knew!

"How's it going with you?"

"Still crippled and still an orphan, and you?"

"That's beginning to be unfunny, Kid."

"I'm still a beautiful person inside and out."

"And a fuckin' pain in the butt."

"Well, I may be having to change my standard crippled little waif image anyway. Got a big deal surgery scheduled. Doc says my leg is developed enough for the prosthesis implant."

"That's wonderful!" Willie Nell exclaimed. "Look kiddo, I'm in traffic but wanted to see if I could come by. Got some stuff to tell you." Although she was on the toll road and had a prepaid tag, she was telling the truth, some yoyo was at the prepaid gate and holding up traffic digging for change! Fuck! Shit! Crap! She looked around for a short line and switched lanes other than the one ol' numbnuts was in. What a jerk!

"You solved the case?"

"What case? You're not supposed to know about that shit! "

"You didn't think Miz Edie wouldn't tell me, did you? And don't worry. I tsk-tsk'ed her good and it got no further. I haven't told anyone, not even my shrink."

"Well, the Task Force is regrouping back in Dallas to launch a manhunt and we'll probably be concentrating in New Mexico. But I think you and I need to talk to your shrink together while I'm in town; I may not be back for some time."

"I always suspected you needed to get your head candled anyway, big sister. God knows I don't need it."

"Seriously. There's a lot of shit for you to hear and for us to sort out. When's your next appointment?"

"What a mouth! Is that the real reason for your call. Getting' down to the nitty gritty, huh? Wanta pick my shrink's brains. And I thought you just missed me. She and I meet every Thursday afternoon at 2."

"When you're right, you're right, you paranoid little troll. Can you see if she'll let me sit in?"

"Only because I'm a wonderful person. But you gotta bribe me a bit; what say you take me for chicken-fried steak at Celebration."

"Deal! Can you make the reservations?"

"Deal," Sunny echoed.

87

As she ended the call, Willie Nell worried about the coming meeting with Sunny and her counselor.

How will she feel when I tell her that Uncle Brock is really my father? Happy for me —us — or more orphaned than she is now that we're not really sisters?

The fear depressed her, so she changed her focus to the task force. Merriweather had called her and said to let Atlee and Ed Soames know the Task Force was regrouping for a manhunt. Then he told her about Prinz' stories in the tabloids.

"Grady says we should try to take Peterson alive, but that he's tempted to issue a 'shoot on sight' order for Derek Prinz," Merriweather said with a laugh.

"Let me get my fuckin' gun, then. Seriously, Jeremy, I need to talk to Grady."

"Sure Willie, let me patch you through to him." After a couple of clicks, Merriweather came back on the phone. "You're connected, go ahead."

"Willie?"

"Hiya Detective Profiler Task Force Honcho Elliott."

"Hi, you beautiful thing, you. You on the road?"

"Your side of Abilene and cruising at 85 per. Hear Derek is no longer one of your favorite writers."

"That sunovabitch outed the Task Force and sent Peterson on the lam. I think he had a source on the inside."

"Surely not one of us!"

"Nah. Probably one of his old cop buddies who overheard something. Had to happen sooner or later, and I think this constitutes later. We've been lucky we weren't made a long time ago."

"Guess you're right. It just pisses me off that it had to be Derek to do it and that he probably sold it to the tabs for a bundle of cash."

Elliott hated that he had to be the one to broach the next part of the conversation, but Willie needed to know, and deserved to hear it from him. "Willie, he's not alone. We believe he has Anita Polanski with him. She called in and said she was taking a sabbatical for a couple weeks. That was the same day he pulled up stakes."

"Could it be a coincidence?" Willie Nell asked, hopefully.

"Well, her Corvette's still at her apartment. And it looks like she's traveling light; one suitcase, very few clothes, but most of her makeup and self hygiene stuff."

"How'd you get a warrant?"

"Didn't need one. Her sister reported her missing and has a key to the apartment," Elliott explained.

"When we told her about the time off and about Pete Peterson, she became concerned because she knew they were seeing each other. We didn't file a missing person report since she called in, but the sister let us into the apartment and told us what was missing."

"Grady, do you think his escape was planned or do you think he just reacts more than he thinks these murders out? You've told us his killings weren't planned, and that some event or thing triggered the slayings."

"I think he's just heading where he's most comfortable. Familiar territory. I don't think he's got an actual plan—just a knee-jerk reaction."

"I was telling Abe I was put in mind of a song Mama wrote about the time our kitten got into the ball of yarn and created a puzzle of string in the house."

"You lost me, girl, what's all this have to do with that song or that yarn?"

"We think we have a string to follow, then here comes a snarl or a knot that throws us into another direction. Pete or Luke or whoever the fuck he is has tangled things into a mess like that kitten made of the ball of yarn."

"That's for damned sure."

"How many of the guys are back?"

"Everybody but you and Abe. Ed just arrived an hour ago. Abe phoned; he's maybe an hour or less behind you."

A white shape shot past Willie Nell's SUV. "Like hell he is. That Cajun bastard just passed me doing a hunnert miles an hour!" Grimly, she increased pressure on the accelerator to keep pace with the speeding Crown Victoria.

88

Talk buzzed around the big conference table as members greeted each other, swapped information, told tall tales, and caught up on gossip. In other words, the men and women of Task Force LJ applied the social oil that held them in suspension as a single, cohesive unit.

Bang.

Elliott had finally commandeered a gavel. The buzz in the room decreased like someone had slowly turned down a volume knob. "Some of you know, a few of you don't, that we have a single suspect for the Lacey Jay murder and most of those similar slayings that Willie Autrey brought to us four months ago."

Elliott was pleased to notice that the group's seating order was decidedly eclectic, cops, civilians, FBI agents all together. No cliques. "Our friend from Louisiana, Abe Atlee, our own scribe, Willie, and a retired detective from the DPS were able to find sufficient cause for us to name Lucas Peterson as our single suspect."

The buzz started again, and again the Task Force Commander banged the gavel. "But most of you saw the tabloid with Peterson's picture. Unfortunately, he saw it too and blew out of town. He took one of our own with him: Crime Scene Analyst Anita Polanski.

"We don't know if she knows he's on the lam. We don't know if she's a hostage. Hell, we don't even know for sure that he hasn't killed her like these other women."

The group buzz didn't arise again at this pronouncement. Instead, dead silence and grave faces filled the room. The Dallas cops all knew and respected Anita. Willie Nell and Anita were best friends. The case of random murders had stopped being random; it had touched home.

"I also have some more profile information on Peterson." Elliott described the short conversation with Lucas' uncle. "I think that after his father left, Dixie Peterson sexually abused her son, possibly as a surrogate for her common-law husband. From Bo's description of this woman, she wouldn't be a very attractive partner for some guy to want to take to the sack."

Then Elliott dropped a small bombshell. "I think we may eventually learn that Lucas' first murder was Dixie Peterson, his mother, sometime in his early teenage years.

"The child was so traumatized by both her abuse of him and by his guilt over killing her that he relives that scene over and over again. All of the victims resemble Dixie, tall, slim, and blonde. We'll probably learn that other women he dated over the years were never so much as mistreated."

"But why doesn't he kill them the first time they're together?" Atlee asked. "That woman out in Fort Hancock, damn. They dated for two years and were in love. In the interview, he showed the detective an engagement ring he had bought for Billie Jean Bollinger."

"I think there's a trigger, something that occurs during the course of love-making, that brings on the rage. It's probably the exact thing his mother was doing when he killed her."

"Oh fuck, fuck, fuck, fuck, fuck!"

"What is it, Willie Nell?"

"It's a blowjob."

The room of cops roared in hoots and laughter.

"Quiet! Right Now!" Elliott turned back to the young reporter. "And just how did you pick that out of thin air, young lady!?"

"Think about it, Grady. It's something that a lot of women don't enjoy, and a lot of the women who do perform fellatio on their husbands, lovers, boyfriends, whatever — well, they only do so when asked."

"And this applies because…?"

"Because Lucas or Pete or whatever fucking name you want to call this son of a bitch doesn't ask."

"That's right," Helen chimed in. "I almost never do it unless a guy pushes for it, and even then not always."

Naomi agreed. "I do it as a special favor, you know, as a surprise or on a special occasion."

"We have to assume that even though we have something in the neighborhood of 20 victims, Lucas has had sex more times than that over 25 years," Elliott continued profiling Lucas. "Police in Silver City and in Fort Hancock polygraphed Lucas, but they also interviewed other women who had been with him. They described him as a perfect gentleman."

He was suddenly interrupted.

"Oh shit! Oh fuck!"

"Willie Nell?" Elliott reacted to the reporter, whose face was a mask of anguish.

"Anita! She's with him."

"Go on. This is a disaster?"

"We had a talk a few days ago. She'd never given oral sex; I tried to talk her into trying it with Pete … uh, Lucas."

"Well, if she's a hostage, she might not be all that anxious to be doing the big nasty with her abductor anyway," Helen Summers volunteered.

"What if she doesn't know he's our suspect and just took off with him for a good time? We might already be too late," Willie Nell wailed.

89

"Take a look at these pictures, Marty."

Detective Elliott and the FBI special agent Johnson, as ranking members of Task Force LJ, found themselves with no pressing duties. They both had dispatched their investigation teams and were steeped in the anxiety that goes with management when awaiting the outcome of a big decision. It was now in the hands of other people and they would be contributing very little at this point in the manhunt. Now they sat in the Command Center with Merriweather, who manned the Communications Center, essentially a radio/telephone desk in the back right corner of the conference room.

Johnson took his feet off the big conference table, stood, and walked around the table to the wall of victim photographs taped to the glass windows between the hallway and the conference room taken over by the Task Force.

"Whatcha see?"

"Don't all these girls look alike?"

"Why, yes. They do. But it's not unusual for a serial killer to target a specific victim profile."

Elliott held up a hand. "That's not where I'm going with this."

"Let's assume that our discussions two days ago about this guy suffering PTSD are correct."

"OK, I'm with you."

"Something has to trigger the blackout, if that's what's happening."

"So?"

"What if he's not profiling his victims, Marty?"

"OK, now you lost me."

"Let's say he's like every other bachelor on the street; he dates a lot of different women. So how come he goes years between murders?"

Marty whistled."Wow, you're saying he doesn't kill every woman he dates."

"Just those who look like this."

"But why?"

"Maybe they remind him of someone?"

"So why's he fuck 'em first, then kill 'em?"

"Maybe the event comes during the sex act at some point." Elliott removed a photograph. "Since there's no premeditation, there's no escape plan in place, either."

"That would kinda explain why some bodies were hidden, and others were left right where they died," Johnson agreed. "And it also fits with the various methods of murder. He just used what was at hand, and if no weapon of convenience was available, he used bare hands."

"OK. So, what could be the trauma that would cause this?" Elliott asked.

"That's your field, Mister Profiler."

"I'm getting there. Give me time to think. Alright, it has to be something related to sex."

"He was raped!?"

"Not likely. That would have been a homosexual encounter. The psychopathology would be different."

"Injury to his sexual organs?"

"Closer," Elliott said. "But no cigar. I'm thinking about sexual abuse, probably as a child and over a long period of time."

Marty mulled over what Elliott was saying. "So these murders aren't premeditated. And that means that this dirtbag could cop an insanity plea, land in a cushy psycho hotel for a few years, then walk away with a trail of a couple dozen bodies behind him?"

Elliott took a deep breath. He knew that if Lucas had been in a blackout state, he couldn't be held responsible for his actions, although he also knew juries were more likely to convict than not, despite evidence of insanity. It was the hardest defense to mount succesfully. "He probably wouldn't walk until after any conviction was lost in the appeals process," he told the FBI agent.

"But if we go after him for only one murder, we have a chance of making it stick."

"Which one would work without him being able to bring up the insanity plea?"

"Only the first one."

Marty buried his head in his hands. "I'm lost again."

"The first murder is the event that Lucas flashes back to. I'm going to presuppose for the sake of our discussion, that he was being abused sexually by his mother, probably had been for years. The rage inside the little boy festered, but he grew bigger and stronger, until, at last, he could overpower her."

"Now I'm back on track," Johnson said nodding. "So he plotted to kill her, a murder case we have no record of, right?"

"You got it, Marty." Elliott continued building on his theory, "We thought the mother abandoned him, according to interviews with Duchamps."

"When, in fact, he'd killed her and stashed her body," Marty was catching up with the profiler now.

Elliott thought he had the complete picture. "And during sex, at some point he flashes back to that event, He kills his mother over and over again. That's what's going on!"

"We need to find out where he hid her body. But we still have a bit of a problem; he was likely a juvenile at the time, preteen or early teens. The premeditation and the cold-blooded nature of the crime could be the hook we hang our efforts on to prosecute him as an adult."

Marty's face hardened and, with a tight-lipped smile, he said, "A judge won't really be happy about any effort by defense to try a middle-aged man as a juvenile."

90

"So, why are we doing this, Pete." Anita wasn't opposed to extemporaneous adventure and road trips, but Pete's little jaunt wasn't making a lot of sense.

"Anita, I care a lot for you, probably falling in love with you, but I can't tell you everything right now. Just give me time to sort things out in my mind."

Love? Did he say love?

The admission of feelings for her caught Anita by surprise. She was stunned and delighted. This gentle man with the big muscles, who could be so forceful when the chips were down — she thought of the Willie Nell rescue — had removed her doubts in a single statement.

They checked into a Motel 6 for the evening, and the lovemaking was everything she had hoped it would be. Lucas was experienced, gentle, considerate, and creative. She had never been more satisfied by a lover. He asked nothing of her, simply attended to her needs so completely and so expertly that she melted like butter at his touch.

Do I love him or am I just excited by how good he is in bed? Do I want to make a life with him or am I just enjoying the excitement of running away with him?

"Pete," she said when he emerged from the bathroom after showering, "will you be going back to Dallas when this ... this thing you're doing ... when it's all over?"

Pete sat on the edge of the bed. And took both her hands in his own. "I know your career and your life is there. I also understand that if I want anything meaningful with you, it will most likely be in Dallas.

"But honey, let's just let this play out awhile before we get into heavy discussion, Okay?"

Anita carefully avoided any talk of Pete's past for the time being as they drove through the seemingly endless West Texas landscape, the Interstate a steady throb beneath the tires of the pick-up. For his part, Pete kept up a steady stream of chatter about the wilderness and its mountains, and about his love for cars and for fixing them. Anita told him about finding the old Corvette and about how she had fallen in love with its classic shape and had become obsessed with restoring the split-window coupe to a showroom appearance.

91

Pete experienced his first flashback episode their third night on the road. They had rented one of the small, picturesque cabins along Bear Creek in Piños Altos.

It was a few minutes before 3 o'clock in the morning when he sat up with a start, the sudden motion jarring Anita awake as well.

"Pete? What is it? Are you okay?

Her lover was drenched in sweat and shaking. He didn't respond to her questions, but he had been with Billie Jean Bollinger. He had revisited the afternoon he had twisted her head so violently he heard her neck snap.

My God, it really was me! They were all me!

The mechanic put his head in his hands and sobbed.

"I had a nightmare, an awful nightmare, that's all," he said after he had been able to regain self control. He lied to her and told her he dreamed something terrible had happened to his mother.

Since Anita already knew his mother had disappeared, she could understand how he could have nightmares of what might have become of her, so she didn't push him to tell more. Instead, she took him in her arms and held him close to her until his shaking had ceased.

"Anita," Pete said into her shoulder, "you're the best thing that's happened to me in a long, long time. I love you so much."

"I love you, too," Anita said, for the first time voicing the true feelings she had for him. They both laid back down and she held him close until he returned to sleep.

Pete ignored the episode the next day as they prepared to hike into the mountains. They would drive as far as the Clinton P. Anderson Overlook, where there were campgrounds, then hike into the wilderness by way of the trailheads at the Gila Cliff Dwellings National Monument. A small general store in Piños Altos was surprisingly well equipped for hikers. They purchased backpacks, trail mix, jerky, water bottles and a first-aid kit. Anita found a pair of hiking boots she liked and paid for them with her debit card. Pete bought an extra bedroll; his tent and camping gear were already in the back of the pick-up.

"Get something we can cook for supper, steaks or burgers, maybe," he told her. "We'll cook over open fire after we set up the tent."

Anita was thrilled. "Sounds like fun. I haven't really been camping since I was a girl."

"Hmmm, you're still all girl to me," Pete said surreptitiously squeezing her ass.

Thirty minutes later, Pete pulled into the campgrounds opposite the overlook. Anita, not a nervous passenger, was impressed with the trip. "Wow, what a drive! On some of those hairpin curves, I just prayed no one was coming the opposite direction."

"Yeah. The line goes something like: 'if you see taillights ahead of you, they could be your own'." Pete replied, beginning the task of unloading their gear and provisions.

"Get into your boots. I want to take you to one of my favorite places in the whole world."

Pete gathered only a bag of trail mix and some bottled water, "Let's drive up to the cliff dwellings. From the visitor center you'll have about a mile climb, but it's worth it. It'll also help you start getting used to exertion in this thin air."

While his sweetheart was preparing herself for an adventure, another flashback rocked Pete. This time, it was Sharon Atlee whose murder he relived.

Am I going to relive others? How many were there?

Pete was drinking an ice-cold bottle of Ozarka° water when Anita pronounced herself all set for adventure. He splashed water over his face and neck to hide the sweat that had accompanied his brief vision.

"Then we're ready?"

"Yessir, Mountain Man."

The drive was uneventful but the scenery was breathtaking. Anita seemed to gasp in awe each time they emerged from a curve on the steady climb to the tourist attraction.

At the visitor center, Anita picked up brochures and placed a $5 bill in the donation box. She could feel a difference trying to breathe at this altitude compared to Piños Altos.

But the mile-long hike up the side of the mountain was gradual and well traveled, not difficult to climb. Anita breathed heavily, but was anxious to glimpse remains of the homes and lives of the people of the Mogollon culture who lived in the Gila Wilderness from the 1280s through the early 1300s.

She didn't notice that Pete, who should be much more accustomed to the altitude and the terrain, was having more trouble than she was.

Pete was behind Anita by 25 yards or so when the third flashback struck. This time, it was Mona. He was dismayed by the bloody recollection of killing the woman and hiding her body.

Okay, God. I know what I have to do. And I will, just not today.

Anita explored the seven natural caves cut high into the southeast-facing cliff of a canyon. Five of the caves contained ruins of cliff dwellings, more than three dozen rooms. Ladders and hand-rails, installed by the park service, made accessibility reasonably simple and the views from inside the dwellings of the canyon and the Gila River made her long for her camera, which was in a closet back at her Dallas apartment.

She suddenly became aware that Pete was missing. Alarmed, she hurried back to the wooden ladders and looked down. He was sitting on a bench looking up at her.

He waved and motioned for her to continue her exploring.

Thirty minutes later, she joined him on the bench. "What's going on with you? You're really acting strange, and it's freaking me out a little."

He only said, "I'll tell you real soon."

Then he said something that scared her, a woman who had seen the worst of what people can do to other people. "That .38 of yours — I want you to keep it loaded and on your person at all times from now on."

92

"I put out an All-Points Bulletin on Peterson's pick-up and for any persons matching either description," Merriweather reported to Elliott.

Johnson was sitting at Elliott's desk when the phone call came over the Task Force Commander's speakerphone. "Good work, Jeremy, and the FBI can see to it that bulletins are issued in surrounding states, too,"

"You know, we'll do better with a paper trail if either of them are using plastic," he said after Elliott had severed the connection with the Comm Center. "Pete doesn't use plastic, but Miss Polanski does. We need to get all her card numbers."

"Got 'em from her apartment already. You can get through the red tape faster than I can with the banks, why don't you handle it?"

"Glad to."

Within hours, they had begun the task of following the trail of purchases Anita had made on her bank card. Because some merchants don't send in the credit card slips on a daily basis, the job of tracking spending can take days. If the charge goes through an automated transaction like a gas pump or card reader, however, it shows up instantaneously. They quickly learned that the couple had spent night before last at a motel in Sweetwater, but had received no word of purchases since.

"We know they're heading west," Elliott told Johnson and Atlee, who were sharing Starbucks with Merriweather at the Comm Center.

Atlee stood. "New Mexico, for sure." He walked over to the map at the end of the room. "His first victims were in Silver City and possibly, at the City of Rocks." He traced the route from El Paso to Deming to Silver City. "Remember, we determined he's not much on planning. I think he's gonna go to ground in country he knows and where he feels at home. The wilderness North of Piños Altos, New Mexico.

"I agree, but before I can commit the money and manpower to scour millions of acres of wild country, I need more than an enlightened guess."

"Sorry, Grady," Atlee said. "Guess we could have Hec and his folks keep an eye out for the truck."

"The APB will do that."

"Not like a personal request will. Police departments get dozens of bulletins. Let's make this personal. Let me talk to Hec."

"Go for it. In the meantime, we can begin the organizational steps for a manhunt to launch once we have confirmation of where they are."

"What constitutes a confirmation?" asked Merriweather.

"A reliable sighting or even a credit or bank card purchase. We can get it all ready to roll now, then just sit and wait."

The wait was three days, and the mood in the Task Force LJ Headquarters was getting testy.

"Why the fuck don't we just go on out there and get them? We know where they are," Willie Nell fumed.

"Duh," Naomi chided her, "There are nine of us — eight, because Jeremy's on the comm — and an area the size of Connecticut to comb through."

The sour ambience hadn't improved when Johnson burst into the room on the morning of the third day with a sheet of paper. "We got 'em!"

"They spent a night in a cabin in Piños Altos two nights ago and purchased a bunch of camping and hiking gear the next day at a local store.

"Let's saddle up."

"What about me and the comm center?" Merriweather asked.

"We'll have a mobile communication van and transfer command and control there. After that, you'll be backpacking a satellite cellular base station once we're on foot. Any communication from outside the Task Force and the search teams will be routed through regular police channels back to us," Elliott answered.

"Now we have a manhunt to organize."

93

Willie Nell stood in the midst of the clutter she called home and dialed Grady's number on a portable phone. One ring, two rings, three rings, four …

Where in the hell did you get off to so early in the morning?

She slammed the phone down on a still-unpacked carton marked "**MISC. CRAP**" in big black letters.

"Be careful what you tell movers when they ask what's in the box you just closed," she taunted herself. Half the second bedroom of the two-bedroom flat was stacked to the ceiling with cardboard boxes, oversized trashbags, and assorted household goods. The other half served as her office.

Almost every box had some terse label, usually a single, indecipherable word, or worse, an abbreviation as mysterious as hieroglyphics. Some boxes had no identification whatsoever. In other words, it was a crap-shoot when she tried to determine where anything might be. It's not that she recently moved. Her lease on the apartment was due renewal next month.

Have I lived like this for a year?

If she needed an article, she simply peeled the tape back and dug in a box until she found it.

One of these days, I'll get organized but not today.

Her promise to herself stayed unfulfilled. Today, she had to share an idea with Grady.

Grady, where the hell are you when I need you?

Deep in her heart, she knew she didn't really have anything new to say to him. She just needed to see him. She needed his strong body to engulf her. She needed to lose herself in him, in the maleness of him.

The doorbell brought her back from her musings. She opened the door to discover the man she'd been craving attention from standing there like an answered prayer.

"Hi," she said. "Did you get my ESP message or something?" She drew him inside trying to bring him closer.

"Willie Nell, behave yourself." He plunked two disposable cups from Starbucks on the carton beside the phone. "When do you think you might get around to settling in here?"

She shrugged her shoulders. "Maybe I won't have to if you ask me to move in with you."

"Like that's gonna happen," he said gruffly. "One day together and we'd be fighting like cats and dogs."

"But think of the making up. Haven't you heard? Makeup sex is the best there is," she replied, coquettishly.

"Girl, if I didn't know better, I'd think you were in heat for me."

Her lower lip protruded, then she said, "Why would that be bad?"

"You're too temporary right now. Even your living space is all boxed up. You can't let anyone in or anything out. How could you ever hope to have a relationship with a man?"

"You could help me change all that," she said. "I'm a quick study. Give me a chance and I'll prove just what I can do for you."

He opened the container in his hand and sipped. "Drink your coffee before it gets cold."

She plopped down on the arm of the sofa, because the cushions were covered with wads of newspaper and stuff taken from one of the boxes. A scrawl on the outside of the box at least hinted of its contents: "**WRITING CRAP**".

"Don't you find me at all attractive?" she asked Grady, her bottom lip still protruding.

"I'm not interested in any man-woman, boy-girl or in our case man-girl relationship at the moment. We have a serial killer to track down. Right now, tell me all you can about your late mother. If we can profile the women, perhaps we can get closer to finding the killer."

94

Grady nodded at FBI Special Agent Johnson. "Marty. ..."

Johnson stood, buttoning his suit jacket. "The FBI will be mounting a manhunt in Grant County, New Mexico, where we believe our suspect is heading, using this task force as its core. We will be joined by Federal investigators and specialists. Naomi has alerted New Mexico authorities and the Grant County Sheriff will take the point in coordinating the actual manhunt.

"We will also have help from State Police and local authorities in Grant County, including police from Silver City. The County Sheriff will be in command, once we cross into his jurisdiction."

Several hands shot up around the room.

Johnson nodded toward Helen Summers.

"I'm confused. What happened to Lucas Duchamps? I thought we were after him?"

"Same fuckin' guy," Willie Nell answered. "Pete Peterson's first name is actually Lucas. His common-law father was Duchamps, but the mother was Peterson. You all know my history with Pete. He came to my rescue when Derek Prinz attacked me, and befriended me in the hospital. I'm as shocked as anyone over this revelation."

"Marty," Ed Soames asked, "What about extradition? Didn't he commit some of the crimes in New Mexico?"

Johnson pointed to the black female FBI agent. Naomi stood. "I've talked to the state attorneys general involved. Because Texas has a more aggressive death penalty record, most jurisdictions, including Louisiana and New Mexico, officials have assured me there will be no problems with Peterson coming here for trial."

"What's Grant County like?" Jimmy Cates wanted to know.

"Abe, you've been there. Want to field this one?"

"Thanks Marty. Folks, Lucas — some of you know him as Pete — Peterson's from Deming and went to school in Silver City. He has spent a lot of time in the Gila National Forest, specifically the Mogollon Wilderness. "It's rugged, few roads and trails, and the altitude alone will be taxing. He knows the area and he's used to the altitudes. For the record, Silver City is higher than Denver, even if it looks like desert. It's 6,300 feet above sea level and the wilderness rises north of there to better than 10,000 feet in places.

"I'm an old coot and I got winded walking a block and a half from my car to the police station, so don't think it won't affect you."

"Is the suspect armed?" Merriweather asked.

Elliott fielded the question. "He has no record of using a weapon in the commission of his killings, but I'd always assume a suspect of this type of crime would be armed and dangerous.

"Pete is a disturbed person, possibly suffering from PTSD. That makes him impossible to predict. Just watch yourself out there. And watch out for your partner."

"So, when do we leave?"

"Willie, I know you have a personal matter to attend to, so probably does everybody else, especially those who have been out of town. Friday morning sound OK?"

When there was no dissent, Elliott continued. "Chief Justin has secured us two black and white units to travel in. Marty and his agents will travel in a specially outfitted communications van supplied by the FBI. Abe and Willie will ride with me in a black and white, and my troops will take the second patrol car. We will travel with lights only in the cities and with sirens on the Interstate. The comm unit will alert highway patrol units and local law enforcement as we come through their jurisdictions because folks, we're gonna be flying."

95

Willie Nell pecked at her laptop as she rode alongside Elliott, who drove the mobile communications van. In the back, Merryweather maintained contact with headquarters and with the other Dallas mobile units. With him sat Atlee, talking to law enforcement officials in New Mexico.

The reporter wasn't working on her story, she was writing a difficult letter to her sister. Willie Nell had been 10 years old when their daddy had died in that awful crash, but poor Sunny was just a baby.

The infant never again lived with them in the little trailer, only visited when her mother could pick her up in Dallas, a real rarity.

The baby had gone from Hudspeth Memorial Hospital in Sonora to Children's Medical Center in Dallas. When it became obvious there would be no money for the long and complicated recovery process the child would require, the baby was transferred to the Scottish Rite Hospital, which provides totally free care to crippled children.

Somewhere, social workers at the hospital found an angel, a donor who would pay for Sunny to remain in Dallas at a children's home near the facility. Sunny would spend almost as much time at Scottish Rite over the next few years as she would in the children's home, anyway.

Just a baby! How did she form such bitter memories from our past?

Willie Nell's thoughts focused on her little sister, now a teenager, and she went at the letter in earnest.

"Dear Sis,

"I'm on the road with my police buddies, but I've been poking around a lot into the lives of our parents as part of our investigation. I've learned some things I didn't know, but I've also come to realize I already had experiences and attitudes that you never had an opportunity to develop.

"I loved living there in Sonora when it was just Mama and me. In the evenings when she was working at The Nook, I stayed over at Miz Edie's, a wonderful woman you barely know.

"Anyway, things were good for awhile. Mama found a band, The Time Travelers, to sing with, and they had a regular gig at the VFW one Saturday a month and at the Rusty Spur, a local bar, the other Saturdays, and some Friday's when the little honky-tonk could afford to pay them. Sometimes they'd play at another place up in Abilene.

"I got to go with her a few times. Miz Edie'd always come along on those trips, too. But that only happened during school vacations. Summers were good. That's also when we'd come and get you to bring home.

"You threw such tantrums when we'd take you back to Dallas. Mama tried to make it more festive; she'd get a bucket of chicken and biscuits from 'the Colonel' and fill a big old jug with Kool-Aid® and we'd picnic in those hills north of San Angelo. Usually, Mama and Miz Edie would spend the day before baking cookies for the trip.

"The ride home was always sad without you. I'd try to keep Mama's spirits up by singing one of those tunes she sang around the house. I learned that Mama wrote all those songs herself, words and music! We just thought they were little cheer-me-ups she'd learned over the years."

Willie Nell felt her tears beginning to come as she recalled the sad moments when she and her sister would be separated after their outings, but she continued writing.

"As I'd sing, I'd still hear you crying as we left you for more tests and operations and rehabilitation. Those partings were hard on us, too, you know. I understood that, even at the age of 11.

"Then came the day The Nook had to let Mama go. With only the money from her singing to live on, she could no longer afford to provide for my needs; she would be touring more with The Time Travelers. I was about your age then. I told Mama I could stay with Miz Edie until she made it

big in Nashville. That was our dream, you know — When Mama Gets to Nashville."

The reporter knew her sister really didn't know about their mother's dream, and the tears began to flow more freely.

I don't know that I've ever missed you more, Sunny, than I do at this minute."

Willie Nell continued the letter to her sister.

"You never knew how hard it was on Mama to give us girls to other people, to let strangers raise her babies. She did what she had to do to give us the best shot at building successful lives of our own. Did you know that Mama kept rooms for both of us, even though we weren't living at home at the end? Edie showed them to me. I got to visit much more than you did, but it wasn't like living in Sonora full-time, across the drive from Miz Edie, riding the bus to Sunday School, playing with the kids I'd known all my life. I couldn't just drop things and go with Mama on a whim anymore. It all had to be arranged."

"Damn it, Tell her how you feel!" Willie Nell chastised herself.

"And I missed you, too, believe it or not. I used to wonder what on earth was so important that two sisters couldn't be together. But then I discovered boys and sports and the usual teenage stuff; I sometimes told Mama I couldn't come with her to Dallas because I had something 'special' to do.

"She never let on how hurt I now know she must have been. She just told me to enjoy my girlhood while it lasted and to not be in a rush to grow up. I took her advice to heart, though. You should too. I didn't rush out to become some cowboy's child bride with a kid to raise before I was even old enough to vote or have a beer. Because of her, I got a good education and I have a career.

"Sunny, I wish I remembered those times even better. They were the last I had with Mama. I had just started high school, which was within walking distance of the children's home. when the call came for me to report to the principal's office. You know me; it wasn't the first time I'd been called to his office.

"It was the worst day of my life. Miz Edie barely coherent through her sobs and tears. At first, she only told me Mama was hurt. When she told me she was dead, we both went to pieces together. But she didn't tell me

it was murder until later, something I resented for years but that I now realize was very wise on her part.

"Did you know Mama didn't use Dude's name when she sang? She was Lacey Jay; she dropped Autrey altogether. She died still thinking Dude was a drunk and drunkenness had crippled her baby daughter. That's why she refused to use his name. I considered changing mine, too, but now I'm glad I didn't Dude was a much better guy than you think, darling sister. I knew him as Daddy until I was 10; you missed that.

"Your only knowledge is that he was driving when the accident occurred that left you a cripple. If I have a prayer for you, it's that someday you release all of that anger and resentment about your past so you can live joyfully in your future.

Elliott glanced from the road to look at the young woman beside him; he had heard the sob. Now he saw the tears trying pouring down her face.

"You OK, Willie.

"Fuck you, Grady. It's Willie Nell!"

96

Silver City, the county seat of Grant County, New Mexico, was founded in the summer of 1870 as a tent city shortly after John Bullard opened a silver mine. As optimism grew, townspeople began to build permanent houses using bricks made from local clay. Many still stand in Silver City's five historic districts.

Once the silver mine was depleted, copper took its place as the major area industry. The original county seat, Piños Altos, is a tourist attraction ghost town on the north edge of Silver City. In recent years, tourism has also become an important economic contributor.

Chief Hector Velasquez was waiting when Elliott, Atlee, and Willie Nell were ushered into his office. Sitting on a sofa to the chief's right was another law enforcement officer in a different uniform. Elliott rightly assumed this was the Grant County sheriff.

Hec shook Atlee's hand and introduced him to the tall, weathered man who rose from the sofa at the mention of his name. "Abe Atlee, this is Sheriff Virgil Crowley."

"Sheriff Crowley, a pleasure. Let me introduce my companions. This is Detective Grady Elliott from Dallas, the commander of Task Force LJ. And this pretty little lady is Willie Autrey, a reporter who initially tied all these murders together. She's a damned fine investigator herself."

Crowley raised an eyebrow, then slowly smiled. "Nice to see a man my age squiring around a lovely young woman. Gives me hope." The sheriff took her hand in both of his bony hands. Willie Nell estimated Crowley was a good five if not 10 years older even than Atlee, but she said nothing.

"I have two more carloads of Task Force with me," Elliott told the sheriff.

"Maybe we should move back to the break room; only place with enough chairs," Hec suggested. At that moment, Larry brought back the other six members of Task Force LJ.

Almost everyone was able to find a seat in the crowded break room, although Summer and Soames ended up sitting on the sink-board. When everyone had found a spot to settle, the sheriff stood with his arms folded. He was lanky with steely, no-nonsense eyes. His lip, a pencil line, connected two weathered cheeks. On his side was a holstered Colt .45 revolver with a 7-inch barrel, worn low, and tied to his leg like an Old West gunfighter.

The sheriff handed Hec a small stack of paper to distribute to the team. "I made everyone copies of some maps of the area," Crowley said. "believe me, you'll be needing them."

Once everyone had maps, Crowley began his briefing. "Here's how it's going to play out, people." He said in a soft, yet firm voice. "I organize and assign the manpower for this little trail hike. I will be teaming each of you with at least three people: a park ranger, one of my deputies and one of Hec's officers or state trooper. These park rangers are with you because they know this terrain better than any of us. My deputy is your search commander. You will all work together and stick to your assignments. "

"However, operational control will be the authority of your people," he said, nodding toward Elliott. "I know you will all be connected through that comm center van you brought with you, so make good use of it."

"From the moment we locate the subject, command and control switches to you and your command post. Your people in the field will relay your instructions to my deputies and the rest of their teams.

"Before anyone objects, I know there are a couple civilians among you. That will not be an issue. I suggest to you, Miss Willie, that you pay attention to the law enforcement officers with you, but when the chips are down, you're running your team with direction from the command post. That also makes you responsible for their lives. Do you read me?"

Willie Nell nodded soberly.

Atlee looked at Willie Nell. He really didn't want to let her out of his protection.

"Alright, now. I talked to Tom Senegal, the sheriff up in Catron. He told me that Highway 159 out of Mogollon is closed for the winter. He's going to run a search from up there down to the Glenwood Ranger Station and the Catwalk area.

"We're going to take the Gila Wilderness area and along the Gila River up to the Clinton Anderson Overlook."

The sheriff nodded at a gaggle of forest rangers. "Todd, I want each of your folks to team up with a task force member and whoever else is assigned with them." The rangers flowed toward the task force members, most heading in Willie Nell's direction.

"Annette, you'll guide Miss Autrey's team," the sheriff said, interrupting the stampede of youthful rangers hoping to share space with the sexy young reporter. Sam Ortega will be the deputy in charge of your group. You'll search from the Mimbres River and Valley to Lake Roberts. Silver City police have agreed to scour the wilderness north of Silver and around Piños Altos."

"Sheriff," Special Agent Johnson interrupted. "I can get a search chopper to help and a lot of experienced man-hunters. Where can you use them?"

"Can you send agents supported by helicopters into the mountains along Highway 15 up to and north of the Gila Cliff Dwellings In Catron County? Gets rid of any jurisdictional friction that could arise."

"You got it."

"If you need a marksman, take Helen Summers," Elliott suggested. "She's about the best rifleman in the department."

"Beats having to beat the bushes for one of our Fed snipers; they're spread pretty thin, Thanks, Grady."

"Sheriff, can I say something?"

"Sure, detective, you got the floor."

"Lucas Peterson — some of you know him as Pete Peterson — doesn't normally pose a threat to anyone. Do your best to take him alive, but don't put yourselves at risk to do so."

"You're the profiler Abe told us about, right," Hec asked. "Can you give us some more insight about the target?"

"I'll try." Elliott said. "Let me first say that Pete threw a monkey-wrench into our assessment of him when he took one of my forensics techs with him. At this point, we do not know if she is a willing companion or a hostage. Hell! We don't even know but what he's killed her and dumped her body somewhere.

"Whatever happens, if you encounter this guy, my cop's safety has to be the over-riding option in apprehending him."

Willie Nell interrupted the profiler. "Pete saved my life when I was attacked and assaulted, then he visited me and brought flowers while I was in the hospital. I don't think he's a bad guy, but he's one sick puppy. If Grady says he committed these killings in a PTSD blackout, then we're dealing with a psychological problem, not a criminal one."

Naomi James smiled at Willie Nell and winked. "Spoken like a bleeding heart reporter for sure," she said with a laugh.

"She's right, but Grady's right, too. Anita Polanski, the forensics tech, is a friend to both Willie Nell and me. Anita's been dating Pete for awhile now. Heck, he could have just asked her to elope with him. I think if he did, she'da said yes."

Sheriff Crowley stood up again and raised both hands. The room slowly quieted. "One other thing to t'all you flatlanders out there: Those cell phones you like so much are pretty useless out here. I've issued all my deputies long-range tactical radios, but I don't have any to spare. The state troopers are on their way here with a bunch of radios commandeered from various substations; there'll be enough for everybody.

"The important thing is to use them. Let people know if you spot this guy or his hostage, or even a sign they might have been in the location where you're looking. With choppers, we have a real advantage if we can just spot them one time. Now, go gather up with your team captains for specific assignments. Be back here at O-six-hundred in the morning to get your radios. Everybody get a good night's sleep, you'll need it."

"How old is that guy? Merriweather asked one of the deputies.

"Virgil? Well, he was named for Wyatt Earp's brother. I understand his father deputied for Virgil Earp when he was sheriff of Yavapai County in Arizona at the turn of the century, so I'd guess Sheriff Crowley's between 75 and 80."

97

It was a glorious morning Anta decided as she stuck her head out of the tent, crisp, cool clear, with very little wind. Pete was already up and was standing barefoot in only jeans as he shaved himself with cold water, using bar soap to work up a lather. Behind him, over a butane camp stove, a coffeepot emitted an irresistible aroma.

"Ready for bacon and eggs, Sleeping Beauty?"

God, I love this guy. Wonder where this will end up?

She slipped on a pair of jeans but didn't bother removing her pajama shirt. Who'd see how she was dressed anyway? But she did slip into her sandals again.

I guess I'm more of a tenderfoot than he is.

The coffee tasted every bit as good as it smelled, and Anita was surprised she enjoyed it so much without any milk or creamer. "I think I could get used black coffee as long as there's some sugar around."

Pete expertly broke two eggs into a skillet and laid four rashers of bacon on a piece of foil covering the second burner. After he flipped the eggs with a flick of the wrist, he laid a slice of bread on top of them and another atop the bacon. Within minutes, Anita was eating the best bacon and egg sandwich she'd ever tasted.

She noticed that Pete didn't ask her to help with the clean-up; he just wiped the skillet with a paper towel and set it aside, then removed the foil from the second burner and tossed it into their carry-out trash bag. The park was strict about its "carry in, carry out" policy.

He ducked back into the tent and within a minute was back, buttoning a long-sleeve flannel shirt and carrying his boots.

"Looks like I'd better get my ass in gear if we're going to do anything today, huh?" Anita disappeared through the flap. She emerged after considerably more time. "Can I be a cover-girl for 'Hikers Digest'?"

"Wowsie, wowser, woo-woo-woo," Pete exclaimed.

In reality, she'd only washed her face, brushed her hair, dabbed a little color to her cheeks and freshened her lipstick. The leggy blonde didn't need a lot of adornment. Even in jeans and a man's denim shirt, her curves were notice-able.

"Now what?"

"We either hit the trail or I take you back into the tent and ravage you."

"Tempting, but I just brushed my hair," Anita sniffed, tossing her head back in mock disdain.

Pete recommended a brisk hike that would keep them out in the rough until late afternoon. "But we gotta get back in time for the sunset. See that rock formation across the road from the entrance?"

Anita looked to where Pete pointed "Uh-huh."

"It's a bit of a scrabble to get to the top of it, but it's flat and a wonderful place to watch a sunset; you game?"

"You should know by now," she said, poking his arm.

98

Four teams were assigned to scour the areas on both sides of Highway 15 from its juncture with Hwy 35 north to the cliff dwellings. Atlee was assigned to a team consisting of a park ranger, a Silver City detective, with a sheriff's deputy in charge. The other three teams, which included the team with Willie Nell, were similarly configured. Atlee's team was led by Al Martinez.

"Robert," the deputy told Ranger Robert Bellamy, "you take the point; you're most experienced in this terrain. We'll keep these two between us."

Bill Jordan, the detective, complained. "You shouldn't be at the rear, Al. Let me walk drag."

"Look, I humped the boonies in Vietnam; the last guy has the best view of any possible ambush of the rest of the patrol. I know what I'm doing."

Jordan didn't say another word.

Atlee, who had kept quiet during the assignments and the briefings, finally spoke up. "There won't be any ambushes. This guy isn't homicidal when he's not in a blackout state, at which point he's a danger to whoever he's with. I'd hate to see someone get trigger happy and waste him just because he sees him."

On the other side of Highway 15, Ranger Annette Ten-Acres, a large, muscular young woman with short, straight hair led her group up the side of a rugged hill toward a black oval at least 80 feet higher than the roadway. "That's a cave and would make a good hiding place," she told Willie Nell.

"Are you an Indian?" the reporter asked.

"No," Annette laughed. "French-Canadian. But I married myself an American Indian computer programmer. I think he wanted me because I look more Indian than he does."

A New Mexico trooper, Larry Milhouse, took the point as they neared the entrance to the cave. Willie Nell realized this was an operational situation if Pete and Anita were in the cave.

"Stop," she told the trooper, who looked at her quizzically. "Try to see if you can bypass the entrance circle to approach from above it. It seems like it would be a lot safer."

The trooper, once he recalled the sheriff's instructions, relaxed. "You're right, Willie. But I need some firepower from another angle, too."

"That would be me, if it's OK with you, Willie," Deputy Ortega said, moving into a track that would bring him up to the right of the cave entrance.

99

Bellamy led Deputy Martinez' team downslope to a narrow trail that par31-leled the highway 200 feet above and a quarter mile away. Trees and rock outcroppings would make their travel almost invisible from above but would silhouette any movement at the highway or ridge against the sky. Atlee found himself impressed by the young ranger. Martinez dropped further behind as dragman once the team was on the trail; although hidden from an elevated view, its openness made them an easier target if they were spotted.

Atlee was mesmerized by the rugged terrain, taking as much in as he could see, swiveling his head from side to side and looking up and the rugged rock formations above him.

This country is breathtaking.

No sooner had the thought crossed his mind than he spotted a splash of red against one of the formations jutting up and out from the ridge.

He raised a fist, signaling the others to stop, and Martinez ran up to him. "Look," the retired cop told the deputy, pointing to the rim. "To the right of the top of that tree."

Martinez motioned him down and the two men squatted and moved to the inside of the trail. Bellamy and Jordan quickly joined them.

"See that point of red on the edge of that rock outcropping?" Atlee whispered.

"Yeah, it could be the corner of a blanket. But, fuck, it could also just be a potato-chip bag. But I think we better check it out."

Bellamy opened a small case at his belt and produced a pair of Nikon mini binoculars. "These might help."

Martinez took the 8-power binoculars and squinted through them. "There's fringe at the edge of the square; that makes it a blanket in my book."

"Angle's too steep to see what's on top of the rocks, though."

"Let's move back down the trail and see if we can't lessen the angle, then," Atlee suggested.

"Good idea. But stay close to the edge of the trail and try not to crop your focus; use your perpheral vision. It will pick up motion if you don't focus on any one thing. And remember, if you can't see them, it's less likely they can see you," Bellamy said.

Quietly, the team worked its way backward about half a mile. Moving inside a relatively thick stand of shrub, Martinez raised the binoculars again, ignoring the branches scratching at his skin and snagging his shirt.

"There are people up there; I can't see them as clearly as when we were closer, but there are at least two human beings on that rock."

"I know that formation," the ranger said, aloud now that they were so far from the rock formation. "That's the Clinton Anderson Overlook. There's a campground about 200 yards or so across the road from it."

Atlee keyed the mike on the portable radio. "LJ3 to Jayhawk, we have a spotting."

Elliott and Merriweather were in the Mobile Comm Center van at the junction of Highways 15 and 35. With them were detective Helen Summer, Sheriff Crowley, and Chief Velasquez. All five cops reacted to Atlee's voice.

"Where!?" an excited Merriweather asked, before Elliott took the microphone from his hand.

"Atop the Anderson Overlook according to our ranger expert," Atlee reported.

"Can you confirm their identity?"

"No sir, I can't; we're at least a half mile south of them and a few hundred below. I don't think we've been spotted."

"Stay put." It was Sheriff Crowley. "We need to move the Comm Center to the campgrounds. I'd suspect they may have spent the night there. We'll be onsite in 20 minutes, but give us 30, just in case. Maintain visual contact."

"You got it, sheriff."

"Keep those binoculars on whoever is up there and report any indication they're leaving immediately."

The time dragged, but Atlee and the deputy traded turns surveilling the people on the rock.

"I count only two," Martinez said, finally.

"Yeah, that's all I could ever account for, too," Atlee agreed. He keyed the mike again. "Grady, we agree there are only two people up on the rock."

100

A tense hour later, the team found the cave empty. But Willie Nell also found it fascinating. The roof of the cave was nearly 20 feet tall and coated with soot from age-old fires where Indians or maybe frontiersmen warmed themselves looking over the picturesque valley. She peered down at the snaking mountain road. Highway 15 was a shoulderless two lanes of asphalt snaking its way through a wilderness along a trail cut first by Mogollon Indians and later by pioneers. In her mind's eye, she could picture wagons of families courageously crossing the mountains in search of new lives.

Willie Nell couldn't believe that her friends, Pete and Anita were the objects of the manhunt. Nothing about this felt real. She kept trying to concentrate on the job at hand and stop dwelling on the fact that she both knew and liked them — they may have murdered her mother! Well, at least Pete. Talk about truth being stranger than fiction!

A crackle of static in her headset erased the vision. "LJ2, this is Jayhawk," Elliott's voice.

"Yeah, boss, what's shaking."

"That's Boss Jayhawk to you, Number two. I wanted to tell you that Abe's team may have spotted them."

The playfulness of the conversation melted. "Isn't he about 300 yards east of us?

"Yes but about four miles north of you, better get your rears in gear. I'm bringing in Helen as a sniper just in case."

"The fuck you say!? Is that really necessary, Grady?"

Elliott ignored the breach of radio security. Pete wasn't listening, and he knew it. "I hope not, Willie, but with Anita's life in the balance, I can't afford to take any chances."

"Shit! I mean, I understand. But, shit!"

"I promise you, Willie Nell," Elliott said, using her middle name for the first time, "I value Pete's life as much as you do.

"I won't give the 'go' for a shoot unless there's no other choice."

"Thanks, I guess, Grady."

"Now get your team moving. Rendezvous will be at the campgrounds. Don't approach by the road; you'll be visible. Circle and enter from the other side."

"What's our role, then?"

"See if there's any indication that they camped there last night," Elliott instructed. "We won't be able to bring the van into the campgrounds; whoever is on that rock will be sure to spot it. Sheriff Crowley says we can get about 1000 yards from it and park behind a curve; we'll have to come the rest of the way on foot and overland in the trees to keep from being seen. You'll be the first eyes there, most likely."

Willie Nell explained Elliott's instructions to Annette and Deputy Ortega. "It's a bit of a rough hike, but it won't slow us too much," she told the rest of the team.

The rugged terrain made travel difficult, unless one was either experienced or native to the area. Willie Nell was neither. The ranger moved forward to take point.

101

"That's the curve coming up." The sheriff told Johnson, who was driving the van. "Pull as far right as you can get."

"I might scrape up the paint on Grady's pretty truck," the FBI agent said.

"That's why the city carries insurance, Marty. Just do it. Real close. We can exit the rear door if we have to," Elliott responded.

Johnson heard the scrub pine branches punishing the side of the van as he slipped the vehicle close to the mountainside. Even with no more room, the van extended nearly a foot into the narrow roadway.

"Hope no one sideswipes us while we're gone," he remarked.

Before they exited the van, Elliott placed one more call to Atlee's team.

"Abe, it's an operational situation now, so you're in control down there. Move your team toward the objective. But do not attempt to take them. Don't even attempt to scale the overlook; you'd be sitting ducks and you could encourage Peterson to kill Anita."

Elliott explained the situation with the van and its inhabitants, estimating arrival at the campsite in 20 minutes. "It's only two-tenths of a mile, but we have to go overland through brush and out of sight, so I expect it to be slow. That should put us in position at 1630 hours. We're exiting the van now."

Merriweather hitched a portable comm center console onto his shoulders and the rest of the occupants carried as much equipment as they could handle. Elliott carried two rifle cases and an ammo box.

102

Deputy Ortega's team, with ranger Como in the lead, emerged from the steep rocks north and west of the campsite. Willie Nell, the tenderfoot of the group, was the last to make it down the mountain slope, sliding, skittering, and finally crashing to a stop at the bottom against a tree, punching a painful gash in her cheek.

"Let me tend that for you, Miss Autrey," the deputy Ortega, extracting a bandage strip and antiseptic ointment from his backpack.

Bandaged and chagrined, Willie Nell joined her team to search the campsite for Lucas's tent or pick-up. Near the rear of the site, south of where they emerged, Willie Nell yelled to the others, "Here's the truck!"

Three nearby campsites were occupied; the one closest to the truck consisted of a domed Kelty four-man tent supported by three arced aluminum poles. The ingenious configuration created a sturdy structure tall enough to stand inside.

Trooper Milhouse took charge at the tent. "We don't all need to go in here — too much risk of disturbing any evidence."

"Evidence of what?" Willie Nell asked.

"If he's harmed the hostage, there could be blood, for one thing, or a weapon."

"She's up there on the rock with him, remember?"

"Maybe not willingly. Just let me do my job, woman!"

Stung, Willie sat on a canvas chair beside the tent door. Sheepishly, the trooper emerged from the tent. "I need someone who can identify Miss Polanski's belongings, I guess that's you, Willie." He opened the tent and escorted her inside.

A search of a suitcase and a duffel yielded recently used toothbrushes, a shaving mug with wet soap, and a woman's make-up kit.

"Whoever lives here slept here last night, and the make-up hints the woman is a blonde, or at least very fair skinned," the reporter inferred.

A plastic trashbag served as a laundry hamper, and a search of it found a pair of crimson panties that Willie Nell recognized. They were crotchless, from Victoria's Secret. She had been with Anita when she bought them at The Shops at Willow Bend, a hoity-toity upscale mall in equally upscale West Plano.

"We better let Grady know, this is the place," she told Milhouse.

"Uh-huh," The trooper said, ogling and fondling the sexy size 5 undergarment.

In less than 10 minutes, Elliott and the rest of the Comm Center team emerged from near the same place Team LJ2 had entered the campgrounds.

Johnson dropped the large pack he carried and, with Merriweather's help quickly turned it onto a three-sided shelter for the communication equipment. Within minutes, the Task Force LJ Comm Center was back in business.

"LJ3, this is Jayhawk, do you read me?" Elliott tested the connection to Atlee's field unit.

"Gotcha 5-by, Jayhawk," Atlee's baritone replied.

"We have occupied the subject's campsite and will apprehend him if he tries to cross the road. I want your team to find shelter near the base of that rock formation so you might be able to capture him if he comes down."

"We'll do our best, but there's not shelter on all sides."

"That's why we're setting up at the road. There's nowhere else for him to go. We're also going to put a shooter on him while he's on the rock in case he threatens the hostage."

"Ten-4, Jayhawk. This thing should play out soon, then?"

"I hope so. Our chances diminish once the sun goes down."

Elliott stared at the brilliant orange sky to the west. It was the beginning of a gorgeous sunset.

103

Helen wasn't sure if she had what it takes to be a sniper, but there was a guy out there with a body count in the 20s; he had to be stopped and she would do what she could.

Detective Helen Summers, after 15 years in homicide, wasn't squeamish in the slightest sense of the word. She was among the toughest of the tough in a man's world and had always been fearless going head-to-head against the men she worked with.

It probably explained why she'd never married. Her martial arts skills ranked among the highest in the department and her marksmanship was the best; she anchored the department's rifle and pistol teams in competition with police departments across the country, beating out even the trained snipers from Special Weapons & Tactics (SWAT) and now they wanted her to do a job normally reserved for SWAT.

When she arrived on-site at the campgrounds, Elliott introduced her to sheriff Crowley, who simply told her to pick a tree.

"The subject has a woman, one of your Texas law-enforcement folks, up there on top of that rock," he said, pointing to a rock formation about 150 yards away across the mountain road from the campgrounds. "He's gotta know we have him trapped up there, but we have to consider Miss Polanski's life is his bargaining chip."

Helen hadn't heard that Anita was involved, and the news was like a punch in the stomach. While her body was trying to decide whether to surrender its lunch or not, technicians were busily attaching a battery pack and wireless sender to her belt. These would supply a two-way telecommunication headset she would put on once she got herself situated in the sniping position two-thirds of the way up the tree.

Elliott offered his sharpshooter a choice between two weapons, a .223-cal sniper rifle that he'd obtained from the Dallas SWAT team, or a specially rigged .308-cal designed for competitive target shooting, that belonged to one of Chief Hector Velazquez' officers. Helen opted for the smaller caliber weapon reasoning that it offered a greater muzzle velocity and flatter trajectory. That it would be easier to haul up to the higher branches of the pine tree didn't hurt, either.

104

Lucas was deep in thought as he held Anita and gazed over his beloved Gila Wilderness. He began speaking to her softly. "I'm in trouble, Anita. *Real* trouble."

Anita sat up a little to look at him.

"I had to leave town. I thought it might be good if you came with me. But now I know better. Anita, I'm going to die here in this wilderness."

"Whoa, big boy!" Anita sat the rest of the way up with a start.

"What kinda trouble and what's all this dying crap you're laying on me? Are you ill?" Her love for this man and a gnawing sense of dread battled for her heart.

"I've done some horrible things and they're looking for me now."

How could this sweet attentive man do anything bad?

"The FBI thinks I killed a woman … several women. The story broke in the tabloids with my picture the afternoon before I came to you."

Dread filled Anita's heart, brutally shoving the love aside.

I don't want to hear this. Stop talking, Pete. Please, stop talking.

But Lucas didn't stop. "Anita. I think I did it … no, I know I did. A lot of women. I wasn't ever sure until just recently, but now I'm having flashbacks. They're horrible; they're memories of the events.

"Anita. I didn't want to have to tell you, but I love you too much not to. This … this little adventure we're on … it's all we're ever going to have. I know it."

Anita sat in silent shock as her daydreams about a life with her Pete shattered like an empty bottle some hiker might throw from this overlook to the rocks at its base. Her mind refused to process Lucas' confession of murder, trying to create a rationale that would save the dream.

"I need to start back years ago. Have you ever wondered how I know how to pleasure a woman's body so well?" He wasn't bragging. Pete's eyes begged for her understanding.

"No, but I want to thank the ones who taught you." But her quivering voice belied the levity of her retort. She shivered as her weak attempt at levity lay unnoticed like a speck of bird shit on a sidewalk.

She tried a more serious tone. "I want you to know that whatever trouble you're in and even if a prostitute taught you all those …" she struggled for the words. "Look, I think I might want to be Mrs. Peterson more than I've ever wanted anything else in my life. If your big secret is that some streetwalker was your mentor in the sex department, I still want you to know I like what she taught you."

"You wouldn't thank her if you really knew her." Pete's response drew a puzzled look from Anita, and Lucas took her cold hands in his work toughened hands, running a thumb over her fingers. "I'm going to miss this, sweetheart."

"Pete, I don't think I like where this is going. You're saying goodbye? I just told you I'm in love with you and this is your response?"

"Call me Lucas, Anita. Or Luke. That's my real name — Lucas Peterson. Derek Prinz hung the 'Pete' tag on me and it stuck. Happens to us Petersons all the time."

Anita suddenly became aware of the height of their perch. She was beginning to get light headed.

God! It must be the altitude.

"I think you're overstating things," she said, gamely trying to dismiss the realities Lucas was forcing on her.

"You wouldn't want to stay with a woman killer. No one in their right mind would."

"A lady-killer for sure, a woman killer? I think not." She inched tighter against him, wanting desperately for Lucas to hold her closer. "I've been picturing little Petersons running all over the house, a couple of boys and a girl or two. Daddies always make their little girls their princesses."

She got no response. "I expect you were the light of your mother's life."

Anita saw Pete's jaw tighten as he clenched his teeth. Then she felt his entire body tense.

He dropped her hands and turned his back to her. Through the rugged place below, he sighted movement. What he'd seen earlier was just what he'd expected. The troops were gathering. If they were this close, it wouldn't be long.

"They're coming for me now … down there." Lucas pointed.

"Who's after you?" Anita still couldn't wrap her mind around the fact that her man was running from law enforcement.

I'm law enforcement. What am I supposed to do?!

"Dallas police, local cops, FBI, you name it," Lucas said. "It won't be long.

"Sweetheart, I need you to be still and listen very carefully. Here, take this."

Lucas extracted a small notepad from his shirt pocket. He always carried pad and pen in the wilderness for notes to remember landmarks when he hiked.

Anita had to be told what no one else knew. The women, some of them merely bones now, needed consecrated ground.

Maybe Reverend Billy should be told.

Lucas sat still looking over the grandeur of the Gila Wilderness and spoke to Anita, unable to look at her. "Until these past few days, I had no memory of doing anything to hurt anybody, but I would wake up with the body — with several bodies. Now I'm remembering."

Again, he saw movement below. They were closing in; he didn't have long and he had much to tell her, much to make her understand.

"When I'm through with my confession Officer Polanski," he said with true agony breaking his voice. "Look through my stuff for the card of a minister in my hometown. He's known as Reverend Billy."

"You're scaring me, big-time! I'm not Officer Polanski; I'm just Anita, a woman who loves you!" Anita was nearly screaming at him now. "Look at me!"

"Why?" He drew a ragged breath. "Do you believe the eyes are the windows to a person's soul? If so, you won't like what you see. It will be black, all black and tinged with the blood of dozens."

"I have looked there. You're wrong. I only see the man I love. When I gaze into your eyes, they're a lovely blue not at all black or sinister." She edged closer to Lucas.

He clenched and unclenched his fists. His arms trembled. His shoulders slumped.

Her man was in deep pain. She had to help him. "Look at me, Pete or Luke or whoever the hell you are." Her voice was firm, confident, commanding.

Without deliberation, he turned to her.

He dropped to his knees. By now she had gotten close enough that he could embrace her legs and bury his face against her belly. His tears were soaking her heavy flannel shirt.

She stroked his hair. "If you've done anything you want to tell me about. I can listen. I won't judge you. I'll try to wait until you've finished with the telling."

He didn't move. His thoughts were nearly audible. She knew he was choosing his words so as not to shock her.

"Write it down. The names. The places. Dates. It's important. Don't fear me, because I am about to describe a monster."

"Don't filter it or try to be inoffensive, my love," she told her anguished man. "Rid yourself of the demons plaguing you. I promised not to judge you, remember?"

He struggled trying to get to his feet. Unsuccessful, he rocked back on his heels and stared up at her, a portrait of agony. She sat before him and took his hand.

Pete sat still looking over the grandeur of the Gila Wilderness. "Until these past few days, I had no memory of doing anything to hurt anybody, but I would wake up with the body — with several bodies. Now I'm remembering."

Dread again assaulted Anita.

I was wrong! I don't want to hear this. Stop talking. Please, stop talking.

"Is that why you told me to keep my gun handy?" She asked cautiously.

"Yes. Sweetheart, all of those women, they include the two serious loves I've had in my life. And I really liked the others. I realized yesterday that you're in danger, too."

Anita had been so excited to see him at her door. Her feelings for this handsome, brave, yet soft-spoken man ranged from sexual to hopes for much more. Now, the guy she was crazy about was virtually admitting he was a serial killer. Her training took over; she reached into the pocket of the light jacket and wrapped her hand around the grip of the pistol, but didn't pull it out, not yet.

Let him talk. Once I arrest him, he shuts down.

But she knew she wouldn't arrest him. She would forsake her career and let him go, if it came to that.

Please, dear, dear Luke, don't tell me anymore. I can't take it. I thought I could but I was wrong.

"I know now it was stupid. I had this crazy idea that I wanted you to come with me. I can hide out for years up here in the wilderness, you know."

"Pete, you need help, maybe a therapist ..."

"No! I'd end up in prison and they'd throw away the key — if they didn't give me the death penalty. Texas is big on the death penalty, you know."

"And what kind of life would it be living up here? You as a hermit with a long beard like the unibomber? That's not what I want for you. For us!

"I love you and I'll be beside you every step of the way through the legal process. You'll probably not go to prison but to a hospital where they can help you." She knew it wouldn't play out that way. To be ruled incompetent, you had to pretty much be foaming at the mouth and unable to understand the charges against you. Pete certainly didn't fit that criteria.

"And if it is prison," she continued, "I'll wait for you."

"Fuck that, Anita! You'd be a little old lady on social security by the time I'd be let go, if they'd ever let me out."

The couple sat in silence, staring out over the canyon to the ghosts of more mountains in the distance. Anita moved closer and Luke turned to sit beside her as she laced her arm through his and laid her head against his shoulder. With his free hand, Pete cupped her cheek and turned it toward him and kissed her tenderly.

"You're a certified peace officer; you can't just let me walk away after what I've told you."

"So, I love you more than I love being a cop or a forensics techie."

As he held her, Pete thought he detected motion below them along one of the wilderness trails.

And here they come.

Lucas patted the blanket beside him and she returned to his side and again placed her arm in his. "It would ruin your life. I want to tell you all about me. It's not a pretty story, but nobody else knows it. Maybe you can tell the world I'm not just a monster inside and out."

Lucas Peterson bared his soul to the woman he loved. He told her about his mother's murder of Bobby Duchamps when he had threatened to leave her the next time he came home from work to find her drunk. She had simply plunged a butcher knife into his stomach and cursed him for making a mess as he bled to death on the kitchen linoleum.

He told her about helping Dixie Peterson bury the body out behind the City of Rocks National Park, and about how she replaced Bobby in the bedroom with her 7-year old little boy. He described the sex acts she taught him, admitting that, at first, it didn't seem wrong, even felt good to be stroked and petted. Anita wept silently as she listened to Luke describe the dawning of sexual awareness and the attendant knowledge of how wrong, how evil his mother had been in stealing his innocence by taking her little boy to her bed from that day on.

Then came the time that he refused her. His monologue tore Anita's heart-strings as she listened to him recount the event.

Please, dear, dear Luke, don't tell me anymore. I can't take it.

But Lucas didn't stop. He told her about killing his mother, deliberately. About how he buried her body with that of his father at The City of Rocks.

Anita listened, numb, tears streaming unwiped down her face, dripping from her chin to puddle in her lap.

He told her about the college girls in Silver City, about Mona and about The City of Rocks. He relived the horror of the death of his beloved Billie Jean Bollinger, and of a nightclub singer in West Texas.

Anita broke the confession with a gasp when she recognized Luke's description of his murder of Lacey Jay, her friend Willie Nell's mother. She wept, then bade him continue. All in all, Lucas told her of 29 murders. In the little pad, Anita barely had room for the names, locations, dates and, in the cases of 10 victims, where to find the bodies.

It was like a horror story — a fiction — and she distanced herself from the emotions of her lover's confession. She commisserated when Lucas told her of his attempts to find out what triggered the blackouts; he told her about the 14-year-old prostitute in Juarez and about all the women he dated who survived.

"It didn't always happen. I was with some of these women for months, even years."

Then Anita shocked him.

"Lucas, dear, sweet Lucas. I may know why it all happened." Anita recalled talking to Willie Nell about the profile the Task Force was putting together. She thought she might know what the triggering element was that tied everything together.

105

As Helen labored to scale the tall pine, Luke and Anita continued to talk. He had recounted most of the details of the murders he remembered, including that of Mona, whose bones were buried less than 100 feet from those of his parents.

Eventually, the two lovers talked of other things. Each spoke of dreams for a family, a home, a life-long mate. Both knew it would never be. Anita grieved the death of her fantasy of living out her years with Lucas Peterson.

Helen cinched the safety harness tight, not for protection, but for increased rigidity to better hold the Remington Model 700 Police bolt-action rifle. She nested the rugged Kevlar/carbon fiber stock against her cheek, peering through the Schmidt & Bender tactical scope. Its 50 mm glass produced a bright view, even at full 12-power magnification.

Lifting her head from the weapon, she touched the Bluetooth miniature headset to open a channel to the Comm Center." LJ7 reporting. The ball is in play."

Elliott didn't need to respond, Helen had just reported she was in position and had sighted her weapon on the subject.

Returning to the sniper scope eyepiece, Helen observed the couple on the rock. She was one of the few people on the task force who had not met Lucas Peterson either as Luke or Pete. But there was no doubt. Peterson's striking good looks were hard to miss. And she recognized Anita Polanski. They were both on the rock, facing each other and talking, at this moment.

Helen relaxed, let her breathing slow. She could hear her pulse inside the shooting headset, a noise-canceling technology that looked like wireless stereo headphones. She practiced holding her breath while she sighted. The most tension in her body was in the muscles that held the stock firm against her cheekbone.

Luke turned to his right. He'd seen a flash, a glint among the trees at the edge of the campgrounds.

A sniper?

He dismissed the thought as paranoia, but kept peering toward where the flash had been; it had only been visible for a split second.

"I said," Anita repeated to her distracted lover, "If they come for you, let me manage your surrender. I don't want them to hurt you."

There it is again. It's either a binocular or a scope.

"Sounds reasonable, hon."

A rifle scope!

Only Anita would truly understand why Lucas did what he did next.

As he held her, Pete slipped his hand into her pocket and extracted the Smith & Wesson revolver.

"What are you doing?" Anita stood and backed two steps away from him.

"I'm not going to hurt you, but I won't let you arrest me." Pete opened the cylinder and ejected the .38-caliber shells into his palm and pocketed them.

Grady's earbud headset crackled. "Jayhawk, the male subject has a pistol."

"Your job is to protect my cop. If Anita is in any danger, you take him out. You won't need to ask permission. Just take him down. Do you understand me?"

"Roger Jayhawk. Understood."

"What are you doing with that empty gun?" Anita asked.

"They have us surrounded Hon. I haven't told you because I didn't want to spoil our time together. But it's over now."

"What do you mean, over?"

"You know I can't survive in jail, away from these mountains, away from you."

Helen placed the crosshairs of the reticle just above Luke's temple

Luke stood. "There's a better way."

He extended his right arm, and pointed the empty Smith & Wesson at Anita's head. He didn't hear the shot that entered just above his right ear and blew the left side of his cranium apart, sending a pink spray of bone, blood and brain matter out over the canyon beneath the overlook. His body collapsed like an accordion.

Through the eyepiece, Helen saw the 'pink cloud' effect of the head shot. The nausea she'd experienced when she heard Anita was the hostage returned with a vengeance and Helen's lunch cascaded down the tree, splattering at Merriweather's feet.

"Do we have a confirmed kill?" Elliott's voice was urgent in her ear.

Gasping, and gagging, she tapped the headset and wheezed a barely audible "yes sir."

106

Willie Nell, like the rest of the Task Force, heard the exchange.

Oh my God! Poor Anita.

The thought surprised her. She thought she'd feel more for Pete, or Lucas, or whoever the hell he was. He had saved her life and befriended her and her friends. But those feelings had quietly been supplanted by the horror of his actions as they emerged during her and Atlee's investigation. Now, she only felt relief that it was over and that the monster who had robbed her and Sunny of a mother would harm no one else ever again.

I have to get to her. She needs a friend right this minute.

Willie Nell ran out of the campground, across the road, and through the sparse trees beneath the rock formation. She stopped, dismayed by the seemingly impossible climb that confronted her.

Then she was aware of someone at her side.

"I'll help you get up there, Willie." It was Elliott.

With his help and instruction, she scrabbled from boulder to boulder, sometimes only with Elliott's strong hands keeping her from toppling back down. At one point, the big man had her get on his back as he pulled them up the face of a large rock with only his arms.

Willie Nell marveled at the big man's strength and at the ripple of muscles moving beneath her body.

Damned, just riding his back is making me horny! At a time like this?

It wasn't an easy ride. Figuring this was what a remora felt hanging on a shark, Willie Nell gritted her teeth as her body swung and bounced against her carrier.

Depositing the disheveled reporter on the flat top of the formation, Elliott went to a weeping Anita. "Willie's here. We came to take you back down, Anita."

Anita looked up to see her friend walking unsteadily toward her. Willie Nell fell to her knees and the two women embraced, both now crying.

Willie Nell knew that Anita's trembling had less to do with the evening chill than with the shock of Lucas' death. "All the shooter saw was that he had a gun on you, Anita!" Willie Nell said to her friend as she warmed her friend's icy cold hands within her own.

"Emp …t-ty," Anita said between chattering teeth. "He took the b-b-bbul-lets out."

"He wanted us to kill him!" Willie Nell said softly.

Anita jerked her hands away from Willie Nell and clutched her arms around herself. "You … you just stand there telling me he loved me, but that he wanted to be executed!? How dare you even think of calling yourself my friend!" The anger finally brought a spark of life to her eyes and voice. "I don't know how he could do it."

"Anita, I can't pretend to know him as well as you, but I can only surmise from the events. I'm sure there was a part of him wanting to disappear into these mountains forever, maybe even take you with him.

"But the Pete, I'm sorry, the Lucas I knew wasn't that selfish; he would not have let you destroy your career for him. And he couldn't live if he lost you AND his beloved wilderness; you know that." Willie Nell stroked her friend's back.

"I need four men to help me get Anita, Willie and the remains of the target off this rock," Elliott said into the mouthpiece of his Bluetooth headset. In less than 10 minutes he was surprised to see ancient Sheriff Crowley accompany three of his deputies to the top of the formation.

Two rangers, two deputies, and Sheriff Crowley made the rugged climb in 10 minutes.

"Glad you're up here, Detective Elliott," Crowley said, not even breathing hard. "We need to start debriefings of all of the Task Force members and any other law enforcement personnel who took part in the take-down or the seizure of evidence at the campground. I'd like to start first thing tomorrow at my office. Can you instruct the Comm Center to get the word out?"

"Happy to do it. And thanks for all the great help. I'm sure we'd have never been able to get close to him without the help of your deputies and the park rangers."

Elliott tapped the earpiece and Merriweather was instantly on line. "What's up boss?"

"Marty's your boss again. Task Force LJ is standing down. Get the word out that all members are to meet at Sheriff Crowley's office at zero eight hundred tomorrow for debriefing. Jayhawk out."

Elliott put his arm around Willie Nell and hugged her close. "You alright?! You're shivering. Come on down, Honey." He took her hand and slowly began the climb down.

She began the descent on wobbly legs. "I feel like a newborn colt!"

"Kinda walk like one, too," he said. "Want me to carry you?"

"You must have me confused with some silly female you know from somewhere other'n Texas. We're made of stern stuff." She gave him her crooked smile. "I know you helped me going up, but my natural ineptness, with the help of gravity, will get me down no matter what."

"Willie, do you realize you just talked for a good 15 minutes with Anita without cussing even once?" Elliott asked, then caught her in his arms as a missed step toppled her from a boulder. "And, yes. I will carry you."

"I'm shooting for a record, my longest time's been 10 minutes," she said looking up at him, her arms around his neck as he cradled her.

"Hey you could do that with your tongue tied behind you!" he parried. "But I think maybe there's a better way to shut you up," he said as he kissed her quickly but soundly.

"What the fuck was that all about?"

"I often wondered how that would feel. Just wanted to get it out of my system. Besides, you're so damned reckless, I figured I better do it before you got your blamed self killed.

"By the way, I think you blew your record at about minute 17."

107

Elliott headed straight for the communication van where Merryweather leaned against the side smoking a cigarette. "I figured we'd be using this rig instead of the glorified walkie-talkie you've had me humping all day," he said to his boss.

Willie Nell trailed behind Elliott a discreet distance. She knew the van had a self-contained toilet, and she was in no mood to squat beside one of the trees in a forest full of rangers, deputies, police, and other searchers.

Within the close quarters of the van, she was forced to insinuate herself very close to the profiler in exiting the small chemical toilet. Elliott was crouched so his head didn't scrape the air conditioner housing protruding from the ceiling. She tried to pass him and her abdomen rubbed against his hips.

"Mmmm, nice buns," she said then, purloining a line from an old Western, "I think this town ain't big enough for the two of us, pardner."

"I believe you're right, little lady," he said in a rough but vain attempt to sound like John Wayne, playing along with the game.

"Well you could have at least pretended to enjoy it."

"Why? Were you trying to seduce me, Willie?" Elliott asked. "If so, wait until you mean it."

Rebuffed, Willie Nell reverted to form. "It's Willie NELL, you fucking asshole! And you can't see what's as plain as the nose on your face. I want you."

"Really?" His voice sounded softer than she'd ever heard it before. "I think you're feeling empty right about now after what happened, up on the rock. You won't admit it to yourself, but any man would do."

"I want more than that, Willie Nell. I don't just want to be someone to satisfy the occasional itch."

Willie Nell was stung; she had completely missed Elliott's inference that there could be something more for them.

Ignoring the furious look on her face, he brushed a rough hand across her cheek. "I do think you're one hell of a woman."

"Thanks for shit," she said.

"With the sweetest mouth out of which comes the foulest of language!" He said, trying to lighten the mood, but she was already gone.

With the help of Elliott and Willie Nell, Anita was able to confirm Lucas' confession about each, as well as a few others not in the files. In addition to his mother, Lucas had told her about Mona Richter, Missy Dawson, a waitress in Pecos, and Gretchen Seitz, a realtor in Houston. Elliott approached her after her testimony. "We need to talk. I'd like to shed some light on why Lucas did what he did. It will help you cope with his death. Call me after we get back to Dallas."

"I don't want to wait," Anita shot back angrily. "Can you at least give me the complete profile before the debriefing. It might help me understand more of what I saw and heard."

Elliott took Anita into the trailer and laid out the profile he and Johnson had put together, then he escorted Anita to Silver City for the debriefing. The debrief at Sheriff Crowley's office was uneventful, except for the chilling testimony from Anita, who broke down several times during the proceedings.

Her testimony verified Elliott's surmise that Lucas Peterson intended to be shot; that he pointed the empty weapon at his companion to force the police marksman to take him down.

"Luke loved the wide open spaces, especially this wilderness area. Prison would have been an impossible place for him to survive," she told the gathering of law enforcement officials at the debriefing session.

"Why did you help him get away?" Crowley asked, bringing an angry and tearful outburst from the forensics specialist.

"I wasn't aware he was fleeing at the time, ours was supposed to be a 'romantic getaway'. I loved this guy, then I learn he's a serial killer. I thought he wanted me to turn him in, until he pulled that trick with the empty revolver.

"I understand. He was really sick. But not remembering the particulars of the crime doesn't exonerate him, since he continued to have sexual partners knowing what might happen. I disagree with Grady's comment that his lack of awareness would be grounds for an insanity plea. He wasn't insane when he courted me, seduced me, and took me with him. According to your profile, if I'd performed fellatio on him last night, I could have been another victim."

Anita's sobbing grew more wracking and her words came hard. "I loved him and now I hate him, rather I hate that he put me at such risk while assuring me that he loved me as well."

With no prisoner, there would be no jurisdictional issues. Johnson refused to consider aiding and abetting charges against Anita. A quick inquest verified Helen Summer's actions as a "good shooting".

The Dallas profiler then asked Merriweather to place one more call for him before closing down the communication center. "Get me Beauregard Duchamps."

The phone call went through quickly. The old cowboy listened intently as Elliott told him about the death of his nephew and how it came to pass.

"Sir," Duchamps said, after listening to the report, "I appreciate that you called me; I appreciate that you did what you had to do; I appreciate that your shooter thought Luke might hurt that woman. But the God's truth is that my nephew would never knowingly hurt a woman under penalty of death."

"I arrived at the same conclusion, Mr. Duchamps. In fact, the woman told us that Lucas purposely emptied the revolver and pocketed the shells before pointing it at her.

"We have a name for that: 'suicide by cop'. I think Luke simply weighed his options and decided if he was never going to see his wilderness again in his life, he might as well end it."

"Mister Elliott, we both read it the same, then," the retired rodeo cowboy said. "I'm glad he's at peace. Goodbye."

"What an adventure, eh, young lady?" Atlee had walked up behind Willie Nell. She turned and threw her arms around his neck, and then kissed him noisily on the cheek.

"Both of our ghosts can rest now, but just because this is over doesn't mean you're rid of me," she said with a mock pout.

"Wouldn't if I could. Girl, you're the closest thing to family I have left in my life. If you're willing, I'd like to always stay that close."

"I found out I actually have a father living," she said cryptically. "I need your help to figure out how I feel about that, maybe over a couple margaritas after we're back in Big D."

"It's a date, but I thought your father died in a car crash when you were 10."

"Not now, dear man. I'm having to compartmentalize just to get through what happened yesterday. But very soon; I really need you."

108

Willie Nell and Atlee sat at the hip Deep Ellum bar where a lot of cops, lawyers, and reporters — as well as assorted groupies and wannabes — gathered to wait out the Dallas drive-time rush-hour. She was having trouble making eye contact with the retired Louisiana cop she considered the closest thing to family she had outside her sister, Sunny. Distractedly, she ran her finger around the edge of her margarita, licking off the tequila-flavored salt.

"Penny for your thoughts," Atlee said.

She looked up momentarily, then returned her attention to the salt rim on her glass. Most of the salt was gone.

"I thought you said you had a lot to tell me. Stuff you learned about … what? You never said."

Atlee thought he wasn't going to get an answer, but after a pause, Willie Nell spoke in a low, flat voice. "What if you learned that a person you thought was your parent turned out not to be? What if it were your father?"

"At my age, who gives a flying fuck?" Atlee said.

Normally, the profanity would spur a rejoinder from his Task Force partner. Tonight, it just lay on the floor.

"What are you trying to tell me about your father. He died in the car wreck that crippled your little sister, isn't that right?"

"No. That was Dude, but it turns out he was my sister's daddy, but not mine."

"Ah, I can tell we'll go through more than one margarita tonight. Go on, dear girl."

At last, animation came to Willie Nell's voice, in the only way she ever really exhibited her anger: profanity.

"My God damned mother got pregnant with a fucking guy at a country commune! She and Dude had a temporary break and she went to a farm and screwed the summer away with this guy — someone I've known all my life.

"Then she came back and married Dude while my real father went off and became a fucking preacher."

"Whoa, Nelly! No pun intended, Willie Nell, but that's quite a secret they kept. How'd you find out?" He motioned the waitress over making a circle with his finger indicating another round.

"It's like I don't know who I am. If Dude's not my daddy, I feel like I never had one. I sure don't get warm fuzzies trying to picture a familial bond with Reverend Brock Taylor."

"That's your father?"

"That's the asshole who was the sperm donor," Willie Nell answered angrily as two more margaritas arrived at the table. She drained her drink in one pull.

"Whooooooooooeeeeeeeeee, pace yourself, girl. I'm too old to carry you outta this place. You know you have me; I meant it when I told you I already think of you as a daughter."

Willie Nell gasped out a sob and threw her arms around the older man. "If you mean that, Mister Atlee, you better be in it for the long haul. You're the only person I've ever had who I could talk to since I was 10 years old."

"You want me to adopt you?" Atlee said, only half joking.

"Well," Willie Nell snuffled back a sob, but she was trying to smile. "My sister is in the market for adoption."

"I'd like to meet your sister sometime."

"You'd like her, Abe. She's not like me. She's tiny, petite really. A songbird and budding musician. About ready to start college." Willie Nell warmed and brightened as she talked about her sister, her only family.

"You know Dexter Morley was the cause of the accident that killed my father ... I mean ... Dude, didn't you?"

Atlee nodded his head but remained silent, encouraging the reporter to continue.

She told Atlee about the accident and the children's home and the numerous painful surgeries. She expressed optimism at the prospects that a final surgery to implant rods to support the shattered bones would finally make Sunny truly mobile. She expressed her fears for her sister's future and her lack of a support system that families provide.

"Sounds to me like Sunny's got a pretty good start, from her counselors at the home to you, and now me."

"You mean it?"

"If you're going to be in my life, Willie Nell, I'm going to be in yours, every part of it. When do I get to meet this young lady, anyway?"

"Oh Abe! Real soon. Let me tell her about you. Let me tell her about me. Let me tell her about Brock and about Dude. I have so much to lay on her first. Bear with me."

"I bet she is less worried about any of it than you are. When will you tell her?"

"Tomorrow," Willie Nell paused to lick the salt on her glass. "Miz Edie and I found music that Mama had written. There was a producer who'd written Mama before she died or maybe after—anyway she never opened the letter. He liked the tape she sent him of a couple of her songs.

"I talked to him. He said he'd buy the music when I told him that the composer/singer had died. Maybe Sunny could re-record them; she's pretty talented."

"Doesn't sound like a bad idea, wonderful actually. So, why the long face?"

"I guess it's the letdown after all the highs I've had these past few days."

"Nope, I can tell there's something else on your mind." Atlee prodded her. "Why don't you let Daddy Abe in on it?"

"Daddy Abe! I've got too damned many daddies now — and not enough either." She laughed.

"But, since you asked, what do you think of Grady?"

"He's a damned good man and a lot of help during this ordeal," Atlee answered.

"Oooh. You're asking how I would rate him as romance material, aren't you?"

Willie Nell felt her face go hot. "Well, yeah. I think I kinda like him, and I think he likes me a little. What do you think?"

"A cop and a reporter? Lotsa room for turmoil, that's for sure. But listen, gal, if you're interested in Grady what the hell are you doing hanging out with an old guy like me?

"If you both want to make it work, you'll find a way."

She stood, kissed him softly on the cheek, hugged him fervently, and grabbed her jacket off the back of her chair. "You're picking up the tab, Pop."

Atlee waved her away. "I guess that's what a daddy does."

109

Willie Nell was pleasantly surprised to wake up without a hangover. In fact, she woke up early; it was still dark outside her bedroom window. That suited her just fine. She had big plans for the day.

She popped into the shower thinking about Grady and humming one of Mama's songs. Deciding her wardrobe for the day might include shorts, she also shaved her legs.

The eastern sky was just beginning to show color when she rang his doorbell. It took three rings before she heard him padding to the door

"Just a damned minute," Elliott said gruffly, yanking open the heavy, solid oak door. "I just got out of the shower ... Willie!?"

"Hi, handsome. Can I come in?"

Without waiting for a reply, she ducked under the arm holding the door and pirouetted into the foyer.

Elliott closed the door and turned just in time for Willie Nell to kiss him on the cheek.

"I haven't shaved yet."

"Ugh. I noticed. Put something on before you drop that towel, but don't shave."

"Why not?"

"I've always had this fantasy of shaving a guy. Let me do it for you."

"Let you hold a sharp blade to my throat? I'm not crazy."

"Puh-leeeeeeeeeeeze," Willie Nell begged.

While Elliott rummaged through his closet for something to throw on. Willie Nell located his razor, a can of shaving gel, and a fresh towel.

"In the kitchen," she yelled toward the bedroom. "And don't put on a shirt or I'll be dribbling shaving gunk all over it."

Grady tossed the polo shirt he'd just retrieved from the closet onto the sofa and walked to kitchen/dining area. The apartment had a kitchenette that faced the dining area.

The reporter placed one of the dinette chairs near the sink and turned on the hot water, mixing cool with it until the temperature was hot enough without being uncomfortable.

"You sit," she told Elliott when he appeared at the end of the hallway that led to the bedrooms. He obeyed.

Willie Nell draped the towel over her left shoulder, laid the razor on the countertop, and moistened his face by alternately holding her hands under the warm water, then rubbing them gently over his features, slowly, sensuously. Next, she squirted gel into her palm — too much — and began lathering his face, enjoying the sensation of watching the gel erupt into foam as she stroked.

"Having fun yet?" Elliott asked.

"Oh yes. I'm gonna build a snowman on that beak of your if you don't stop talking, though."

As she began shaving one side of his face, she was aware that Elliott was staring at her braless breast only inches from his face. The thought aroused her and she felt her nipples hardening.

Good. That'll give him something to look at while I work.

Willie Nell realized that shaving under his nose and chin would be difficult from a standing position, so she straddled his lap and sat. Now she was too close for comfortable arm movement; she leaned back — and nearly tumbled to the floor.

Elliott's strong hands grabbed her at her waist and held her so she could lean.

"Lower," she ordered.

Elliott cupped her hips so she couldn't slip back off his knees, enjoying the feel of her firm, round buttocks in his big hands.

Carefully, the reporter negotiated the sharp razor around and under his nose, careful not to nick his lips. She didn't fare so well on the chin and a tiny drop of blood appeared beneath the left edge of his mouth. Instinctively, Willie Nell licked the droplet away, and found the taste electric.

Is this what he tastes like? Will I find out today?

She continued shaving him with no more damage. As she wiped the remnants of shave foam from his face, she saw the nick was bleeding again. Willie Nell applied finger pressure to the nick to stop the bleeding, holding Elliott's face in both hands. She looked straight into his eyes, and then she kissed him.

It was a soft, gentle kiss, At first. Elliott's grip on her buttocks tightened and his lips parted. Suddenly her tongue probed between his lips and she crushed her upper body against him, her back arching.

Elliott's right hand insinuated itself inside the edge of her shorts; he was delighted to find no thong, no panties, nothing but girl, warm, inviting. He accepted the invitation.

Her tongue was a living thing, darting over and between his lips, slashing, seeking his soul. Her moan was a low hum. When his hand touched the wetness and followed it up to touch the tiny nub of her desire, the moan turned guttural.

Without breaking the embrace, Willie Nell raised herself a few inches above his lap to allow him to move the soft material of her shorts aside and to undo his pants.

Then she engulfed him, completely, both mouths working hungrily on him until he exploded. She spasmed in unison with him, over and over, her body jerking, but Willie held him fiercely close. At last, passion spent, Elliott cupped her hips in his hands and rose, feeling her legs cinch around his waist.

He carried her to the couch and sat, then leaned over with her laying atop him, still enfolding him. Within minutes, he felt arousal again and began to grow inside her.

The sensation was something Willie Nell had never known, it overwhelmed her, and she cried.

"God, Grady. What if I love you? I wanted this but … but I thought we'd take it slow, see if there's anything to build on, you know? I've wanted you ever since I was hanging onto you as you climbed up to the top of the overlook, the feel of your muscles beneath me, protecting me. You coulda laid me down right there on the rock."

"Bet you didn't know I had a semi-erection all that time I was hauling you up that rock formation," Elliott responded.

Willie Nell laughed and moved rhythmically again atop her lover's fully aroused body. "You dirty old man."

"When we finish I can take you to breakfast," he said.

"Shit. By the time I'm finished, It'll be time for lunch," she said.

Elliott arched his back and lunged upward impaling her with his full length.

"Better plan on making that dinner," she sighed.

110

As Willie Nell approached the crippled children's home, she tried to visualize the coming encounter with Sunny. It was going to be an emotional exchange, that much she knew. She was still trying to wrap her mind around her own fear that the revelation of her birth might affect their closeness. She dreaded telling Sunny that, technically, they were only half sisters.

Damn it all, I've faced killers and bloody crime scenes, and here I am agonizing over giving my little sister some good news.

Willie Nell knew that was an "apples and oranges" argument. She'd had nothing to lose and everything to gain in her confrontations with crime suspects and hard-boiled cops, she reminded herself. But Sunny was something else, a vulnerable young woman about to graduate high school and strike out on her own, facing a hostile world with a disability

She's crippled in body, and fearful of mind. Don't give her another handicap by changing everything she's ever believed.

The reporter knew Sunny needed to know that she's based all of her feelings about her parents on misinformation. She slapped the steering wheel. She didn't have to dump it all on her at once.they could go through the Lacey and Dude boxes together. She'd let her see the letter, if not now, maybe later."

That's called sandbagging! But you have her interests at heart, after all what's it to her that you're the bastard of the family?

A sign announcing Dallas City Limits appeared, so her internal conflict was suspended for the moment. Once off the Interstate,Willie Nell stopped at the

431

little donut shop near the home to pick up the tension easers the two had shared all their lives.

"Hidee, Miss Autrey, I haven't seen you in a month of Sundays," the jovial woman behind the counter said.

She should be calling me Miss Taylor … maybe someday … or maybe not.

"I've been working out of town." She slid her card across the counter.

"I've seen you on TV a few times. You're mighty good," the woman said.

"Thanks. Stay tuned in. I've been working on a humdinger."

"More at eleven as they say in the business, right?"

"More truth than poetry, Maud."

They laughed conspiratorially.

She beeped her SUV open, then placed the box of donuts on the seat beside her. A box for two donuts?!? She opened it. Inside were a half dozen filled and a half dozen cake donuts. She checker her receipt. Maud had only charged her for the two she had ordered and drew a smiley face with curly strands for hair.

Thank you Maud. Maybe it's a sign that this is going to go well!

She cut through the residential area and up the incline to the building perched on a hill. With her boxes stacked on a pull cart intended for luggage, crowned with the box of donuts, she entered the smoked glass doors.

Stopping at the reception desk, she presented her ID.

"Oh, I recognize you Miss Autrey. Your sister's in the music room but you know where her room is."

"Yes, I do."

I'm a phony! My name isn't Autrey. it's Taylor! Will I have to change it?

Willie Nell was messing in her own mind; she knew that a lot of on-air-personalities used pseudonyms. She'd even considered, taking her mother's last name for a professional name herself.

I'll just continue as usual. Brock wouldn't make waves.

"What the fuck do I care what he thinks about what name I use!" she challenged herself once again.

She felt more than saw her sister enter the room. "Hey, you're pacing like a caged leopard. What's going on?" Sunny asked.

"I have a lot on my mind, kiddo. I brought donuts want to go get milk or coffee to go with them?"

"You usually only bring treats when you have something distasteful to tell me. Are you off on another Big Story?" Sunny clomped over to the bed and sat down with a plop.

"Heavy, not distasteful," Willie Nell countered. "I want to share some of the things I discovered about Mama and Dude."

"You used to call them Mama and Daddy. What's changed?"

"Hey, who's the investigative reporter here?" Willie Nell gave a mirthless laugh.

"Come on, give." Sunny leaned back on her arms to take some of the tension off her lower back.

Taking a deep breath, Willie Nell began to tell her sister what she'd learned about Mama's death, Willie Nell joined her sister on the bed, tucked her feet underneath her body and reached out. Sunny willingly went into her sister's arms and began to weep. "I feel so bad for her. She was so young to die so violently. You got the guy who did it, right?"

"Yes and no. We discovered who he was, but he died, too."

"How? I hope it was as gruesome as Mama's was."

"If you want the truth, he allowed himself to be shot. He turned an empty gun on Anita and a law enforcement sniper shot him."

"Good. So is that your big news?"

"Only in part. There's more. I read the police report of your accident."

"We know what caused it and the results. That asshole can't be punished either. Dude's dead."

"That's no way to talk about your Daddy, Sunny," Willie Nell's fragile composure cracked. "I don't ever want to hear it again. For your information, Dude wasn't drinking; he'd been stone-cold sober for months at the time."

When she'd regained control of her emotions, Willie Nell continued. "Someone else caused the crash. He confessed. And he'll pay for what he did to our family.

"Somebody from the task force went and talked to the other driver on the road that night, a guy named Dexter Worley. He told me something astonishing, something not in the accident report."

Sunny's attention was riveted. "What? What could he have told you?"

"Sunny, my dear, sweet sister. Your father didn't cause the accident and that means he didn't cause your injury. Worley admitted that he caused the wreck and forced Dude off the road.

"Mister Worley said his guilt has been eating at him for years; he just spewed it all out as soon as the agent mentioned us."

"I don't see how that's going to change anything."

"Restitution. My lawyer says he'll have to make restitution. You'll get a settlement."

"Dexter's the man's name who ran Daddy off the road and made me a cripple?"

"Yes. I think he was glad to be found out. He was also the anonymous donor who paid for your tuition at the children's home."

"I always kinda figured that musta been Uncle Brock or his church."

"Me too," Willie Nell said.

"You know, big sister, " Sunny said her voice beginning to sober," I wish I could say I have happy memories of our parents like you wrote in your letter, but I don't, not many, anyway. Oh, I remember going back to Sonora for vacations, short stays. But I also remember how I felt when I was brought back time after time. My first memory is as a tiny girl, maybe age four or five, in a wheelchair. I cried when you left. I cried a lot. I was so lonely; that's what I remember."

Willie Nell opened her mouth to speak, noticed that Sunny was staring at the ceiling, and decided to let her continue.

"Then one day, I was tinkering around with the old upright piano in the meeting room where visitors waited when they came to take one of the kids out for awhile. Mama had just left; she had played a few songs on that visit. You and I sang. Do you remember, Willie Nell?"

The reporter listened and nodded, but let the teenager continue.

"You, Miz Edie, and Mama. You all left me alone again. But I had that music running around in my head. So I sat down and picked them out on the keys. When the music teacher walked in, I figured I was in trouble; taped above the piano was a sign 'HANDS OFF'. Instead, I was complimented. She asked me if I'd like to take music lessons with her.

"Oh, boy, didn't I ever!" The memory brought a smile to Sunny's face. "I loved music; it was how I kept myself feeling close to you and Mama. When I played the piano and sang, I wasn't just 'that little crippled Autrey girl' anymore; I was the girl who could make music for her friends.

"Did Mama tell you about hearing me play on her last visit? She said you couldn't come, you had some kinda school thing."

The older sister searched her memory. Yes! Mama had said Sunny sang beautifully. She hadn't mentioned the piano, and Willie Nell had shrugged off the conversation.

How could I not react to that? I was so full of myself, I didn't even give it a second thought.

"Yes, Sunny, she told me," was all she could say to her sister.

"Mama finally got to see me when I wasn't angry and kicking and screaming," Sunny continued. "You know, I wasn't mad at the world; I was mad at Daddy. If it hadn't been for his beers and that icy road, I'd still have been home with my wonderful, beautiful sister, and I wouldn't be alone all the time."

Both sisters were wet-eyed now.

"Now you tell me I've wasted all that anger and blame on Daddy when he didn't do anything wrong? How am I supposed to feel?"

Willie Nell broke her silence. "Sweet girl, that anger served you well; it may be what made you strong enough to endure all you've had to go through. I am so proud of how you've handled the surgeries, the physical therapy, and all the pain. You're a rock, baby sister."

"Okay, so our parents weren't scumbags like I thought," Sunny changed gears quickly. "Is that why you brought all these boxes?"

"I thought you'd find them interesting. What I've seen of them, I did. Mama's journals are sweet and she wrote about us a lot."

"All those boxes are full of her diaries?" Sunny gasped.

"I truly don't know what else is in them. I only saw part of them, the things that brought resolution to their deaths. We should go through the rest of the things together, if you're willing."

"I don't think donuts are going to be enough to sustain us through all this!" She waved an arm towards the stack of boxes.

"It'll get us started. When we need a break, we'll go down to the cafeteria."

Sunny made a gagging sound and put out her tongue. "Tonight's liver night. Can't we go get a burger or something?"

"You got it, Babe." Willie Nell said with a grin.

Once they got into the second box in the stack, however, food was forgotten. Sheet music, hand-scored, filled the box. Each song had its own folder and Sunny clasped the first one to her chest. "Ball of Yarn!"

"She wrote the song she sang to us?" Willie Nell asked. "I had no idea that she composed."

"I've got to take these to the music room, Willie Nell. You want to hear them, too, don't you?"

"I thought you wanted a burger!" Willie Nell teased. "I can run get some and bring them back while you tinker with Mama's songs."

This is the first time I've seen Sunny live up to her name. Her smile is like Sunrise.

Willie Nell observed her suddenly effervescent little sister. "Even the new surgery didn't cheer her up like this." She thought. "Thanks, Mama for bringing Sunny back to life!

111

On her way back from Wendy's with burgers and fries, Willie Nell tried to steel herself to the scary part of her visit with Sunny, the part about Reverend Brock Taylor and their mother. She was going to have to tell her that she wasn't an Autrey, that there wasn't a drop of Dude's blood in her veins.

The music filled the hallway. Already, Sunny had graduated from "Ball of Yarn" to another ballad, a love song. It was amazingly good, Willie Nell thought.

She's her mother's daughter, for sure.

"Ready for death by burger?"

"Double meat, double cheese, double-bypass specials?"

"You know it, and I assume you want fries with your coronary."

"No other way, sis."

The word brought back Willie Nell's fear, but she decided to attack the issue right now. "Careful how you use that fucking word, squirt!"

"And just which word would that be, potty-mouth?"

"Sunny, I learned something else in Sonora, not about Mama and Dude, and not about you. It's about me."

"From that look on your kisser, you musta found out you're pregnant by the Prince Derek," Sunny laughed. She knew Willie Nell detested the ex-TV reporter.

"What would you say if I told you Dude wasn't my daddy?"

"Get outta town!" Sunny's eyes and mouth formed perfect "O's".

"Before Mama and Dude married, she had a thing. An affair at a commune out at Janine's place."

"Oh, wow! Cool! Way to go, Mom!"

"Not too cool. She was pregnant with me when she and Dude tied the knot."

"Big whoop, so she kept you legal."

"Sunny!" Willie Nell cried in exasperation. "Be serious. You know this means you and I are just half-sisters, don't you?"

"Hey, we're sisters, period. Family is relationship, not a gene pool. But just for giggles, didja learn who the sperm donor was?"

Willie Nell was crying too hard to continue. She grabbed her sister and squeezed her.

"Hey, don't break the cripple."

"Reverend Taylor is my biological father, Sunny," she said through blubbers.

"Uncle Brock? Well, that explains a lot, like why the preacher took so much interest in us kids, huh?"

"I guess so." Willie Nell took a deep breath. "Reverend Taylor wants to have a relationship with me as a daughter, and with you, too."

"What on earth for?" Sunny studied her big sister. "You know, Dude's the only daddy you ever knew. I grew up more in the Children's Home than in the trailer with you guys, but Dude's my Daddy. End of story. You're gonna hafta do what you gotta do, but leave me out of it."

Willie Nell's voice softened and Sunny found she had to listen carefully to hear her sister. "Do you think God mighta looked down at us and say ' Those girls need a Daddy?' Then poof! All of a sudden, here's Brock wanting to be the father he never was. Then there's Abe."

"Uh-oh, I'm lost again. Who's Abe?"

"My Task Force partner, Abraham Atlee, a man whose daughter was among Peterson's victims. He and I bonded. He's the sort of father I wished Dude — or Brock for that matter — would have been. And he wants to get to know you, too. He's a real dear man."

"For a kid who grew up in the orphanage, you sure got a shitload of daddies, big sister of mine."

Willie Nell sighed.

"Do you think you might feel that way about him because he's an older man who just happened to be there at the time? I mean, would any father figure have been the same to you?"

"I believe that Abe and I needed each other to fill the gaps left by our losses, so maybe God led us to each other. Maybe it was God's plan. But what do I do about Brock?"

"If you and this Abe are all tuned in and comfortable, don't feel any responsibility to change it. Brock only finally admitted he was your father, but where was he while you were in the orphanage?" An impish smile crossed Sunny's face. "So, y'gonna change your name?" she asked brightly.

"You little shit, I'll change the shape of your head!" Willie Nell was relieved that her terrible secret had just been brought down to size by this runt of a teenager.

"Just try, bastard sister." Sunny danced a little jig, surprising the older woman.

"What's that you just did?"

"My leg is getting stronger." Sunny said. "Doctor Price says it's pretty close to time to put the rods in. He says the muscle tone's good and that after about six months of rehab, I won't have to hobble around anymore.

"And, get this: Miz Edie's going to come to Dallas to live with me and help out during the rehab. She said we could get an apartment. Ain't life just grand!?"

"So I won't be able to refer to you as 'Sunny The Cripple' to all my friends?"

"You do, I'll kick you with my bionic leg. And I'll thank you to use my given name," Sunny skipped back to the music room and picked up a guitar.

"Call me Sunrise." Sunny said, then, ignoring her sister's astonished stare, "Want to hear some more of Mama's music?"

Willie Nell's smile was inward and pleased that Sunrise Autrey was finally claiming her birthright. She was beginning to be proud of the name her parents gave her. With that simple sentence, Sunny had resolved her sister's dilemma about her own name as well. She was Sunrise Autrey. Willie Nell was proud to be her sister, proud to be Lacey Jay Autrey's first-born. She would not discard the name that spoke her heritage.

With a straight face, she replied, "Only after we do justice to our cholesterol-on-a-bun suppers."

"With donuts for dessert. We are sooooooooooooo bad!" Girlish laughter and music filled the hall for the rest of the evening.

Epilog

The house lights dimmed and the loud, frenetic audience dialed the noise down a few decibels. The Willie Nelson concert in Dallas always sells out, but seldom does the warm-up band get everyone into the auditorium so quickly. Jaded country music fans often ignore the opening acts and filter in slowly during their performances to take reserved seats just before the headliners come on.

Tonight was different. Tonight, one of their own was debuting, a little Dallas girl with a big voice and a first-album release that was well on its way to a gold record.

Willie Nell sat between Atlee and Elliott, as proud of her little sister as Lacey Jay would have been had she lived to see it.

The record, "A Ball of Yarn," consisted of a dozen songs written by the girls' mother and heard for the first time on the debut album. Tonight, most of them would be performed on a live stage for the first time.

A lone steel guitar hit a note and reverberated. At the end of the reverberation, a drum intro thundered to life, and quickly found itself competing with the anticipatory roar of the audience. Then a slim young singer in sequined denim and an impossible purple Stetson ran onto the stage.

The audience erupted so loudly Willie Nell could hardly hear the first two lines of the song that announced Sunrise Autrey's arrival to the world of country music, "A Ball of Yarn".

Printed in the United States
74095LV00003B/34-60

9 781425 980078